Praise for Novel Women

When a group of women have monthly book club together for 10 years they discuss more than story arcs—specifically their own! The intimate details they share guarantee a fun and juicy read. When they're lives enter a transition stage—divorce, empty nests, restlessness—these life changes risk altering the group dynamic forever. It is utterly enjoyable being a fly on the wall of these Novel Women!

—Eva Lesko Natiello, New York Times
bestselling author of *The Memory Box.*

Being of "a certain age" myself, with my own empty nest and thoroughly enjoying my personal "second chapter," I completely identified with the women portrayed in Novel Women. They spoke to me in ways no pert young protagonist could. I admired their close friendships, worried when they faced crises of love and life, and rooted for them to prevail. Novel Women is a fun read, and I'm waiting for book two!

—Michelle Cameron, Author of *The Fruit of Her Hands and In the Shadow of the Globe*

Ultimately a celebration of resilience and friendship, Novel Women weaves together the strands of several lives—each character more compelling than the last. For ten years, Brianna and her reading group have confided in and comforted each other, even as rivalries and resentments have simmered in the background of their meetings. Now after a decade of discussions, the women are poised to confront their futures (and in some cases their pasts) to see what the next chapters of their lives hold. Novel Women is the ideal read for rainy afternoons and shared bottles of wine; you'll find yourself rooting for the characters and cheering on the steps they take to embrace chances at rediscovered love and newly rewritten endings.

—Eireann Corrigan, Author of
Accomplice and Ordinary Ghosts

novel women

· BETWEEN FRIENDS BOOK CLUB ·

*To Between Friends Book Club – always
and forever my sisters, my friends.*

In the depth of winter,
I finally learned that there was in me
an invincible summer.

Albert Camus

Brianna

10TH ANNIVERSARY – BOOK CLUB MEETING

"YOU NEED TO pull harder!" I cried.

Madeline jerked the bottle of champagne away from Hanna, her face plastered with her usual smug expression.

"Ah," was all I managed to say before the cork popped and flew into a nearby column, ricocheting and smashing into my wall unit.

"Holy shit!" Hanna jumped up to inspect the damage.

All eyes followed her, but no one said anything.

Picking up the broken object, Hanna brought it to where the group was sitting around my fireplace and looked directly at Madeline. "Nice! That's what you get for grabbing the bottle out of my hands."

Madeline's face bloomed crimson as she captured the last of the bottle's runoff in some cocktail napkins.

Hanna cradled my husband's broken "Man of the Year" award, which he received last year from his law firm.

Feeling the tension in the air, I said, "Don't worry about it,

Madeline, Eric always hated that award." My lips tightened over my mouth in an awkward smile.

My attention snapped back to the group when Ava muttered something I couldn't quite make out. The tone, however, was clear. That was all they needed. The rest of the ladies of the Novel Women Book Club began to roast Madeline, some even standing and clapping.

Madeline stood ramrod straight. After a minute or two, she regained composure as the pink tinge on her face faded and she poured champagne into the crystal flutes set on the coffee table.

Wanting to deflect any further criticisms, I stood and took the award away from Hanna. "Well, that's one way to get rid of this awful thing." I bent over the couch and placed the award on the floor.

Turning back to the group, I said, "Can you believe we've been together for ten years?" I handed each member a champagne flute, then raised my own for a toast. "Here's to you, my friends. I can't tell you how much it means to me that we've reached this milestone together." I looked at each one, beginning on my right with Charlotte, my adventurous lifelong sidekick; and ending on my left with Madeline, my very own narcissist, whose daily dose of *the right way to do things* has probably helped me more than I care to admit.

My eyes welled up, so I kept the toast short.

"Well…" I paused, swallowing. "I started this club so I would have someone to talk to when I finished a great book." I took a deep breath. "But instead of just discussing books, it's become my oasis away from my crazy life. We began sharing books, but over the years we've shared our lives, loves, triumphs, failures, and losses. You've become so important to me. I love you dearly. Thank you!" I raised my glass and we clinked the flutes together.

I sat on the couch, concentrating on keeping my tears at bay and felt my stomach twist into a knot. *Why can't I tell them how scared I am? How lost I feel? Is it just my kids leaving for college? Or…*

"Bri, please, we should be thanking you," Charlotte said. "Hell, you've made me read! And what would I have done without all of you during my divorce? This is my oasis, too!" Charlotte tipped her glass to me and winked. Reaching into a pocket, she pulled out her gloss, and smoothed it over her lips.

I twisted my wedding band around my finger.

"Here's to Bri!" Staci stood too fast and wobbled.

Hanna grabbed her arm until she regained her balance.

Everyone rose to toast me with a tinkling of crystal.

"Thanks, everyone." I inhaled deeply. "Instead of an assigned book this month, I thought we'd all share a favorite novel that we've read during the last ten years. Who wants to start?"

"How the hell do you remember all those books?" Staci asked, talking with her hands as usual. "I had to look on our blog and read the book reviews you wrote to freshen my memory."

I kept my eye on her glass, waiting for more champagne to spill over. "I don't remember every single book, but if it moved you, you'd remember it."

"I'm with Staci on this one," Hanna said

The others nodded.

"Don't be ridiculous!" Madeline cried. "How hard is it to remember a favorite book? Jesus, I wonder about all of you." She shook her head hard and not a single strand of hair fell out of place.

Oh boy, she's starting early tonight. God, I hate refereeing all the time. I reached over to Madeline and patted her arm to calm her rhetoric before it escalated.

I cleared my throat. "Okay, then, let's start. Hanna. What was your favorite book?" I looked down at my finger. It was glowing red. I stopped twisting my ring.

At forty-two, Hanna was the youngest member. Her husband's long hours at work and excessive travel irritated her. I knew she wanted more from her marriage.

"*Anna Karenina*," Hanna blurted out. "Anna followed her heart.

3

I loved that, even if it didn't end well." She wrapped both arms tightly around her chest.

Bad mood or not, she always managed to look like she'd just come off a soccer field with an outdoorsy, apple-cheeked glow. Her blond hair and freckles completed her athletic-schoolgirl look to perfection.

"God, I remember that book. It just went on and on," Staci said. "I was glad when I finished it." Crossing her legs, she banged them into the coffee table.

"That's a classic and certainly shouldn't be demeaned by you. I mean, really." Madeline strongly brushed something off her skirt.

"What? I wasn't demeaning it. What's up with you now?" Staci asked.

Out of the corner of my eye, I saw Ava putting her phone down and knew I had to do something before they got into it.

"Staci, I liked your blog post on the Mohonk Mountain House. Maybe we all could go for a weekend?"

"That'd be great," she said. "Thanks for reading it. My writing is still rusty, I think."

"Ladies, how about it?" I asked. "A weekend trip to New York this fall?"

"I don't have my calendar here," Madeline replied. "I'll let you know when I'm available."

I heard some rumblings around me but thought back to an online article I just read on friendship, "Seven Signs You're in a Toxic Friendship." Out of the seven signs, Madeline fulfilled three definitely, but probably four realistically. We all struggled with her perfectionism and control issues. I toyed with the idea of taping one of our book clubs to let her watch it back. Would she see how offensive she sounded? Probably not.

Ava pushed her bangs back. "So! This is all about *your* schedule?" Her voice low.

Madeline gave Ava a frosty glance. "No, of course not. All I'm saying is I can't commit to a date right now. I'm surprised you actually heard me. You've been glued to your phone all night. Besides, keeping a calendar might help you to keep better track of your schedule. Then we won't have to reschedule book club so often." She cocked her head in an exaggerated *so there* expression.

Ahhh... I needed to deflect and looked for the bottle of champagne. "Staci, can I have some more champagne?" I asked a little too loudly.

As she stood and handed it to me, I remembered that Staci was leaving the next morning for Burlington, Vermont. She wanted to revitalize her career in journalism now that she was divorced and her sons were on their own.

Quickly, I asked her, "What was your favorite book?"

Sitting, she said, "I liked *The Paris Wife.* I related to the wife in the story, working hard to keep her marriage together, even though her husband was just as controlling and self-centered as mine."

"How are you doing, now that it's all behind you?" Hanna dropped her crossed arms from her chest to her sides.

"Great, never better!" Staci chirped. She looked like she wanted to get up and dance. She'd told me the other day that she felt twenty-one again, not forty-nine. She sat there beaming with her perfect California bathing-suit model smile.

"You look amazing. Divorce agrees with you," Hanna said. "Maybe I should try it?"

Staci looked up and shook her blond ringlets off her face. "Are you unhappy with Mark?" she whispered, reaching over to grab Hanna's hand. The question pulled all eyes to Hanna.

"No. I don't know. I do wish Mark was home more. I'm waiting for the kids to ask me who he is one day." Hanna sank deeper into the couch. "You know, all those years of playing sports in high school and college taught me about teamwork. Where's my team now?" Hanna shoved both hands into the space between the couch cushions.

No one said anything for a minute or two.

Madeline broke the silence. "You should appreciate your hard-working husband more and not complain all the time."

Hanna dropped her head to her chest.

"Madeline, she does appreciate him. She just wants to see him more." I interjected. "Even you can understand that."

Madeline looked off and muttered, "Whatever."

Hanna looked up at me and mouthed, *Thank you.*

Surprised that Ava again didn't react to Madeline's terse comment, I reached across the table and tapped her on the knee. "What's your favorite book?"

Ava, voluptuous and exotic, owned a real estate business she'd built from nothing. I met her fifteen years ago when we accompanied our first graders on a Girl Scout camping trip. Only a higher power knew how we survived the entire weekend sleeping in hammocks in a platform tent. Ava and I still moan about the ants and tripping over tree roots trying to find a toilet in the middle of the black night.

Hearing her name, Ava looked up from her phone. She'd been texting most of the evening. "My favorite book was..." She hesitated and sat up in her chair. "I'm not sure. To be honest I haven't thought about it, so come back to me." She looked back down at her phone. *"Mierda!"* She pushed her bangs out of her face, but they fell forward again. "Staci, by the way, you are so much better off without that pretentious dick of a husband. He was an insufferable ass."

"What?" No, he's not! He's totally charming, handsome, and intelligent. He'll be a fine catch for some lucky lady." Madeline raised her chin and looked back to Ava.

Staci looked first to Ava then to Madeline. "You weren't married to him, Madeline." She drew out the words. "You don't know anything." Taking a deep breath, she said, "He isn't what he appears to be. I'm so relieved to be away from him."

Madeline opened her mouth, but I put my hand on her arm again and managed to talk first. "Let's not rehash Staci's divorce or trash talk her ex." I looked to Staci and smiled. "Hanna is right though, Staci, you do look good."

I looked over the group stopping at Tess who'd been quiet tonight.

"Okay. Tess, what was your favorite book?"

She had been laid off last year after thirty-two years with ASH Media. Her husband, Stephen, who was just about to retire from his New York City law firm, had comforted her by saying they had plenty of time to travel now.

"Let's go to Italy," he told her. "Who needs that job? Pack a bag, let's start."

But just as Tess finalized the travel arrangements for their three-week trip to Italy, Stephen had a heart attack and died.

I'd felt helpless. I tried to involve Tess in some of my charity events to distract from her pain. The few things I managed to pull her into, she performed in a perfunctory way—just like a teenager doing chores around the house, counting the minutes.

Tonight, she sat looking at her hands, picking at her cuticles.

"Hello, Tess? You there?" Madeline reached over and swatted Tess's hand away from her nails.

"Ah…" Tess looked up at the group.

Ava stirred and began to look up at the commotion but refocused a moment later back onto her phone. I was glad. I was tired of refereeing Madeline already, but if Ava joined in it would be like dealing with two bitchy teenage girls. I hate confrontations—they seemed to thrive on it.

"Let's see…" Tess stammered, staring at a spot on the wall above Madeline's head. A smile crossed her lips. "Maybe it's because of where I am in my life right now, but I would say any steamy bodice ripper with a cover picture of Fabio's bare chest rippling with six-pack abs glistening in the moonlight." Tess paused, letting her words hang in the stunned silence.

"Just kidding." She started laughing.

Whoa! That's wonderful. Maybe she was beginning to heal.

Staci pumped her arm in the air and howled. "You go, Tess!" When she brought her arm down she knocked over her empty flute.

"Oh, God, sorry, Bri, you know what a klutz I am. At least I didn't break it."

"Don't worry," I said, refilling her glass.

I tensed, knowing Madeline as I do, that she was on the verge of saying something to Staci about knocking over the glass. I looked at her and asked, "When are we getting together this week for the charity?"

"Not you, too. Don't you keep a calendar?"

"Yes, it's on my calendar. I don't remember offhand and thought I'd asked you."

"We're meeting on Tuesday at 9 a.m." Madeline chided and rolled her eyes.

I turned away, tired of deflecting.

I saw Staci give Charlotte a half smile. "Hey, speaking of sexy men—who were you talking with at the McManns' party?" she asked.

All heads turned on the same beat.

"What, holding out on us, Charlotte?" Ava tossed her hair back and glanced up from her phone.

Charlotte shrugged, clearly wanted to avoid answering the question. "We should finish everyone's favorite books first."

"Well, darling, we can certainly make an exception. Spill it," Madeline ordered. She uncrossed her legs, leaning forward in her chair not to miss a single word. "After all, it would be good to finally stop this adolescent behavior of sleeping with every Tom, Dick, and Harry and settle down." She lowered her voice. "Don't you worry about your reputation?"

Oh jeez. I rubbed my temples. *Not her sanctimonious shit again.*

"Madeline, that was crass—even for you." Ava uttered, her eyes still glued to her phone.

Charlotte started to say something, then leaned back and laughed. She usually ignores everything Madeline says. But this...

Charlotte turned toward Staci. "His name is Maxwell. That's all. I barely know him. But I can tell by the way he carries himself, he'll be a tiger in bed. Just the type of man I'm looking for." Charlotte closed her eyes.

Staci bounced in her seat. "Tell us more."

Charlotte smiled at Staci then turned toward Madeline. "You sound like an old schoolmarm from the nineteen hundreds. Lighten up." Charlotte reached into her pocket and reapplied her lip gloss.

I watched her attach the top. "That's a nice color."

Ava looked up at Charlotte, reached over, and grabbed the lip gloss. "It's called Désir." Ava elongated the word.

Charlotte's cheeks bloomed. "I just bought it."

"A new Chanel lip gloss, a new man. Hmm..." Ava handed the gloss back and picked up her phone again.

Charlotte was my oldest friend and the first to join book club. Four years later, she'd gotten divorced. Everyone was stunned, and for her, it was as if a tornado had blasted into her life, in seconds claiming her best friend, her confidant, her lover, her provider. She was left spinning in the tails of the wind, alone, frightened, and so very sad, broken like remnants of furniture scattered after a storm.

"Charlotte, when are we going to meet him?" I asked.

In the six years since her divorce, Charlotte had maintained a cavalier attitude about dating. She didn't seem to care about the men she spent time with. She had certainly never blushed when we asked about one of them before.

"Let me see if he calls first." The pink smudge deepened and crept across her doll-like face to match her lip gloss. "By the way," she said, "I liked *Fifty Shades of Grey*."

"What! Are you kidding? With all the amazing books out there, you pick that? Really?" Madeline placed her glass a little too hard on the coffee table.

"Yes, that book!" Charlotte snapped, sitting up perfectly straight. "I want to be more adventurous and spontaneous. Freer. I don't ever want to be the woman I was before." She set her jaw, staring first at Madeline, then at the rest of us, as if daring us to contradict her choice.

No one asked her anything more. I don't think anyone wanted to know what she meant by "more adventurous...and freer."

We moved on to Madeline.

I took a deep breath.

Madeline should've been born in the Victorian era with its inflated sense of morals. Everything in her life was perfect, according to her. Even her dark hair was cut into a perfect, precision bob. None of us had ever seen such an impeccable haircut.

"I loved *Rebecca*. I'm so glad we occasionally read the classics. 'Last night I dreamt I went to Manderley again.' All those elegant descriptive passages." Madeline sighed rapturously.

"I thought you would say *The Great Gatsby* or *Madame Bovary*," Charlotte offered. "You talked nonstop when we read those books."

"Oh, I loved those, too. I just don't understand why you have to have an affair to experience true love," she remarked. "Why embark on an affair? They're dangerous, stupid."

"Oh, come on!" Hanna replied. "Aren't you ever tempted? Don't you ever look at someone else and wonder?"

"Of course, I *look* at other men, but that's it." Madeline nodded curtly.

Ava put her phone down.

My heart rate picked up.

"Okay, Madeline, hypothetically, what if you met a man at a charity event, and you thought he was handsome, charming, and sexy as hell," Hanna began, pushing herself to the end of the couch. "You both flirt. The conversation's lively."

"Why pick Madeline? Why not one of us single ladies?" Staci chimed in.

"I'm making a point here," Hanna said. "Then a few days later you run into each other at Starbucks when you get your morning coffee, and you strike up another conversation."

"Why Starbucks? I go to Dunkin' in the morning," Staci interrupted again.

A few of the ladies giggled.

Hanna pressed on, "Then, you see him at the health club and a few other places in town. You chat every time you see him. You notice him at restaurants when he's having lunch with clients." Hanna threw her hands around emphatically.

"Why can't this happen to me? I never meet anyone like that." Staci sighed.

Hanna gave Staci the just-a-minute signal and proceeded. "One night you see him when you're out to dinner with your husband. You go over to his table to say hi, but it's really to check out his date."

"Was she beautiful?" Ava asked.

"Wait, Hanna, are you making this up?" Bri interrupted. "Staci, this could be a good story for you to write about."

"Hold on!" Hanna took a deep breath. "He seems to be popping up everywhere. Was he always around? Isn't it wonderful someone new is paying attention to you? After a few months, you begin to look for him everywhere. You think about him all the time."

"Oohh, ahhhh," Ava murmured.

Even Tess grinned a little.

"'Oohh' is right…I'm getting goosebumps," Staci said.

"Then you find yourself in the same bar one night when you're with your girlfriends celebrating a birthday. He's with some buddies. The two groups mingle and everyone has fun. At the end of the night he walks you to your car, touches your arm softly, and keeps his hand there while you talk. He's so close you can smell traces of his lingering cologne. You feel butterflies in your stomach. Your arm tingles under his touch. He leans down and kisses you so gently, almost innocently, but on the lips. Then he leans back to see how you react." Hanna paused.

Staci immediately jumped in. "Wow, forget Madeline. I'll take him! Send him my way."

We laughed.

"Everybody, wait!" Hanna held up her hand and turned to Madeline. "Don't tell me you wouldn't kiss him back."

"I bet Madeline would jump his bones," Ava squealed, louder than the rest of us.

"No, I wouldn't!" Madeline protested loudly. "I'm married and I don't associate with adulterers. It's immoral. I would, I would... push him away. It's disgusting." Madeline crossed both arms in front of her chest, nostrils flaring.

"You don't really mean that, do you?" Hanna crossed her arms.

Madeline nodded emphatically and looked with distaste at the other women.

"Good for you, Madeline," I said. "I'm glad *someone* can resist Temptation." It always shocks me when I agree with her.

"Well, not everyone's happy in their marriage. Maybe they're just lonely." Staci offered, shrugging.

"Lonely? Come on, the guy's a home wrecker—like a termite destroying the foundation of everything you've built until the house collapses around you," Charlotte spat out. She inhaled, calming herself, and sank into the chair.

Hanna blurted. "Well, I don't know what I'd do if my dream man made a play for me."

"There is no such thing as a 'dream man.'" Madeline looked exasperated. "You girls are soooo delusional." She stood up and huffed off in the direction of the bathroom.

I exhaled. My muscles relaxed.

"I hope she's wrong. I'm looking for one." Staci looked down at the table.

"'Dream man' might be hard shoes to fill," I offered. "Okay, enough. Ava, let's get back to the books." I reached for more champagne.

"Ugh, me again?" Ava grimaced, almost as if in pain, pushed her bangs away, and reached for her phone on the table.

Madeline returned and sat down. "Where have you been, anyway? Certainly not with us. Who have you been texting all night? You know that's rude, Ava? Right?" Madeline pointed at Ava's phone.

"*I'm* rude. Do you realize you say the most abrasive things to us? You have no filter whatsoever. You're like one of the *Housewives* on TV. If this is the way you treat your friends, I guess I'm glad I'm not your enemy." Ava sputtered. "Here—I'll give you my undivided attention." Ava dropped her phone in her purse.

"I'm just trying to help you. You don't have to be so combative." Madeline hissed.

Tess interrupted the two and asked Madeline, "How can you be so sure you'd never have an affair?"

"Don't be ridiculous. Stan and I have a long, strong marriage. He would never stray and neither would I." She waved her hand in the air dismissively. "Divorce happens over money problems or when people are mismatched from the start. That's not us on either score." Madeline sat up, looking superior.

"O-M-G! Talk about delusional. You live in a bubble. You are absolutely ridiculous!" Ava shouted.

"Again, you're being so aggressive and I'm just telling you how I feel." Madeline scolded.

"Jesus, you are the most frustrating person to be around. You are too sheltered or something." Charlotte shook her head and pulled her gloss out of her pocket.

Ava spat out, "You know, Madeline, you are wound so tight... I...I can't imagine you having sex." She wiped some spittle off her lips.

I grimaced and everyone instantly quieted. The knot in my stomach tightened. I looked at Ava pleadingly.

"You probably only do it for poor-old Stan on his birthday." Ava's tone softened.

Madeline eyes bore into Ava. "We have a wonderful sex life—if you must know."

Ava crossed one leg over the other. "Well, not all of us would be satisfied with Tea Party sex!"

Thank God for Ava tonight. Instead of her usual arguing with Madeline she was handling it with humor. Her comment made us all laugh and let the tension in the room dissipate.

"What? Tea Party what? You just made that up!" Madeline's hands flew in the air, smiling slightly.

Ava grinned like a Cheshire cat, goading Madeline. "I did not. You know…it's…lights out, missionary style."

Madeline retorted, "And I suppose you're a master at Kama Sutra."

A roar erupted before the words were completely out of her mouth. Somehow talking about sex always seemed to soothe feelings.

"Yup, here we are back at sex." I stood to get a bottle of wine and let them settle down. *They always make me laugh no matter what mood I start off in.*

"Well, aren't we the witty one tonight?" Madeline pointed to Ava's purse. "Remind me not to interrupt your texting again."

Returning with an open bottle of wine, I stopped in front of Ava. "Come on. What's your favorite book?"

"Okay, okay. I liked *The Women's Room*," Ava offered. "Growing up Puerto Rican I thought if you were white and educated you didn't have problems, but that book showed me that every woman has issues."

Ava's marriage had been stormy the last few years. I wasn't sure they'd make it.

"I'm lost. Why would you pick that?" Madeline asked.

"Hey, you wanted a book, that's my book, live with it." Ava flipped her hair.

Charlotte shook her head. "And you, Bri, what was your favorite?"

"I loved *Memoirs of a Geisha*. The writing was so good that I actually felt I was on those cliffs in the tipsy house with the wind blowing hard." I closed my eyes for a minute, remembering. "I loved the fact that Sayuri ended up with the love of her life and that she had been right about him all along."

I caught some murmuring to my left where Ava and Madeline were trading jabs. I felt my stomach tighten until I saw them both smiling.

The members began side conversations about their upcoming summer plans. The book club was going on hiatus for the summer for the first time in ten years—too many conflicting vacations. For some reason, this made me uneasy.

It wasn't just the time apart. After all, we would see one another over the summer, just not as a group. There was more to it than that. I detected some subtle shifts occurring among us. Most of the members were empty nesters now, and some were newly divorced. Would our paths continue together? I prayed they would.

Pushing my anxiety aside, I told everyone, "E-mail me what book you'd like us to discuss at September's meeting."

Madeline reached over and grabbed Tess's hand again. "Hey, 'Miss-I-want-Fabio's-glistening-abs-in-the-moonlight,' he's not going to want someone with bleeding cuticles. Stop doing that."

"Oh, right—like not picking will make that happen." Tess wrapped both hands around her glass, smiling tightly at Madeline.

Around 11:30 the girls began to leave. I gave each one a huge hug at the door, saying how much I'd miss not having book club this summer.

When the last member left, I closed the door and leaned on it, the silence overwhelming. I looked into my beloved family room. Its massive two-story fireplace had kept my family warm in the winters when we played board games or watched movies. Without warning, a tear dropped down my cheek.

My gaze moved to the painting above the fireplace, the one we had purchased in Prague last summer. Eric loved the painting. I hated it, but never told him so. I knew most people found it striking for its bold colors and intensity. The painting depicted a path flanked by trees sublime in their transient shades of amber, crimson, and orange. But what drew my eye was the path, strewn with discarded, withered, faded leaves. I could almost smell the musty decay and hear the whistling of the wind around me.

Rubbing the heel of my palm against my chest, I dimly recalled a tree-lined path from my childhood, that time after my mother died.

Exhaling, I wondered why I was thinking so much about my early childhood lately. The memories seemed to follow me around like a gnat that you had to keep swatting away. *Enough!* I told myself.

I plopped down on the chair closest to the fireplace and picked up my son's senior portrait which I had framed just that afternoon. It made me smile, remembering his superhero phase when he wore capes everywhere, even to bed. I must have watched him hundreds of times, half hidden in the kitchen, while he walked on the hearth pretending to be Batman on a rooftop. My finger traced the outline of his face.

Memoirs of a Geisha lay on the table next to his portrait. What did I have in common with a geisha? I couldn't think of any book that really matched my life; well, maybe *The Divine Secrets of the Ya-Ya Sisterhood*. I could certainly relate to the theme of things left unsaid. Should that have been my book pick instead?

Or maybe I should have chosen something about a middle-aged woman whose children are about to leave home. Too bad there's no book titled *What to Expect When You're Empty Nesting*.

SUMMER
PART 1

STACI

BURLINGTON BOUND

MY RADIO BLASTED, "I'm ridin' solo…" *Yup, that's me. I'm finally free!*

I drove up and away from my old life on that sun-drenched day, turning onto scenic Route 22A in Vermont. All I could see were rolling pastures speckled with farms, cows, and horses. I cruised with the top down on my rented white convertible, my hair flying this way and that. I felt giddy, more like a teenager escaping to college for the first time rather than a forty-nine-year-old divorcée.

Am I allowed to be this happy? It had been so long, and it felt so good.

Up and over, hill after hill, farm after farm, bordered by the Adirondacks on one side and the Green Mountains on the other, this roller-coaster landscape seemed as if it ought to be in a movie or a coffee-table book. It hadn't changed in decades. I had traveled this road back and forth during my college years and it still took my breath away. I was headed back to the last place I'd lived when I was single—just for a visit, to reinvigorate myself, enjoy the jazz festival, and begin again.

The undulating road was in sync with the radio. I sang along at the top of my lungs to Jason Derulo's song, totally out of key. It always amazed me that a song could so exactly nail a mood.

A few miles outside of Fair Haven, an odor began to waft over the windshield, growing stronger with each mile. In the heat of late spring, the manure stored on all the nearby dairy farms takes on a life of its own, especially when the wind blows toward the highway. The malodorous scent immediately brought me back to my college days.

The stench becoming too much for me, I decided to put the top up. A large sign ahead read *Devil's Bowl Speedway*. As I pulled into the parking lot, I remembered passing this track on my way to college, but it was different now, more professional, with a large asphalt driveway and spectator stands.

A black pickup truck with a trailer attached was the only other vehicle in the lot. I parked next to the truck and raised the convertible top.

Looking at the stunning mountain range behind the racetrack, I was struck by the beauty of the swirling clouds. My spirits soared, and I felt an urge to twirl around like Julie Andrews in *The Sound of Music*. Instead, I grabbed my tote bag, with my camera in it, out of the back seat. The mountains naturally framed the racetrack and the surrounding fields. Memories floated in, of me sitting with my dad on our old, beat-up Adirondack chairs, talking and laughing. My dad would look up into the sky and point to a passing cloud formation.

"Staci, do you see that spaceship up there?" my father once asked. I must have been eight or nine.

I told him I did. Off we journeyed to a planet called Paragon in the Sunflower Galaxy where the inhabitants dressed in the finest silks embellished with rare gems that changed colors in the light and dark. Dad built a world around the Paragonians' lives. Somewhere buried in all these stories were life lessons, the kind my children would later read in the Berenstain Bears series or Dr. Seuss.

We always ended with a few lines from Shelley's cloud poem:

I am the daughter of Earth and Water,

And the nursling of the Sky;

I pass through the pores of the ocean and shores;

I change, but I cannot die.

I miss my father every single day even though it's been ten years since he passed away. An eternity really. I lowered my head as my eyes welled up.

A strong breeze blew from the valley, catching my orange floral silk scarf, a gift from my sons. The knot must have loosened around my neck while driving with the top down. It lifted up and above my head. The breeze died quickly, sending it floating back down, landing a few feet away from me. My thoughts turned to my ex-husband, George. My father never told me what he really thought of him. When George and I told my parents that we were engaged, my father had looked down at the ground before shaking George's hand and hugging me. Looking back on it now, I'm certain my father knew I was making a mistake. All those years of my dad's stories and life lessons had managed to fly off in the wind just like my scarf.

My cell rang and I rummaged in my bag, pulling it out only to discover it was George. I hit decline and turned the volume off.

I threw my phone back into my purse. My ex-husband was nothing like my father. George could be so charming, having the perfect response for every situation. But he would drive by a car accident and never think to stop to help or even call 911. After all, if he did, he might miss an important call. The next business deal was his true love. Stories were just a waste of time to him, and only cold, hard facts and deals mattered.

George complained when I encouraged him to look at the beauty all around us. He would usually say: *Let's go, what's taking so long, who cares what the sunset looks like, we'll be late for my client dinner.* Remembering that now, I shuddered.

For years I listened to his rants. He'd wind himself up, saying: *My mother could handle the home, her children and have dinner on the table seven days a week, without breaking a sweat, and all with limited means. Not like the money I give you.* I closed my eyes and shook my head trying to shake away the memories. How did I make such a huge mistake? I still can't believe I married him and stayed married for twenty-five years.

I walked through the parking lot into the field beyond where a huge sugar maple caught my attention. I took a picture, then snapped a few more of the mountain range beyond before putting the camera into my bag and heading back.

Reaching the car, I looked at the track. A few pictures might be nice for my blog. I was in no hurry.

A simple chain-link fence surrounded it with a large open gate just beyond the black truck. I walked through and stopped at the stands, pulling my camera back out of the bag.

A loud roar erupted behind me. Startled, I dropped my bag and the contents spilled everywhere. Luckily, I was holding my camera in my other hand.

Jesus, what an idiot.

The noise grew louder, closer. Out of my peripheral vision, a dark blur appeared. My arms reacted quicker than my mind and I lifted the camera and snapped a few pictures to capture the moment.

Thank God my ex wasn't there. I could almost hear him raging about my lack of coordination and how much the items I had dropped on the ground cost. Still stunned by the noise, I bent to retrieve my makeup bag, jamming it and the rest of the fallen stuff back into the bag. Only one car was on the track and it was so loud. How could people tolerate the volume with several cars on the track, race after race?

Looking for a different angle to photograph the car, I climbed up the bleachers and snapped a few more pictures as it rounded the curve. I hoped one of the shots would be clear enough for my blog. I had invested in a good camera because blog posts need lots of images. No one likes to read anymore, now the goal was fewer words, more pictures, like grammar school workbooks.

I missed writing for a newspaper with all its hubbub and those insane deadlines. Being a journalist had been the most exhilarating, stressful and adventurous years of my life. But when the kids came my husband had insisted I quit. He hadn't wanted anything to interfere with *his* career.

After so many years out of the profession, and with jobs being scarce, I began blogging and freelancing. Certainly not the excitement I was used to in the newsroom, but it was a start. Hoping to reinvigorate my career, I had traveled to Burlington to write about the annual jazz festival.

Back in the car, I resumed my trek up the highway, turning the music as loud as my ears could handle. In my car all alone, no one cared that I couldn't carry a tune.

My stomach growled—either to protest my singing, or because it needed food—so I stopped in the small city of Vergennes for lunch. I couldn't believe how much Vergennes had changed since I'd last been here. As students, we always just blew through it.

Once inside Gianni's Italian Specialties, I ordered a number 23 with ketchup from the sandwich board.

"You must be from Jersey! Only people from Jersey put ketchup on a chicken cheesesteak," said the man behind the counter.

I laughed. "Guilty as charged, but is that really true?"

"Trust me, only people from Jersey put ketchup on everything." He squirted ketchup up and down my sandwich. Still laughing, I walked outside the front door to a small patio with petite café tables overlooking the street, putting my plate down on the table closest to the railing.

The sun warmed without burning and beauty seemed to pour out of every flower, plant, and building. Vergennes was adorably quaint, with its own New England distinctiveness. In the late nineteenth century, the small city had once bustled with a Navy shipyard, but all that had remained by my college days was a broken-down remembrance. Now restored, it had regained some of its past charm. I sat back, enjoying the town's afternoon rhythm.

Savoring my sandwich, ketchup and all, I noticed a shiny black pickup truck with a race car on a trailer drive by on Main Street. It looked like the truck from the speedway. Idly wondering what the race-car driver looked like, I watched as the truck continued up the road and made a right out of my line of vision.

"Miss Cindy, can we get ice cream?" I turned toward a small, squeaky voice to my left where a group of preschool-age children were walking up the sidewalk toward the restaurant, all holding hands, with adults in front and at the rear. Some sort of school or daycare outing. The children were cute, and my thoughts flashed back to my own boys at that age. Chris and Jeff, only thirteen months apart, were now out in the world making their own memories. I fell into a reverie thinking of my sweet, sweet little boys.

"Excuse me," said a strong, deep male voice directly behind me.

Startled, my arms flew up and knocked over my soda. *God, do I always have to be such a klutz?* I bent to retrieve the fallen drink, and when I looked up, a tall man stood before me, dressed in jeans, T-shirt, and a baseball cap. To my utter astonishment, he held my scarf in one hand. A food tray was in the other.

"Sorry for startling you," he said, his smile mischievous. "Is this scarf yours?"

"Yes, that's mine. But where did you find it?" I spun around and opened my bag to check. The scarf wasn't there. It had clearly embarked on its own adventure this trip.

"At the track, in the bleachers," said the stranger.

After a moment, I realized I was staring and quickly reached out to retrieve the scarf from his outstretched hand. His dark brown hair spilled out from under his baseball cap and halfway down his neck. His features were chiseled, with a strong jawline. When he lifted his head after setting down his lunch at an adjoining table, I noticed deep green eyes that popped against his tan skin. The café tables were so small and close together, it was as if he was sitting right next to me.

"Thank you so much for returning this. My sons just gave it to me last weekend. But how did you know it was mine? How did you find me?" I asked, putting my scarf back into my bag.

"When I was doing laps at the track I noticed a woman in the stands." He took his soda and sandwich off his tray, placing the tray on an empty chair. "The next lap I didn't see you and I slowed down going around the gate. I saw a white convertible with out-of-state plates parked by my truck." He finished unwrapping his sandwich and looked at me. "It's only a chain-link fence, you can easily see into the parking lot.

"When I was leaving I noticed something colorful lying in the stands. I picked it up. There is no lost and found at the track, so I put it in my truck."

"But how in the world did you find me?" I asked, amazed at how observant he was.

He turned and pointed to my car. "I live about thirty miles up the road toward Burlington. When I passed I noticed the same white convertible I'd seen at the track. So, I decided to see if the stranger sitting on the patio was missing a scarf. Plus, I was hungry."

"Wow," was all I could muster.

"I've never seen anyone taking pictures when the track is closed. Are you a photographer?" he asked.

"No, not even close. One of my friends is trying to tutor me so my pictures aren't a blurry mess." I went on and on about catching the light and focusing on a moving object." *Why am I babbling?*

He interrupted my monologue. "I'm John Marshall, by the way." His gaze seemed intense, taking in everything, without breaking eye contact.

"Ah, I'm Staci Hughes." I reached across both our tables to shake his hand but banged my arm on its return, shaking both our tables and almost spilling my soda again. He quickly reached across and caught my wavering drink.

God—I'm even more spastic than normal.

"You okay? It's a tight space with all these little tables so close together."

"I'm fine." I tried not to blush, placing my napkin on my lap and looking into his face as if nothing had happened.

He smiled at me and I wondered if he'd already pegged me as a clumsy oaf.

"Why were you taking pictures of the speedway? Do you like racing?" he asked.

"Well, honestly I just needed a place to pull over because the manure smell from the farms was so strong with the top down."

We both laughed.

"Is this your first trip to Vermont?" He took a bite of his sandwich.

"No, I drove to and from college ages ago, it really hasn't changed much. The drive is a beautiful as ever." My gaze fell on his rough and calloused hands; the left one without any sign of a wedding ring. Did he have a girlfriend? He probably did, he was just too damn attractive—like a Ralph Lauren model. Women must swarm him.

"What brings you here now?" He sipped his drink.

"Just going to attend the jazz festival." My heart picked up a beat or two as he moved closer. Normally, I wouldn't care for the tables being so tight together, but for some reason I enjoyed the closeness, almost like we were eating together at the same table.

I, the alleged journalist, appeared to be tongue-tied. I felt moisture beading on the back of my neck.

"Are you meeting up with friends or classmates?" Leaning back, he picked up his drink.

I watched him sipping his soda, then answered, "No, going solo. A little me time." I found myself wondering what my hair must look like after the convertible ride. Did I need a little lipstick?

Leaving my answer alone, he talked for a while about the changes to the area in the last decades since I attended college. I felt my cheek muscles straining from grinning so much.

Other patrons came and went, enjoying lunch on the patio on this pristine day. How long were we there, talking?

I hadn't considered meeting a man on this trip. He was smiling, maybe even flirting a little. Could he actually be interested in me?

Feeling warm, I noticed sweat glistening around my wrists. It dripped down the back of my neck under my hair and between my breasts. Was I having a hot flash? Without thinking, I blurted, "It's so hot!" *Whoa! Why did I say that? What is happening to me?*

John Marshall laughed. His laugh wasn't condescending but playful. He must have realized I was nervous.

His phone vibrated in his shirt pocket, but he ignored it. My ex had never ignored a phone call, even on those rare occasions when we were in the middle of sex. Somewhat befuddled, I didn't know what to say or do next. Luckily, he did.

"Do you work?"

I faltered through this simple question. "I'm between lives right now, but hope to go back into journalism, possibly freelance." *Between lives? What the hell am I saying?*

He didn't ask what I meant. How do you tell a stranger that your marriage of twenty-five years had died a slow death? I looked down at the table and felt my face flush.

John must have sensed my unease and looked away, out over the road.

We finished our sandwiches. I stole glances at him and he at me. *He must be around 6'3",* I thought, *with the physique of a much younger man.* It was hard to pull my gaze away. John Marshall was so damn appealing. A few awkward moments passed as I tried to calm my stumbling thoughts and think of something else to say.

Finally, I asked, pointing at his cap, "I guess you're a Patriots fan." We locked eyes.

"Of course, what else would I be? And you must be a Giants fan." He smiled. We joked back and forth about who was a better quarterback, Manning or Brady, before moving on to the jazz festival and how many bands were going to be there this year.

He looked at his watch and said he needed to get back to work. Two hours had slipped by with this handsome stranger. I sighed.

"You said you live outside of Burlington. Where exactly?" I asked, not wanting him to leave.

"I own a farm in Ferrisburgh on Porter's Bay," he said, standing up and gathering his tray and plate.

A million things ran through my mind: Did he have a girlfriend? Was he married and just didn't wear a ring? Why didn't he ask me for my number or where I was staying in Burlington? He seemed attentive. Had we actually connected or was that just wishful thinking on my part? How could I prolong the conversation?

"Are you going to the jazz festival?" The sentence just popped out. "Maybe I could buy you a drink for being so kind and returning my scarf?" Embarrassed out of my wits, I found my bag on the ground, rummaged around for my cards, handing him one. "Call me if you have some time to go for a drink."

"Okay." He smiled down at me. His whole being seemed to light up. There was none of that insincere glint to his smile that my ex had.

He turned and left.

Feeling flushed, all my mind could conjure was: *That's a farmer? Really?*

Now what? Time to call Bri. I went back into the restaurant to use the restroom first.

"Hey, Jersey, was that your scarf John had?" the owner asked me on the way out.

"Yes, you know him?"

"Of course. He owns a farm a few miles up the road and comes in here often after racing. I haven't seen him spend so much time with a woman since his wife died, though," he said.

"That's terrible. What happened?" I asked.

"His wife died of cancer about five years ago," he said, and then immediately began to clean the counter with gusto, perhaps realizing he probably shouldn't have said anything. "Hope you enjoy your stay, Jersey," he mumbled, turning to walk into the back.

I felt awful prying. It was none of my business. John had a down-to-earth genuineness about him, as if he had no time for airs or pretentiousness. Not like my Brooks Brothers, Wall Street, man-about-town ex.

I rushed outside, jumped in my car to call Bri. I noticed five calls and one voicemail from George. I ignored them and called Bri.

"Hey!" I blurted, barely containing my glee.

"Hey yourself. Sounds like your adventure has begun," Bri replied. "What's going on?"

"You are never gonna believe this." I related my meeting with John.

"Well, that's great! Trip's off to a good start."

Bri didn't sound like her normally cheerful self. "Something wrong?"

"No, nothing. I'm just feeling apprehensive about my kids leaving for college. They haven't even left yet and I'm already missing them. Taking care of them is all I know. That and folding socks, which I'm doing right now." She sighed.

"You'll find something. Don't worry."

"Tell me more about John," Bri sounded more cheerful. "Jesus, you've only been gone seven hours."

"Well, he's a farmer and a race-car driver, and a widower. And he's gorgeous!"

"He's a *farmer?*"

Bri's emphasis on the word surprised me, diminishing my excitement a little. "What do you mean by that?"

"Just that it's different from your hedge-fund ex."

"Yeah, it's different, an amazing, wonderful, breath-of-fresh-air difference," I gushed.

"Tell me everything again," Bri said. "What's that *devil place* you stopped at? A stripper bar?"

Laughing, I retold my story. "Can you believe it?"

"So, you basically did the old drop-the-scarf-around-a-handsome-stranger trick." Bri chuckled.

"I guess I did, didn't I?"

"Did he take your number?"

"No, but I gave him my card and invited him for a drink."

"You did? Wow!"

"Although, maybe he was just trying to do the right thing and return my scarf and then I practically pushed my card down his throat." I started feeling awkward about it. "It's been a long time since I've been with anyone else."

"Hey, you gotta start somewhere!"

I ended the call and listened to George's voicemail.

His terse voice choked out: *Staci, don't ignore my calls. What are you a child? The landscaper has trimmed the bushes and trees absurdly. Tell him he's fired. I refuse to pay for that botched job!*

Furious I texted him back too angry to even speak. *This is my house, my landscaper, my trees and bushes—not yours. None of this is your concern.* I got out of the car and walked up the street trying to shake him off. Eventually my mind calmed and I went back to the car to continue to my destination.

Back on the rolling highway, I fantasized about kissing John. Intimacy with someone else still felt scary. Sex with my ex-husband had been obligatory—and boring! Thinking about John Marshall sent a shiver up my spine. A half hour melted away in blissful fantasy before I pulled into the Marriott by Lake Champlain.

After I checked in, I walked to Church Street, turned right onto Main and continued up the hill until I reached the top. Always one of my favorite spots in Burlington, my alma mater, the University of Vermont, stretched out on both sides of the hill. Down below lay the city, with Lake Champlain glittering beyond in the sunlight and the blue haze of the Adirondack Mountains in the background. With so many gorgeous layers, this hilltop always struck me as a magical place—a real-life Norman Rockwell painting.

Still jazzed from my encounter with John, the afternoon and evening flew by. I stopped for dinner at a cozy place off Church Street, sitting at a table outside. After dinner, I slowly made my way back to the hotel and unpacked. Sleep, however, eluded me as I replayed my lunch with John, but this time we touched and kissed and…

*

The moment my eyes opened the next morning, my thoughts flew to the dreamy stranger I'd met. What would I wear if he called and asked me to go out? I wanted something new, just because.

I sang in the shower, using the small soap as a microphone until it melted away and my skin shriveled around my fingers. My concert continued while I dried my hair, ending only when I banged the top of my knee doing a hip-thrust move with the dryer.

My sore knee didn't squelch my mood as I shopped, purchasing a pair of black skinny jeans, a pair of black leather open toe high-heeled boots, and a silky royal blue top.

Returning to my hotel room, I scanned my research on the jazz festival and decided on a course of action for the afternoon. I picked up my camera and notebook and headed back to Church Street. Writing wasn't like riding a bike; you have to practice all the time and my skills were decidedly rusty. It would take time, but I was excited to get started.

*

My euphoria over John waned by the next morning. I needed to push him out of my mind and focus completely on what I'd come to do—to figure out if writing could fill my empty days.

But I couldn't help thinking: Could a relationship really work living in different states? At best, it would be complicated.

A touch deflated, I left my hotel with my backpack, camera, and notepad. I met with the managing and artistic directors of the festival, who answered my questions and gave me a tour of the Flynn Center for the Performing Arts where the headliners would perform. I was pleased—not only did they take me seriously, but I felt the information I was getting would make a great story!

Before dinner I headed back to the hotel for a shower. During the festival, jazz bands played all day and into the night. Dinner would be a good time to check out some of the bands that only played in the evening.

Opening the curtains in the room, I paused to admire Lake Champlain, the water glittering like tiny diamonds in front of me. The lake had settled into a sweet-tempered, tamer current after the demanding afternoon of boat traffic. The sun perched on top of the distant Adirondack Mountains as if waiting for its final bow.

My phone rang.

*

An hour later, I waited outside on a Church Street bench, listening to a local jazz band, tapping my foot to its soulful rhythm. Jazz was so sensuous with its staccato beats. My hips loved to sway to the music.

A mere whisper of a breeze blew down from the top of the street onto the cobblestones. People congregated all over the roads, sidewalks, and parks, listening. Some stood, some brought folding chairs, while others sat in groups on large Hudson Bay blankets. As I sat, I took some notes about the dynamic atmosphere. I knew I should mention how Church Street had been transformed into an open-air mall in 1981, and now boasted around one hundred shops and restaurants. While live entertainment was common here year-round, the jazz festival featured hundreds of bands, from novice to legendary. The streets sizzled, and the air was charged with the spicy, redolent rhythms of drums, guitars, pianos, and saxophones. It felt heavy with the beat.

John Marshall strode up the street toward me, his stride sure-footed, and I slipped my notepad into my purse. As he walked closer, I noticed that the baseball cap was gone. In its place was a luxurious head of thick brown hair with a slight wave falling below his ears, striped with gray at the temples.

His walk looked so confident. I thanked God he was walking toward me and not me toward him; I knew I would have fallen over my feet. My hands began to shake slightly. *How silly is that?* You'd never know that I was a forty-nine-year-old woman who had met a lot of men, including famous ones.

Please, I pleaded with myself, *don't let my voice betray me, no high notes or squeaks.* I watched him, trying to keep my jaw from dropping. *God, he should be in a jeans commercial.* John looked directly at me as he strolled up the hill. My mouth grew dry. Seeming to move in slow motion, it took him forever to reach me, making me even more nervous. Intelligence used to be my aphrodisiac, not looks. *Does everything change in middle age?*

He came close and looked down into my face. "Hi," he said,

with an impish grin. He seemed to realize how nervous I was and was enjoying every moment of it.

Looking up at him, I simply smiled.

"What a beautiful evening!" He offered both hands and gently pulled me to my feet, then led me down Church Street. "I thought we'd grab a drink by the lake before we go see my friend's band."

Noticing my feet struggling in my new high-heeled boots on the cobblestones, he held on to my arm.

"Sounds great," I blurted, attempting to keep my balance and not clutch at his arm. The boots may not have been my smartest choice, but I loved being able to wear heels again. My ex-husband wasn't very tall, and it had bothered him when I hovered over his head. I certainly didn't have that problem with John, though I had to focus on keeping up with his long stride. Somehow, my body stayed upright.

The bar overlooked Lake Champlain with a huge outside deck area for dinner and drinks. We were lucky to get the last table by the water. Even there by the lake, blocks away from the main stages, the streets bustled with people and were filled with music.

After being seated, we locked eyes for a moment, smiling. A flashback flickered into my mind of my middle-school days and a kid named Harry, who I'd been crazy about. When he sat across from me in lunch one day, Harry flashed me a big smile, like John's, but Harry's smile wasn't for me. A couple of boys had dared him to sit at the girls' table. Harry always took the dares and won the bets, but for just one moment, I'd thought he'd come over specially to talk to me. I had felt crushed when he bounced right up and walked back over to his friends, slapping high fives.

We ordered drinks, a cosmo for me to help calm my nerves, and a vodka tonic for John. Feeling shy, I fidgeted with the cocktail napkin. He seemed as calm as he was two days ago at lunch, while I was anything but.

I tried to pick up my cosmo gracefully, which was filled to the brim. My hand shook slightly, and tiny droplets cascaded onto the table. I took a large sip to prevent any more spillage. *Well, at least, I didn't drop it. Yet.*

John watched me make a mess. My mind ran a marathon trying to think of something to say. I blurted: "What makes you smile?" *Ahhh…such a lame-assed question!* It sounded like a question you'd read on the Internet under "Tips to Avoid on Your First Date." *Christ, I'm a grown woman.* I felt my cheeks burning and turned away.

"Hmm…well," he said, actually considering the question. "Lots of things. My children, a good joke, a movie, a book." His smile drew me in and held on. So unlike my ex, whose brittle smile looked like his mouth would break if he extended his lips too wide.

"What makes *you* smile?" he asked, interrupting my comparisons.

Not wanting to give myself away by saying that *he* did, I changed the subject. "Oh, you have children?"

"Yes, two girls. Sophie is twenty-four and Natalie is twenty-one. You?"

"Two boys, Chris is twenty-three, and Jeff is twenty-four; both on their own now. I live in a suburb in the northwestern part of New Jersey, out in the country." Of course, I wasn't sure John would think of it as country, more like *Town & Country*.

John kept his gaze focused on me when I spoke, listening intently. This level of attention was new for me: no obligatory glances or nods, no one ignoring me and talking on the phone, but someone's full attention.

John told me about himself. His mechanical engineering degree was from Northwestern. After college he had worked in Boston, then came back to the family dairy farm to help his dad and ended up taking over.

"My father and I spent a great deal of time outside together. He would have loved being a farmer instead of a CPA," I said. "Maybe you could show me your farm sometime."

John grinned and reached for his drink.

No answer. Was I being too forward? Could he hear me? "How did you get into racing?" I asked, my voice rising a few octaves.

John caught my eye and I flushed. He'd definitely heard me this time.

"I've always loved racing. I started about five years ago. It's only a hobby, a part-time kind of thing."

Lowering the volume, I asked, "Do you race often?"

"I'm racing on Saturday night at Devil's Bowl." Laughing, he told me about his first smash-ups. His eyes glistened in the candlelight, exposing tiny gold flecks that drew me in and held me captive.

"I'd love to see you race." I held my breath, hoping he'd invite me.

John looked at me but said nothing. The waitress saved the awkward moment by presenting the check.

"My treat, remember." As I handed the credit card to the waitress, my mind considered our conversation. I wanted to see more of him but felt some vague hesitation on his part. After all, he hadn't responded to my not-so-subtle requests to see his farm or to watch him race.

John's friend Mike was already playing when we arrived. A family sitting on a nearby bench were getting up and offered us their seats. The four-piece band played New Orleans–style jazz with Southern embellishments.

An hour or so later we walked back to Lake Champlain. At night, you can't see the Adirondack Mountains, but you can see, hear, and feel the water. At dusk, humidity visits the shore and sticks around for a few hours before receding back out over the water. We strolled to Battery Street Park, enjoying the crisp, clear night. We found a bench and sat looking out over the lake.

He held my elbow as I settled onto the seat. John's tenderness was refreshing. The way he talked about his daughters made my heart flutter.

"My older daughter calls me every day. I love that about her." John turned slightly on the bench to face me. "I certainly didn't call my father every day when I was her age. I guess she feels she has to look out for me since her mother passed." John swiveled back on the bench and looked out over the water.

My mind raced for something profound to say about his loss, but instead I just stared out over Lake Champlain.

"Well, I have an early start tomorrow. May I walk you back to your hotel?" John said. He stood and faced me, holding out his hand.

"Sure."

His smile went way up into his eyes, the skin crinkling around them.

My hand found his and I stood facing him, wishing I could run my fingers through his hair and entwine them in the soft curls at his neck. But John pulled me to the left around the bench and toward my hotel.

The Marriott was only a five-minute walk, and before we entered the lobby, he gently grabbed my arm and pulled me back to him. Catching me off-guard, I looked into his face as he guided my chin with his index finger until my lips reached his mouth. We kissed, a long, soft, slow, gentle kiss filled with tenderness. I think a small moan escaped from me when he moved in closer and his kiss probed a little deeper. His mouth was moist and longing, with a hint of lime lingering from his drink, melting any inhibitions I might have had.

We stayed tight together with his forehead leaning on my head and his hands on the side of my face, our breaths united. "I had a wonderful time tonight," he said, backing slowly away from our embrace.

"Yes, me, too," was all I could muster, not sure if my body would hold me up. *Wow. I felt that kiss down to my toes!* He must have felt it, too.

"Good night," he said, turning up the hotel driveway.

"Good night." My voice was barely audible. I steadied myself on a column. In my haze, it dawned on me that he hadn't asked me out again. *He does have my number*, I told myself. *Yes, yes, he does.*

Alone in my hotel room, the evening played itself over in my mind. To be hopped-up on some unknown love potion at my age was exhilarating, and I hoped he felt the same. Sleep eluded me, but the Chardonnay in the mini bar calmed me.

I glanced at my phone and saw a text from my ex. I ignored it and put my head back on the couch.

George lived a life centered on work. That excited him. He wasn't always that way, but once his career took off, his family became secondary to the next deal, the next meeting, the next business trip. His dream of success came at a price. I'd tried to be a good wife and mother, but my marriage had turned hollow, just going through the motions without the emotions. Did he cheat? Who knows? Somewhere along the line it didn't matter anymore. We just kept up the pretense for our sons.

In bed, John's scent lingered in my nose and in my hair, a faint odor of an earthy musk warmed by the sun. A simple trace of a man who had nothing to prove.

*

The sunny morning matched my mood. As soon as I knew she'd be up, I called Bri.

"Wanna hear about my date?"

"Your what? How? Where? Tell me," Bri enquired.

Bri listened avidly to every detail.

"Do you think he'll call?" I asked.

"Maybe, but he's a guy and they can be dicks."

"Oh, don't say that! Tell me: Of course, he'll call. Let me live with this fantasy for a little while."

"Just relax, you're overthinking the date. It sounds like you had a wonderful evening." Bri's voice was soothing.

"I know, it scares me. To have a man interested in me after all these years is so…I can't even think of the word…exhilarating, maybe."

"Enjoy every moment." Bri changed the subject, bringing me up to date about Madeline's recent party and her new friend, Natasha.

Duty called. I sat at my laptop and started writing a blog post. But after a sentence or two, I detected a touch of musk and my mind wandered back to last night. I wasn't focused enough to write. I grabbed my backpack and ventured out to interview more people and take pictures. I needed to move.

Burlington has soul, a gentle serenity that runs deep, not just during the jazz festival, but throughout the year. I've always been able to unwind and relax there. My years of living in a fast-paced metropolitan area had frazzled my senses with so many unnatural time pressures. I wondered: Would this be a better place to live?

Later in the day, after I showered and ate dinner at the hotel, I returned to Church Street to mingle in the hubbub and ended up outside of Ben & Jerry's ice cream shop. The sweet smells of sugar, chocolate, and cream pulled me in. Like most of the divorced women I knew, twenty pounds magically disappeared after the divorce. I smiled, thinking how it must have annoyed my ex.

Thoughts of John persisted as the night wore on. Back in my room I uploaded the pictures I had taken. So many happy faces. But were they really happy? I clicked on the app on my phone where our family photos were stored. Staring back at me was a woman whose head was angled toward her husband with a huge smile plastered on her face. No, there was no way anyone would know how unhappy I'd been.

My phone vibrated, and John's name popped up.

"Hi," I said in the sexiest voice I could muster.

"Would you like to come to the races at Devil's Bowl tomorrow night?" John asked. "I'm not sure it's all that exciting, but you did say you'd like to go."

"Yes, absolutely," I said, trying to keep the excitement out of my voice.

"Can you drive down yourself around six? The racers have to be there hours before. I'll be in the fourth race, black car number thirty-five, and after that we can watch the last race together and maybe catch a drink after."

"That sounds great. By the way, I had a wonderful time the other night."

"Me too," he said quietly. After a long pause, he softly said good night and that he'd see me tomorrow.

He called and asked me out, but... Why did he become so quiet at the end of our conversation? Men! My mind grew fatigued thinking about all subtle nuances of dating.

*

Saturday was a bedazzling, sunny day, alive and full of promise. In my excitement, I rummaged through my clothes trying to decide what to wear and made a mess.

I felt just like a young girl going out on a first date, even though I wasn't.

Because I was so nervous, I finished getting ready much too early. I stopped for a sandwich in Ferrisburgh on the way to the race. Vermont must be calling forth the diva in me. I moved and grooved to the Queen of Rock and Roll herself, Tina Turner, up and over the hills to the racetrack.

Unlike the last time I was there, the Devil's Bowl Speedway parking lot was jammed, and newly arriving cars were funneled to an adjoining property. Lights, noise, cars, people, vendors—a lot of hullabaloo. I realized as I got out of my car, that I knew nothing about car racing and should have done a little research before coming.

I saw a few open spots in the bleachers where I had taken the photos that first day. Excusing myself, I inched my way to the top and put in earplugs before the cars started and the noise overwhelmed my hearing. I always carried a spare set in my overnight bag because of my ex's snoring. My ears tingled the other day at the track with only John's car. With multiple cars, I anticipated a pulsating throbbing in my ears, the same as after a concert. So, I brought my earplugs.

The announcer gave the five-minute warning for the first race.

The couple next to me laughed when they saw me putting in the earplugs. I took them out. I smiled and asked, "What kind of cars race here?"

"It's short-track stock car racing, ma'am," said the young man next to me. The young girl with him giggled and twisted her hands together. "If we're lucky we'll see some paint swapping tonight," the young man said.

Ugh! I hated being called *ma'am*. "Is that dangerous—'paint swapping'?" I asked, not sure I wanted to know.

"Nah, not really," he replied just as the cars lined up for the first race and started revving their engines.

"I've never been to a race before. It's exciting," I shouted. The young man gave me a thumbs-up.

The collective roar of the engines assaulted my ears and any chance at conversation.

The first race began. The crowd was up on their feet.

The leaders of the race seemed to collide around the second curve and stayed glued together for a few laps until one of the cars pulled forward.

The crowd ignited into a thundering roar every time two of the race cars banged into each other. But this entangled kind of racing at a high speed had me panic-stricken, and I jumped every time the cars bumped together.

Suddenly John's race was next. What if his car flips over? I've seen multiple deadly race-car accidents on the news. What if he's killed or injured? Before I could ask the young man next to me to explain, the announcer commanded the drivers of the fourth race to "start your engines."

My leg twitched up and down. *Am I actually nervous? I barely know the guy.* But what if he gets hurts.

The green flag waved and the cars rushed forward.

Oh God!

AVA

FIRST LOVE

THE HOUSE LIGHTS were out when I pulled into my driveway after book club. Paul still wasn't home. *Gracias a dios.*

I checked my cell again for any messages. None. I dropped my keys on the counter, collapsing into a kitchen chair. Maybe he went to play racquetball? I pushed my overgrown bangs out of my eyes and rested my head in my hands. Thank goodness book club gave me time to think, even if the girls kept asking me why I was constantly checking my phone.

I walked over to the bar and fixed a drink.

Two dirty gin martinis later, I realized I had forgotten to tell Tess about a prospective buyer for her home. Was it too late to call her?

Looking up at the clock, I realized it was way too late for racquetball. Where the hell was Paul? Then I noticed the flashing light on the home phone. That blinking red light drove me nuts whenever the lights are out at night and I've forgotten to listen to my messages. I pushed play.

The last message was from Paul. "I can't believe you pulled the plug on the sale," Paul snarled. "Just what the hell are you thinking? Oh, I forgot—you don't think." He continued to attack before informing me he was disappearing for a while. He needed space. "Don't call me. I'll call you."

I guess that was supposed to upset me. *What a coward!* Didn't want to call my cell and risk me answering. *"Pendejo!"* I said aloud. *You're nothing more than a pubic hair.*

The martinis started to work and I lay down on the couch, closing my eyes to calm my agitated thoughts. I took deep breaths, inviting the darkness to push my feelings away. I floated in a quiet, dark sea for a few minutes, but I couldn't sustain it. Today's events kept demanding my attention.

I thought back to this morning's ride into the city. The mist collected on the car's windows and the wipers strained to keep the windshield clear. The wet cold seeped into my bones as we drove silently into New York City.

Paul and I met our attorney in the conference room in the old Pan Am building overlooking Central Park. On a good day, it had views of the Hudson and East Rivers. Today, I could see nothing but a seamless gray haze.

In our conference room, I said hello to Sam Wells, our attorney for twenty years. Because I trusted him, I'd asked him to look over the closing documents. Paul pushed them across the table, shooting me a look of disdain. I ignored him. I hadn't been involved in the negotiations for the sale and needed to know what I was signing.

"Ava, we talked about this last night. All we need is your signature. Everything is already settled." Paul slammed his hand on the table, making me jump. "You didn't have to come in today. I told you that last night."

"Well, it's my business, too." My voice rose, then I paused. He'd barely talked to me last night about anything, much less the closing details. "I want to look over the documents. And Sam, too."

Paul stood and began to pace up and down the conference room.

"I only need a few minutes to review and to talk to Sam," I said.

A headache throbbed in my forehead. Something felt off. Maybe how quickly the purchase had gone through. Usually negotiations are haggled over for a few weeks, even months.

Paul had initiated the idea to sell. He said he couldn't handle the stress anymore. I'd agreed to the sale, hoping against hope that it might help our failing marriage. The last few years with Paul had been bad. He had become a monster—condescending, disagreeable, sometimes even cruel. Was it the stress of the business that made him act this way? I wasn't sure I cared anymore.

The strain of commuting into New York caused such anxiety in me especially after becoming a mother. I grew fearful at being too far from my two children. Stress or no stress, though, I never acted like Paul. Instead, I had branched off of our New York management company and opened a real estate business in New Jersey. I earned my Realtor's license and started Aguiar Realty with one office in Chester and eventually another in a neighboring town. The move to New Jersey allowed me more time with our children.

I had just opened the closing documents folder, taking a pad and pen to write down any questions, when Sheila, our secretary, announced that the buyers were here.

"What? Aren't they early? I just started reviewing the documents." I turned to Paul. "I don't even know who they are."

"Well, you're about to find out." Paul stood to greet the buyers. "Good morning, gentlemen."

I pushed my chair out and walked over to Paul. The buyers' attorneys introduced themselves. One of the buyers looked vaguely familiar. He was quite old and his hands shook when he removed his hat. Paul introduced him as Bruce Bass.

My head started to pound again. Bass— *Ay caramba!* I knew a family by that name before I met Paul. *It can't be.* The father was a *shark* and the son…

"I'd like to introduce my son, Neil," said Bruce, who turned toward the door as his son walked through it.

My mind instantly cycled back thirty years. *No way!*

Neil and I locked eyes as we shook hands. The room suddenly shifted as if the floor was going to swallow me. Unsteadily I returned to my seat while my husband showed our guests to their chairs. *Just what the hell is going on?*

I looked up. The man sitting across from me hadn't changed much. Warm blue eyes, sculpted chin, and the aquiline nose that dominated his face. His beautiful blond hair was now replaced with a trendy shaved head. Regardless, he was still handsome. Time had been kind to him.

I thought I saw a flicker of recognition behind his steely demeanor. *Stay calm,* I ordered myself. *Don't let anyone know.* The irony struck me. Neil sat across from me, wanting what was mine, when thirty years ago he had walked away. Back then, I wasn't good enough.

My mind raced, trying to figure out how to escape the room. My breath was labored and my face felt like it was on fire. I could feel a hot flash coming on. I had to get out of there. I couldn't think clearly.

Our attorney, Sam, started handing out the documents. I hadn't even reviewed the closing summary sheet yet. The Basses' attorneys handed out their clients' personal financial statements and a check made out to us. Sam gave the buyers our last few years' profit and loss statements. My head throbbed.

I stood, my hands on the table for support. Paul must have known who these people were. "I'm not signing the documents. We are not selling the business."

Paul tried to grab my arm as I turned to leave, but I pulled away. I heard gasps around the table as I fled the room.

I collapsed into a chair in my old office a few doors down from the conference room, slamming the door shut.

It took several minutes but eventually all parties from the closing walked by, murmuring quietly to one other. Paul sounded gracious, telling everyone that he would work out another arrangement within the week for when I felt better. He was anything but gracious when he burst into my office as soon as they were gone.

"What the fuck happened to you between eleven o'clock when we agreed to sell and eleven-ten when the buyer walked in the door? Are you crazy?" Paul kicked a chair out of his way, moving closer to me. "What the hell?"

All I could muster was: "This isn't right. And you know it." I turned and looked out the window.

Paul approached and grabbed my shoulder, spinning me to face him. His face was beet red. He clutched my shoulders with both hands and shook hard. "Do you know what you've done?"

Between clenched teeth, I sneered under my breath, "If I knew why we are suddenly selling our business, maybe I could answer that question." Met with an enraged stare and no response, I added spitefully, "And by the way, those damned people are never getting anything of mine!"

Paul stormed out of the office.

My mind drifted back to the present. *Ah.* I rubbed my head. The martinis have stopped working. I was as angry now as I was this morning. I opened my eyes, desperately trying to push the chaos from my mind. I rose and walked over to the window, searching the dark for a clue. Was it a midlife crisis, another woman? Why did I go along with this idea? And how in the name of hell did Neil get involved?

Wandering aimlessly through our family room, I wondered if another martini would help calm me down. Oh, what the hell! I moved toward the bar.

*

My cell phone woke me in the morning. I must have fallen asleep on the couch sometime in the wee hours. My headache from yesterday remained but had increased in intensity thanks to an unknown number of martinis. I could barely lift my head and my hair tangled on a pillow button when I did. *Que hodienda! Fuck.*

I finally managed to stagger to my cell on the kitchen counter. I didn't recognize the number. Needing coffee, I opened the freezer and pulled out the ground beans. No Keurig pods for me today; I needed an extra punch of strong, old-fashioned coffee. I took three aspirins and choked down a piece of bread while I waited for the coffee to brew.

Within a half hour I began to feel human again and ate a muffin. I thought about Paul, but my mind kept returning to Neil. I took my coffee to my computer and Googled him. Neil still lived in Manhattan on Central Park West. Clearly, he had continued to prosper. I checked him out on LinkedIn.

Ping. An invite to connect with Neil popped up on my screen. *What the hell is he thinking? That I really want to be a business associate of his? Is he crazy? He dumped me thirty years ago with no explanation and now he wants to buy my business and be on LinkedIn with me?*

I shut my laptop. I needed to get to the bottom of this business transaction between my husband and Neil. Whose idea was it? With Paul off the grid, I had to do some digging and maybe Neil was a good place to start.

Opening the laptop, I tapped my finger on the side of the computer, still torn between logging out and connecting. *What am I waiting for?*

I hit the connect button and inhaled deeply.

Ping! I had a LinkedIn message within a minute:

Ava,

Need to talk to you without Paul.

Please call me today.

Neil (212) 867-5305

Oh God, I don't know what to do. What could he possibly have to talk to me about?

My hand shook as I reached for my cell and dialed the number.

"What do you want?" I barked.

"Ava. Are you all right?" Neil asked

"Yes. No. I don't know." I answered, surprised that I just blurted out the truth. I should have hung up on him.

"I want to see you, please. Come into the city and we'll meet for lunch, dinner, whatever you like. Or I'll come out to you."

"Why do you want to meet? I need more time to review the transaction." I didn't want to explain myself to him.

"Ava, it's not just about the business."

My heart suddenly skipped a beat.

"Ava?"

"I'll come to the city. Where would you like to meet?"

*

My mind raced through every conceivable scenario to try to figure out what Neil wanted. I felt both hyper and exhausted. Nothing made sense.

After I showered, I rummaged through my closet. I wanted a casual, no-big-deal outfit. I needed to look relaxed and confident even if I felt anything but. At least the shower and the aspirin had helped lessen my headache.

I decided flats and my favorite jeans would give me a carefree look. I threw on my new leather jacket. The leather was so soft to the touch that I found myself stroking the sleeve. I looked in the full-length mirror. My hands were trembling from nerves. I wrapped both arms around my chest before turning to leave.

Still not a word from Paul. Should I call him? The longer he stayed silent the angrier I got. How dare he yell and shake me like that? What was he trying to pull? I'd had enough of his craziness.

We met at Il Molino, my favorite Italian restaurant. Wherever Paul might be, I knew he wouldn't show up here. He hated the restaurant because of a bad waitress more than three years ago. Paul had left in a huff and vowed never to return.

I took a deep breath before entering Il Molino. Neil was sitting at a small table in the back of the restaurant. Should I turn and run?

Too late. Neil spotted me and waved me over.

He stood to greet me. I slid into my chair before he could offer a hand, a hug, or to push my seat in.

"Ava, you look beautiful." He smiled, staring.

I looked at him, my expression deliberately blank. I used to dream about meeting him again and didn't want my thoughts to betray me. I ordered my usual gin martini to calm my nerves.

Neil was dressed in jeans and a button-down shirt. He looked fit and fantastic. *Damn him, he looks even more carefree than I do.* I almost laughed out loud at the thought.

Neil started talking after the waiter brought my drink. "Thank you for agreeing to see me. You must have a lot of questions, but please listen to what I have to say first."

I glared at him. "You have some nerve, thinking I might ever want to hear what you have to say about anything."

"Ava, please listen. You can yell at me all you want afterward."

"Okay, talk." I slouched in my chair, trying to conceal my pounding heart. I needed to keep my guard up. His beautiful, melodic voice used to be able to lull me into anything.

"My father ran a background check on you when we were dating. He was not happy I was dating a *shiksa*." Neil looked down at the table. "That means a non-Jew. My dad knew the owners of the building where you lived and where your father was the superintendent. He threatened to have your father fired. I didn't want your family hurt because *my* father was a prick."

"What?" My cheeks burned. "Just what the hell are you talking about—that's ancient history." I threw my napkin on the table and started to get up.

"No, Ava, please just hear me out. I was twenty-four years old and felt helpless. As much as I loved you, I didn't think I had a choice. I had to walk away. I never explained because...I don't know: I was a coward, confused, afraid of my father and what he might do."

My body trembled as I sat down and looked at the love of my life telling me this crazy story. Had I entered the Twilight Zone?

"So, you thought you might ingratiate yourself by waiting thirty years and going into cahoots with my husband? *That* was a good idea?"

"No, that's not what I meant." Neil reached for my hand across the table. "I wanted to tell you how sorry I am for what I did."

I pulled my hand away.

"I have never forgotten you, us." Neil's eyes pleaded for forgiveness.

How could so much change in my world in one day? I shook my head, speechless.

"I've kept tabs on you over the years. You seemed happily married and successful and I was genuinely pleased for you." Neil stopped talking abruptly, almost as if he cut himself off mid-thought.

"I don't understand what this is all about. Why did you offer to buy our business? Because of your guilty conscience?"

"Paul approached me directly about a month ago." Neil said. "The sale didn't go through a broker."

Totally stunned, I couldn't speak. Why did Paul go to Neil? The room pixelated like a grainy, antique picture.

"Ava, are you all right?" Neil asked, reaching for my hand again.

"I guess I don't know what the men in my life are up to." I gulped my martini. Why did Paul want to sell so quickly? A few years ago, we had to sell some stock to pay his online betting debts. I had insisted he go to counseling and thought his addiction was over. Was it back?

"Neil, I can't stay. I feel sick." I stood up and left as quickly as I could. I just didn't know whom I could trust anymore.

*

I went directly to our Manhattan office. It was a Saturday, so no one was there. I looked through the closing documents that were in a folder Paul had left on his desk. Neil and his father were paying a premium for the business. Why? Out of guilt?

The papers appeared to be in order. I looked at the company's profit and loss statement. Everything looked fine.

Nothing out of the ordinary turned up in Paul's desk, either. Maybe my suspicions were unfounded. I turned the lights out and locked the office door.

*

Sunday came and went. My life was on hold. Who the hell did Paul think he was? I called his cell and it went directly to voicemail.

"Paul, where the fuck are you? Call me back right now!" I screamed into the phone.

Hours seemed to pass like days. Tick, tock. I worked aimlessly around the house washing laundry, gardening, paying bills, doing anything and everything to keep my mind occupied.

Around two o'clock, I knew I had to call Tess about her prospective buyer. I washed my face with cold water and pulled her file out of my briefcase.

"Hi, Tess."

"Hey, Ava. Have you got an offer?" Tess asked eagerly.

"A pretty solid offer may be coming within the next couple of days. It's the young couple with the toddler. They loved your home and are hoping their parents can lend or give them some money. They can make the monthly payments but are just shy of the 20 percent down they need for the mortgage approval. I'm sorry. I forgot to call you or even mention it at book club. I was pretty distracted on Friday."

"Why? Is everything okay?"

"Not really sure yet." I said tentatively.

"Ava, what's the matter?"

"Paul is gone. We had a fight and I don't know where he is. It's been coming for some time. I simply don't understand what is at the root of his dissatisfaction with me, with his life." Choking on my words, I finally allowed my pain to engulf me and indulged in a long, overdue cry.

*

Monday melted into a repeat of Sunday. Maybe Paul really was having an affair? That would explain how distant he had become these last few years. We don't even spoon anymore. Our infrequent couplings were always at my prompting, and were perfunctory and lackluster. I'd assumed it was due to our diminishing rapport, but it made sense if Paul was having a liaison. Snooping in his private and business e-mails, verifying out-of-town reservations, and stalking his phone while he slept had become a way of life for me. But he'd always checked out clean. I couldn't approach his assistant with my suspicions, either. Rick would be the first to throw me under the bus, to tell Paul. Those two were as thick as thieves. My cell rang and I looked at the number. It was Neil. I didn't answer it. *"Por favor, deja me quieta!"* Please, leave me alone. *"I need to figure this out and you're just complicating things,"* I pleaded, as if Neil could hear me.

When my hundredth call to Paul went unanswered, I wanted to throw the phone across the room. I tried to reconstruct the events of that day. He'd tried to keep me home. He was annoyed that I wanted to look over the closing documents. Why had Paul sought out Neil to sell him the company? Could Paul be gambling again? Yet I hadn't found any evidence.

My phone rang. I prayed that it was Paul. *Ay Dios mio! Es mi hijo!* It was my son, Gabriel. *What am I going to say to him?*

"Hi, honey! How are you?" I said, trying to sound normal despite my clenched jaw.

"Hey, Mom. I'm fine. Thought I'd call since I didn't hear from you guys this weekend. Were you away?"

"Your, your father is away…" I stuttered.

"Where did he go this time? He doesn't usually travel without you on the weekend."

I didn't know what to say, so the truth came tumbling out. "I'm not sure. We had a fight and he left three days ago."

"Three days ago, and you didn't call me? Or Alysia? What's wrong with you? What if he is dead? Have you called him?"

"I've called him a thousand times, but he's not answering my calls. Why would I involve you and your sister?" I firmly state. "This is between us." My tone surprises me. I suddenly felt braver than I had in the last few days. Talking to my son fortified me. I could suddenly face whatever might lie ahead. Paul might wish he were dead after I got through with him. Putting me and now the kids through this distress was the ultimate act of selfishness.

"Mom, he's never left before. This must be pretty serious."

"It is serious. He asked me not to contact him, to give him space. I have to assume he's safe. He's a grown man." I thought for a moment, fuming. "I'm going to report his wallet stolen and freeze his access to his debit and credit cards. He'll be in touch soon enough."

*

The next morning, I went back to work. Work I knew.

My assistant seemed giddy when I walked in.

"What's got you so excited?" I asked her.

"Go into your office," Kylie said, a huge smile lighting up her face.

When I opened the door, the fragrance hit me first. *"Ay car-amba!"* There were flowers everywhere. Long stemmed red roses in vases of varying size. This had to be Neil. It was like a scene in a movie where the girl falls madly in love with the sender. But I'd already been there, done that.

"You sure do have an admirer out there." Kylie giggled.

"I guess I do. Was there a card?" I asked.

"No. No card. Aren't they from your husband?"

I stopped myself from answering and looked at Kylie. "Oh, of course. But it's nice to get a message, too." I picked up a vase on the window ledge. "Help me move these to the outer office before I start sneezing from so much perfume." The flowers made me smile for the first time in four days.

I bent down to smell the roses on my desk and the barrette holding my bangs to the side unclipped and fell to the floor. Kylie walked in as I was searching for the barrette on the floor and helped me find it.

"You could wear a hairband until your bangs grow long enough to put behind your ears," she offered.

No friggin way, I thought. I would cut my bangs again before running around like a Catholic schoolgirl.

After we brought most of the flowers to the outer office, I texted Neil to thank him.

He immediately called me back, but I didn't answer.

The office phone started ringing and I fell into my normal work rhythm. It was comforting to be there, doing what I had been doing for years. The rest of the day flew by and before I knew it, it was late in the evening.

I arrived home after ten. I made a drink. Exhausted, I changed and climbed into bed.

My cell rang. It was Bri.

"I talked to Tess today and she told me what happened with Paul and the closing. Can you talk? Do you want to talk?" Bri asked.

"I can talk, he's not here. Things with Paul are escalating."

"How?" Bri sounded concerned.

"You know, it's almost like he has a girlfriend and resents me.

He's restless and irritable when he's around. Maybe he's gambling again. I don't know, and I'm really starting not to care. He's hiding something, buying time and trying to make me the heavy. Why did I ever trust another man after what Neil did to me?"

"Well, can I help in any way?" If you need a place to stay till you sort things out you can stay with us," Bri offered.

"I'm an idiot for not being more involved with the sale of the business."

"Does Paul know you dated him?"

"Yes, he knows all about him." A pain shot up my back. *"Que voy a hacer?"*

"What?" Bri asked.

"What am I going to do?" I translated.

"With Paul or Neil?"

"Both!" It helped to talk about this lunacy. We talked for a while, but, of course, neither of us could figure out what to do next.

After we hung up, I turned on the TV to mask the suffocating quietness of the house.

My chest ached from the vice grip of the last few days between Paul and Neil. I closed my eyes, willing my body to relax. My mind traveled back in time to the first man who'd broken my heart.

Neil and I met when he struck my car from behind at a stoplight. I was devastated because my rusted Dodge Dart wasn't covered for collision and I didn't have the money to fix it.

The man who approached my driver's window was extremely handsome, dressed in a dark suit and tie, with dirty blond curly hair. When I leaned out of my car window, I had to look up at him—so tall and athletically built. *Ay, yai, yai!* For a moment, I almost forgot about my car.

"Are you okay, miss? I'm so sorry. I saw the light turn green and…" the tall, blond stranger bent down by the window to talk.

"Didn't you see that old man cross the street at the last minute? I had to stop for him."

"No, I didn't. I'm running late for a show and I guess I was distracted. Now I'm really late."

I got out of my car to survey the damage. His black Porsche had a bad dent on its front, worse than my bumper.

"I don't have collision insurance," I cried.

"Don't worry. I'll take care of it." He moved back to his car and reached inside.

"I'm really late," the stranger said. "Can we exchange numbers? I promise to call you tomorrow to get this sorted out. Maybe even tonight, if I don't get home too late."

"What? No way! Why should I trust you?"

"Here, take my insurance card and file a claim if I don't call you by tomorrow. All my information is on that card." He smiled a broad infectious grin. "Can I please have your phone number and address?"

I glanced down at the insurance card and saw his name was Neil Bass. I could just hear my friends: *What kind of a fool are you?* "Sure," I told the handsome man with the black Porsche.

Neil was as good as his word and called. We met after I got an estimate of what it would take to repair the bumper. He actually asked me out afterward.

"I'm glad you agreed to meet me instead of my just mailing the check to you," Neil said when we sat down at Monte's for a cocktail before we headed to see an off-Broadway play.

We stayed out late. Neil walked me to the front of my apartment building. He wrapped his arms around me and kissed me good night. Not a peck, but a slow, moist dream of a kiss. It literally took my breath away. Light-headed, I didn't think I'd survive another. But I did.

I sneaked quietly back into the house without waking my old-fashioned parents. Since I couldn't afford my own place, I had to live by their rules.

The Bronx was the last place I wanted to live, but my father worked there as a building superintendent and a free apartment came with the job. The Irish and Italians who lived in the area could be quite cruel to us Puerto Ricans. Our last name, Delmar, didn't instantly scream Hispanic, so they assumed I was Italian, and I let them. I felt if someone really loved me, my ethnicity wouldn't matter.

After Neil and I had been dating for a few months, we met, as usual, at the Bronx Zoo, which was conveniently placed between his home in Manhattan and mine in the Bronx. And it was one of our favorite places. I had decided it was finally time to tell Neil the truth.

"I have a confession to make. I'm not Italian," I began.

"Really?" Neil's eyebrows rose.

"I'm Puerto Rican." I closed my eyes, expecting the worst.

Neil laughed out loud. "I don't care."

I was giddy with relief. My big secret was out and he didn't care. I skipped all the way to our next exhibit, World of Reptiles.

Watching the lizard crawl up a rock, I wondered if his parents would care.

*

Our love grew. Bewitched, we carried on for almost a year like no one else in the universe existed. I thought I was Cinderella.

But one day, at the beginning of summer, Neil dropped by my family home unannounced, his arms full with a bouquet. He'd never been there before. Embarrassed by our tiny basement apartment, I always arranged to meet him somewhere else or I waited outside the building if he insisted on picking me up.

I was horrified when my sister showed him into our crammed living room. I don't know how I'd thought I could have kept him from coming to my home or meeting my quirky family. Aghast, seeing the gold crushed velvet couch encased in plastic on a thread-bare sky-blue rug through Neil's eyes, I thanked him for the flowers and hurriedly put them on the table, pulling his arm to leave.

My father teased us as he blocked the front door with his massive shoulders, drawing out every word. "So, we finally get to meet the mysterious Neil."

Reaching out to shake Neil's hand, my father said, "I'm Dan. And now you've met my wife, Paquita." My father then issued an invitation Neil couldn't refuse: "You must stay for dinner. We would love to get to know the person who's captured our Ava's heart."

"Paquita, we have a special guest for dinner tonight," my father proclaimed proudly, having snagged the long alluded-to Bass on his fishing line.

If I died once, I died a thousand times that evening. We had *pollo guisao* for dinner, a family favorite with white rice and red beans. Neil even followed the family's lead, picking up a chicken thigh and eating it right off the bone, claiming, "This is my new favorite meal. Ava, why didn't you invite me over sooner? Your family is so much nicer than mine." You could tell that he thoroughly enjoyed the meal and was sincere about enjoying his time with *mi familia*.

Neil gave me a sweet tender kiss outside my apartment door. "I really enjoyed spending time with your family. Why were you afraid of my meeting them? They're really warm and sincere people. My parents, on the other hand, are neither warm nor sincere. When I finally introduce you to them, you'll understand why I'm putting it off as long as possible."

A few days later, Neil called. "Can we meet me for a cup of coffee?"

"Coffee? You don't like coffee. Is everything okay?" I ask.

"It doesn't have to be coffee. I just need to see you before I leave on a business trip. I don't have much time. Pick you up at five?

I don't know why the alarm bells didn't go off, but the day flew by. "So where is this trip? Timbuktu?" I asked as I jumped into his car. "You sounded so grim on the phone."

"We're opening up a new office in L.A., and I'm leading the

project. I need to sign leases, hire staff, run marketing programs, find housing," Neil voice trailed off, as though he were deep in thought.

"Housing?" I plead.

"I'm going to be there for a while. It could be a long while. I'm staying at a hotel in L.A. for the time being." Neil's voice cracked, his shoulders sinking into his chest, "I'm sorry, babe, but it could be a few months before I see you again."

He drove around in circles aimlessly, not saying a word as I tried to find any good side to this disaster. "We could still talk on the phone," I stammered. How did I manage to summon the strength to support him when I was crushed? I couldn't help but wonder if this was the end. Did his parents not want to meet me? I didn't dare ask. Somehow, I knew instinctively this was his father's bidding. Neil parked in front of my building and as he opened the driver's door, I noticed his eyes were brimming with tears.

Something was terribly wrong. Neil opened up my door and embraced me tightly. He kissed me gently while holding my chin so as not to break his gaze. "I love you, Ava. I will always love you. I'll give you a call as soon as I get settled." Neil's voice fought to disguise the torrent of emotion he was holding back. And then he sped off.

I ran into the house, my stomach twisted and knotted like sheets from a dryer. By the time I reached my bedroom, reality hit hard. We were over. My gut had told me that this could happen one day. We came from different worlds. But my heart had refused to listen.

Brooding, stuck in slow motion as the sultry days of that summer slipped by, I mourned my loss. Neil never called again. Brokenhearted and betrayed, I reflected on the *why* until I just couldn't anymore.

By the end of that lonely season, I decided that if I couldn't have Neil, I was going to have something else. Money. It never disappointed. I wanted the financial security that my parents never had. I would have the best clothes and dine at the finest restaurants.

I channeled my pain and anger and refocused it. Nursing school would never give me the life I wanted, so I quit.

I found a job at a small real estate business in Yonkers, owned by a family friend suffering with some health issues who needed an extra hand. The economy was staggering with high unemployment, tight credit, and exorbitant mortgage rates. While learning the business, and studying for my New York Realtor's license, I made my mark as a property manager. I persuaded the owner of several neglected properties that I could turn them around if given the opportunity and he gave me a crack at it. Who knew that being a super's daughter could pay off?

Everyone thought that I was insane for leaving school and working in the real estate industry at that crazy time, but I knew I would show them. I would show Neil. I was strong, smart, and determined to make a fortune on my terms. Nothing would derail my dream. I swore I would never again be cast away or easily forgotten.

My cell rang, bringing me back to the present.

"Hello," I answered.

"Ava, it's me, Neil."

CHARLOTTE

SINGLE AND SATISFIED

L ATE SPRING PACKED eighty-degree temperatures when June began. The warmth was intoxicating. Springtime always brought out my passionate side, but this year my fever spiked to a fiery level. Maybe the beginning of menopause was good for something after all.

Moving away from the kitchen window, I noticed the latest Victoria's Secret catalog mixed in the mail on the counter. Flipping through it, I decided to purchase two lingerie slips: both satin with eyelash lace trim in white and pink, along with a new bra, panties, and garter. I like to be prepared, especially when there's a new man on the horizon.

Ordering done, I closed my laptop and reached in my pocket for lip gloss. Dry lips drive me crazy. I smirked, thinking back to last night's book club and Ava's reaction to my new gloss.

I threw out the junk mail and sorted the rest into piles. My cell buzzed. *Speak of the devil.* "Hello."

"Hi. It's Maxwell. How did your meeting go?"

His question brought me up short. "Ah, good." I must have told him about that meeting to review new strategies to cut expenses at our local schools. Hmmm, a man who listens.

"I called to see if you'd join me for dinner next Saturday?"

"Sure, that'd be great." We talked for a while about his upcoming business trip to Chicago. He had a smoldering, velvet voice. I found myself zoning in on the voice and not the words. *Oh my, my. I would love that voice in my ear whispering...*

"Charlotte?"

"Ah...Sorry, I dropped something."

After we ended the call, I turned and looked out the window again. A tinge of sweat trickled between my breasts and my face felt flushed. Another hot flash? I had an urge to go for a long, fast drive somewhere, anywhere.

My cell buzzed again.

"Hey there." Bri's cheery voice filled the kitchen.

"Hey yourself. What's up?" I sat at the kitchen table, feeling calmer.

"Can you please chair the silent auction of the Build-a-Home event?"

"For you—sure." *Ugh*. I'd do anything for Bri. But I hated the thought of banging on doors, asking for items to auction.

"Thank you so much. This is such a relief. I'll e-mail you the list of the last few years' donors."

I told Bri about my upcoming first date with Maxwell.

"That's great!" she said.

"Yeah, he's hot."

"Where'd you meet him?"

"At Mary and Jim's party."

"Oh, that's right. So, you think you might like this guy?"

"'Like' is a strong word. I'm more comfortable with lust. He's damn sexy."

"Don't you want to meet someone you could share things with?"

"I share, Bri. I share." I laughed.

"Very funny. But seriously…a real relationship."

"Dating is a bitch. Take my word for it. No reason to lose yourself in these passing affairs. I just wanna have fun."

After we hung up, Bri's words whirled in my head. Meeting men could be frustrating. Some of the men around my age had referred to me as chilly, uninterested, solitary, and uppity. That was fine with me. My girlfriends' husbands tell me it's my independent, self-assured vibe. I don't think they mean it as a compliment.

Well, to hell with them. It took a lot of work to love myself again after my spouse cheated on me. I felt ugly, unwanted, and stupid.

On the flip side of dating, a lot of younger men were interested. I guess my "cougarness" was hip to them. I loved the attention—and the sex. But I set an age limit. I drew the line at ten years. I wouldn't date anyone in their mid-thirties or younger.

Of course, as soon as I drew that line, a younger man made me rethink my decision.

Last week I went to our neighborhood restaurant/bar, Bradley's, with Hanna. Her husband was away and I thought a night out would be good for her.

Bradley's traditional ambience was like most of the bars and restaurants in Morristown. Its dark paneled walls and stained-glass windows framed a large oval bar in the center of the main floor. Hanna and I sat on bar stools and ordered drinks.

The place was packed with a lively after-work crowd. Clusters of people gathered around the bar.

Hanna leaned in close. "A young man across the way has been staring at you for a while. He's coming this way. Don't turn around."

"How young?"

Hanna pushed her face upward indicating that he was behind me.

My curiosity piqued, I turned around.

He smiled. "Hi."

Oh boy. This little tadpole must be my son's age. He introduced himself as Chris.

He told us that he had come from work with a group of his colleagues and pointed to them. "We've been here for about an hour."

"Are you celebrating something?" I asked.

"Yes, someone got a promotion." He leaned in closer.

We ordered drinks and Hanna and I both talked with Chris.

Two hours later, when Hanna bagged out, I ordered a Coke. Chris flirted with me shamelessly.

"Why are you wasting time with me and not meeting someone your age?" I asked.

"My last girlfriend was probably older than you are."

Feeling a little dizzy and well past my limit, I ordered another Coke. Those pale blue eyes combined with alcohol and my libido could spell trouble. Looking at Chris reminded me of all the dinners I'd had with my son and his friends, trading jabs, joking. He was just too close to my son's age. It wasn't happening.

Chris insisted on walking me to my car, trying to convince me go on a date with him. As I turned to open the car door, he pulled me to him. I looked into those baby blues. He placed my face between his hands. His kiss was the kind you see in the movies, where the woman swoons, breathless.

But I pulled out of his embrace. This wasn't the answer to my longing. I smiled at him as I got into my car. "Thanks for a wonderful evening."

*

Saturday arrived quickly. I decided to get a mani-pedi for my first date with Maxwell. I wanted to wear a pair of open-toe high heels and my little piggies needed to look their best. Kim, my manicurist, loved to hear my dating stories. I told her I had a promising date tonight.

"How'd you meet?" she asked, filing my nails with an electronic file.

"At a party at my friend's home." Mary and Jim McMann were old friends. The party celebrated their daughter's college graduation. Mary had confessed that she had an ulterior motive for inviting me. She wanted me to meet Jim's fraternity brother, Maxwell.

This wasn't the first time one of my friends had set me up. I hated blind dates: at best, they're awkward; at worst, horrible. And then you have to report back.

Mary told me Maxwell was divorced with children in college and had recently moved back to New Jersey. Divorced men always come with bundles of baggage. But Mary was a good friend that really tried to find a nice man for me to date, so I kept an open mind.

While I was daydreaming, Kim finished my manicure. I followed her over to the spa chair for my pedicure.

"What'd you think when you met him?" she asked.

"At first glance? Surprised. Shocked, almost. Like when you fill out one of those dating site questionnaires about your ideal man." I chuckled and put my feet into the water.

Kim dug deeply under my nail and I winced. "Ouch…"

"So sorry," she said.

I hate this part of the pedicure. "Anyway, after Mary left, he said, 'I see you need a drink. Let's go fix that.' We headed toward the bar with his hand on my arm, and I sensed a—I don't know—an animal magnetism about him. The kind that James Bond wears like a second skin."

"So he's hot." Kim eyed me. "Looks like new Bond."

"No, more like… Harrison Ford, but not really." I closed my eyes and brought Maxwell's image to mind. "He has a full head of brown hair sprinkled with gray."

As Kim massaged my aching feet, I relaxed. "He's about six two, which is great because I'm so tall. Beautiful, soulful hazel eyes. And his voice—the sexiest I've ever heard."

"Sounds good. Yes."

"Yeah." I remembered how he held himself. Confident, strong, like he knew where he was going and what to do when he got there. I felt warm all over. Another hot flash?

"Did I tell you he has a dreamy, luscious voice like Sean Connery?" I shrugged. "Just sayin'."

"Lucky girl," Kim said.

"Maybe. We'll see."

*

When the doorbell rang, I inhaled deeply. Every nerve in my body was pinging.

The initial few minutes of a first date always made me anxious. But when Maxwell swooped into my house, he disarmed me with his charming manner and funny stories. He was light on his feet the way a dancer almost glides through a room. I wondered if he could tango. I was halfway to the restaurant before realizing how comfortable he made me feel. I didn't feel the usual awkward first-date jitters.

The Italian restaurant on the Jersey side of the Hudson had breathtaking views of the city. It was decorated with lovers in mind, with warm tones on the walls and floor, and soft textured fabrics on the sofas and chairs. Ceiling windows or French doors swept the entire back wall of the restaurant, curving around to its right. Sheer-flowing drapes floated down from the ceiling, dancing to the rhythm of the Hudson, arching sensually in the light breeze.

Maxwell looked over the wine list. "Have you ever had a Brunello di Montalcino?"

Maxwell's smooth voice made me look away from the swaying drapes, returning my gaze to meet his. "Ah. No, I don't think so."

He ordered a bottle. "I think you'll enjoy it."

When the sommelier brought the wine to the table, Maxwell

poured just a little into my glass. "Take a sip now, and then we'll let it breathe and have it with our dinner."

"Okay." The wine had a lushness to it already and I was excited to taste its full bouquet later.

We shared an order of fried calamari, one of the house specialties. He suggested we pair it with Ketel One martinis. *That voice, the martinis stirred, not shaken—so very Bond. Ooh, the possibilities.* I couldn't help smirking.

"Something funny?" he asked.

"No, nothing really." I caught myself hoping he'd be like James Bond—a great lover, who would then vanish.

Maxwell poured a glass of wine for both of us. "Tell me what you think."

I swirled the garnet liquid, inhaled the aroma and took a tentative sip. "It was good before, but now…the flavor is smoother with a smokier taste." I closed my eyes and sipped again. "A hint of a berry, strawberries maybe."

Opening my eyes, I watched Maxwell's skilled swirl and inhale. I loved how he savored the taste. I hoped he savored women the same way. I cleared my throat. "Well, I think I have found a new favorite. Thank you."

We talked about wine and the vineyards we'd visited. When dessert was served, Maxwell asked, "So, what did Mary and Jim tell you about me?"

The wine had seized my imagination as I watched the drapes behind Maxwell gently bend in the breeze. The undulant graceful floating had a come-hither pull that stimulated me like an aphrodisiac. It reminded me of all those romantic movie scenes I saw as a young girl in the 60s. Directors often used these billowy wonders in place of more obvious sexual props, luring the couple in with a promise of sheer pleasure.

Jesus, one martini and I think I'm Liz Taylor in Cleopatra. My cheeks grew warm and I hoped Maxwell couldn't see my blush.

I looked at him and realized I hadn't answered his question. "Sorry, I was thinking about the wine." I reached for more but the bottle was empty.

"Would you like another glass? I'll get another bottle."

"No, I was only looking for one more sip. It's so good."

He reached his hand over and lightly stroked mine and poured the last sip of his wine into my glass. "I'm really glad you like it."

Warmth spread up my arm. When he withdrew his hand, I immediately picked up my water glass and drank it down. Maxwell made me rethink my three-date rule—three dates with a man before we have sex. I longed to pounce on him right there. I reached into my pocket to reapply my gloss. My lips kept soaking it in, so dry tonight.

What in the world had he asked me? "Ah...Mary told me the essentials: married your college sweetheart, now divorced, kids in college, just moved back here." I smiled at him, hoping now that we'd covered the basics, we could talk about anything else—the weather or the stock market, maybe. I don't want to know the intimate details of his life. The less I know the better.

But then Maxwell asked me about my divorce.

My ex—instant lust kill. The heated fantasy I'd been conjuring all night began to fizzle. Nothing sobers me up faster than thinking about Grant. *I just want to continue fantasizing about kissing Mr. Bond here.* "We just grew apart. It happens." I shrugged my shoulders and smoothed my napkin in my lap.

Grew apart my ass. That SOB couldn't have hurt me more. Stabbed me directly in the heart. I thought he was my soul mate, my friend, my lover. I was his *"Stepford Wife."* Bastard cheated on me with a half dozen women, including some of our acquaintances. I hoped he'd rot in hell. I looked up at Maxwell and forced a smile, hoping it didn't look venomous.

"I'm sorry." He looked down at the table. "My wife and I divorced eight years ago."

Okay. That's enough. Bring back Mr. Bond. Let's just have sex and forget about all this life stuff. "That must have been hard on all of you. I know it was hard on us." All my dirty little thoughts vanished. *Please, please bring back Bond. I could use a little night tonic, some horizontal refreshment.*

"Yes, it was. Somehow my daughter, Emily, and my son, Kevin, turned out okay." Maxwell looked away and when he turned back, a small smile seemed plastered on his lips.

What can you say? I reached my hand across the table and held his protectively. "I'm really sorry."

Maxwell looked down. "Now I'm sorry. Didn't mean to go there. Sometimes it still gets me when I least expect it."

"It's okay. It gets to me, too."

Maxwell motioned to the waiter, gesturing for the bill. "I want to show you the garden in the back of the restaurant. It's amazing. When it's not overcast and threatening rain, I prefer to sit outside."

He held my elbow as we entered this masterpiece of a garden. It was the same width as the restaurant but twice as long, winding down to the river with tall hedges and raised flower beds. The beds contained begonias, lilies, and impatiens bordering the boxes in bright yellows, reds, and purples. Some herbs, maybe basil and rosemary, were scattered about. Back by the river some fifteen tables were filled with patrons. The threat of rain hadn't deterred them.

We stopped at the end of the patio and gazed at New York. The sheer size of the city overwhelmed me. Inside, framed by windows, the sight might be spectacular, but outside, freed from any constraints, it felt surreal, something like you'd experience in a 3-D movie. Maybe it was the martini and the wine, but I felt I could reach across and touch it. We stood silent, looking out.

The dampness seeped into my bare legs and I shivered. Maxwell's arm, looped through mine, must have felt me tremble. He offered me his coat. Even with the eighty-degree day, the night had turned cold and wet.

"Will you be warm enough without your coat? I should have brought one tonight."

Maxwell shook his head and placed his coat around my shoulders.

"Thank you." I stopped shivering, grateful for the warmth.

"I'm traveling to L.A. for a few days next week. I'll be back by the weekend. I just happen to have two tickets to the Harry Connick, Jr., concert at the Mayo Theatre. Would you like to go with me next Saturday?"

Let's just go back to your house or mine—why wait till next weekend? "Saturday works for me." I turned to face him, hoping for a kiss.

"Perfect." He stepped back and turned to leave, pivoting me with him.

*

On Wednesday, my new Victoria's Secret lingerie arrived. I ripped open the box and rushed into my bedroom to try them on. Oh yes, very nice. Maxwell's voice stuck in my mind all week, like a catchy piece of music. I heard him over and over again. In the shower, in bed, at work: that lush, smoky velveteen tone with his perfect intonation rolling out words like precious works of art.

Looking in the mirror at my new lingerie I felt a hot flash coming on. Maybe, or… God, that voice.

I needed to get out and do something. It was still early evening, so I went to the gym for a good workout and a steam.

*

Nathan and I were going out to dinner for what I called our Friday night special. We'd met soon after my divorce and had enjoyed a casual relationship ever since. No strings: basically, friends with benefits.

I met Nathan at Oscar's around eight o'clock for dinner. Usually I looked forward to dinner together and our antics later in the bedroom, but tonight, something felt off.

He rose to greet me when I entered the restaurant. "You look lovely."

"Thanks." I sat down.

He was dressed in a dark Armani suit with a white shirt, no tie. Nathan wore relaxed elegance well. He was handsome, with soft feminine features. My dad would have called him a dandy, stylish to a fault.

Our conversation was light, refreshing. Chatting about current events and local politics used to stimulate me, but not so much tonight. After a few glasses of wine and dinner, I just wanted to go home. But I soldiered on—old habits and all. But the sex was a letdown.

Afterward, I was exhausted. He wanted to drive me home from the hotel, but I called Uber.

We agreed to meet again next time he was in town, but I wasn't sure it was a good idea. Maybe our tryst had run its course.

*

I made phone calls to solicit donations for the Build-a-Home event all the next morning. I met Bri at the mall for a little shopping that afternoon.

"How was your date with Maxwell?" Bri asked as soon as when we met at Bloomingdales' cosmetics department.

"Nice."

"That's it—'nice'?"

"Yeah. Haven't had sex yet, to my great dismay." I applied a few new Chanel lip gloss colors to the back of my hand trying to decide which one I wanted to buy.

Bri laughed. "You only had one date! How about getting to know someone first?"

"You sound like my mother." I motioned for the salesperson and held up the tube I'd selected. "You want to get a drink in the coffee shop downstairs?"

"No work for you today?"

"I haven't used any of my vacation time this year and just felt like a day off. The school superintendent's office is busy with year-end stuff, but they gave me the day anyway."

"I'm going to try to get a job as soon as Logan leaves for college. I haven't worked in twenty years, not sure what I could do now." Bri shrugged.

"Are you kidding? Look at all the charity stuff you've done. You haven't just been doing your nails and shopping."

The coffee shop was crowded but we managed to find a table. I went to the counter and ordered for both of us.

I brought over a chai tea for me and an ice tea for Bri.

"Thanks," Bri said. "You know, it took my friends, Lea and Mary, years to get a job. I've been out of work longer than they have. Companies don't want to hire people in their fifties and sixties." A melancholy shadow crept over her face.

"You'd think businesses would hire older people because they don't have childcare issues anymore."

"Yeah." Bri sighed, looking out into the mall.

I'd noticed lately how she'd drift off into her own thoughts. Her usual uber-optimism seemed forced. "Is everything okay with Eric?" I asked.

Bri continued staring. "Hmmm…sure…why?" she answered in slow motion.

I reached over and put my hand on her arm. "Hey. Are you here? You're not your usual bouncy self. Is something wrong?" Something was definitely bothering her. I hoped it wasn't marital issues. Then I remembered a conversation I'd had with my gynecologist.

"Is it sex?" I asked. "My doctor told me that fifty percent of couples who are married a long time tend to lose their passion." I was talking a bit too loud and heads turned toward us.

"What? What are you talking about?" Bri's head snapped

around. "Lower your voice, would you? Eric and I are just fine." Her voice had a tight edge to it.

"I'm not saying you aren't. I just wanted to share this conversation I had with my doctor."

"Fine." Bri's smile looked forced.

"The year before my marriage fell apart, I went for my yearly exam. The gynecologist asked me about my sex life. It startled me a bit. I told her we were fine, great even."

Bri squirmed in her chair, recrossing her legs.

"The doctor then told me that a large percentage of longtime married couples don't have sex on a regular basis. Some as little as once a year. I remembered being blown away by that statistic."

Bri waved her hand. "Well, that's not Eric and me, so you don't have to worry."

"Let me finish. It's just a decrease in estrogen and women need a little extra…you know…warming up."

Bri hung her head, but I charged on.

"The doctor said that men love physically and couples need to have a satisfying sex life throughout the marriage."

"No duh." She flipped her hands outward.

"Well…"

Bri's elbow dropped down on the table and landed on my spoon, shooting it across the room. She got up and retrieved the spoon.

"Okay. What exactly are you trying to tell me?"

"Go get a Butterfly, it'll do you some good." I said. "It'll do you both some good."

She rolled her eyes and started to laugh, sitting back in her chair. "A what?"

I leaned across the table and lowered my voice. "The doctor told me to go to the Dain Shoppe for some proactive libido boosters."

Bri roared with laughter. "What?" People who'd turned away when I'd lowered my voice turned back.

I dropped my voice even lower. "You know, sexy lingerie and some other stuff."

She shook with amusement. "Like what?"

"Butterfly, Bullets…"

Bri almost fell out of her chair she was laughing so hard.

This wasn't going as planned. "Ah…never mind!" I went to the counter and asked for some water to give Bri time to settle down. I pretended not to notice the stares and whispers from the surrounding tables.

"I'm so sorry, Charlotte. I don't know why I'm laughing like a hyena. I should be used to the way you talk by now. I haven't laughed that hard in a long time. Thank you."

"Sure, I think. But, I'm bringing you to the store anyway. Maybe we'll go with book club? Wouldn't that be a blast?"

"Maybe. You can bring it up in September when we meet again. I can't wait for Madeline's reaction." Bri rolled her eyes.

"Don't be such a prude! And Madeline might surprise us."

*

I couldn't figure out what to wear for my second date with Maxwell. I toyed with the idea of opening the door in my new lingerie, but then decided it might be too bold. He did, after all, buy tickets.

I settled on a wrap dress in a colorful print that hugged my curves but didn't show the lines of my garter and thigh highs.

Maxwell picked me up right on time and whisked me out in moments. My thoughts of skipping the concert and heading straight to the bedroom were dashed.

When we pulled into the parking lot, I realized the concert would be over in a few hours. Then what? Maybe I'd get to show off my new purchases after all.

"Do you have any vacation plans for the summer?" Maxwell asked as we walked to the theater.

"Not yet. I tend to be spontaneous and just go."

"What are some of your favorite places?" He pushed open the theater door and held it for me.

"I love the beach." I entered the theater's foyer and he guided me to the bar for a drink. "I've spent summers at the Outer Banks in North Carolina and had a property there for a while. I own a time-share in Aruba, so that's high on my list. But, as far as my favorite… it has to be Hawaii."

Maxwell smiled broadly. "You're kidding. I love Hawaii. Have you gone all the way out on the Hana Highway in Maui?" Or walk through the Bamboo Forest?" Maxwell handed me a white wine and we moved away from the bar. "I try to go every year to one of the islands."

"Last year I went to Oahu twice to visit my youngest son, Chad. He was stationed at Kaneohe Bay his last year in the Marine Corps. I spent two weeks each time." I closed my eyes, savoring the memory. "My first trip to Hawaii was to Maui when the kids were young. I remember Hana Highway. Not sure that we ever saw the Bamboo Forest."

I listened to him tell me about his first excursion years ago with his family. They'd swum in pools at the bottom of waterfalls, snorkeled off the reefs of Molokini, and watched the sun slip into the sea at dinner.

Maxwell gestured enthusiastically as he spoke about his trip last year to Punaluu Beach on the Big Island and its jet-black sand.

I smiled, encouraging him. His irresistible tone made me weak.

"The Hana Highway is truly the drive of a lifetime. Just amazing." He sipped his wine and seemed to be lost in memory.

If you think that's amazing, just wait…. I tried to read the poster of coming attractions next to me to divert my racy internal dialogue, but every time he spoke, his voice drew me back.

Maxwell returned to the bar for a quick refill before we were seated. "What do you like to do in your spare time? Do you have any hobbies?

"I like to walk and work out at the gym." *I wonder what he'd think if I said sex. Can sex be a hobby?* I smiled coyly. "Um…I like movies and reading. I've been in a book club for ten years with my oldest friend, Bri. I'm glad she talked me into it.

"What types of books do you read in book club?"

I drank my wine down fast. "Anything, everything. Each member gets to pick a book. Last year we read a book my great uncle wrote back in the thirties. What a hoot that was. I've been trying to find a first edition, but no luck so far."

"What's the book?"

"*Topper* by Thorn Smith."

"Wasn't there a movie with Cary Grant?"

"Yup."

"Wow. Do you write?"

"No. His wife was my grandfather's sister. Not a blood relation. No cool writing genes here."

Maxwell chuckled. "No cool writing genes here, either. My writing is limited to business planning and tends to be done in bullet points." He talked a bit about his business consulting firm. "After my children left for college I wanted to do something new and started up my own business. Plus, I love to travel."

Once we were seated, Maxwell asked if I had a good relationship with my ex. My expression must have told him everything he needed to know. He reached into my lap to cup my hand.

"You know," I said, my eyes on his hand clasped over mine, "my ex would often tell me stories about his coworkers and their courting woes. He repeatedly said to me, 'Thank God we don't have to be in the dating world anymore.'" I looked directly at Maxwell. "So how ironic was it that he would end up *dating* while we were still married? That's how *I* ended up in the singles scene after twenty-one years." Bitterness rose up from my stomach, flooding my mouth. I drank some of my bottled water.

He rubbed his fingers over my hand. "I'm sorry," he said softly.

At least he didn't say "The man's a fool." If I had a dime every time someone told me that... I took a deep breath. I rummaged around in my purse for my gloss and applied some, trying to avoid eye contact with Maxwell.

The houselights dimmed and a spotlight showcased Harry Connick at the piano and the next few hours melted by as the retro crooner lavished us with his sultry voice.

"You know, he's just so damn likable, too." Maxwell said as he walked me to my door after the concert.

I asked Maxwell to come in.

He hesitated.

Annoyed, I turned around to unlock the door. "Thanks again for the lovely evening." I uttered and started to push open the door. Maxwell turned me and tenderly kissed my lips. A sweet kiss. Not the devouring smashup of urgent hormones needing release kind of kiss I was hoping for.

He pulled back.

Now I hesitated. I didn't know what to do. I wanted to be crushed into him right here and now. Have him pull my hips in tight while running his hand up my legs to the tops of my thigh highs.

Instead he ran his hand down my arm. "Would you like to go out again?"

I looked into his eyes and stepped into him wrapping my arms around his waist. I leaned my cheek on his. Not moving, I savored his warmth and the scent of spice and wood. Not able to resist, I took a half step back and kissed him hungrily.

Maxwell responded, pressing his mouth harder against mine, tongues exploring.

I pulled his hips into mine. A smoldering warmth erupted inside me. If he said something in that deep voice, I knew I'd climax right at my front door. I freed my arm, pushed open the door and guided him inside, still lip-locked.

My back was against the wall when Maxwell released my lips.

My need was so strong I didn't think we'd make it into the bedroom. Maxwell kissed me again. His lips found my ear and slowly moved down my neck.

I closed my eyes, feasting on his desire. His sweet kiss was forgotten, replaced by a smoldering intensity as we touched and fondled each other.

He struggled out of his coat and helped me take mine off, still standing behind my front door. The coats dropped onto the floor. He placed one hand on the side of my head and untied my wrap dress. My heart began to hammer.

Our lips connected again and heat soared through me. I pushed off the wall and we stumbled our way to my couch, still kissing. I nudged Maxwell down and stripped off my dress, letting it fall to the floor.

"You're so beautiful," he slowly uttered and reached out for my hand.

Carried away by longing, I pressed him onto his back and took what I wanted. When he whispered my name, I exploded.

Lying against him, panting, drowned in ecstasy, I thought that Maxwell could shake and stir me anytime.

TESS

THE DREAM

MY EYES FLEW open.

That stupid dream again.

I was looking around the entrance to an airport terminal. It felt like I'd been here many times before. I hadn't.

The escalator was directly in front of me, carrying hurried travelers up to the concourse. To my right a wide hall branched off into the unknown.

Should I go up or go right? Which way to my assigned gate? Decide, Tess...decide...the plane won't wait for you!

I began to move, but was weighed down by enough baggage to make a socialite look empty-handed. My feet moved in slow motion. I began to sweat.

I finally arrived at my gate. Sometimes in the nick of time. Other times, a second late, forced to watch the plane back away from the jetway. Leaving me lonely and alone.

That's when I always wake up—disorientated and upset.

I had no idea where I'm going, why I was making the trip, or if I will arrive at my destination.

Damn it! When is it going to end?

Instinctively, I turned to Stephen for comfort. But my husband's side of the bed was cold and empty. A heaviness in my shoulders pushed me back down. I pulled the blanket over my face and fell into a deep and dreamless sleep.

*

Buzz...buzz...buzz.

"Go away!" I swatted at the mosquito buzzing in my ear.

Buzz...buzz...buzz.

"Ugh! All right, already."

Looking toward the sound, I groggily recognized the sound of my cell phone set on vibrate. I must have forgotten to switch the ringer after last night's book club. Unlike the other ladies, I'm not a wine drinker. But I did partake of a couple of gin martinis. Maybe one too many. I sounded a little worse for wear as I answered the phone.

"Mom...you okay?"

"Good morning to you, too, Liz. We had the last book club meeting before our summer break and I guess I celebrated a little too much. You know what a lush I am."

"Right." Her tone sounded no nonsense, as usual. "I'll be there in two hours. I'm heading to the train right now."

"Huh?"

"Geez, Mom, how much did you *ladies* party last night? Remember, I'm coming over to help go through Dad's stuff today."

"Yes, yes, yes...and we didn't party that much. I had trouble sleeping last night, so I'm just a little out of sorts. I'll be fine after coffee."

"Well, have two cups and I'll be there in a couple of hours." Her voice lightened up a little bit. "Love you, Mom!"

"Love you, too, sweetheart."

Liz was the older of my two children, but only barely. She and her twin brother arrived only a minute apart. My tough, practical, hardheaded firstborn. I have a mental image of her brother starting to make his way out first. I just know she grabbed him by the umbilical cord as if to say "Oh, no you don't!"

"I'd better get my act in gear or there will be hell to pay in a couple of hours." I said out loud, tossing the phone back on the nightstand before heading in to shower.

I wasn't looking forward to the day's chores. Stephen had died a year ago. I just couldn't bring myself to clean out his clothes, his belongings and our shared memories. Liz had volunteered to come over and help.

"Might as well get this over with." The words and my tears were drowned out by the spray of the water.

Two hours later, my confident, no-nonsense daughter breezed in the door.

"Would you like a cup of coffee before we get started?" Anything to delay.

"No thanks, Mom. Let's just dive in and…"

Stopping short, she looked straight into my eyes. "Have you been crying? Your eyes look red."

"Oh, it must just be water from the shower." I lied. "Let's get this show on the road."

Liz followed me into the basement.

"There isn't all that much left. Dad and I had started cleaning out a couple of years ago in preparation for downsizing."

My eyes began to betray me, tears starting to form. "When Dad and I were rummaging through the tons of grammar, middle, and high school stuff that for some reason I thought I *had* to save all of those years, I ran across a stack of homemade cards addressed to 'Mommy,' with hand-drawn hearts, proclaiming *I Love You!* Sorry, sweetie. Today may be one big trip down Memory Lane."

"It's okay, Mom. I understand. Take your time. I'm here for you." She wrapped her arms around my shoulders and gave me a squeeze.

I wiped away the tears and took a deep breath.

"Well, there were a couple of things I set aside to show you. Come here."

I handed her a framed photograph. "Look at this. I love this picture of you in this outfit. You were four years old and insisted on wearing it virtually every day to preschool." I laughed. "I still can't get over that I paid fifty cents at a yard sale for that purple fleece sweatshirt and skirt. You wore it with pink tights and black Mary Jane shoes. I wanted to wash it every night, but most mornings it just moved from the hamper back to a hook beside your closet."

"I love that picture, too, Mom."

"Quite a contrast to today, huh? A Wall Street attorney dressed for success with an attitude to match." My voice started to shake.

Reaching into another box, I pulled out a faded construction paper booklet, the pages held together by tarnished brads. "And look here. Jackson's first screenplay from second grade. 'The Funny Bunny Meets Godzilla.' Four lines long and self-illustrated."

"Definitely destined to be a classic." She chuckled at her brother's early brush with the film industry.

"I'm just so proud of both of you. Dad was, too."

"I know." I could see tears forming in her eyes.

"Look at the two of us," I said, wiping the tears from my cheeks. "Come on. I have trash bags ready to pack up Dad's clothes and take them to the thrift store."

We worked for two hours, starting first with the clothes stored in the basement and eventually moving upstairs to the bedroom closet.

"Let's take a little break." The emotional side of the project suddenly outweighed the physical one and I felt weary. "I have some cold cuts in the fridge for sandwiches. Plus, I made a chocolate cake yesterday and one slice won't hurt either of us, given all of the work we've done today."

We lingered over the crumbs. Neither of us wanted to go back to work yet.

Liz broke the silence. "Mom. It's been a year. It's time. You need to get out there. You're still young."

I had to speak carefully not to show my sudden flare of anger. "I know you mean well. But everything I built my life around is gone. I don't know if I have the strength to start over." I wanted to scream *Why can't you understand that?* But I held my tongue.

"Mom, you are the strongest woman I know."

I didn't say anything.

"Besides, it's what Dad would have wanted," she added so gently it made me tear up.

"You're right about that last part. Dad and I had the if-I-go-be-fore-you-go talk several times over the course of our years together. I always laughed it off, saying that was a long time in the future." My voice trailed off. Then I added: "Liz, I know you want me to be happy and Dad would, too. It's just too early. I'm not ready."

"Okay, but don't wait too long."

"I'll make you a deal. When I am ready, you'll be the first to know. It's just that I miss your dad so much." The choked words sur-prised me. "I was just thinking about when your dad and I met..." My voice trailed off as I stared at the plate on the table.

"I still remember that party as if it were yesterday. Both of us like fish out of water completely uncomfortable strangers among strangers. But somehow we found each other and talked for hours.

Then, later as Sarah and I walked to the subway, I blurted out, 'If I had to marry anyone I met tonight, I would marry Stephen Norton.' She thought I was drunk, but a year later, she was my maid of honor."

"Just like a fairy tale." Liz began cleaning up the table.

"Maybe...but aren't fairy tales supposed to have happy endings?"

By early evening everything was boxed up and labeled for the thrift store pickup scheduled for Monday.

"I have to get back to the city, Mom."

"I can't thank you enough, sweetheart. I knew this would be

hard, but it's taken a lot out of me. I'm probably heading to bed soon. Have a safe trip back home."

I climbed the stairs and walked into a bedroom whose closet and dresser drawers were now half empty. It felt light years away from the bedroom I'd slept in the night before.

I decided to take a quick nap and then have a light late dinner. As I lay down on the bed, my mind swirled with disjointed memories all converging on me at once.

For some reason, the one I couldn't shake happened just a little more than a year ago. I stopped trying to push the thought away and let myself remember.

I had been walking by the printer at ASH Media after the higher ups announced that the company was being acquired. John was talking to two younger team members; their backs toward the door. "You know there will be layoffs. I just hope they start with the older ones first. Isn't it about time Tess retired? What is she waiting for, anyway? They should have kicked her out years ago," he'd said snidely.

I remember thinking: *How can he be so cruel? I hired him; John wouldn't be where he is today without me.*

The following day, John got his wish. I was the first on the team to be laid off and escorted out of the building.

Stephen met me at our front door when I arrived home. Despite his expression of concern, his eyes twinkled.

"I hear you got laid off," he said. "Well, at least I still love you."

As bad as I felt, I fell into his arms, knowing that everything would be all right.

And it was…for a while.

Stephen decided it was time for him to retire, too. We planned world travel adventures. I booked our dream trip to Italy. We spent days clearing out the accumulated stuff of our life together and evenings talking about Rome, Venice, Florence—the wine we'd drink, the food we'd eat, and the places we'd see.

Unlike the graceless way my firm had dismissed me, Stephen's law firm wanted to honor his retirement. They planned a farewell dinner. It would be a bittersweet moment.

The evening of the dinner, I was surprisingly ready before him. Normally, he was dressed and pacing the floor downstairs long before I even put my earrings on. But my adrenaline was pumping as I prattled on about how exciting it would be to finally begin traveling.

Stephen seemed distracted. I figured it was my nonstop talking combined with his feelings of leaving the firm he'd helped build. To give him some space, I went down to putter a bit in the kitchen.

Sorting through the day's mail, I tossed half into the recycling bin. The other half could wait until tomorrow once we'd recovered from the night's festivities. I started the dishwasher so it would be finished when we got home, just in case we brought a piece of cake home and wanted a midnight snack.

Minutes ticked by and I was anxious to hit the road. Stephen always hated to be late, and with this being his party, he no doubt wanted to get there early.

"Stephen, we need to be heading out. Are you about ready?"

No answer. Was he in the bathroom?

I lightly ran up the stairs, planning to give him a hard time about being late on his last day.

I walked through the open bedroom door and knew instantly that he was gone.

*

Now, a year later, I lay in my empty bed crying myself to sleep over everything I had lost.

I woke up the next morning still dressed in the same clothes as the day before. It took me a minute to shake the cobwebs out of my head. I had slept for twelve hours. After a hot shower, I headed downstairs to grab some breakfast and coffee.

I booted up the laptop on the counter to check the weather before I decided what to tackle next. Maybe a little yard work?

I was surprised to see an e-mail pop up. It was from an old college friend, David, whom I hadn't talked to in ages. I filled my coffee cup and moved the laptop over to the table.

Hey, Tess. How are you doing? I still can't get over Stephen being gone. My heart breaks for you, my friend.

I've been trying to get into a sabbatical program in France. For some reason or another, I never got a spot in the program...I guess they thought I was too smart. :-) Just yesterday, I got a call that they had a last-minute opening...either they decided I wasn't that smart or someone dropped out... I'm guessing a little of both.

The good news is that I got the spot. The bad news is, I leave for Paris June 15 and I need a house sitter. I was wondering if you would like to come and spend the summer down the shore and stay with Mac."

Mac? I wondered. Mac who?

You haven't met him, but Mac is my best friend. He's an eight-year-old, hundred-pound golden retriever. He's named Mac, well, because it's short for Machiavelli, always one of my favorites of the old dead guys...Just kidding, he's more like Mac & Cheese in personality.

The house, well, more of a cottage, is only four blocks from the beach. I seem to recall that you were never much of a Jersey Shore gal, but maybe you're looking for a change of scenery?

Please think about it, but don't think too long. It is a great way to spend the summer. You don't need to rattle around all by yourself in that big old two-story colonial up there in soccer-mom land.

Think of it as a favor to your old friend and partner in crime. Remember when we...no, I'd better not put that in writing. Just please say you'll do this. I know it sounds cliché, but it might be good for you—you know, the beach, sun, a new environment. And it would save me a fortune in dog-sitting fees...hahahaha! Mac says, "woof," which means "please come stay with me," in dog.

Hey, I'm probably taking a lot for granted. And, yes, I could make some good cash renting it out, but I want Mac to be able to stay here with someone I trust. Let me know and we can work out the pesky details.

David

I stared at the screen. It was a lot to take in, but he did have a point...several points. I wasn't tied to anything. My house had been on the market for the past six months. With the New Jersey real estate market, who knew how long it would be before it sold? It would be easier to show it without me there and I could certainly use a change of scenery.

I thought about it for a few minutes and then with uncharacteristic speed, hit reply:

David, thank you for thinking about me. Yes, I can't believe it's been a year since Stephen left me, either.

I'll do it. What should I bring? How do I get there? What else should I know? Oh never mind—I'll call you.

Love you always,

Tess

*

The next two weeks flew by. I told Liz about my plans. She wasn't quite sure what to make of it all, but didn't try to stop me. I contacted Ava, my book club friend and real estate agent to let her know where I'd be in case there was a bite on the house.

Before I knew it, I was turning my black Lexus into a seashell gravel driveway. "Cottage" definitely described David's house. It was cute, well-maintained, with a beautiful flower bed on either side of the front door.

A huge blue pickup truck was parked in front of the house. A late model, clean and shiny, not something I envisioned David driving. Maybe it belonged to the neighbors?

The front screen door opened.

"Darling! You're here!"

David hadn't changed a bit. His smile still made you wonder what he had up his sleeve. He wore a Princeton sweatshirt that had seen better days and faded jeans. His once dark hair was a lot shorter and sprinkled with gray.

"David, so good to see you again!" I threw my arms around him.

"Enough pleasantries. I have things to do, planes to catch. Come inside and I'll show you around; not that it takes much time."

The place was small, but clean and immediately comfortable. It had everything I would need, most of which I could see from the front door. A living room with a futon and a couple of sturdy, padded chairs. A compact kitchen with a small dinette and two mismatched wooden chairs. To one side was a bathroom with a clawfoot bathtub. The door to the bedroom was open, but I couldn't really see in.

"Well, this is pretty much it. The bedroom is in here."

I followed David through the door and gasped. The bedroom was huge, as big as the rest of the house put together. In the middle was a king-sized bed.

David laughed when he saw my raised eyebrows. "You don't like my boudoir?"

"It surprises me," I stammered.

"This was originally two bedrooms, but since it's just Mac and me, I made it into one large room with a decent-sized closet. You'll understand the reason for the king-sized bed when the first thunderstorm rolls in."

The front screen door opened and banged closed. A soft "woof" came from its direction.

"They're back. Come on, I'll introduce you."

Just inside the doorway was the biggest golden retriever I'd ever seen in my life. He looked at his master with soulful, adoring eyes. His tail swept back and forth with enough force to knock over a small child. He "woofed" again, this time with more emphasis.

"I'll get you a treat," David told him.

I swore I saw the dog smile.

"Oh, but before I do, let me introduce you to Brian. Brian, this is Tess. Brian is sort of a handyman/friend/dog walker/all-round-good-guy...I don't know...how would you describe yourself, Brian?"

"I like to think of myself as being 'in construction.'"

His clear blue eyes were pools of appeal. It took me a split second to return his handshake.

"Pleasure meeting you, Brian. David didn't mention you in his e-mails."

David laughed. "Brian is driving me up to Kennedy for my flight and he took Mac for a little walk while I was waiting for you. He's single and totally straight."

"Um...okay...um...Didn't really cross my mind..." I was stammering again.

Brian smiled and walked back outside. "Speaking of planes, we have to hit the road or I will miss mine. Just a quick rundown of the essentials. By the phone—yes, I still have a traditional landline, which also provides the Internet connection—you will find a list of important numbers, starting with the vet. I hope that you won't have to use that one, but I did tell them you were coming and will be looking after Mac. They are good people." David paused briefly and scratched Mac behind his silky ears.

"Next is the people hospital…you never know. Mrs. Kelly lives next door and this is her number. If you need her right away, you might want to just go over there and *bang*. And I mean *bang* on the door. She's a sweetie, but deaf as a post. Don't be fooled though, she notices everything and is the sheriff of the street." He gave his I-call-them-as-I-see-them shrug.

"Last but not least is Brian's number. As you may recall, I have the mechanical skills of a gnat, so if anything breaks, just call Brian. He'll put it on my bill." David laughed at his own joke as he winked.

"At what point are you actually going to pay that bill?" Brian shot back from the porch, though he clearly wasn't worried about the payment.

With much overstated flourish, David said, "I continue to pay you with my undying gratitude each and every day."

Turning back to me, he said, "Now, I stocked the fridge with all of the major food groups: fruit, vegetables, bread, butter, milk, jelly, and beer. I know you're not much of a beer drinker, but you never know when it might come in handy." He grinned at me and I rolled my eyes.

I opened the refrigerator. "Wow. You really did stock it. Exactly how many people were you expecting?"

"I also packed the pantry with dog and people food. Forage as you wish. The rest of the stuff you need you can get in town. It's only three blocks from here and only three blocks long. You can't miss it," David closed the pantry door.

"There's a combination coffee shop/bookstore. You can't miss that, either. It's called Browse and Brew."

I giggled at the name.

"Don't look at me like that, I didn't name it. They have great coffee and a nice selection of breakfast muffins and pastries. Feel free to walk down there with Mac; they all know him and his penchant of begging for attention and treats. Don't they, boy?" David reached down and scratched Mac's neck.

The dog groaned with delight.

"Just tie his leash to the hitching post out front and he'll shake down the passersby like a furry Artful Dodger." With a sigh, he ran his hand through his hair and looked around. "Now that we've completed the Chamber of Commerce tour, any questions?"

My head was swimming. "No, I guess not. Oh wait, what and when does Mac eat?"

"He would like to eat as much as he wants whenever he wants. But you should give him a cup of kibble in the morning and one at night. Try to ignore those puppy dog eyes begging for more, but if you can't resist, a couple of treats won't hurt him."

"We better get going," Brian said in a firm but gentle voice.

"Right, let me get my stuff." David grabbed his backpack and bulging duffel.

"Oh, hang on before you head out. Um…what about the yard and those beautiful flowers out there? I've killed every plant I've owned and am nervous about being responsible for them. And you never said when you're coming back. When does this program end?"

"At the end of summer, around August twenty-ninth. Don't worry about the yard, Brian will take care of it." He buried his head in Mac's silky nape. "You be good, you hear?"

I could tell that for all of his bravado, David was trying to leave before he fell apart. Leaving Mac was no doubt the hardest part of his adventure.

"We'll be fine. We'll take care of each other," I assured him and put my hand gently on David's shoulder.

Then they were gone.

Mac and I looked at each other as if to say: *Okay, what now?*

"I don't have a clue, pal, I don't have a clue. I have no idea what I have gotten myself into."

*

For the longest time, Mac lay in front of the door staring at the screen, chin resting on his front paws.

I dragged my bags from the car into the house. There wasn't that much; I didn't figure I'd need a lot.

Every time I went into the bedroom and saw that king-sized bed, I laughed. Everything else in the cottage was almost miniature in comparison. I guess I didn't have to worry about falling out.

I discovered two areas David had left out of his whirlwind tour. One was a cozy screened porch just off the kitchen with a cabaret-type table and a couple of rattan rocking chairs. I could foresee evenings out there reading a book or just watching the sun go down.

The other was an outside shower, tacked on the side of the house and surrounded on three sides by a tall, solid enclosure. It was roofless, so when you stood on the pallet that made up the floor, all you could see was the blue sky and some fluffy white clouds.

I took it all in, sighed and realized I was ravenous. I hadn't eaten since I left home. It dawned on me that Mac hadn't been outside for a while. He still seemed a little apprehensive about me.

"So, Mac, what do you say that I get a little cleaned up and we go out and take a walk downtown to get a few additional supplies?"

Not sure if it was hearing his name or the word "out," but for the first time, Mac lifted his chin from his paws and even swished his tail.

I went into the doll-sized bathroom and washed my face. Looking in the mirror, I contemplated my unruly short brown hair and decided a quick brushing would have to do.

I grabbed Mac's leash and, luckily, the house keys were right behind his leash on the peg because David had forgotten that detail.

I opened the screen door and let Mac roam the yard while I locked up. Clearly, Mac was feeling perkier as I snapped on the leash.

"Lead the way." Off we went on our first adventure together.

Downtown was exactly how David described it: three blocks from the house and exactly three blocks long. I arrived just in time, because it looked like they were getting ready to roll up the street and it wasn't even 6 p.m.

"I will have to remember that for future reference," I said to Mac.

I tied his leash to the small hitching post with a bowl of water on the sidewalk next to it. Mac eagerly lapped up the contents. I went into the grocery store, which seemed more like a general store than a modern supermarket.

"Hi, I'm Tess and I'm staying in David Lowes's house on Fourth Street," I told the lady behind the register.

She smiled back. "Oh, yes. David told us you were coming to stay with Mac. Plus, Mrs. Kelly was just in here and gave us a complete rundown of your arrival today. She described you to a T, right down to your lovely smile."

"David told me she was the sheriff of the street, but I didn't expect a thorough report this early. I guess I better be on my best behavior."

"Don't worry. She's harmless and sweet. You should go introduce yourself. She'll tell you all about the town and offer you some freshly brewed iced tea and homemade cookies at the same time." She looked past me through the window. "Is Mac outside?"

"Yes, and I'm afraid he just drank all the water in the bowl by the hitching post."

"Don't worry, saves me from having to dump it out when I bring it in. I'm Mindy and the person behind the meat counter is my husband, Jack. We own this fine establishment."

Her smile was warm and inviting and I instantly felt at home.

"Well, I don't want to keep you from closing; I just wanted

to get a few supplies, like something I could make into a quick salad for this evening. I'll just grab some tomatoes, green peppers, and carrots. David was kind enough to provide me with a head of lettuce."

As usual, I couldn't seem to stop yammering. Like they cared what I wanted to have for dinner.

"Oh, and maybe some roast chicken to throw in," I added.

"No problem, we're here as long as you need us. I'll throw a little extra chicken in for Mac, even though I'm sure David said no snacks. Don't worry, he never follows his own rule. Come by anytime. We're glad to have you, if only for the summer."

When I walked out, I realized I had been holding my breath. I let out a hefty sigh and Mac looked at me with a goofy doggie grin. His eyes were riveted on the bag of groceries. *No snacks, right,* I thought. You don't get to be that big on kibble alone.

We returned to the cottage and Mac made another round, inspecting the front yard until he found the perfect spot.

"Come on, pooch, let's see if I have anything in this bag for you," I said, holding the door open for him.

The words had barely left my lips before Mac was inside standing over his empty food bowl.

"I guess a before-dinner snack never hurt anyone."

I unwrapped the chicken and tossed a piece in his bowl. At least, I think I did, because by the time I blinked, the bowl was empty again and Mac was looking at me with puppy-dog eyes.

"You'll have to settle for kibble for now. If I feed you too many treats, you'll be ten pounds heavier and look like a wooly mammoth when your dad returns." A cup of kibble clattered into his dish.

If he was disappointed, he didn't show it. He buried his face in his dinner.

I unpacked the rest of the groceries and tossed a salad, pouring a glass of tea from the pitcher David had left in the fridge. I headed to the screened porch. Dusk was falling and the night was alive with sounds of cicadas and crickets. Fireflies flitted around the backyard. It was so tranquil that I nearly nodded off before finishing my meal.

"What say we pack it in? One more quick trip outside and we'll call it a night?"

I opened the screen door for Mac. He was out and in quickly. Mac had a bed in the corner of the big master bedroom and he went straight to it.

"At least your bed looks appropriately sized." I cracked open the window and took a deep breath of the ocean breeze. *I guess I'd better put my nightgown on in the bathroom. The bedroom is on Mrs. Kelly's side.*

I'm not sure who was snoring first.

*

After a week, Mac seemed less mopey, not as apt to stare at the screen door.

"As long as your food bowl is filled regularly, I think you're going to do just fine. Let's go hang outside. It's such a pretty day already."

I found some gardening supplies in the small shed behind the house, along with a lawn mower. I'd never mowed a lawn in my life and I had no intention of starting. Thank goodness David had arranged for Brian to take care of the small yard.

I weeded and watered the flower beds, and to my surprise, didn't detect a silent scream coming from any of the flowers.

"I guess time will tell," I said tentatively to the nearest black-eyed Susan.

I sat on a lawn chair and thought about all those times I ran the kids to soccer practice, ballet class, friends' homes, not to mention all of the PTO meetings and teachers' conferences. It's strange how much of a hurry I'd been in, while doing basically nothing.

I looked over at Mac resting under a tree. He was my sole responsibility now. No rushing anywhere.

"I could get used to working up a sweat like this," I said, speaking and smiling at no one, turning back to the flower beds.

The day grew warm and humid. Before long, my clothes were soaked with sweat, clinging uncomfortably to my skin.

Mac and I headed in and I got some cool water for both of us. He curled up on the kitchen rug.

Grabbing some clean clothes, I half stumbled into the outdoor shower enclosure. It really was getting hot.

I'd been a bit hesitant about showering in the great outdoors the first few times. But soon I felt completely comfortable, even exhilarated, being surrounded by just three high walls and the blue sky above.

I figured that the only people who might see anything were the pilots of those propeller planes who fly overhead in the summer, their banners extolling the virtues of "The Best Bar on the Beach."

Layer after layer, clothes landed on the pallet floor. Yellow tank top. Navy shorts. White sports bra. Lavender panties. I didn't care if they got wet. It felt good to peel them off my hot skin.

The cool water sprayed the top of my head, dripping down my hair before falling onto my naked, somewhat sunburned, shoulders. The rivulets followed the curve of my breasts, streaming over my stomach, and landing in a puddle at my feet.

"Yup," I said aloud, turning my head up to the water, "I could definitely learn to like this."

*

There it was, taunting me again. Should I take the escalator down and try to find my gate, or turn right and continue to the upper floor of the airport terminal? This time, I picked the escalator and stopped at the snack bar before proceeding on to my flight. But I couldn't find the gate. I was going to miss my flight. Sweat started running down my back and I began to hyperventilate.

I woke up. That damn dream again. I heard snoring. Stephen? Was I still dreaming?

I reached to touch his arm. There was nothing but space next to me. I looked at the clock. 4 a.m. Ugh!

I sat up and felt small in the giant bed. Alone and lonely.

A wave of sadness erupted within me, like a tsunami. The same sadness that would hit me when I least expected it, dragging me down like an angry riptide. I'd felt lonely and alone so often since Stephen's death, but this was the first time since I arrived a week ago. Tears burned my cheeks.

I heard snoring again and looked toward the sound. Mac.

Just push through, I told myself. Funny, back when life was one big hustle-bustle, I'd longed for days when I would be able to put my feet up. Now all I wished for was to have that life back.

Deep breaths...one...two...three...

I tried to clear my head only to be startled by the image that popped up...Brian. How odd was that? I'd only met him once. I shook my head, but his image remained.

"We might as well make use of the time. Come on, Mac...let's take a walk."

I grabbed the leash hanging by the door and the old hoodie sweatshirt on the other hook. It was early enough it didn't matter that I was wearing my sleep shorts and an old tank top. I still didn't know many people here, so who cared?

The cool, salty air was refreshing during the four-block walk from the house to the beach. The sun wasn't up yet, but the charming, old-fashioned streetlights provided enough light for us to make our way on the uneven sidewalk.

After thoroughly inspecting and approving several trees, Mac fell into a comfortable walk by my side. As we moved closer to the beach, he started trotting eagerly.

Well, at least I may finally get in shape this summer, I thought, quickening my pace.

Turned out, lots of people were up at before sunrise. *Geez, don't these people sleep?*

Undaunted by the pounding footsteps of joggers coming from behind, Mac and I took our time. We stood by the railing on the boardwalk and watched as the sun began its ascent. I was transfixed. Mac sat patiently at my side, not quite as thrilled as I by the sunrise. Instead, he watched the people on the boardwalk, undoubtedly hoping that someone would drop a morsel of food.

I really wasn't paying much attention when he barked at another jogger coming toward us. My arm was nearly jerked out of its socket by a tug of Mac's leash. I tried to turn to see what Mac was so excited by. But instead of turning, I was thrown off balance, bracing myself to hit the boardwalk with my backside.

Just as I was about to land, hands slipped under my arms, saving me from bruising both butt and pride.

Regaining my equilibrium and balance, I found myself looking straight into a surprisingly familiar face.

"Well, hello." The jogger reached down to scratch a happy Mac behind the ears.

Brian.

He was dressed in running shorts and a T-shirt that fit very well in just the right places, stretched over his washboard abs.

"Hello. What are you doing out at this time of the morning?" I stammered.

"I was just going to ask you the same question. I try to run a couple miles every morning before work. What brings you out when all sane people are sleeping?"

"Oh, I just woke up and couldn't go back to sleep. Figured I would come down and see the sunrise. It's beautiful."

"Yes, yes, it is."

I turned to face him again, and realized he wasn't looking at the sun or the beach or the surf. His eyes were traveling from the top of my head to the tips of my toes. I grew acutely aware that I was dressed in ratty pajamas and a Princeton hoodie two times too big for me. Plus, I had bedhead hair and unbrushed teeth.

He raised his eyes back to mine. "How have you been settling in?"

"Good. Really good." I felt like a teenager having her first conversation with a boy she liked. It was a feeling that I hadn't felt in many, many years and it shocked me.

"Um...Mac and I have just been hanging out," I continued. "What time do you go to work...and what exactly do you do, again...wait a minute, isn't today Saturday, or have I completely lost track of time already?"

I was mortified that the words kept spewing from my mouth, running together in one tangled sentence, but I couldn't stop myself.

"I'm in construction, but as David so eloquently said, pretty much a jack-of-all-trades. During the summers, I try to get as early a start as possible and work as late as possible, with a few Saturdays thrown in. It makes up for the slower winter months."

"Oh."

Oh? Is that all you can say? Come on, Tess, get hold of yourself. I ran my hand through my tousled hair. Damn, why hadn't I at least worn a baseball cap or left the hood of my sweatshirt up?

"Well, I don't want to keep you. We were just heading back." He's going to think I'm an idiot. I was squirming to get way.

Brian nodded. "I probably should run along, too. We should get together some time now that you're settled."

"Ummm...yeah...that would be great." My sixteen-year-old self was still doing the talking.

He turned and started running in the same direction as before. I couldn't help but linger on his backside as he ran off. *Damn, he has a nice runner's ass!*

Just as that thought popped into my head, he abruptly turned, ran backward a few steps and waved at me, smiling his crooked smile. "Call me if you need anything!"

I felt the blush rising into my cheeks. Was I betraying Stephen, or was Liz right about moving on? I shook my head.

Back at the house, I took a quick look at myself. Oh, man, I'm sure he was thinking, does the woman even own a mirror?

*

The next morning, I didn't have any trouble sleeping late. Mac and I took a walk to the Browse and Brew for brunch. I tethered Mac to the dog-sized hitching post on the sidewalk.

Since it wasn't quite noon yet, the small place wasn't crowded. I kept an eye on Mac, a magnet for every child carrying something to eat.

"Egg with bacon on a croissant and a mocha latte, please," I told the teenager manning the counter. "Is it okay if I look through the bookshop while I'm waiting?"

"Sure...that's why we have 'Browse' in our name. I'll call your name when it's ready."

"I haven't read a book in ages. Maybe I should pick up a couple. Thanks."

The book club ladies would be so proud. Perhaps I should get that bodice ripper I mentioned at the last book club, something light on plot but heavy on the breathing.

I glanced out the window and saw that a small girl was feeding Mac part of her cookie as her parents stood by patiently. I started perusing the cover of a potential purchase, when I heard someone behind me.

"Well, we meet again. Twice in as many days."

Stunned, I spun around and there he was, looking tanned, handsome, and tall. Brian. He was holding two cups of coffee, one being the latte I'd ordered.

Steadying myself as gracefully as possible and catching my breath, I managed to respond with a very sophisticated, "Oh, hi!"

"Hi!" He was obviously mocking me, but smiling while he did so. What a smile it was, too.

"Umm…how did you know this was mine? Were you here the whole time I was? How did I miss seeing you?" The words wouldn't stop flying out. Jesus, what's the matter with me?

"I wanted to check on a small job I did for the owners in the supply area earlier this week. I was just walking in from the back room, but you were absorbed in this plethora of literary genius. I figured I would surprise you. Did I?"

"I certainly wasn't expecting to see anyone I knew. Plus, you look different today. Why aren't you at work?"

"My dear lady of leisure, today is Sunday. Remember? Yesterday was Saturday."

My head was spinning so much that I couldn't even remember my own name, let alone what day it was. I let my eyes drift down his white polo shirt skimming those abs to the khaki shorts on his slim hips.

Realizing that he had noticed me staring, I looked away. A telltale blush swept across my cheeks and headed toward my neck.

Still…that smile…that twinkle…those blue eyes…

"So, doing a little browsing?"

The spell broke and I snapped back to reality.

"Yes. It's been a while since I've read a book. Never enough time. I'm looking for something mindless to read."

"Well, looking at that cover, *something* certainly springs to my mind." He was grinning.

"Um…yeah…"

Great, I was once again turning into that sixteen-year-old girl. I tried to regain at least a modicum of composure, looking toward Mac, who was licking a different child's ice cream cone. *Clearly, unlike me, he is doing just fine.*

"So, what have you been doing since you've arrived?"

I was grateful for the change of subject. "Not really a whole lot. I can't believe how much time it takes to do relatively little. I've been taking walks on the beach, although usually not as early as yesterday, puttering around the house. Watching Mac chase squirrels. You know."

I paused, searching for something to add, and suddenly blurted out, "Oh, and I've discovered something wonderful—the pleasures of the outdoor shower."

Ohmigawd! Did I really just say that? Out loud? To him? And did I really use the word pleasures? My face was now burning hot. "I think I shared a little too much information just then. Sorry."

"Not at all. In fact, I was just picturing you in the shower. Quite a nice image, I must say."

"Okay, would you look at the time…I'd better…um…go check on Mac."

Afraid he would sense the tingling moving through every inch of my body, I turned and rushed off, nearly toppling a stack of books in my wake. I stumbled awkwardly out the door. The sea breeze cooled my burning cheeks.

Pulling Mac from the pool of melted ice cream he was happily lapping, I quickly prodded him toward home. It was two blocks before my breathing returned to normal. My heart felt like it was going to pound out of my chest.

Get a grip. Don't read anything into what just happened. Deep breaths.

It was then I noticed I was empty handed except for Mac and his leash. I hadn't purchased a book or taken my latte, let alone remembered to check on my sandwich order.

HANNA

RUNNING THE SHOW

I SLAMMED ON THE brakes to avoid hitting a doe that had launched itself in front of my car. The sound of screeching brakes didn't startle the dim-witted beast. Unfazed, the deer stood inches from my front bumper, staring into the windshield at us, sniffing, before walking away, oblivious to oncoming traffic. Chester's deer population seemed genuinely annoyed by the invading humans. Maybe they were right.

The rush-hour traffic on Elm Street backed up the typical mile. My weekly carpool duty required the logistical planning of a military operation. Stress mounted as I glanced at the car clock and calculated my ETA. I had lost precious minutes jockeying around Arial's crowded driveway and was further delayed by a quick conversation with Lucy's mom at her house. But with luck, I would still drop the girls off at the soccer field at exactly five o'clock.

"Girls, please lace up your cleats and make sure that you have your water bottles and gym bags ready. I'm going to have to drop you off without parking."

"Again?" whined Katie. At six, no shrinking violet, she already knew her own mind. Most of the time her independent attitude pleased me. At others, like now, it tried my patience.

"Yes *again*, pumpkin. Don't worry—you'll be on time."

We pulled into the parking lot adjacent to the field, and as the gravel crunched beneath the skidding tires, the girls, well trained, popped open the Expedition's doors, pulled out their drinks and bags, yelled out quick "Thanks," and ran onto the field.

"I'll be back to get you at six-thirty," I called, before pulling away to go get Brandon and shuttle him to karate.

I hated when my soccer week carpool duty coincided with Mark's business travel. It left me feeling overwhelmed, like a hamster cycling feverishly on a wheel. Thankfully, summer break was just around the corner, with its pared-down schedule and a vacation at the Outer Banks. I peeled off to grab an Iced Skinny Mocha at the Grounds Crew, counting on its stimulation to help me through the rest of the evening's activities: karate and soccer pickups, dinner, homework, bedtime, and an hour or so of stripping the wallpaper in Mark's home office.

I darted into the coffee place and ordered my drink, thankful the line was short.

"Hey, Hanna! Come join us!" Four mothers I knew from Brandon's class were drinking coffee, undoubtedly taking a quick break between shuttling children, shopping for year-end teacher gifts, or baking for one of the many concerts, picnics, graduations, presentations, art shows, and school plays packed into the exhausting final two weeks of June.

"I'd love to, but I've got to get Brandon to karate, then pick up Katie and the girls. The only reason I can fit this in is because I washed and pressed Brandon's *gi* this morning before the kids were up. Gotta run, but I'll see you at the second-grade concert on Thursday. We'll catch up then!"

Freshly caffeinated, I zipped home to get Brandon. Pulling into our driveway, I beeped the horn, and Brandon dutifully came running out, a purple trail from his PB&J sandwich dribbling down the front of his crisp white karate robe. *Oh, well.* I sighed. Ally, our college student babysitter thankfully home on summer break, waved to me from the doorway. *Am I horribly selfish for hoping that she doesn't find a "real" job anytime soon?* Driving through our neighborhood, we passed Bri's BMW. Bri and Eric looked sharp, probably heading out to a movie and dinner. I envied their freedom, wondering if the day would ever come when Mark and I would be able to just do whatever we pleased.

I thought back to the neighborhood block party last September where I had struck up a friendship with Bri. We had both been hovering around the wine table, watching the kids enjoy the moon bounce rented for the occasion.

"I miss the simplicity of life when they were this age," Bri said wistfully, more to herself than to me.

I belly-laughed. "Funny—I was just wondering if these Energizer bunnies ever stop. I can't wait until they grow up, get drivers' licenses, and start dating!"

I felt more connected to Bri, a woman nearly a decade my senior, than to many of the younger mothers in the neighborhood. I was thrilled when she asked me to join the Novel Women Book Club. The other women were in their late forties and fifties, some divorced, and most with grown children. I found them a refreshing change from my friendships with younger mothers, who incessantly discuss teachers, kids' activities, PTO, house projects, and their husbands' jobs.

Undeniably devoted to their families and jobs, most of the book club women operated with a self-confidence and a "who gives a crap?" attitude foreign to me. Menopause may contribute to some of their more candid emotions, but I sensed it was something more—a deep sense of security, either earned or learned. I was sad that book club had adjourned for the summer. I won't see the group until the weekend after Labor Day at the Build-a-Home Fund-Raiser, which Bri and Madeline were chairing. While I was not looking forward to finding a dress for that stuffy event, I was counting the days until I could see the group together again. In the meantime, I thought, just let me get through the end-of-school whirlwind with my sanity intact!

*

I was in a foul mood the next day, having barely slept. I'd waited up for Mark to check in after his dinner meeting in California, only to miss his call while I was in the shower. I hadn't slept well lately, still upset by the lingering terror brought on by my latest bedtime reading selection, Anna Quindlen's *Every Last One*. I was absolutely haunted by the book and couldn't shake a sense of impending doom. My uneasiness was intensified by the physical and emotional distance caused by Mark's new job. When he received his promotion, his new boss said he'd only be traveling to the Midwest and East Coast. But he began making trips to the West Coast and overseas almost immediately, and it's been that way ever since.

I went through the motions of getting the kids to the bus stop, straightening their rooms and the kitchen, watering the plants, feeding the dogs, and letting them out. I glanced at the tree-house-in-progress, and, shuddering, closed the blinds.

"Ugh!" I groaned out loud.

Mark had promised to build the kids a tree house more than a year ago. Right now, it was a monstrous skeleton of two-by-fours in the corner oak in our backyard. It was a wonder that any of the neighbors—including Bri and Eric—didn't complain about the eyesore. So many things about the house were being neglected, me included. I studied my reflection in the mirror. Although my blond hair disguised any grays, my face looked haggard. I was still the same weight as when we married, but I carried the weight differently and looked flabby. I never had a muffin top when I was a runner.

Surprisingly, I was free until after school. My English as

a Second Language student had to go to work and canceled our lesson, and they'd moved my food bank shift last week. I decided to go for a run to work on the muffin top. Mark and I used to run together a lot, in college and then when we were newly married and lived in the city. We loved running over the Brooklyn Bridge to the Promenade where we would grab a cup of coffee and the Sunday *New York Times* settle onto a bench overlooking downtown Manhattan. When had we run together last? After the promotion, Mark joined the Wall Street Athletic Club near his office, and when he wasn't traveling, he left the house at 5:00 a.m. to work out, showering there before heading to the office. Recently, all the exercise I got was running into the Grounds Crew for a jolt of caffeine and walking the dogs. I slipped on shorts, an old T-shirt, and running shoes, and jogged down the beautiful tree-lined streets of my neighborhood, armed only with my cell phone and a water bottle.

Insecure about running after such a long hiatus and not wanting to be seen in my decidedly non-chic attire, I kept to the side streets for several blocks. Turning onto the high school campus, I headed to the track where I completed four slow laps without injuring myself. I was huffing like a bull about to charge, and my arms were sore from the awkward position I had adopted, but I finished without collapsing. *Wow! Am I out of practice!* I cooled down by slowing to a walk, then sat on the bleachers to enjoy the sun on my face, well pleased.

A school bell rang and a gym class filed onto the field. A group of girls walked around the upper campus, while a coed group played badminton on the field in the center of the track. A cluster of eight strapping young men ran around the track, pushing each other.

"Settle down, gentlemen. Line up for your sprints, then work in a couple of relay races. Let's burn off some of that excess energy." The gym teacher, clipboard and whistle hanging from a lanyard, positioned himself to keep an eye on everyone in the field.

As they began running sprints, the boys—probably

seniors—exuded testosterone. Amused, I watched them compete with one another, enjoying their playful banter and roughhousing.

With the finish line directly before me, I had a center-stage mezzanine seat to the show. At the end of every race, the victor glanced my way, seeking a reaction. I smiled and looked away, only to see two boys engaged in push-up contest, oozing sweat and throbbing biceps. Closer to me, one ripped athlete used the railing of the bleachers to hoist himself in a display of pull-up prowess. It was a regular three-ring circus of the testosterone of youth.

"Marty, quit showing off for her, man," one boy shouted to the tallest, darkest, and most handsome student.

As the boys shed their shirts, I couldn't stop myself from out-right staring at their buff legs, arms, and abs. They were full-grown men, with hair on their legs and chests, rippling muscles, drenched in sweat. Their boundless energy enthralled me. I mused that what they probably lacked in experience they undoubtedly would make up for with stamina. *Do they realize that women hit their sexual peak in their late thirties?*

The gym teacher strolled over to the boys. "Hey, who do you think you are? Adonises? All of you: Get your shirts back on and jog four laps."

Blushing, I realized this exchange was my cue to head home. I took a couple of healthy sips from my water bottle, stretched quickly, and began jogging away, shaking my head at my horny-old-lady thoughts. Hopefully the gym teacher hadn't noticed me gawking and wouldn't report me as a suspicious pedophile. As I instinctively glanced down at my phone, I saw that I had missed a text from Mark.

Heading to Napa now with the group, Babe. Sorry I missed you last night. Love you. Will call you before I fly back tomorrow. M

That afternoon brought Brandon's piano and Katie's art lessons, timed inconveniently back to back, within a few miles of one another. Katie and I sat in Mr. Paterson's living room as Brandon ran through his lesson. Katie quietly worked on her homework while I checked my to-do list for the rest of the week, trying to decide on a healthy snack for the soccer team that the adults would approve of and the players would not leave uneaten on the bench. I closed my eyes and wondered when my life had been overtaken by such trivial details. I adored my husband, children, and our lovely home, but what had become of the art major who spent weekends in galleries and museums? I couldn't recall the last time I had picked up a sketchbook or dabbled in watercolors, and my latest art excursion was as a school field trip chaperone to the Morris Museum.

I tuned in to Brandon's playing. He wasn't half bad and he always seemed eager to practice at home. His expression mixed concentration and enthusiasm in equal measure.

I glanced at Mr. Paterson. He was handsome for an older man in his fifties. His demeanor was patient and calm, yet his hands, I just noticed, were unbelievably graceful and strong. The tendons of his hands and forearms bulged, visible as violin strings as he softly corrected Brandon and demonstrated the proper technique. He radiated creativity and a quiet strength. I was fascinated by those hands, touching the keys so lightly and quickly with such tensile strength. *How must they feel roaming over your body? Oh, my God! What the heck is wrong with me lately? It's a good thing that Mark will be home tomorrow night.*

*

The next day Katie had a soccer game followed by the annual parent-child mini-match. Mark had called earlier from the San Francisco airport saying that his flight was delayed, but he'd head straight to the soccer field for at least the second half of Katie's game. I brought snacks for the team, and as I went to drop off the trail mix, fruit, and water, Katie's coach, Jim Snyder, approached the bench. I tensed as he neared, bobbling and dropping the mini water bottles. I only knew him slightly as Gracie's father, Katie's teammate and friend. I had never gotten the girls to practice late, but I thought he might not be thrilled with the just-under-the-wire arrivals, and feared a mild reprimand. *Good God, I'm acting like he's my team coach from college!*

He bent to help me pick up the errant bottles. "Wow! Orange slices and homemade trail mix! Sure beats pretzels and Red Bull." Yes, one parent had actually brought this for the six-year-olds, a snack that would live on in infamy. Jim's smile was dazzling, his blue eyes crystal clear, and his dark thick hair shimmered with strands of gray.

I laughed and returned his smile.

"Thanks for stepping up in the nick of time to coach the girls this season, Jim. They're really enjoying themselves out there."

"I guess that's one reason to be happy for downsizing; being out of a nine-to-five job allows me time to hang out with Gracie. Katie is having a great season. She really gets the game and has some natural talent. She gets her athletic ability from you?" I noticed how he glanced at my calves below my Bermuda shorts as he asked the question.

"Not a chance! I was never much of a soccer player. I used to be a runner, and I'm thinking of getting back into that. It's just hard to fit it into my routine. I went out for a quick couple of miles yesterday and didn't feel horrible. I'm thinking about some strength and flexibility work, too."

"Good for you! I was a bit of a jock in high school, but a pharma desk job and years of wining and dining clients left me thirty-five pounds heavier. Since the layoff, I reinvented myself as a certified personal trainer at Platinum Performance downtown. I'm glad to be back in shape and I love helping my clients get there, too. I train a bunch of guys and women working toward half and full marathons."

"I always wanted to run a marathon. Maybe I'll give the gym a call. I hadn't realized how much I missed running."

"Maybe you could train for one of the shorter races at the shore this fall. It's nice to set a goal, and usually the weather is comfortable. No pressure, but here's my card, just in case you were serious." He handed over the simple matte-finished rectangle. I couldn't help but notice that his left ring finger was bare.

A giggling gaggle of girls suddenly appeared.

"Coach Snyder, we finished our warm-up laps. What should we do now?" They squealed. I had the sensation of being swarmed by a flock of twittering birds. No adult conversation could compete with that racket.

"Good luck, girls!" I called out as I walked over to the bleachers, my head lowered to hide a smile.

I couldn't take my eyes off Jim during the girls' game. Probably in his early fifties, his full head of dark hair didn't sport the ever-present baseball cap favored by men of that age. He looked youthful, with the physique and gait of a former football player, as opposed to the chiseled, too lean look of many younger trainers. He was definitely handsome, but also patient and filled with humor around the girls. Unlike other parent coaches, he didn't bellow from the sidelines or mumble about the gaffes on the field. He seemed genuinely to enjoy the girls and their chaotic energy.

Jim's wife, Marci, hadn't been around for several months, not showing up at games, practices, or play date drop-offs. Rumors were rampant. Tales circulated of an affair, a divorce, a stint in rehab, even a plastic-surgery recovery isolation. You have to love a small town—plenty of gossip and probably a few home-cooked meals delivered by concerned neighbors. *Is he just a newly divorced hunk on the prowl?* I wondered. But I couldn't deny that it felt good to have someone notice me, to be recognized as something other than a "mom."

At the post-game scrimmage between the parents and the girls, Coach Jim played on the girls' team. Most of the moms had surreptitiously departed just before the end of the first game, which left one other mother, all of the fathers, and me to play on the adult team. *No sign of Mark yet. Damn.* I retied my Keds and launched myself into the game, hoping not to embarrass myself.

I was flattered when Jim positioned himself directly opposite me on the line. There was a lot of playful jostling, nudging, and laughing. The girls were having a blast, and I was glad that I wasn't totally winded or uncoordinated in my attempts to move the ball toward goal.

"Not bad for someone who isn't a soccer player," Jim teased

"Thanks." I gasped. My cheeks were flushed, my spirits high.

The game continued, and at one point I swiveled too quickly and ended up on the ground. Jim extended a chivalrous hand to pull me up. A prickling sensation ran the length of my forearm as he hoisted me effortlessly, flashing that million-watt smile. Tingling from his touch, I cast my eyes downward, like a guilty child caught in a lie. The game ended with the girls "winning." The sun was still out, but people were late for dinner and homework, and families began piling into their cars to head home.

"Great games, Katie! Did you have fun?"

"Yes, Mommy. It was the best day! Too bad Daddy wasn't here."

"I know, pumpkin. He should be home soon." We packed up the car and filed out of the parking lot, both of us beaming even though we were annoyed at Mark's absence.

Mark's car service was just pulling away as we arrived at the house. Fox Business News was blaring on the family room TV.

"Where's my petunia?" he cried out when he heard the kitchen door open.

"Here I am, Daddy!"

"I missed you all very much," he said, handing Katie a miniature cable car. He placed a model replica of Alcatraz Island for Brandon on the kitchen counter. I received a kitschy scarf depicting the Golden Gate Bridge. And a hug and kiss on the lips and a two-handed squeeze on my rear. No mention of missing the game.

"Sorry, it was one of those airport-gift trips," Mark said cheerily.

"Anything big happen while I was gone?" Just then Brandon burst in from his playdate, still carrying the McDonald's Happy Meal toy that accompanied his chicken tenders dinner.

"Daddy! You're home!"

"Hey, little man, how was everything here while I was gone? Any problems to report?" At eight, Brandon was more serious and focused than Katie. Since Mark started traveling more, our son had begun double-checking that all doors were locked before going up to bed. I had to make sure he didn't feel too responsible when his father was away.

"No, we were good." Trained like Pavlov's dog to associate Mark's suitcase with a souvenir, Brandon scanned the room until he spotted the Alcatraz figurine. "Is this for me? Thanks, Dad!"

"I'm beat. I'm going to take a quick shower. What would you like to do for dinner, Han?"

"How about I feed Katie some leftover pizza and you and I have some omelets and wine later?"

"Sounds great. I'll be down in a bit, babe." He squeezed my shoulders affectionately before heading upstairs. I watched him as he walked away. Perfect posture and a lean, boyish physique made Mark appear taller than his six-foot frame. He had the easy movements of an athlete, with thick dark blond curls. So far he retained all his hair and no gray intruded. College girls and elderly women alike often flirted with him. But I saw that the areas around his clear green eyes and his jaw revealed stress and fatigue. *He needs to slow down*, I thought.

After serving Katie dinner and Brandon dessert, I began setting the table and assembling ingredients for a ham, cheese, and tomato omelet. Uncorking a bottle of red wine, I let it breathe as I checked the kids' backpacks for notices and supervised their bedtime rituals. *Thank God tomorrow is Saturday!* I lit several votive candles on the table. Lately, Mark and I generally took a day or two to re-acclimate after his trips. It hadn't always been this way. In the early years of our marriage, we couldn't wait to get our hands on each other after a separation. We would talk late into the night to catch up on each other's lives and dreams. Even after the children were born, we would still manage to reserve time to cocoon ourselves immediately after any time apart. Lying close together, we fit like jigsaw puzzle pieces. Recently, our conversation seemed stilted and the edges of the puzzle pieces frayed, no longer smoothly interlocking. *When did we turn from an absence-makes-the-heart-grow-fonder to an out-of-sight-out-of-mind kind of couple?*

While Mark tucked the kids into bed, I showered, dried my hair, dabbed on a little cologne and made a fast pass with lipstick, then slipped on the snug black V-neck T-shirt and tight jeans that Mark loved. Until we knew Katie and Brandon would stay in bed all night, the Victoria's Secret nightie dinners of the past had had to remain on hold. I hurried downstairs to cook the omelet, then quietly called up to Mark. Getting no reply, I looked upstairs and found him in Brandon's room, fast asleep in the boy's upper bunk bed, a hardcover copy of the latest *Mystery Tree House* book opened flat on his belly, rising and falling with each loud snore. Brandon, displaced from his regular sleeping berth, had moved to the lower bunk and was nestled under the covers, sleeping soundly. I kissed them both on the forehead, closed the door behind me, and went downstairs, where I put on some quiet music, ate my omelet, and slowly enjoyed several glasses of wine. I let the wine and music wash over my disappointment and stared into the flickering candlelight until the votive sputtered out. Fidgeting with the candle, I took the Platinum Performance business card out of my purse and put it on the table. *Is it normal to feel neglected and stale? Why do I feel like Mark's taking advantage of me? Is he cheating on me when he is away? Does everyone feel this way after years of marriage? Or is this just a temporary rough patch?*

I lumbered upstairs, crawled into bed and slept uncharacteristically late the next morning. On the dresser was a note from Mark.

Wanted to let you sleep. Taking Brandon to art class and Katie to the Fun Fair at school. See you for lunch.

I took a few Tylenol, got dressed, and called the gym to arrange training sessions with Jim starting next week. I looked online and registered for a half marathon at the shore in September. Goal-driven, that's me. While I was at it, I chose an evening watercolor class at the art center. I needed to buy a watercolor set, and some new workout clothes and running shoes. Time to reclaim a little of my former self.

*

Sunday dawned void of any planned activities other than church. Mark wouldn't be traveling this week, so maybe we could get back on track with some together time. We made love last night, but I had felt detached, distant. There were no kisses, talking, or snuggling afterward. Mark surrendered to sleep almost immediately, leaving me to worry about our strained relationship. *We need a long conversation about something other than the kids' schedules or his work.*

I couldn't share these troubles with my mother or friends. Mom and Dad had such a close marriage. She was a school nurse, he was a small-town doctor in Illinois. Only the rare emergency call interfered with our nightly family dinners. Mom simply can't wrap her head around all of the lessons, sports, and chauffeuring that consume our time. Sarah and Candace are great friends, but their husbands each lost their jobs in the past two years, forcing them to work part-time. Both women are afraid of losing their homes, so they would have no sympathy with the marital strain caused by my husband's new promotion. Bri was the only one I'd feel comfortable confiding in, but lately she's seemed distracted. I sense it's about more than the upcoming gala, but she's not saying.

Mark and Brandon watched the Mets game on the family room television and Mark came into the kitchen to grab some snacks, whistling. He seemed relaxed, but I knew that his Sunday afternoon pre-gaming had already begun. Each Sunday around noon, Mark began isolating himself emotionally, preparing himself for the intensity of the workweek ahead.

"Do you think that you might be able to work on the tree house a bit today? Or maybe we can carve out some time to scrape wallpaper tonight?"

"Maybe. I have some projections to sort through before tomorrow, but I can put in a little time out back today. I really want the kids to be able to enjoy the tree house this summer and I'd love to get the office finished by the fall."

Working on Mark's home office was a task both of us had once enjoyed doing after the kids went to bed. Tackling a panel or two each evening, music gently playing, sharing a beer or wine, we talked and worked together to coax the stubborn and hideous gold paisley paper off the walls. The work definitely felt a chore now, especially since I had to tackle most of it solo. Although Mark's promotion meant we could afford a contractor, I stubbornly wanted the two of us to complete the project together. But now Mark could barely muster the energy to look through the mail after work, never mind strip wallpaper. As I might have predicted, we made no progress on either the tree house or the office that Sunday.

*

I kicked off the school week on Monday excited and a bit nervous to start my new physical training. I spent an inordinate amount of time choosing my exercise outfit, finally settling on a pair of flattering shorts and a purple V-neck tee which amply covered my muffin top. I joined Jim's training group of two other women and a man. The women, both mothers of toddlers, were younger and had the bodies of college students, along with perfect hair and nails. I marveled that they could train while raising young kids and still look like glamour queens. The man, Thomas, appeared to be in his forties. He didn't have an athletic build, but he was running for a charity team in the New York Marathon in November and was dedicated and hardworking. The first training session ended with a three-mile run to the county park. Jim and I slowly led the way. The supermodel moms certainly could've kept up with us, but they were chatting about new stores and spas rumored to open in the neighboring town of Weston.

"How about we do Indian Runs halfway back to the gym and then pick up the pace with solo runs for the final mile?" Jim glistened slightly with sweat; the heat and humidity was already oppressive. Dark clouds to the west, though, meant that hopefully a short thunderstorm would cool us off.

"I'll try," I managed to wheeze.

At the two-mile mark, Jim, Thomas, and I broke off into a quick run. My lungs were burning but my legs felt loose and strong. By the time we approached the gym, Thomas had fallen back and Jim and I sprinted our final hundred yards into the parking lot.

"Not bad at all!" Jim's breath seemed to adjust to normal immediately. "I don't think you're going to have any problem building your endurance, so we can concentrate on getting your speed up for the race. We just have to make sure that you stay injury-free. Here, let me stretch you out."

Gasping for breath, I was grateful not to speak. As I lay self-consciously on the mats spread in the yard leading to the gym, Jim stretched my moist hamstrings and massaged my calves. *Thank God I shaved my legs and wore my lined running shorts.* I'd never liked massages. A near-stranger's hands on me always seemed invasive and inappropriate. But Jim's strong hands guiding and pulling my legs felt glorious. Maybe endorphins were to blame, but it was all I could do to stifle a little gasp of pleasure. Our eyes met briefly and what did I see? Longing? A small, sad smile passed Jim's face before he looked away. A clap of thunder sounded and large cool raindrops plopped onto my face and legs, almost sizzling on my hot skin. Thomas broke my reverie just then by puffing into the parking lot.

Jim began to stretch him out before the sky opened up in a full-blown, summer thundercloud burst.

It took me a moment to steady myself and get up off the mat. "Thanks. I'll see you Wednesday."

"Don't forget hamstrings keep stretching and drink plenty of water," Jim called over his shoulder.

I ran to the car and sat waiting for the storm to settle down. I checked my phone for any missed calls or messages and turned the car radio on. The music and the rhythmic pounding of the rain were strangely soothing. The storm picked up. The rain thumped on the car roof, punctuated by rattling claps of thunder. The music was drowned out. I felt my pounding heartbeat as I recalled how Jim's hands felt on me. *What game am I playing here? Is Jim flirting or just being friendly? Am I so desperate for attention that I'm throwing myself at him? Or am I just lashing out at Mark?*

The rain slowed to a steady patter just as the interior lights and dashboard lights flashed and went dark. *Oh God! The battery's dead. How can that be? Serves me right!*

I checked my phone for the time. I had to be at school for Katie's closing kindergarten graduation ceremony in an hour. Luckily, Mark was working from home this morning so he could attend the school program. Frantic, I punched his speed dial number. It beeped, rang, and went to voicemail. I tried the home number and left a panicked message as well. *He must be on a business call. He knows I don't bother him needlessly. Shouldn't he interrupt his call if I call in the middle of a huge thunderstorm?*

Just then, a gray pickup pulled up next to me. "Everything okay?" Jim shouted.

My car windows were steamed up and I had to open the car door to respond. "Battery's dead." I flushed, my recent daydreams making me feel guilty.

"No problem. I can give you a jump or drop you at home if it's something else. I know that you have kindergarten graduation this morning, too."

"If you don't mind, it would be great if you jumped me." *Ugh. Unfortunate word choice.*

Jim deftly sprang from the cab of his truck, took out his jumper cables and latched them with conviction onto the Expedition's battery. He knew which cable went where. I wondered just how many damsels in distress he had rescued.

"Okay, turn the ignition."

As the engine hummed, Jim unhooked the cables and flashed me one of his brilliant smiles. The rain had slowed to a misty drizzle. I rolled down my window. "Thank you so much, you really saved me!"

"My pleasure. You might want to have your battery, or your alternator checked out. It could even be an electrical problem. Check it soon. Let me know what it turns out to be."

He waited for me to drive away, then drove off in the opposite direction.

When I pulled into my driveway I bristled at the sight of Mark's parked Audi. Mark had his cell phone pressed to his ear when I walked into the kitchen, soaked, red-faced, and tense. Seemingly oblivious to my disheveled appearance, he waved, his eyes bright. I knew that look. His adrenaline was pumping and he was on a high from an invigorating deal. He hung up.

"Hey! How was your session? Sorry I couldn't pick up when you called. That was Bruce calling from Japan. The Everall acquisition looks like it's going to happen. All of our hard work paid off, and I get to head the close. Man, I'm pumped! Great news."

"Congratulations," I spat out.

Mark totally missed or ignored my sarcasm—as well as my drenched Raggedy Ann appearance. *How self-absorbed can he be?*

I let out a huge sigh, deciding to play the supportive wife. "You've been courting that one for ages. When will it all go down?"

"Bruce is taking care of most of the prelim on-site work. It looks like I'll be on a plane to Japan the week after next."

My stomach lurched and my mouth went dry. "But that's when we're supposed to be on the Outer Banks!"

Even in my shock, I wanted to gauge his reaction. His mouth drooped and his eyes flashed worry for a millisecond, then he said, "Oh, honey, I am so sorry. I've been looking forward to vacation as well. Maybe your mom and dad can come out and join you and the kids. Or maybe we can push it back another week."

I was fuming. He knew that we were boxed into our week because it was one of the only available when we booked the vacation last December. We'd never find something down there at such a late date, and, frankly, the prospect of spending a week with my happily married parents was not enticing.

He came up to give me a hug. "Oh, baby, I'll make it up to all of you. Maybe we can get away somewhere at the end of the summer, or even over the November teachers' convention break."

I was numb, dumbstruck, and didn't respond. *Did he even notice?* I could see that his mind was already firing on all cylinders planning the Japan deal.

*

Mark spent the week before his Japan trip working late at the office, working out early at the gym, and working his way back into his children's good graces after having upset their vacation plans. He hoped that extravagant gifts would placate them. He gave Brandon a mini low-power go-kart and Katie a certificate good for an afternoon party for ten at the Kidz Fun Zone sports complex. The kids, thrilled, forgave him, but I knew I would be saddled with policing Brandon on the kart and organizing and running a party with ten shrieking girls at the Fun Zone. Mark was the generous Santa doling out generous "some assembly required" gifts on Christmas

Eve, while I was the sleep-deprived, frustrated parent struggling to put everything together.

We did manage to have a nice dinner out on the night before his trip.

"You seem quiet tonight, hon. Everything okay?" he asked, swirling his cabernet in his glass.

"I'm just tired and still disappointed about our vacation, I guess."

"I understand. I promise I'll make it up to you, babe. But this is such a high-profile deal. If all goes well, even the CEO will know who I am."

I clenched my fists, deliberately letting go of my wineglass, afraid I'd snap off the stem. "I know. But it's hard managing the home front alone. I don't want to whine, but I feel like a single parent. I miss our family time and—I miss you. You just assume I can handle everything alone." I blinked back my tears, picked up my drink, and gulped from my glass.

His eyes darted from side to side, not accustomed to seeing me on the brink of waterworks. He grabbed my hands, almost wrestling the wineglass from my grasp. Lowering his face to catch my eyes—a familiar consoling maneuver I use on the kids—he sounded exhausted.

"I'll ask my folks to babysit so you and I can get away after Labor Day. You love that place in the Adirondacks. Want to head there again? Or we could try that fancy resort on Saranac Lake, maybe go with Bruce and his wife. It could double as our fifteenth anniversary celebration."

Leave it to Mark to multitask when it comes to celebrating milestones.

I sat up straight, fixed on his gaze. Breathing in and releasing my best yoga breath, I launched into the speech I'd been rehearsing in my head for months. "It's more than just needing to get away. I feel we're growing apart. You love your new job, and, believe me,

I'm thrilled for you. It's just, you are so unavailable to the kids and me. I miss having you around to talk to, to share experiences with, and to help out. That means more to me than the money and things it can buy. Even when you're home, your head is still wrapped in your work. Do you even like spending time with us anymore? It feels as if you can't wait to leave the house in the morning. Like you are sharing yourself elsewhere. I don't know what to think. Is there someone else?"

The last sentences spilled from my lips frantically, as if the words would elude me if I didn't blurt them out. Why was I so afraid? Why did he seem so unconcerned? Was I the only one sensing that we were adrift?

My eyes welled up as I struggled to compose myself.

"Don't be silly. Oh, baby, never!" Mark grabbed my hands across the table, almost knocking my wineglass over. "Honey, you and the kids are everything to me. Sure, I love this job, the high, the power, the sense of accomplishment, but I also love what it gives us: the house, the lessons, the financial security. I have been tired, but things will settle down after the Everall deal. I will make it up to you, I promise. I love you more than anything, Hanna. What do you say we get dessert at home and get out of here?"

He winked at me playfully, but then the vibrating of his cell phone interrupted our conversation. Scowling, he glanced down, hesitated a nanosecond, and said, "Crap, its Bruce. Must be a problem if he's calling at this hour. Sorry, hon. I have to take it."

Mark went outside to take the call. I knew we wouldn't finish our talk. At least I had said my piece. Letting my eyes wander around the restaurant, I took in the room. Scarlatti's was a favorite place of ours. The food was delicious and not too heavy, the wine selection was wonderful, and the service was courteous yet friendly.

"Would you like coffee or dessert while you are waiting, Mrs. Feldon?"

"Yes, Patricio. I would love a decaf cappuccino, please."

The place was crowded for a weeknight, with eleven couples populating the dimly lit room. On the far side of the room was a group of six. They were quiet. I hadn't heard or noticed the three couples at the table earlier, but now I recognized two of the couples from town. Seated with them were Jim and an attractive blond woman, fortyish. My heartbeat quickened. Watching them inconspicuously, I noticed that Jim looked wonderful, tanned, wearing a dark jacket over a white Oxford shirt. He was smiling and chuckling with the man to his left. The woman to his right seemed to be waiting for his attention. After a few minutes, Jim turned to her and lightly touched her on the hand. Not a familiar gesture, more a polite, apologetic one. It looked as if Jim's friends were trying their luck at matchmaking. I studied his face and detected only friendliness, but the woman seemed very interested in him. I was overcome by a flash of jealousy, then an overwhelming need to escape without being seen. I gestured to Patricio for the check and quickly paid it. As the group readied to leave from the back of the dining room, I darted into the ladies' room to hide.

Huddled in a bathroom stall, I was surprised to hear the three women come into the restroom. *Idiot! Of course, they would come in here before driving home!* I flashed back to memories of high school, hiding in a stall while the mean girls smoked cigarettes by the sinks. I was afraid to move, or have them spot my shoes under the door. Why was I running from them? What's the worst that could come from a conversation? Before I could bring my mind fully back to the present, I found myself perching on the toilet seat.

They immediately started talking the minute they were through the door. "So, what do you think? Isn't he great?"

I hazarded a peek through the thin gap between the door and the frame and saw that one of the women from town was talking to Jim's date, who hunched toward the mirror, refreshing her lipstick.

"He is definitely a gentleman, gorgeous, great body, funny,

but are you sure he's over his ex-wife? He doesn't seem interested. Friendly and lots of fun, but I'm not sensing he's attracted to me."

"Oh, don't worry about his ex. They had problems for a while, and then over the winter when Jim lost his job, he found her in bed with the contractor who was doing their addition. We all thought it was just a fling, but Marci moved to Florida with the guy and they are still together. What kind of woman leaves her family like that? Don't get me wrong, Jim was heartbroken, but he's certainly not pining over her. He's too focused on Gracie and trying to pay the mortgage. He's a sweetheart. We just want him to have somebody to share some fun with."

"Okay, if he asks me out again, I'll woo him with my womanly ways." Blondie chuckled.

After they exited the bathroom, I unsettled myself from my toilet perch. Hopeful that Mark was off the phone and we could get out of there, I walked to the valet-parking placard and asked for the Audi. Mark had the ticket and was pacing around the parking lot, still engrossed in his animated cell phone conversation. But the valet knew us and sprinted away to fetch Mark's car. That's when Jim walked up behind me.

"Fancy meeting you here! What a nice surprise? Did you have a nice dinner?"

I almost toppled off my heels. "Yeah." I gulped. "We love this place."

"You certainly clean up nicely." He looked from my calves to my neckline. "You look lovely tonight. I always see you in gym clothes."

"You're not so bad yourself." I blushed and hoped he would think it was because of the wine.

As my car approached, Jim went to the driver's door, and sidled between it and the valet to hold the door open for me. He gently touched the small of my back as he ushered me into the car. "Thank you," I whispered, before he closed the car door. My back tingled from his touch and I felt a rush of warmth in my lower body.

"See you on Friday morning at the gym." His eyes searched mine for a moment as I put the car in drive and pulled from the curb. In the rearview mirror, I saw him looking after me.

The high drama of my departure was short lived, as I only drove thirty feet to pick up Mark by the side of the restaurant. He wrapped up his call soon after.

"Ugh. I'm so sorry about that, Hanna. Bruce needs major projection revisions before I get on the plane tomorrow. I'll be burning the midnight oil tonight." He sounded exasperated but I could hear a tinge of excitement in his voice.

Jim was just getting his pickup truck as we passed by the valet station on the circular driveway of the restaurant. He waved briefly as I drove by.

"Hey, isn't that Katie's soccer coach? Anyway, do you think that I could get a rain check on that 'dessert,' honey? We'll celebrate just the two of us when I get back. I promise." Mark leaned over and kissed me slowly on my neck. Usually that move made me melt instantly, but tonight I was distracted by a sizzling sensation at the small of my back.

Brianna

A FOX IN THE HEN HOUSE

"**Y**OU WHAT?" I threw the socks in a drawer and plopped on the bed to listen. "Staci, start when he picked you up."

"Bri, you should see him in a pair of jeans!" Staci described her date in vivid detail.

"Wow, sounds wonderful. Just be careful!"

"Yes, mother hen, I will." Staci replied. "You know, Bri, I don't ever remember feeling this way, not even when I was first dating my ex. There's just something about him."

I hung up, looking down at my feet dangling off the bed. For a moment, I lost myself to the first time I had felt that enchanted. So long ago. *Ah, that naughty passionate love.* I used to daydream the day away, playing out intimate scenes between us, drawing little hearts in the margin of a legal pad with our initials in them. My coworkers had to nudge me during client interviews at the law firm where I worked at as a paralegal. Sometimes I'd blush, thinking someone could see the steamy scenes playing in my mind. After a few months, the heat cooled, then chilled, and then, as with all intense relationships, we broke up.

"Bri!" Eric called from downstairs. "Where are my clean boxers?"

"In the laundry room," I yelled. *Back to domestic bliss.*

"No, they're not!"

Men. "I'll be right there." I picked up the empty laundry basket and stomped downstairs.

My husband wasn't my first love. We met later. I thought I knew everything about him after all these years together. But, I didn't.

Last month, out to dinner with Doug and Marie, Eric told us about catching cutthroat trout with his father on the Skagit River in Washington when he was fourteen and how excited he was finally catching a fish on the last day of the trip. He regaled us with anecdotes: setting up a tent for the first time, hooking anything and everything but a fish, his father patiently trying to teach him to cast a fly-fishing rod. Eric had us laughing from dinner into dessert. That trip held a special place in his heart that he shared exclusively with his dad. My heart had swelled with love for him. I only wished I had heard those memories before.

I pulled freshly laundered boxers out from a folded pile, and handed them to Eric, who now demanded to know why the laundry wasn't put away.

"I didn't get to it yet! You want them upstairs? Put them upstairs! What do I look like, your personal maid?"

Eric grinned and wrapped his arms around me. "Well, maybe if you wore a maid outfit, we could have a little fun with it."

"Oh, please." I broke away from him. "Just go to work, and remember we promised to go to Madeline's party on Saturday night, so don't plan a late tennis game." I tossed the folded laundry into a basket and walked to the kitchen.

"The party's late in the day, I can play in the morning," he yelled. *God forbid he should miss a tennis match.*

After Eric left for his job at Simon Crane where he specialized in litigation trademark and patent cases, I roamed the house, picking up whatever everyone had dropped and left. We lived in a large five-bedroom colonial built in the 1990s—almost a McMansion.

But in fewer than three months I would be an empty nester and no longer saw the need for all this house, if there ever had been a need for it. It made me feel small.

Putting away the cereal boxes in the kitchen, I didn't know how to fit into this new chapter of life. I felt like a long-term employee being laid off, but without a severance package. Sleep eluded me. When I was lucky enough to fall asleep, I'd wake up boiling hot in the middle of the night.

Most of my friends were returning to work. Now that Logan and Julianna would both be off at college, I knew I needed to do something. Before children, I'd worked as a litigation paralegal. But working with litigators and coming home to one every night struck me as too much around-the-clock arguing. I couldn't face it. But what else could I do after all these years?

I sighed and sank into a kitchen chair.

After a few minutes, I pulled myself together, picked up the laundry basket off the counter.

"Mom!" Logan jumped in front of me in the hallway. I dropped the basket. Clothes flew everywhere.

"Stop doing that!" I yelled. But my wide-open smile betrayed me.

"Why? It cracks me up every time." Logan picked up the basket and piled the laundry back haphazardly. "I'm going over Sam's house, be back at dinner." He handed me the basket and shot out the door.

"Okay." I watched him go.

Logan's baseball shirt was on top of the stack of laundry. How many baseball shirts had I cleaned over the years—thousands? We signed him up when he was little more than a toddler for sports like T-ball, soccer, and lacrosse, hoping to focus his enormous energy. He'd inherited his adventurous, hyper-energy side from his father, but at least he didn't have his dad's overwhelming need to control everything. Instead of going nuts when things were out of place, he thrived in chaos.

Looking at his baseball shirt, I remembered how, when he came home, I'd pick him up. He'd wrap his small arms around my neck and hug as tight as he could, bestowing big wet kisses on my cheek. He always smelled like apples and chocolate chip cookies.

I turned back toward the kitchen sink, realizing a tear had escaped and was halfway down my cheek.

My daughter, Julianna, a rising college junior, worked as a nanny for the summer for a couple across town. I hardly saw her. Julianna and Logan would both leave for college in about ten weeks.

Julianna, my serious child, excelled in school and at anything she tried. But she held everything back. I didn't know if she was upset after the breakup with her high school boyfriend. I had to ask Logan, since she never mentioned it. I hoped she hadn't learned to hold in her emotions from me.

After I put away the laundry, I picked up the family room. Eric's latest books were piled high by his favorite chair. I looked through them: some business magazines, this year's Pulitzer Prize fiction winner, and an anthology of America's greatest poems. Both of us are passionate readers, but Eric reads more widely than I do.

Chores done, I walked through the house. Its quietness unnerved me. I changed and went out for a walk. Hanna was struggling to walk her Saint Bernard and her Labrador together. They were pulling so hard that she almost fell over.

"Hanna, wait!" I called. "Want some help?"

I ran across the street to catch up with her and we continued down the hill.

"I'm glad I ran into you," Hanna said. "I had a great time at book club."

"Me too," I said.

Bringing up book club reminded me of the upcoming fundraiser that Madeline and I were chairing. I was a little anxious. "You know, as a group we worked together really well on past charity functions. This time, Madeline and I may need everyone's advice, but we aren't meeting until after the event. When we brainstorm together we usually come up with a solution quicker than any think tank."

Hanna laughed. "There's always the phone, Bri."

"I don't think it's the same as us all being there, bouncing ideas off one other."

"I know. Don't worry—we'll all be there for you."

Why am I so anxious? Changing topics, I asked, "What's up with your tree house?" I could only imagine what Hanna's other neighbor, a pompous and house-proud doctor, must think about that eyesore so close to his impeccably manicured home. I was surprised he hadn't complained to the town.

"I know, sooo sorry." Hanna pulled as hard on the choker collars as she could, but the dogs barely budged. If they kept going, they'd trample the neighbor's flower garden. I grabbed one of the leashes and together we stopped them.

"You know Mark's been working and traveling a lot. We barely see him." Hanna looked at the ground.

"Don't worry about the tree house. Eric and I don't care," I said, seeing the upset look on her face. "But I was serious at book club when I asked if you wanted to go for coffee and talk. We can talk now or go for coffee or a drink later—whatever works for you."

"I'm not sure what's on the kids' schedules today. After our walk, I'll look and call you."

"Okay," I said. "Are you going to Madeline's party on Saturday?"

"I think so," Hanna said. "Yes, I mean. I'm going with or without Mark."

We continued to walk around the neighborhood together. "Do you ever wonder what really goes on in our neighborhood? Is this McMansion life really all it's cracked up to be?" I asked.

"Perfect homes, perfect lives—right?" Hanna reached for the dog's leash when we arrived at her driveway. "My white-picket fence is a bit tarnished, but at least I'm honest about it."

"All of our fences are tarnished one way or the other," I said. "Listen, if you need help, call me. I'll babysit." My arm twitched from Hanna's dog yanking me. How did she manage to walk them both?

I had forgotten how hard it was when my kids were young and Eric was always working, but in a way, I envied her as I watched her haul the two beasts down her driveway.

*

The smell of the barbecue hit us as soon as Eric and I walked up Madeline's driveway. Her backyard was full of people and the aroma of juicy, sizzling, grilled steak was everywhere. It made my stomach growl. The party was already in full swing by the time we arrived.

Madeline's backyard looked like an ad out of that luxurious lifestyle catalog, *Frontgate*. Staged to perfection, it looked like some top designer had waved her magic wand, but we all knew she hadn't. Madeline didn't need magic—she made her own.

I snagged a shrimp from one of the serving staff and got in line at the bar.

As Madeline passed by I tapped her on the shoulder. "You have outdone yourself this time. This is amazing." I hugged and kissed her.

"It was nothing." Madeline waved her hand in the air, but a huge smile beamed from ear to ear.

We were friends long before book club. Our children were always in the same grades in school and she and I worked together in the PTO. A part-time pediatric speech therapist, she was precise and exacting in everything she touched.

I often thought that there must be another side to her—one maybe not so precise, more like the rest of us. But even with her daughter's science fair project she tried to get the results to turn out her way. Her daughter's experiment was on what snack food choice says about someone's personality. The book club members were guinea pigs, and we all gained a few pounds from eating enormous amounts of snack food. Madeline kept making her daughter repeat the experiment because she felt the findings were wrong. Madeline's snack food of choice was pretzels and she denied that the "pretzel personality" suited her, which her daughter described as a novelty seeker who thrives in a world of abstract concepts. No, that was not our Madeline.

"Staci met a man in Burlington," I whispered into her ear.

Her mouth fell open. "No way, she's only been away a few days! Besides, I thought she went up to focus on her career and not to find a man."

"She stayed in that sham of a marriage until she felt her boys were old enough, and now she's free to find some happiness," I confided. Staci and I had become closer friends after she separated from George. Neither Eric nor I liked him.

Madeline clapped her hands together. "Well, I guess I'm happy for her. Listen, I think you know everyone here, except maybe Natasha who is talking with your husband." She gestured toward the deck. "She just moved into the neighborhood a few weeks ago, so I thought I'd introduce her to our gang."

"That's nice of you," I said. "Where is her husband?" I looked to see who she was.

"Oh, she's divorced." Madeline excused herself to greet some new arrivals.

Natasha's back was to me. She was dressed in a short, brightly colored beach design skirt that looked like a Lily Pulitzer, and a tight tank top showing off her gym-tailored, perfectly balanced curves.

I yanked my top down.

Hanna waved me over. I made the rounds and then managed to grab Eric so we could eat dinner together on the patio. "I haven't met Madeline's new neighbor yet, is she nice?" I asked, noticing him staring at the deck where Natasha was leaning against the wall.

"Oh, yes, she'll fit right in," Eric commented. "I met her last week at the club. She plays tennis and golf."

"Of course, she does. Am I the only person around here who doesn't play tennis and golf?" Eric hadn't mentioned meeting Natasha, but, of course, we didn't tell one another every little detail of our lives.

His smile turned impish. "Well, I've only been trying to get you to learn for about twenty-five years." Eric leaned closer to me in his chair and took my hand. "How do you like your new car?"

"It's wonderful," I replied.

"Did you check out all the new features yet?" Eric asked. He'd skimmed the car's manual last night and said that the front seats had a cooling element similar to his car.

"No, I only got the car yesterday, remember?" I smiled, knowing that he'd tell me all about it. I hated reading manuals. I'd rather push a button or knob and see what happens.

But Eric changed topics. "How was Logan today? Did he clean his room?"

"You're kidding, right? He ran out of the house about ten minutes after he got up, just like he's been doing all summer. Haven't seen him since."

Eric dropped my hand and sat back in his chair, annoyed. "You should have made him do it!"

"Oh, come on. He's leaving for college soon. His room will be immaculate then." I sighed. "Don't worry. He'll do it."

Eric gets his shorts in a bunch when things aren't carried out according to his instructions. Me, I let things go. I picked at the food on my plate.

After dinner, I introduced myself to Natasha, who had remained perched on the side of the deck for most of the party.

Beautiful in a striking Eastern European way, she exuded confidence despite knowing only a few people at the party. She moved fluidly, her gestures graceful. Her silky voice was pitched almost too low to hear, and she had a gift for small talk. Highlighted hair accented high cheekbones. But what struck me most were her lips. So temptingly full, they oozed sex appeal; she was exactly the kind of woman men flocked to and tonight was no exception. I felt a little pale in comparison and went into the house to apply some lipstick.

The men brought out some tequila and started doing shots. They liked to act like fraternity boys at our gatherings, raising the noise level and growing rowdier as they downed drinks, except, of course, for Stan, Madeline's husband. She would never allow him to participate and admonished the wives for allowing their husbands to behave in this raunchy manner.

I looked up at the deck and saw Eric speaking with Natasha again. He waved when he saw me, his snappish manner long forgotten. Amazing how easy he got over his bad mood.

When he drank too much, our entire bedroom rumbled loudly with each breath. I would lay awake next to him counting snores until sometime around 3:00 a.m. when exhaustion let me lapse into sleep. As grateful as I was that he wasn't doing shots, I wondered why he was spending so much time talking with Natasha. Was it just that she was new to the neighborhood? That seemed unlike him.

While helping Madeline clean up at the end of the party, I thought back to when I first met Eric. We both worked in Oak Park and frequently got coffee at the corner newspaper store before work. One day we noticed each other, the next day we smiled, the next we nodded, and then finally he said hello. That was the eighties, so everything was puffed up: our hair, our shoulders, our skirts, and our egos. Eric wore his hair a little longer and fuller than was customary for attorneys then.

We joked around, getting to know one another slowly. I was seeing a few different men and thought of Eric more as a friend, but I loved to flirt with him.

One day I bluntly asked, "So what's your zodiac sign?" I didn't know anything about zodiac signs, except mine, but the dating scene back then was choked in clichéd rhetoric.

Eric's eyes had flickered. He paused for a second before answering, "I'm a Pisces."

"A what? What symbol is that? What month?"

"It's March, and it's a fish."

His eyes darted around my face. Always the lawyer trying to figure out where this was going.

"A fish, a fish! An itty-bitty fish?" I couldn't control my burst of laughter.

"Why is that so funny?" Eric asked.

"Well, you are speaking with a lion, the ruler of the universe, the king of the zodiac, or queen in my case, and a fire sign, and you're just a little bitty fishy." I basked in smug delight.

Eric placed a hand on each shoulder and looked directly into my eyes. "Yes, I am, but I'm also a water sign and I believe water puts out fire!" He began to laugh, this time sounding genuine.

I laughed with him and for the first time noticed his deep blue eyes.

I wish I still had half that hubris now. I was so in control of my life back then, or at least believed I had control. Life since then had taught me differently.

After my juvenile ploy at being witty, I noticed small things about Eric: how he took his coffee, how his eyes lit up when he discussed a case, how well his suits fit. Eric could be intense and controlling at times, but I had more fun with him than anyone else. He worked out at the gym and played tennis, claiming physical activity was better than any pill on the market.

We began to date and came to realize we wanted the same things: the white-picket fence, a couple of kids, yearly trips to the shore. We made each other laugh. Within a year we were engaged. Our gentle sparring continued over the years, teasing, but no real fighting. Eric had made me notice him out of all the other fish in the sea.

On our way home from Madeline's party, I asked Eric if he had fun with Natasha.

"I had a nice time at the party with everyone," Eric said.

Always the lawyer.

"You certainly spent a lot of time with her." I couldn't remember the last time that Eric drove home from a party, but he hadn't been drinking with the boys tonight—too occupied with Natasha.

Eric broke into a wide grin. "Oh, don't tell me you're actually jealous."

I shook my head no, but he laughed. "Good, now you know how it feels."

"What's that supposed to mean?"

"You always seem to have some man hanging on your every word," Eric said. "But you're so cool and collected, you don't even notice."

Maybe that was true twenty years ago. Certainly not now. But why correct him? It was nice that he still thought so.

"I hope the kids aren't around, we can make a night of it," he said and grabbed my hand. The next thing I knew, Eric's hand went up my leg and under my skirt.

Tired or not, there's nothing like a little jealousy to stimulate the hormones.

The kids were out when we got home. Eric made drinks and we went up to our bedroom. We sipped our drinks, talking, teasing, and then found our passion's tempo. The warmth of Eric's flesh was intoxicating and I responded eagerly. The tightness in my stomach eased.

The next morning Eric was back to his usual self before I even managed to get out of bed. "Bri, these socks don't match. I can't believe that you can't match the socks up. They all have little patterns on them." Eric waved them in front of my face. "Wear your glasses when you sort them."

"Ugh," I moaned, pounding my head into the pillow. "My degree isn't in sock sorting, so sorry." I walked out of the bedroom before he could see me smiling. "My, bad," I yelled back. The monotony of household chores could bore anyone into a little carelessness now and then.

What would it be like to be single now? I could be out and about with my friends without a care in the world. On the other hand, I'd be alone without an anchor. Was that anchor a stabilizing element in my life—or just weighing me down? My left-brain husband could be so testy at times. Eric re-wiped the kitchen counter after I had already done it, every night. Ironically, this meticulousness didn't extend to his bathroom sink. Every morning after he shaved, the basin looked like a child had bathed in it, with water running down the cabinets and puddling on the granite surface at the base of the sink. *Consistency, dear, I should have demanded, shaking him by the shoulders.* But I hate confrontations. Even small ones rattle my sense of control. I always let it go.

The phone rang. "Bri, it's me, are you ready?" Madeline asked.

"Give me ten minutes and I'll pick you up at your house." I was already late. I pictured Madeline tapping her fingers on her kitchen counter, counting the seconds.

Madeline and I were going to the White Orchid Arboretum to see if the venue would work for the Build-A-Home fund-raiser. The widely attended charity event was usually hosted in a conservatory, botanical garden or arboretum. Hosting outside adds an extra level of preparation to include in case of weather issues. With hundreds of people attending, we had to bring our A-game.

The arboretum had a huge, renovated barn where we would host the dinner dance. The property was well groomed with a pond and cobblestone walks. Wildflowers carpeted a huge field to the right of the facility in vivid yellows, reds, and purples. The greenhouse to the left of the barn held the arboretum's famous white orchids.

Chairing an event of this size was like operating a small business. I knew the summer would fly by, so it was smart to start planning early. And it gave me something to think about other than my children leaving home.

Madeline pulled a graph pad from her tote. "Okay let's get down to business." She walked around, deciding what would go where and how many tables we'd need. I realized that she didn't need my input, didn't even ask for it, really. Did she ask me to cochair because somehow she sensed how I was feeling? I don't share my emotions, but had she figured it out?

"Bri," she said, "I was thinking of letting Natasha be responsible for the event decorations. Are you okay with that?"

"I already asked Ava to do that because of all her connections." I held my breath. It was a lie. I would have to call Ava as soon as I got home.

"Oh, okay." Madeline shrugged. "I just want to bring Natasha into our group a little more. Maybe she could join book club."

I looked up and smiled, quickly changing the subject back to the layout of the tables. I would not invite Natasha into my book club. Why did I feel so negatively about her? All she'd done was talk to Eric at a party. And after all, Madeline seemed to like her a lot.

After I dropped Madeline off I decided to run my new car through the car wash. The birds at the arboretum had left presents all over it. Maybe they liked its silver color.

Charlotte phoned me as I was pulling into the entrance, my first phone call in the new car. My old one didn't have the Bluetooth feature, but Eric's did. I pushed a round knob located in a similar spot to answer the phone. Nothing. I quickly scanned the dash and pushed a few more buttons. Still nothing. I rummaged in my purse for my cell and pushed the phone button. *Eric's right. I really should look at the car's manual.*

Charlotte's voice boomed all over the car. "Hey, Madeline sure complained a lot about my favorite book pick at book club. Remember how she said, '*Fifty Shades of Grey,* with all the other books out there you pick that one'?"

"Yes. I have to tell you, though, even I was confused about that." I tried turning several knobs to turn down the volume on the phone.

Charlotte continued to talk loudly about her book selection as I asked the attendant for a regular wash and got out holding my phone. I hoped the car wouldn't lock going through the wash with the keys in it. I should have looked at the settings. The last thing I'd want would be to call Eric to tell him I'd locked myself out at the car wash.

"Bri, Bri are you there?" Charlotte's voice screeched.

"Oh, yes sorry. I'm getting out of my car. Do I have to do something to disengage the phone?"

"No. It's automatic, silly. Didn't you have Bluetooth in your old Lexus?"

"The feature wasn't available when I bought it. Remember I had it for six or seven years." I walked around the back of the building where the cars were dried. I recognized most of the people standing around and talking.

"Hello? Charlotte? What were you saying?"

I couldn't hear her anymore. My connection must have died. I ended the call, then called her back, but her phone was busy. I waited a few minutes again.

"Sorry, Charlotte, my phone disconnected. What were you saying?" I walked back to the entrance.

"I was talking about the Red Room in *Fifty Shades.* Wouldn't you just like to try some of those moves with Eric?" Charlotte asked.

"Ahhh?" I didn't know what to say and turned around. My car was out and being wiped down. I headed toward it.

"Oh, stop. Don't tell me you're like Madeline, all straitlaced and proper! I don't believe it."

"Madeline could be kinkier than any of us, for all we know. You shouldn't assume you know about her sex life unless you've been with her." I laughed.

"Well, I can tell you that I want someone to..."

"Charlotte, hello." My phone must have disconnected again, but when I looked at the phone's display it was still connected.

As I got closer to my car, I understood what had happened. My car's Bluetooth had picked up my cell phone and Charlotte's booming voice was telling everyone in the vicinity about her sexual desires.

"I would love a good spanking from Christian Grey. Wouldn't you?"

"Charlotte, stop talking," I screeched into my phone. I picked up my pace. "Charlotte, stop talking." Of course, she couldn't hear me.

I noticed the attendants laughing as they wiped down my interior. A few women were still congregated around the exit, listening to Charlotte's sexual fantasies, and then looking over at me. One of them, Kathleen Scape, stood with her arms crossed. She was this year's president of the high school PTO. I've only had a few brushes with her, but they were enough. I knew this conversation would be all over town by tonight.

"How about being handcuffed to the ceiling and blindfolded with your hands in those feathery handcuffs, Oooh..."

"Charlotte! Shut up!" I yelled.

"Thanks so much, the car looks great," I told the young man wiping my dashboard. He didn't seem to want to stop. "I'm late for an appointment. Thanks again." I almost yanked him out of the car.

"You've got an appointment?" Charlotte asked.

"No. Charlotte, everything you just said was broadcast all over the car wash. I'm so sorry. I'm an idiot. I should have read the car's manual. I guess I'm as technology challenged as my family keeps telling me I am."

Charlotte roared with laughter.

"No really. I'm so sorry. Kathleen Scape, the PTO president, was there with some of her cronies."

"Who cares what she thinks? I don't live there. Let them talk. If anything, maybe a Red Room is just what she needs to put a smile on her sour face." Charlotte laughed. "Right?"

"Right!" I laughed, wondering when Charlotte had gotten so carefree about what other people thought.

*

"Let's squeeze in a family vacation this summer," I said to Eric a week after my car wash incident.

"Absolutely. When?" he asked.

Eric was litigating a patent infringement case over the summer. I was trying to get the kids ready for college and keep up with Madeline's to-do list for the charity event. Julianna's schedule was actually the hardest to work around. She only had one week off from the family she babysat for—next week, when they were attending a relative's wedding in Chicago.

I never organized a trip so fast. Luckily, Eric managed to rearrange his calendar quickly.

*

Late morning risings were followed by lazy afternoons at Seven Mile Beach in the Cayman Islands. At night, we meandered to a casual restaurant by the water and watched the sun set off the patio. By the end of the week, our energy returned. We snorkeled off Rum Beach and traveled into George Town for a little shopping.

My uncertainty about the future faded to the recesses of my mind. On the flight home I felt invigorated, ready to face my new chapter with renewed energy, just like I used to feel at the beginning of each school year.

Within an hour of our return home, Eric left to play tennis, Julianna and Logan went out with friends, and I started the laundry. As I washed and folded, a plan began to form in my mind for my next phase in life. I ran to boot up my computer and—humming, happy—started searching for résumés and cover letters.

The phone rang.

"Hi. Is Eric home?" said a silky-voiced woman.

"No, who's calling?"

"Bri, is that you? It's Natasha. I wanted to know if Eric was playing in the league match tonight. We really need him!"

Without thinking, I told her he'd left about ten minutes ago and should be there soon.

My stomach cramped a little. The vacation glow dimmed.

SUMMER
Part 11

SWIPING RIGHT

"COME ON, JOHN!" I screamed, standing with the crowd on the bleachers. My pulse raced to the roar of the engines as the cars thundered by. As nervous as I was that John might get hurt, it was thrilling to watch. This is just what I thought it'd be like when I gave my ex-husband a race-car driving experience for his fiftieth birthday.

I remembered how he'd frowned when he opened the envelope. Handing me back the gift certificate, he had said, "Are you kidding me? Make sure you get my money back."

Of course I laughed, infuriating him even more. He hated my nervous laugh. God knows I'd tried a million ways to change it.

I knew the gift was stupid. Madeline had even warned me at our book club meeting the week before. "Darling, I don't think George will appreciate this type of gift."

"Why? He's an adrenaline junkie," I answered, but I'd known then that she was right. Maybe I had just wanted the experience— pushing the pedal to the metal. Anything to escape his perfect life.

"Dear, his thrills come from mergers and acquisitions, beating out high-stake players, not from some blue-collar need-for-speed crap." Madeline pursed her lips, accentuating the *p.*

Ava had replied, "Madeline, you're a stuck-up bitch. What's wrong with racing?"

"Oh, please. Do you see any racetracks around here? It's just not what we do."

"What? We…you…" Ava's response faded as vibrations pumped my feet, bringing me back to the racetrack.

I tried to steady my legs, to not fall forward. The bleachers shook hard from all the stomping. The crowd around me climbed up onto the bleacher seats once again. Not trusting my balance, I had stayed seated during the first races. But this time John was racing and I couldn't see.

I didn't care if I fell. *God, look at me. My engine is racing as much as his.* I took a deep breath and steadied myself as I extended my leg. The young man next to me reached his hand out and helped me up. Smiling my thanks, I looked over the track and found John's black car. Black, the perfect color for a race car. Sleek, sexy, and dangerous.

My ears hurt from the crowd, the cars. Burning rubber crept up my nose and the air tasted of exhaust, but I cheered lap after lap until my voice grew hoarse. What did Madeline know, anyway? I couldn't remember feeling this jazzed, this excited.

John moved closer and closer to the front of the pack.

Vroom, vroom tingled up my spine as the crowd revved to a fever pitch.

The leading two drivers were now neck and neck. One lap, two laps. The cars looked cojoined.

As the drivers approached the last curve, John was on the outside. I held my breath. My heart pumped, hard. *He can start my engine any day.*

John edged out the leader by a small margin and crossed ahead by a fender.

The adrenaline-infused crowd exploded at the photo finish.

Both my arms waved in the air as I made a high-pitched squeal of delight, jumping up and down on my seat.

Spectators climbed down off their seats and I realized that, somehow, I had stayed upright. For as long as I could remember—certainly as long as I'd been married—I would fall, trip, bang into things. Not today. The young man next to me jumped down and offered me a hand.

"Remember I mentioned swapping paint at the beginning of the race?" he said.

I leaned in close to hear him. "Yes."

"When two cars look like they're touching, that's swapping paint. Like the last two before the finish."

"Oh, got it. Thanks." I looked out over the track to find John. *I wouldn't mind swapping a little paint with the gorgeous man in the black car.* I loved the term and rummaged in my purse to make a note of it on my phone. I found a lozenge and unwrapped it, thinking it might soothe my raw throat.

The track announcer introduced John, along with the race sponsor, awarding him the trophy. His black racing suit piped with red and white outlined his powerful physique. His shoulders and arms strained against the fabric, while his hair was in wavy disarray from the helmet. *Damn!* He should be on the cover of *Sports Illustrated.*

John thanked his team and sponsors, then posed for pictures before exiting the podium with his crew. *Will he find me in this crowd?*

As the cars lined up for the last race, I looked for John. I hoped he'd find me soon.

Then I saw a bit of commotion at the bottom of the stands. John, in a T-shirt, jeans, and a baseball cap, was talking with three women. One of the women wrapped her arm through his and started to pull him away. John stopped and pointed at me. I waved. The woman uncurled her arm, stared at me, and whispered in his ear. As she walked away with her friends, her long, dark, glossy hair swayed like she was in a shampoo commercial. *Who the hell was that?*

I watched John make his way up the stands, moving with a dancer's rhythm, his evenly spaced strides in time with his own internal beat. Spectators congratulated him, and he would pause to nod, thank them, move on. I danced all through school, even in college, but I never acquired a dancer's walk. Growing up, I'd always been a little awkward. My friends would say "Have a nice trip," every time I stumbled. I'd never really minded. My ex, however, tore into me every time I banged a wall or missed a step, and, suddenly, I had grown increasingly anxious every time I fumbled.

John squeezed through the people sitting in my row and sat next to me.

My breath caught as he squished against my thigh. I was glad it was so loud. I didn't trust myself to speak.

His body seemed to echo the energy of the crowds. "Did you enjoy the race?"

"Yes, definitely. It was so exciting."

"It was a good run today. You must be my lucky charm." John grasped my hand. "I sent my crew home with the car and my pickup, so we could ride back to my house together. I need to shower and I'd like to take you to my friend's bar."

I nodded. "Sure." My heart pounded in my chest. Our knees touched softly in the crowded stands, and neither of us shifted away. The last race started and the cars circled lap after lap around the half-mile track. My ears hurt from all the noise, but I was happy as hell.

After the last race, we started moving to my car. More spectators congratulated John, some asking him to pose for pictures with them. The balmy night called for a convertible drive, so down went the top. Backing up, taking extra care because my passenger was a race-car driver, I didn't hear John's question. "What? Sorry, I'm trying to focus on my driving."

I heard him snicker. I didn't have a rearview camera on the rental and twisted around to see behind me to pull out of the parking spot. As I did, I noticed a huge, mischievous grin on John's face.

"What's so funny?" I asked.

"Nothing, nothing at all." He stopped grinning. "Make a left out of the parking lot and head toward Burlington." Another smile formed at the corners of his mouth. He was thinking of something, but wasn't sharing.

It was a picture-perfect evening with pinpricks of light just beginning to break through as we drove to John's farm. It was hard to talk with the top down, so we rode the half hour silently, with an occasional glance or light touch of a hand.

John leaned over, tapped my shoulder, and said, pointing, "The next left at the stone gate is my driveway."

The sign at the entrance read: Champlain Valley Farm. The driveway was long, paved, and lined with maple trees. The expansive outside lighting made it look more like an estate than a farm. A beautiful red-roofed stone home finally came into view. I drove around the circular driveway to the front door.

"This is a farm?" I asked, turning to John.

"Yes, a dairy farm that's been in my family for three generations. We've owned the property even longer." We walked through the front door and into an oasis of Vermont granite and wood.

"John, your home is beautiful," I said, looking up at the beamed ceilings and a huge stone fireplace in the great room.

"It was built in the early 1900s by my grandfather." John walked over to the wall of French doors and opened them to a massive stone-covered patio that looked out over Lake Champlain and the Adirondacks.

"Can I get you a glass of wine?" he asked.

"Sure." I didn't know where to look first.

He returned with a glass of Pinot Grigio. "I noticed you drank this the other night."

"Thank you." I wanted to grab and hug him, but instead he wandered off to shower. He had no idea how happy he'd just made me. My ex was always embarrassed that I didn't drink expensive red wine, preferring lighter white ones. He refused to order the wine I liked when we went out, cavalierly ordering an expensive bottle of red and asking the waiter to bring glasses for everyone. When he'd finish ordering, I always asked the waiter for a glass of white wine, knowing full well I was making him gnash his teeth.

A door closing somewhere in the house brought me back to the present. It seemed awkward to roam around John's home uninvited, so I went out to the patio and sat. The pinpricks from earlier were now glistening stars that had broken their nighttime binds. I sipped my wine, hoping it would settle my thoughts and allow me to relax.

When John returned, he immediately began to tell me how a friend of his grandfather's had designed the house. "It's a cross between a Cape Cod and some sort of French country design. My grandfather was really particular."

But I wasn't listening. All I could do was look at him. His wet hair framed his chiseled cheeks and jaw, accentuating those amazing eyes. What he did for a pair of Levi's would create chaos in the fashion world, turning upside down the thought that jeans had to be expensive to look good.

"Would you like a tour?"

"Sure." I hoped he wanted me to agree.

He put his hand out to me and I held it as we walked through the downstairs, passing by the master bedroom with its shut door.

John recalled a few family memories, like the time a football went crashing through the French doors.

"Oh no, was anyone hurt?" I asked.

"No." He laughed. "My sister had thrown it, then took off and left me quite literally holding the ball." John grinned at the memory. "I was always playing football, so naturally I got blamed and had to pay to repair the window out of my allowance. But my sister owed me after that, so it wasn't so bad."

He seemed to have a story for every room. I laughed nervously like I always do, giggling at almost everything he said. *God, I hate it when I can't control myself. He must think I'm an ass.*

John stopped abruptly when we came to the kitchen. His playful stories ceased. "My wife, Jess, was going to remodel the kitchen, but then she got cancer." John just stared into space, probably somewhere back in time.

I lightly put my hand on this arm and told him how sorry I was for his loss, then quietly turned to give him a few moments, walking out to the patio. I wasn't sure how to handle a man who had so clearly loved and lost his wife. Was it unwise to get involved?

After a few minutes, I sensed John was standing directly behind me. The hair on my neck stood at attention and a prickling sensation shot down my spine. All I could think was: *Please wrap your arms around me.* He stepped so close that our clothes lightly touched, but then he backed away and we both looked out onto the water for a few minutes.

He cleared his throat. "I'd like to take you to Sammy's. It's my friend's bar on the lake. They have the best local brewed beer around. I know it's late, but if you're hungry they have really good bar food." He moved in front of me, and looked down into my face.

A clean soap smell filled my head; he didn't wear overbearing cologne. He touched my arm to indicate which direction to go in. The only direction I wanted was wrapped around him, but instead he led me to his truck.

When we got to Sammy's, John ordered some local brews for us both. We sat outside on the deck. I'm not much of a beer drinker, but it was quite good. A woman played the guitar and sang, sounding like Carly Simon.

When the singer took a break I asked John, "Do you know a lot of people at the track? Or were those ladies fans of yours?"

"Both. The three women at the bottom of the stands were my friends' wives and...well...I guess I do know most of the people there."

"You said you started racing five years ago. Did you always want to?"

"No, it started after Jess died. A diversion, I guess." John turned his head and seemed to drift away.

"I'm so sorry for you and your family." I wanted to say so much more.

Our awkward moment lingered until I broke the silence. My mouth went into overdrive, telling John all about my marriage.

"We actually met after work on a subway platform in New York City on our way home," I said. "We were young, working in New York at the start of our careers, his in finance, mine in journalism." My hands kept time with the beat of my words. I didn't tell John that my ex-husband was all I had ever hoped for at that time, ambitious, intelligent, good-looking. His unrelenting drive made us wealthy, but the pressure changed him. After a while, all I wanted was to get away from him. Money always costs something.

I took a breath and noticed John was watching me. "We dated for a year, got married and moved to the suburbs," I continued. "I quit work as soon as my first child, Chris was born. I loved every minute of being a stay-at-home mom and our early family life. But the marriage changed and didn't survive after the kids went off on their own." No need to tell him any more.

John nodded, listening attentively. He didn't say anything for a minute or two. I guessed he was considering what I'd said.

He cleared his throat. "I met Jess after graduating from Northwestern; we were both working in Boston." John met my gaze. "Like me, she had also been brought up on a farm, but in Kansas. Marriage soon followed, then two daughters. My youngest, Natalie, is interning this summer in Boston. She'll be a senior at BU in the fall. Sophie works in Hartford, Connecticut, for an insurance company." John smiled as he talked of his daughters, and slowly became more animated.

I told John stories about my sons and their never-ending antics. One of my favorites was the day my youngest, Jeff, was ten years old. I was washing his jeans, and in his back pocket was a wad of crumbled up bills. When I confronted him, asking where he got the money, he simply said, "Oh that's because I sell information. You know, gossip!"

I laughed as I told John how I'd shrieked at him. "What?"

John laughed with me.

I continued: "Jeff told me that he asked his friends what they wanted to know about each other and he would find out for a price. According to Jeff, his classmates were too afraid to ask the questions, so why shouldn't he make money doing it?

"Of course, we stopped him from *selling gossip* before he got in trouble with the school or a parent, but he was always entrepreneurial." I ordered a vodka tonic and it made me even more talkative. John seemed amused by my babble. We talked about our kids for a while. It grew late. We were the last ones left on the deck when the bar closed. I was pleased that I'd made it through the evening without once spilling my drink or banging my knee.

When we pulled up to his front door, John turned his body in the truck and leaned toward me, cupping my face in his hand. We kissed slowly, his lips soft against mine. As the kiss lingered, my hand entwined in the curls at the back of his neck. Light-headed and longing, I bent forward, pressing harder, demanding more. John broke off the kiss.

"Good night," he said. He kissed my forehead and moved to open his truck door. I fell forward a little when he exited the car.

I took a deep breath and got out of his truck, my knees weak.

He held my car door open and I got in quickly.

"Thanks for coming tonight." He kissed my lips one last time, then smiled and walked to his front door.

"Yes…thank you." I tried to smile. Waving as I drove off, I wondered if I'd said something wrong. *What just happened?* The drive back to the hotel seemed longer than it really was.

By the time I was back in my room, I realized just how deeply John still loved his wife.

*

The afternoon was quite hot while I listened to a local jazz band. I ducked into a small high-end food boutique for a cold drink and sandwich. The woman in line before me at the checkout counter was the woman I saw talking with John at the race. Her glossy locks were pulled into a tight ponytail.

She turned and stared at me. Her small features were set into a delicate heart-shaped frame, but her beautiful face turned rigid. Did she know who I was? She couldn't possibly remember me from the track. She looked like she was about to say something, but then abruptly turned and rushed out with her grocery bag.

I didn't know what to make of that.

*

It was two long days before I heard from John again. The jazz festival was all but over, and I was ready to give up, check out of the hotel, and head home. When I heard his voice on the phone, my breath caught. He asked if I'd like to spend the afternoon touring his farm. He told me to dress casually and no heels. He would grill me the best steak I ever had. I believed him.

I was tingling. Our third date, his house. I was so ready.

John met me in his driveway and we walked into the barn nearest the lake. Inside, two horses were already saddled.

"So, you think I can ride a horse, do you?" I arched my eyebrow.

"Well, show me what you've got!" John smiled, baiting me.

"I can ride." I hadn't been on a horse in twenty years and had never been fond of the big beasts. No way was I going to admit that.

156

"However, it's been a while, so don't gallop away on me. I prefer my bones unbroken." At least it was a western saddle.

"Oh, you city girls." He laughed and helped me mount and adjust the stirrups.

"No city girl here, I live in the country!"

"Uh-huh. We'll see."

We spent a few hours touring the three-hundred-acre farm. At one point, John pointed to a collection of trees and we headed there. He helped me dismount and took my horse's reins. We walked to a wooden bench overlooking the lake. I tried to walk naturally, but the inside of my thighs were killing me.

"What a beautiful spot: the lake, the mountains—breathtaking, really." I tried to absorb the beauty all around me, but all I wanted was him. We sat close, our bodies touching. A flutter began in the pit of my stomach.

He began to tell me about the lake, but I was riveted to his face. Every time our eyes met, my heart turned over in response.

He stood and pulled me with him. I hoped he would wrap his arms around me, but he walked us over to the horses. Ugh. I had to get back on that damn beast.

We rode to a huge barn. I prayed this would be it, no more riding. My thighs ached and my lower back was tight and spasming.

My first steps were tenuous, but I tried to pretend nothing was bothering me. *Sure, I'm a country girl. Uh-huh.* At least I stayed on the horse and didn't fall off. I seemed to have regained my balance around John. What a change from my awkwardness around my ex.

John reached out his hand and I took it, ignoring the ache in my body.

We continued down a long walkway with cows on either side. "We've been using new technology," John said. "Helps keep the cows happier and they produce a higher quality milk."

The cow's teats were connected to some sort of contraption. "Do they stay in this gizmo all day?" I asked.

"No." He laughed. "They wouldn't be happy if they were stuck in the parlor all day." John motioned for me to follow.

"Every time I drink milk I'm going to remember this day." I smiled, looking desperately for a place to sit down. There wasn't one. I took a deep breath.

John turned around and asked, "Would you like to feed a calf?"

"Yes, absolutely." I looked up at him. John's eyes were like a warm summer day on a Caribbean beach, so inviting. My ex had piercing eyes that took in every detail, calculating, always calculating. A place I never wanted to see again.

John guided me into a sectioned-off area of the barn and handed me a bottle from one of the stable hands. He took another bottle. The area was filled with hay and he motioned for me to sit down in it. I cringed knowing how hard it would be to get up again. But I did it anyway.

John taught me how to bottle-feed the calf. It reminded me of bottle-feeding the two abandoned puppies my father had found years before. My father would have loved this.

"My daughters and I fed the calves every Saturday morning. It was our time. I would find out all about their week and what was happening at school," John said.

"Sounds like you bonded over the bottles." I smiled, thinking what a lovely memory it was.

"Yeah, we did."

After the calves were fed, John stood and helped me up. We gazed into each other's eyes. I could barely breathe. I thought about falling back into the hay, dragging him with me, but instead he pulled me toward the door.

As I began to walk my thighs and back were screaming. I really didn't want to get back on that damn horse.

"Well, I promised you the best grilled steak of your life, so let's get back to the house, clean up, and start dinner. That's if you're not too sore from riding?" He hooked my arm in his and we walked out of the barn.

"How did you know I was sore?"

"Well, it could be the hunched way you're walking, or the grimace on your face every time you move. Not too much country where you live." John laughed and gave me a hug. "Come on, we can walk back to the barn with the horses and take the Jeep back to the house."

"Oh, thank God!" I laughed.

*

The steaks *were* delicious, literally just melting in my mouth. John took the first steak off the grill. He cut a small piece and fed it to me. My imagination kicked in as he slowly, carefully cut it, watching me with a gleam in his eyes. *That's it—I've either got to give up those romance novels or lay off the wine.* My hand shook as I picked up a glass of water.

The food filled me, but as I watched John eat, another hunger grew. "John, you were right, these are great, better than the steak houses in New York City. Fabulous!"

"Yup, told you. My friend raises beef cattle about twenty minutes east of here and it's the only steak I eat now."

We finished dinner. John stood, picking up my plate, and said a few friends were stopping by to pick up some cuts of beef. "One of us gets the side of beef and we share it. It's too much for one order if you want it fresh."

As if on cue, a knock at the door interrupted him. "Hey, Maryanne, Leslie. I've got it all wrapped and ready to go. Come in and meet Staci."

I stood as the two women entered the patio. John introduced us. There across from me was the raven-haired beauty. Her name was Maryanne. I extended my hand, but neither lady offered up a hand.

"You're not from around here," Maryanne said, with censure in her tone as she looked me up and down.

"No. I'm from New Jersey."

The women continued to stare at me and said nothing as John left to get the beef.

"Here you go, girls. You'll love it. We just had two steaks from the side. Superb." John made a lip smacking noise.

Both women approached him with their backs to me. "Thanks, sweetie. You going to the Smiths' big BBQ?"

"Wouldn't miss it for the world."

"Bye, handsome. We'll show ourselves out."

Neither looked back. I didn't exist.

"Come on." John held out his hand. We strolled down to the lake. The walkway was softly lit. At the dock, we put our feet in the water.

"Aren't those the same women you were talking to at the racetrack?" I asked, kicking my feet.

"Yes. Their husbands and I go back to grammar school. Been friends forever."

They would make my life hell. They're so transparent. I'm an outsider moving in on one of their own. Sounded like an episode from a bad daytime soap. My stomach churned.

"It's such a beautiful evening." He grasped my hand.

By the time we returned to the patio, it was late. John offered me a nightcap and poured us small brandies. We nestled into the couch on the patio. The view had an exotic feel to it with the unobstructed view of the lake and a bright, full moon in the background. A light breeze blew the humidity back out into the lake.

John put his drink down and turned toward me. I looked up into his eyes. He guided my mouth to his and we kissed slowly, gently, while he ran his fingers through my hair. His lips were incredibly soft, and kissing them felt like falling into a caressing cloud. How could such a large, outdoors man be so tender, so soft?

We kissed again, and this time our tongues explored and min-gled gently. We pulled each other closer, lingering as the warmth in my stomach spread. Then he stood up and grasped my arms, pulling me to him. His hands cupped my face and brought my face up to his lips again. My heart pounded an erratic rhythm as a strong, tin-gling sensation shuddered down my spine.

Just as his hand began to roam along my collarbone, a phone vibrated in his shirt pocket. *What timing!* He looked at the caller ID and said he had to take the call. It was from his daughter Natalie.

"Of course," I whispered.

He walked into the house. A minute later he returned. "Staci, I'm sorry, but my daughter has an issue at work and needs some advice. She's upset."

"No problem. Why don't we go out tomorrow night?" I blurted out, disappointed that our evening was interrupted.

"Sure, yes, definitely," John walked me to the door and gave me a light kiss on the cheek. "I'll call you tomorrow and arrange some-thing." John turned back to his call.

Unsatisfied, again. But, I wasn't giving up.

I drove back to Burlington in a daze.

*

The next morning, I called Bri. "Do you think I should extend my stay?"

"Ahhh…What do you think?" Bri asked.

"Oh no, just tell me what you think. No question with a ques-tion shrink stuff please. If I leave now, I'll never see him again. I'm sure of it."

"Then you should stay. You don't have anything you have to be home for and you don't want to regret it," she said. "Are you ready for this? A relationship?"

"Absolutely!" I almost shouted. "I've been ready my whole life. But, I'm scared, too."

"Go for it!" Bri told me to call anytime.

*

At the front desk, I asked if a room was available for another week.

"Yes, Mrs. Hughes. We have one room available, but it's a suite," said the clerk.

"A suite? Sure, I'll take it." I enjoyed spending my ex-husband's money any way I could. Should have opted for a suite in the first place!

*

That night, I hurried down the street to our rendezvous. He was waiting outside the restaurant and the sight of him made me stop. He was speaking to a group of women. He looked like a rock star surrounded by groupies.

He turned as I approached, reached for my hand, and pulled me toward him. His touch sent shivers down to my toes. I reached up and kissed him softly on the lips, wishing there weren't a hundred people around.

"You look beautiful," he said in a raspy voice, gliding a finger down the side of my face. He moved close. I could feel his warmth, and smell the soap that lingered on him. There was an unquenchable passion in his eyes.

Our names were called for dinner and the spell was broken. He held my arm as we made our way into the restaurant. I took a few deep breaths and focused on my wobbly legs. *Don't let me trip or embarrass myself. Can he see how nervous I am? He always seems so calm.*

"Was everything okay with Natalie?" I said.

"Yes, just an issue at work." John unfolded his napkin and placed it on his lap.

We ordered drinks. "Did you write a blog today?" he asked.

"Yes." But I didn't. All I did was think about him. "How about you—did you practice at the track today?"

"No. There's always so much work to do on the farm. I squeeze in a practice run whenever I can." John shrugged his shoulders. "When are you planning on leaving Burlington?"

"Well, sometime next week, but no definite date," I answered. "Why do you ask?"

This time he blushed and looked down. "Well, I'm enjoying your company—a lot," he managed.

Words failed me, so I reached over and cupped his hand in mine. Our eyes met.

We broke contact when the waiter returned for our order. My breathing felt like it did after a spin class, with a little heart palpitation thrown in for good measure. The menu blurred. Was it my failing eyes or the lightness in my head? It took a few moments before everything calmed enough for me to speak again. "Have you always wanted to be a farmer?"

"No, I didn't plan on being a farmer, it just happened." John said. "I'm grateful things worked out that way, though."

John told me that when he came back from college he worked for a few years as an engineer in Boston. He met Jess at a friend's party. Within a year they were married, and when Jess was pregnant with Natalie, his dad had a stroke, so they moved back to the farm.

"As you saw, the house is quite large and we all lived together," he said. "My parents were aging and needed help; we had one child and another on the way, so it worked out well for all of us. I ended up loving the farm. We were a big happy family in that old house and we cared for one another. It was the best decision I ever made."

"Will your girls take over the farm?" I asked.

"I don't know, maybe one of them will someday. You just never know."

A coolness settled over the table, and John seemed to withdraw. I needed to steer the conversation away from his family. "Have you ever considered racing outside of Vermont?"

John bowed his head. "No, it's just a hobby, nothing I want to pursue further." His glance shifted to the window and the pedestrians walking by. I wanted to reach out and touch him, but thought better of it. He looked as if he were back in the past with his young family and I was intruding.

My stupid questions had brought this about. An uncomfortable few moments passed.

"John, how are you?" asked a tall, balding man in a white shirt and jeans. The same dark-haired woman I met at John's house was hooked on his arm. "And who's this?" The man pointed in my direction.

John stood and shook the man's hand and gave him a bear hug. Then he turned and embraced the woman.

"Staci, this is Carl. You remember Maryanne from the other night. Carl and I have been friends since high school and Maryanne is his lovely wife. In my opinion, she's crazy for staying with this gnarly old bear!" John whacked Carl on the shoulder.

"Hi," I said, grateful for the interruption.

As John and Carl talked, I noticed Maryanne staring darkly at me. My smile lingered through their brief conversation, but Maryanne never returned my smile, never said a word. As the couple moved off to their own table, I saw Carl give John a thumbs-up.

"Sorry about that," John said, sitting back down at the table.

"No, it was a pleasure to meet your friends." *Sorta.*

"Where were we?" John smiled.

"We were talking about how sexy racing is?" *It just slipped out.*

"We were? So how sexy is it?" John leaned across the table.

"Well, according to the press it's at the top of the charts."

He laughed and leaned even closer. "And how sexy do *you* think it is?"

I immediately blushed. *"Very,"* I said in barely a whisper. I hoped it sounded smooth and sensual and not like a squeaky child.

"Well, there's a good reason to continue it then." He beamed.

Our dinners arrived. I listened to his stories of Carl and was astonished by his affection for his friend. I can't remember when my ex ever spoke fondly about anyone.

When we finished dinner, Carl asked us to join them for a drink at the bar. *Crap, I didn't want to share John's attention. And, how would I engage Maryanne when she wouldn't even look at me?* But John said sure and off we went.

After a round of drinks, Carl started giving John the full buddy treatment, holding nothing back.

"Did John tell you about the time he got pushed out of the locker room naked in high school into a crowded hallway?" Carl howled, punching John in the arm.

"Another time, he hit the principal's parked car because he was kissing a girl. You weren't a race-car driver then. Were ya?" Carl gave John a small push and both men laughed loudly.

John grinned impishly. "Okay, Carl, you sure you want to trade stories?"

Carl jumped in again. "John passed out after drinking beer in the woods with friends. When he woke up, he discovered he was sleeping in poison ivy."

John blushed.

Eventually Carl stopped teasing and started telling me about all the things John had done for others. How as a sophomore in high school, John took on some seniors bullying a younger boy, and how he'd helped a classmate after a fire had destroyed the family's barn.

Before Carl could continue, John said, "Okay, okay, enough!" He slapped Carl on the back and asked him how the new feed was working out.

"Good, though I'm not sure it's worth the money."

When they started talking about management of their herds, I excused myself and went to the restroom. As I left the stall, Maryanne was leaning on the wall closest to the door.

I smiled at her. "Hello."

"You know," she began, "John is a special person around here, well thought of in every way." Maryanne looked me up and down, staring while I washed my hands. "There are local women who tried to get close to him since Jess died, but he wasn't interested. He needs a real woman like Jess, not some spoiled city girl with two-hundred-dollar haircuts and designer clothes. He's special to us and he doesn't need to be hurt again." Turning, Maryanne didn't wait. The door slammed with a *bang* as she left.

What? How do I go back to the bar with her there? Do I look like a spoiled woman with some expensive haircut and fancy clothes? I looked in the mirror. Maybe I do. After a minute, I went back to John.

"Carl and Maryanne said to say goodbye. Maryanne wasn't feeling well. Is everything all right? You were gone for a while."

"Yes, everything's fine." There was no way I was going to tell him what had just happened.

We left the bar and headed onto the cobblestone streets of Burlington with jazz music piggybacking on the wind and spiraling in all directions. A band playing old sixties and seventies caught our attention. They were performing a mean rendition of "Tighter, Tighter," by Alive 'N Kickin'.

John stood behind me, his arm draped around my waist. I rested my head on his shoulder. We swayed to the beat. *"Hold on… a little bit tighter…"* I wanted to stay cocooned in his warmth all night, but the song ended. John grabbed my hand and we walked off to the lake.

He stopped at the highest point of the park above the water and pulled me to him. He confessed in my ear. "Staci, I haven't been with anyone since Jess. I don't know if I'm ready."

What could anyone say to that? I pulled him even closer.

"You're so beautiful, you've bewitched me." John stared into my eyes.

I didn't waver. I had no love left for my ex-husband. John's confession and the deep love he still felt for his wife only made me want him more.

"Is anyone ever ready?" I whispered into his ear. "Come back with me to the hotel. I have an amazing view of the lake from my suite." I tugged his arm.

He hesitated at first, but I grabbed his hand and we slowly walked back to the hotel.

We didn't talk on the way, but Burlington serenaded us with its intimate, passionate beat. My sexual thoughts seemed in perfect harmony with the music.

We entered my hotel room and I rather awkwardly offered John a drink. My hands fumbled trying to open the bottle of white wine I'd stashed in the mini-fridge. My heart pumped hard and I snapped on Pandora to mask the sound.

"Staci," John said, standing by the bay window.

"Yes?" I offered him a glass. "Isn't this a great view?"

"Yes, it is." We looked out, sipping our wine.

The sky was dark, but a last tail of the sun lingered in the middle of the lake, lighting up a small cloud formation in front. I thought of my father and smiled.

I turned to John and said, "Growing up I spent a great deal of time with my dad. He was such a storyteller. He could make up a story about anything and there was always some sort of life lesson in it." I turned back to the window and pointed to the backlit clouds. "Those clouds would have been a spaceship from somewhere with an important mission."

"Those are wonderful memories to have." John put his arm around my shoulder.

"Yes, they are. I miss my dad." I touched the window as the last trace of light disappeared.

I placed my wineglass on the window ledge so I could embrace him. The ledge was too small for the glass and it fell off, shattering. I nervously giggled, stepping away, and waited for the reprimand.

"Oh, let me get that. Don't cut yourself." John moved in front of me and picked up the broken glass, then got a towel from the bathroom and cleaned up the wine.

I watched, embarrassed at my clumsiness. "I'm so sorry."

"As long as you didn't cut yourself. Spills happen all the time." John rinsed out the towel in the small kitchen.

My ex would never find a spill amusing, nerves or not. Nor would he ever think to clean it up.

John brought me another glass of wine and we watched the moonlight peek through the clouds.

"Where were we?" he asked.

"Here," I said, taking his hand in mine.

John seemed to relax a bit. "My dad wasn't as creative as yours, but he did try to instill what he thought was important," he said. "Although, I'm sure I was a bit more of a handful than you were growing up."

"What makes you think so?" I asked coyly. "My mother was always complaining I gave her migraine headaches." I tilted my head to the right and gave him my best so-there look.

"I still don't think you were a bad girl." John faced me.

I felt flushed from laughing. Or was it the wine? "Well, not bad, but I can be naughty."

John closed the space between us, grabbing my waist with his free arm. His mouth found mine and this time I tasted passion, not his teasing, softly addicting kisses. I closed my eyes and let his desire engulf me.

"Ohh," I whispered.

John, his movements swift and light, took both of our glasses and put them on the table. Frozen, I watched him. He came within a few inches of me and looked into my face. I thought for a moment he wanted to say something. Was he teasing me? He ran a finger down my arm to my hand, sending an electric current with it.

I pulled John into a tight embrace. He buried his head in my neck, nibbling. I let out a gasp. His clean, soap scent filled my nose, filling me.

We began to sway, slowly at first. Our bodies pressed together, so warm. His hands roamed up my sides, tingling every nerve he touched. He lavished hot, deep kisses on my neck and chest. Looking deeply into my eyes, he unbuttoned my shirt.

I felt anxious for a moment. I wasn't twenty anymore! But for the first time in my life, desire overrode my concerns.

My shirt, then my bra fell to the floor. I inhaled sharply when his warm mouth caressed my body, nearly sending me over the edge.

I reached up, unbuttoned his shirt, and pulled it off him, resting my head on his impressive chest. I had wanted to do this since the day he had returned my scarf. His upper body was strong from hard work; not the pumped-up steroid look from the gyms. I ran my hands all over it.

"Staci," his voice thick and unsteady. "It's been so long."

He bent over, picked me up and tenderly placed me on the bed. He lay next to me. Our arms entwined as we explored each other.

My hands rubbed his back and moved to the top of his jeans. His kisses became deeper and more probing. He tasted sweet with a little kick of salt.

He moaned when my hand moved to his belt. He stood, let his pants fall, and helped me pull my skirt off.

John lay back down and began to gingerly massage me, his calluses only adding to the pleasure. I did the same. We began to move to our own tempo, turning, trembling in anticipation. Our hands stroked and caressed each other until we could no longer stand it, and John settled into me.

I sighed. For a moment, his long, slow, juicy kisses were the only movement between us. A rousing need raced through me. John began to rock slowly, then moved more steadily to the pace of the music or to his own internal beat. It didn't matter. I was beyond awareness.

Slowly, our rhythms became one and passion seared through us. The pleasure made me frantic. I wanted to stay like this, but exhaustion finally set in. John looked intensely into my eyes as his jaw clenched. He pulled me tighter and tighter until his need was drained.

*

My mind stayed in a dreamy haze in the hotel café as I stirred my coffee endlessly without drinking it. I relived last night over and over until every detail was etched in my mind.

My thoughts turned to Bri and the rest of our book club. I hoped their summer was turning out as well as mine. I couldn't wait to tell them all about John.

The boats below were traveling to unknown destinations and sloshing waves on the shore. The lake had a luminous sparkly sheen next to the brilliant blue sky. The colors outside were magnified to a higher hue.

I knew I wouldn't be able to write today. I was tired and love-sick. My mind wouldn't settle down and my body wanted movement. I put on shorts and sneakers and went for a long walk along the lake.

My elated mood continued well into the afternoon when I stopped for lunch at a small restaurant known for its farm-to-table freshness. After lunch, I walked through town. My stomach began to ache. An uneasiness settled over me, probably due to lack of sleep. Desire had its downsides, too. All the constant thinking about John was starting to make me jittery, fueling a constant need to keep moving.

Totally exhausted a few hours later, I headed back to the hotel to shower and get a late dinner. As the hours ticked away, my euphoria began to peel like old paint on a house, first in tiny cracks, then in large strips. At dinner, I barely touched my soup. I knew something was wrong.

I called Bri when I returned to my room. "We had a great night, made love, and today—nothing, not a word."

Bri tried to calm my anxiety. "Staci, it's all new and you need to give it some time."

"Yes, of course, I don't know what's happening to me. I've gone a little crazy."

"Everybody gets a little crazy in a new relationship," Bri said.

"I guess, but I'm not sure that makes me feel better. John is usually so kind and attentive. Not calling just goes against his character."

Bri paused for a moment. "You will be all right, whatever happens."

"I just want to be with him!"

"I know you do and I want that for you. Give it some time. Call me if you need to talk." It took three glasses of wine and total exhaustion, but I finally fell asleep.

*

The morning was gray and drizzling, which matched my mood. Waiting around for someone to call had never been my style and never would be, no matter how strong my feelings were. I drove around for a while to distract myself and in the afternoon, I went to see a movie. By dinner, John still had not called. I sat on the bed and, with my hands slightly shaking, called him, reaching his voicemail.

"Hi, John, it's Staci, give me a call when you can. Thanks." Short and sweet.

An hour later John called. "I'd like to meet you for a drink tonight if that's possible?"

"Okay. Is something wrong?"

"Well, I'd like to talk with you in person." John's tone was serious. There was no playfulness in his voice. Instead, a hardened inflection had crept in.

What had happened?

Two hours later we met at the hotel bar and sat at a corner table facing the lake. It was excruciating waiting for John to tell me what was bothering him. My hand shook as I picked up my glass of wine.

John turned toward me and took my other hand.

"Staci, there's no easy way to say this. I'm not ready for a relationship and don't know that I'll ever be ready for one." John's face was stricken and he didn't look me in the eyes.

My whole body tensed immediately and a knot pulsed in my throat. I didn't trust myself to speak.

"I've been alone all these years and then you entered my life out of the blue. You were a vision that day at the racetrack up high on the bleachers with your hair waving in the breeze. You nearly made me crash the car." John held my hand tighter looking out over the lake. "Then I actually found you in Vergennes. It had been so long since I had even noticed a woman. And you, well, you are...so beautiful." He faced me.

I looked at the ground, commanding myself to stay calm.

"When I called you, I thought it would be fun to go out on a date with a gorgeous stranger."

His face was only a few inches from mine, I could feel his warmth.

"You were someone safe, no ties to the community. I wouldn't have to explain anything to my friends or family, who are constantly trying to set me up. They don't understand why I haven't moved on."

I sat back in my chair and faced him.

"What I didn't expect was how much I would enjoy being with you." John took a deep breath. "If we tried to make this work, I would only hurt you. I'm just too shattered." John dropped his head.

I clenched my right hand hard, my nails pinching the palm.

When he spoke again his voice was tender, almost a whisper, and he inched closer to the left side of my face. I felt his breath on my face. "I don't think it's wise for us to see each other anymore."

I looked at my aching palm. I stayed like that for a few seconds fighting tears, disconcerted. I pushed my chair back a few inches so I could see him. My thoughts drifted to the occasions when John had seemed distant. I'd known, somehow in the recesses of my brain, that this might happen. But it still surprised me. Had Maryanne said something to him?

Finally, I said, "John, something special happened between us. That just doesn't happen every day."

He nodded. "Yes...but...I was so happy when I left your room the other night, but during the next day all I felt was guilt. I'm... not ready for a relationship."

I said nothing; just looked at him, trying to find something in his eyes, but he looked away in the fading light.

Turning back to me he said, "I've had a wonderful time with you and I...It's too much of a struggle for me right now." John wilted in his chair.

My breath kept catching. I tried long, deep breaths to keep the tears at bay, but I felt his restlessness, his flight reflex to escape. I steadied myself. He needed to hear what I had to say. "I can't imagine for a moment the pain you've endured, watching someone you loved so much die." My voice quivered. "I don't want to take her place in your heart, but you do deserve some happiness, John."

A long, awkward silence followed. "When Jess died I just went through the motions, because the farm had to keep running and my daughters needed their father. Without my daughters, I don't know what would have happened."

"Did you talk with anyone about your grief?" I inquired, realizing how intense it still was. *Why did you sleep with me if you felt this way?* I wanted to ask.

"No." He told me that they had worked hard for years, without vacations, to get the farm in good shape, took care of his aging parents and their young daughters. By the time they could begin to enjoy their lives together, Jess had gotten cancer. "It was...so unfair." John's face contorted.

"I don't want to cause you any more pain or put any pressure on you. But, there *is* something special between us and it might help you find some peace." *I had no anger, just sadness for me, for him—for us.*

"Even if that's true, we come from different worlds. I…I don't belong in your world and I can't see you in mine." John sighed.

Maryanne had definitely talked to him.

John looked away again and was quiet for a moment. "You live seven hours away. At best, it would be a long-distance relationship."

He still seems to be hesitating. Is he trying to convince me or himself?

"Maybe that's the best thing for you, a relationship that has some natural boundaries, geographic or otherwise." I flicked my hand. "As far as different worlds—well, that's just ridiculous, we live in the same world. My life is in flux right now, too, and I can design it any way I want."

"Right now, I can't…I'm really, really sorry." John stood, eyes moist, anxious to leave.

Before he turned to go, I stood and pulled him back to me. I balanced on tiptoe and touched my lips to his. The gentle kiss turned passionate, but a moment later John drew away.

I grabbed his arm and he turned toward me. "If you feel differently sometime in the future, call me."

John Marshall turned and left the restaurant.

My eyes welled with tears and my body collapsed into the chair.

I must have stayed like that for close to an hour, drifting, swirling around in my head with no direction, no sense of time and place. John's presence still lingered like a shadow. By the second time the waiter asked if I needed anything else, I realized that I was alone. Even John's scent had vanished. I rose slowly.

It was time to go home.

AVA

SURRENDER

I WOKE UP FEELING better than I had in days. I'd made it through tough spots before and knew I would again.

When I got to the office, I went online and viewed our bank accounts and credit cards for any withdrawals or purchases. Nothing. Maybe Paul was using the management company's account. I hadn't looked at those books in years. Being too busy with our realty company, I had left it all to Paul. I called the New York office and spoke with our secretary.

"Hey, Sheila," I said.

"Hi, Ava. How are things going? Is Paul coming in today?" Sheila asked.

"I don't know."

"Oh." Sheila paused "A—"

I interrupted, afraid of what she might ask. "I need the latest bank accounts, credit cards, and passwords for the company. I'm not sure I have the current information."

"Ah…" Sheila's voice broke. "Is something wrong?"

"No. Why would you ask that?"

"No reason. Sorry. Sure, I'll send you the information right away." She hung up.

Had I spooked her with my request? Did she know something I didn't?

Sheila sent me all the information about the accounts five minutes later. I looked through the company's checking account. Nothing came to light.

The heavy scent of roses still permeated the office. *Neil.* I closed my eyes, remembering how I used to melt at his touch. A quiet groan escaped my lips. *Que Macho!* My eyes popped open. I couldn't think about him now.

*

The year after Neil and I broke up, I met Paul in New York. The son of Portuguese immigrants, he owned a residential building on the Upper East Side of Manhattan.

We were both attending a conference in the city about the new East River waterfront development. I noticed him when he spoke to a small group after the meeting ended. Joining them, I thought he had a good grasp on the issues, and that he was smart, comical, and charming. I also noticed how he managed to dodge questions he didn't want to answer—like a seasoned politician. The group continued the discussion across the street over drinks. Within two months we were dating exclusively.

My family loved his sense of humor and my sisters thought he was handsome. I did, too. His smooth, flawless skin accentuated large brown eyes. His smile was quick and effortless. His poker-straight brown hair was cut into a feathered back style, popular in the eighties, that no mousse could tame. It always ended up wilting in his face.

As I held his hand on our first date, I glanced down and noticed his ring. "That's an interesting ring," I remarked.

Paul looked at it. "It was a graduation gift from my parents and means a lot to me. See that diamond embedded in the center? That was my father's and before that my grandfather's. My great-grandfather gave it to him and started the tradition. Someday I hope to give it to my son—that is, if I'm lucky enough to have one."

He talked for an hour about his parents and family. We had similar backgrounds, both first-generation Americans from working-class families. I could be myself around him, unashamed about my ethnic roots.

Paul's ample charm could turn churlish on a dime. While I didn't like that, I looked past it. His love for his family warmed my heart, but it was his drive that won me over. He was no Neil, but I thought we'd make a good team.

*

"Paul, this is my last phone call before I speak with an attorney. I suggest you return it quickly." Enough of this crap.

I called Bri. "Can Eric suggest a good attorney?"

"For what? Divorce or business?" Bri asked.

"Both, I guess."

"Do you want me to call him at work? Do you need somebody immediately?"

"No. Ask him tonight. I have a bad feeling about this. Remember when I had to dip into our savings and sell some stocks to cover Paul's online betting? I thought that was over with. Maybe it isn't."

"Have you looked over your accounts and the business ledgers?"

"Yes, everything seems to be in order."

"Check the invoices. Make sure they're real. When I was a paralegal we had a case where an employee handling the company's checkbook paid invoices to a fictitious company and pocketed the money."

"Oh God! What has he done?" *Que ha hecho...*

"Ava, I'm not saying that's what Paul is doing. It's a possibility, that's all. Do you want help?"

"No, not yet. Just find me a good attorney."

"Will do. Call me if you need anything."

After I hung up, I noticed my hand shaking slightly. I reviewed all the invoices posted. Nothing stood out. I entered the first company name into Google. Central Heating was located in Brooklyn and appeared legitimate.

My cell rang. It was Paul.

I took a deep breath. "Where have you been?"

"Just what the hell are you doing asking Sheila for my account information?" Paul barked into the phone. "That's my company. You ran away from it years ago, gave up your rights."

"We'll see what my attorney thinks about that!" Who did he think he was dealing with? Some weakling afraid of her own shadow?

"Wait, wait, Ava. What's all this talk about attorneys? Just sign the damn closing papers and everything will be fine!" he shouted.

"No, it hasn't been fine for a long time."

"Listen to me. I can't take the stress anymore." He calmed his voice, but the anger still bled through. "We need to sell the business. Then things will get better between us. We can work together again, like we once did."

"It's not the job, it's you."

"What? That's bullshit! You're bullshit! Sign the damn papers."

"Call me when you want to tell me what's going on. Until then I'm not signing anything." I pounded the end call button.

He sounded desperate. *Dios Ayudanos,* I thought. *God help us.* I stood and walked to the window overlooking the parking lot. I couldn't keep either of my shaking hands still.

Maybe God couldn't help me, but an attorney would.

My cell rang. I walked over to the desk and looked down. It was Neil.

"Hello."

"Ava. Please meet me for lunch or dinner. Please," Neil pleaded.

"No. Why are you calling and sending me flowers?"

"You know why."

"Now isn't a good time. I'm confused about my life right now and don't need any more complications."

"Let me help you, please."

"No," I whispered into the phone. As much as his caress had soothed me years ago, now it would only make me feel more unstable.

"Ava, please meet me."

"I have to go." I ended the call.

That night I dreamed of kissing and holding Neil, feeling warm in his arms. The same dream I'd had for thirty years. The only place I allowed my longing to exist. We never aged in that recurring dream: still stuck in our twenties, in our bliss. Tonight, however, everything changed. Tonight when I pictured us, we were thirty years older.

I woke up.

Sitting at the edge of the bed, I wondered if my dream, against all odds, was coming true. I shook my head. Better not believe that. I knew I couldn't survive losing Neil a second time.

*

Bri's husband, Eric, called me late in the day. "What's going on, Ava? I want to make sure I refer you to the right attorney."

I ran down everything, starting with the closing and ending with the invoices. "I'm worried because we had to pay off half a million dollars of Paul's online betting debt a few years ago. I thought that was behind him, but now I'm not so sure."

"All right. I'm going to talk with Thomas Kane. He specializes in divorce and has a forensic accountant on his team. They'll be able to drill into the ledgers and find any inconsistencies immediately. They're expensive, about five hundred dollars per hour, but you need someone at the top of his game."

"Thank you." I felt some relief. Someone qualified would help me with this mess.

*

I met with Tom Kane and showed him everything I had. He asked when I wanted to start divorce proceedings.

"Give me another week or so. I want to be really sure." I already knew I wanted out, but still hesitated.

I resumed my normal life, even going back to tennis league on Thursday nights.

My first match was a rigorous one that left me winded, but feeling great. I sat down with my doubles partner for a cold beer at the clubhouse afterward.

Looking out the bay window above the courts I saw Eric finishing a game. I stood, wanting to thank him for the attorney referral. However, before I turned to walk down the stairs, a woman in a tight, white tennis dress approached him. She stood so close that I thought for a minute it might be Bri in a blond wig, playing some kind of role-playing game. The woman seemed to almost coil around him. They talked for a few minutes before Eric turned and left.

I made a mental note to find out who the woman was and let Bri know.

*

The following Thursday after tennis I opened the door from the garage to the kitchen and jumped a foot when I saw Paul sitting on the family room couch. He was drinking scotch. The bottle on the table next to him was half empty. I dropped my purse on the kitchen table next to the door, but kept my cell in my hand.

"What are you doing here, Paul?" I asked.

His eyes were droopy, his face flushed. He was clearly very drunk. "It's my home, too. You forget?" He stood up on wobbly legs and slowly made his way toward me, bumping into chairs and tables along the way.

I walked back into the kitchen, positioning myself behind the island. "You need to leave now."

"Sign the damnnnnn papers," he slurred, bouncing repeatedly into the island as he moved closer to me.

Wanting to get him out of there fast, I said, "Sure, Paul, next week."

I started asking him questions. Trying to focus on them, he stopped moving and supported himself on the edge of the island. I pushed my Uber app and requested a car while continuing to talk to him. The app showed the car was five minutes away.

"I've got a car coming to take you home."

"I am home, damn it!"

He began to mutter things that made no sense. I pretended to listen, counting the minutes. Finally, I heard a car horn outside.

"Your ride's here." I turned and walked to the front door. Before I could open it, he pushed me into the wall. The family photos on the wall shook. One fell to the floor with a crash, the glass shattering.

Was the shove deliberate or just because he was drunk? Would he hurt me?

"Sign the papers," he screamed, his face so close to mine that he sprayed me with spit. He squeezed my wrist.

"Why, you…*maricon!*" I stepped into him, put both hands on his chest and pushed as hard as I could.

He stumbled back and fell to the floor.

I pushed 911 on my phone. "Get out and into that car or I'll hit dial and call the police. Now!" I screamed, holding my finger over the call button.

Paul struggled to get to his feet. He fell back—twice. He finally pulled himself up on the seat of our living room chair.

The car horn honked again and I flung open the door.

"Now, Paul."

Steadying himself on the back of the chair, he bumped his way out of the house. I watched from the door. He fell over a planter on the porch. I didn't envy the driver.

I shut and locked the door. That was the last straw. I ripped my wedding ring off my finger and threw it at the wall.

After a horrible nightmare-induced sleep, I called a locksmith and told Tom Kane to start divorce proceedings.

*

Once I decided to divorce Paul, I had to make two hard phone calls to our kids, Gabriel and Alysia. Neither seemed surprised. I promised them that Paul and I would always put them first and not involve them in any of our stupid squabbles. I just hoped Paul would keep his part of the bargain.

Work kept me moving forward, focused and happy. I had one house closing after another as buyers needed to move into their new homes before the school year began.

Neil continued to call almost every day. At first, I didn't answer, then I answered one call a week. Then two.

"Ava, come out to the Hamptons with me this weekend." Neil left a voicemail when I didn't pick up. "Come on—you remember how much fun we used to have there."

I remembered walking on the beach at sunset, playing house in his parents' oceanfront mansion, and never leaving bed on rainy days. The memory tried hard to lure me back into his arms, but I resisted the temptation. I knew I had to keep my desire locked up in my thoughts where I could control it.

*

Paul and I now talked exclusively through attorneys as we negotiated dividing the assets and selling the management company. Once the company's ledgers and accountants were thoroughly reviewed, I learned that a Shelton Enterprises had been paid something in the range of $750,000. There was no such company. Where had the money gone?

I might never have found out about the missing money if the forensic accountant hadn't gone over every inch of the books.

After several meetings, I decided to not press charges against Paul, or to ask for my share of the missing money. Instead we used the $375,000 that should have been mine as leverage.

"I want him out of the Jersey realty company. I started that from scratch and made it a success. Give him the management company and all proceeds from the sale and sever him from my company forever," I instructed my attorney.

"Are you sure? Paul will net about $1 million for the company after expenses," said my attorney.

"I am. I want a clean break and I'm willing to pay for it. And I certainly don't want the IRS coming after me for some tax liability that Paul didn't pay because he gambled the money away."

Paul and his attorney readily agreed and we finalized the property settlement. The management company was put up for sale through a broker. Neil and his father no longer wanted to buy it.

*

We had to meet to sign the agreement. I thought Paul looked better than he had in months. He was clean shaven and crisply dressed.

His demeanor was charming, polished, ready for his new phase of life. He flirted shamelessly with his attorney's secretary before entering the conference room.

After the signing, Paul followed me outside the building. "I'm sorry, Ava. Can you forgive me? We should try to work things out." His statement was flat, delivered without a shred of sincerity.

"No, it's too late for that." I continued walking to my car down the street. "What are you thinking? We just signed a property settlement agreement."

Paul walked alongside of me. "All I wanted was for you to sign the closing papers for the sale of the company. But, no. You did this to us. Not me."

"Where did the $750,000 go, Paul? More gambling debts?" I

stopped at the entrance to the parking lot and handed my ticket to the valet.

"It doesn't matter anymore, does it? Is it Neil Bass? Is that why you don't want to try to work things out?" Paul stood before me, his face turning red.

My anger flared. "No. It isn't. And exactly why did you ask him to buy the company in the first place?"

His hand gripped my arm. "I needed to sell the business. The stress was killing me. Remember? I thought it would be a quick sale because of your past relationship with Neil." Paul released my arm. "And, it would have been a quick sale, but you—you fucked it up."

"You need help, Paul. Professional help. You have a gambling addiction." I watched as the valet brought my car down the ramp.

"What? That's ridiculous. It's not an addiction, just something I enjoy. You enjoy drinking. Does that make you an alcoholic?"

"Please, for the sake of our children, get help." I walked over to my car, finished with the conversation.

But Paul had to have the last word. "So that's the thanks I get for bringing you out of the slums and into the life you always dreamed of."

Fuming, I used every ounce of willpower to ignore him and get in my car.

*

A week before Labor Day, Neil walked into my realty office after lunch. We locked eyes through my open door. His warm smile sent a shiver up my spine. He was much easier to ignore on the phone. When he stood there, in person, it took all my strength to appear nonchalant.

Kylie came bounding in and said I had a visitor. She winked at me with a thumbs-up after she ushered him into my office, closing the door behind her.

"You're a long way from home. What's up?" I said, staring at a file on my desk.

"Ava."

I looked up and watched his smile turn into a large grin.

"Why are you here?" I forced a bored look on my face, impressed with my self-control. What I really wanted to do was leap into his arms and taste his *delicioso* lips. I wondered if he believed I really was indifferent to him.

"Stop ignoring me."

"I'm a busy woman. What do you want?"

"You!"

Such a small, inconsequential word—but what enormous implications! I started to say something, but stopped.

"Ava, I want us to be together again. I want you," Neil said in that warm, raspy voice that had seduced me so many years ago.

I started to shake my head, but he countered with: "Just go out to dinner with me tonight. Please."

Hesitating, my mind a jumble, I blurted, "Okay." I told him I'd meet him at 7:30 at Redwoods down the street. "I have a closing in an hour and have to get back to work."

He rose and walked to the door. "Until tonight."

Giddy at the prospect of seeing him later, I clicked my killer red heels together, chanting under my breath: "Neil, baby, take me back to Kansas."

*

Shades of pink, purple, and yellow bathed the sky as twilight unfolded. Neil and I watched the majestic light show from our outdoor table. I could never have predicted in a million years that I would be sitting here with him tonight. I didn't think I'd ever see Neil again after he'd left me all that time ago.

We ordered drinks and continued watching the close of the day.

The stress of the last few months seemed to fade with the sunset's afterglow. Was this my new beginning?

Neil reached across the table and held my hand. "I've missed you, Ava. A lot."

"Neil, we are not the same people. That was thirty years ago." I looked into his eyes. The same eyes I'd once loved, eyes that had sent me spinning in all directions, hopeless, lost.

"Let's give us another chance." Neil leaned toward me. "We have nothing to lose and everything to gain. It's so rare that two people find each other again. Please." His finger slid my bangs out of my face and behind my ear.

I was so mesmerized that I didn't even register the fact that my bangs were finally long enough to tuck behind my ears. All I could grasp was the smell of his cologne. Gone was the Paco Rabonne he used to wear. "You've changed your cologne. What is it?"

"Straight to Heaven, which is how I feel with you right now." Neil laughed, squeezing my hand.

"I walked right into that. Didn't I?" I smiled at him.

"No, it really is called 'Straight to Heaven' by Kilian."

We both chuckled and relaxed.

"Thanks for going out with me," he said after a moment of contented silence.

"Well, what was I supposed to do after you showed up at my office?" I felt connected to him by a retractable leash, being pulled closer and closer. "I'm not even divorced yet."

My comment hung in the air as the waitress came over. I flipped open the menu, stammered out the first thing I saw, and then watched her retreat.

"Neil, I still have feelings for you, but I'm not sure about us dating again." I sat back in my chair, shifting away from the table.

Neil looked down.

"Our relationship ended when you threw me away like a child discarding his worn-out toy. Now my marriage is ending. Do you really think I should jump back into a relationship so soon? Especially with you?" If I were truthful, I knew that I wanted him, had always wanted him. My dream tugged at my heart as I looked into his eyes. But, I would not tell him that. He needed to prove to me that he had changed. I refused to be tossed away again.

"I really loved you, Ava, and it hurts me that you think I threw you away." Neil's shoulders drooped. "I was weak, but I'm not that person anymore. How many people ever get a second chance?" His eyes pleaded with me. "I understand you need time. I'm not expecting us to return to where we left off. But, I'd like us to date. Then we can see where it goes."

I had no idea what to say. "I can't answer that right now. I..."

Dinner arrived just in time. I didn't know what I wanted. After we started eating, I asked him if he had ever married.

"I was married twice and clearly neither of them worked out."

"Any children?"

"No, wasn't in the cards." Neil put his fork down and continued, "I married a young woman that my parents set me up with after we broke up. Her name was Leah and she was what they thought I should have in a wife." He took a large sip of wine. "I was pining over you and angry at my father and she was a comfort. We parted amicably a year after we married."

I ordered another drink. "And what happened with the second wife?"

"It was a total disaster. Sarah changed completely once we were married. All she seemed to care about was spending money. More, more, more was her mantra." His nostrils flared. "I was an idiot. How could I have not seen that in her when we were dating?" He told me that he became cautious about dating after that. He asked me about my marriage.

Handsome as he was now, I found myself wishing he hadn't lost his hair. What would I run my fingers through after we made love?

"Paul and I met about a year after we broke up," I said. "We came from similar backgrounds and both wanted to succeed in business. Most of the marriage was good. At least I thought so. But the last few years…" It hit me that I had never once cried at the breakup of my marriage. I remembered crying all the time after Neil left me.

"Ava."

"Sorry, I got lost in thought."

The waitress removed our dinner plates. I ordered coffee. Maybe it was the wine, the stars, his smile, or my internal yearning, but I felt content. It couldn't be this easy to fall back in time. Could it?

Neil walked me to my car. I touched the door handle to release the lock. He came directly behind me—so close. Every nerve in my back sizzled. My breath caught.

I turned around and Neil closed in on me, pinning me against the car. He kissed me deeply, his kiss no longer a memory or dream. I gave myself freely to his passion, my resistance completely dissipated.

"Ava, you must feel this," Neil whispered in my ear.

A moan escaped me. "I do." Our physical connection came roaring back to life right there in the restaurant's parking lot. We tried to fill our aching need for one another with one kiss after another. I didn't even notice the people getting into the car next to us until the engine started.

I pulled myself away from Neil, my lips burning. If I had doubts, they weren't enough to dampen my desire.

"What's wrong?" Neil asked.

"I need time. Please, let's get to know one another before we complicate my life any further."

*

I spent Labor Day weekend with family and friends, going from one picnic to the next. Neil and I talked for hours every day that week, getting to know one another again. We made plans for Sunday night dinner. I thought to myself, I'm going to have to spend every day at the tennis club to shed the pounds gained from so many rich meals.

I had just chilled a bottle of white and set out an appetizer plate when the doorbell rang. Neil was right on time. He'd made an eight o'clock dinner reservation at a new French restaurant in Morristown that a client had raved about.

Neil scooped me up the moment I opened the door, giving me a huge, wet, sensuous kiss hello.

"Down, boy," I said, trying to catch my breath. "We are going to take it easy, right?"

"I couldn't help myself." Neil closed the door.

I poured two glasses of wine. We talked and munched on cheese.

By the time we were ready to leave, I had finished two glasses of wine and felt a happy glow taking over.

The doorbell rang.

"Are you expecting anyone?" Neil asked.

"No." Startled, I opened the door. Paul was supporting himself, clutching the doorframe. His face was bloody and bruised.

"What happened? Neil, help me get him in."

Neil strong-armed Paul inside and we propped him up on a kitchen chair.

"What happened, Paul?" I asked.

"I want to speak to my wife alone!" Paul barked, glaring at Neil.

"There's no way I'm leaving Ava alone with you when you're in this condition." Neil stood tall and firm.

"Ava, I need to talk to you. Please." The blood on Paul's face dripped on the countertop. I wet a few paper towels at the sink. I started to dab at the cuts on his face.

"What happened to you? I think you need stitches over your eye. It looks deep." I cleaned the blood from his face and scrubbed the countertop.

"Ava, I'm not gonna hurt you. I just need to talk to you."

"Absolutely not. I'm not leaving her with you!" Neil curled his right hand into a fist.

Ahora van a pelear por mí. Increíble. Now they're gonna fight over me. Unbelievable. "Both of you calm down—right now!" I shouted. Both men looked at me. "That's enough!" Surprised by my commanding tone, they backed off. I threw out the bloody paper towels and went into the pantry for some antiseptic and Band-Aids.

When I finished cleaning Paul up, I grabbed Neil's arm and brought him into the family room. "Why don't you go to the restaurant and I'll be along in a few minutes?"

"No way. Not happening." Neil kept watching Paul in the kitchen.

"I'll be fine. I want to find out what's going on. He won't talk with you here. Please."

Neil wasn't happy but he left. I heard his car pull out of the driveway.

"Okay, we're alone," I told my soon-to-be-ex. "Talk."

Paul got a glass from the cabinet and drank down two glasses of ice water. "I owe you an apology—a big one. You were right. I have a gambling issue." He looked to the floor.

"Is that what happened to your face? Do you owe more money?" I wanted to run away and hide. God only knew what he'd done to himself, but he was still my husband and that meant I was still involved.

"Yes, I owe someone a hundred thousand dollars. That's why I wanted the sale to go through so quickly. I need a hundred thousand dollars now."

"This debt is for online betting?" I asked, shocked that he'd been beaten. Just like in the movies.

"No. Off-track racing. Look, it doesn't matter what it's for!" He slammed his glass on the counter. "I need the money now. It will take months, maybe even an entire year, to sell the business. And that's your fault."

"You should have thought of that before you got yourself into this."

Paul poured himself another glass of water and drank it down. "So what's up with Neil? You two shacking up again?"

I didn't dignify that with an answer. "I'm late for dinner. What do you want?"

"I want you to sign off on a hundred thousand dollar loan from our retirement money." He put his glass into the sink. "I'll pay it back when the business sells. I will e-mail the paperwork when I get home."

"I guess you thought this out." I looked at him. "But I'm not signing anything until I speak with my attorney. If this is a reasonable way for you to get the money you need, I'll do it under a few conditions."

"Like what?"

"First, since we have already agreed on the finances, I want a thirty-day divorce. Secondly, you must leave me alone."

"Ava, why get a fast divorce? I'm gonna go into rehab and when I come out I want you and me to get back together again." Paul moved closer to me. The scent of sweat and blood choked my nose.

"No way, Paul. We are over." I put my hand out to stop him. "We haven't been good for a long time. We both deserve to be happy."

Paul saw my outstretched arm and halted. "I'm sorry, I really am."

"I know." I told him to send me the papers and I'd have my attorney reach out to his lawyer tomorrow about the loan.

Paul stared at his cut hand. "You know, the asshole beating me up was trying to wrestle my ring off my hand, but somehow I kept it on." He walked over to the sink, turned on the water. Soaping up his hand, he twisted his great-grandfather's ring off his finger. "Give this to Gabriel. I don't want to take a chance of losing it. I don't deserve it."

"I will. Or better yet I'll hold it till you get out of rehab. You should give it to him yourself." I smiled and placed my hand on his arm. "Go and get well." I walked over to the family room and looked outside to see if his car was there. "I'm glad you didn't drive. How did you get here?"

"Uber."

"I'm late for dinner. Can I drop you somewhere?"

Paul shook his head, got his phone, and ordered a pickup. "Are you absolutely sure you want a divorce? I'm gonna get better."

"Yes." The finality of the word felt refreshing.

*

Neil had called my cell twenty times before I could bundle Paul into a car and head to mine. I called him back.

"Are you all right?" he asked.

"Yes. I'm on my way."

"No, don't drive. I'm only a street away. You didn't think I was going to leave you alone with him and drive a half hour away?"

I laughed and turned my car around in the cul-de-sac. Neil pulled up my driveway a minute later.

He got out of his car and wrapped both arms tightly around me, kissing my forehead. "Are you sure you're okay?"

"Yes." I didn't want to talk about it. "Let's go to dinner. I'm hungry."

We got into his car. Neil reached over and kissed me.

We kissed and kissed and kissed until the car had steamed up as if we were teenagers necking in the back of a parking lot.

"I can't believe we are here together," Neil murmured in my ear. "I feel like my life's been on hold until this very minute." He caressed my face. "It's always been you. Always."

A tear rolled down my cheek as we embraced. "I guess we found our way back." *How ironic that it all happened through Paul.*

"Do you want to go to dinner now or…?" Neil shrugged, a deep longing in his eyes.

"Yes, I'm starving. Let me freshen up first. Come into the house. We've given the neighbors enough to talk about." I laughed.

Walking up my front stairs with Neil close behind me, an old song of ours popped into my head: "Do You Believe in Magic." I turned and looked at Neil. *Well, I guess I do.*

CHARLOTTE

UNEXPECTED LOVE

A STEPPENWOLF SONG STREAMED over Pandora as I put my lip gloss back in my jeans pocket. "Lookin' for adventure." Yeah, that's me. Though I doubt Mars Bonfire had me in mind when he wrote that song—late forties, divorced with college-aged kids, dating.

I laughed out loud. *Mr. Bond hasn't seen my latest Victoria's Secret purchases, though.*

Smiling, dancing around in my kitchen to the chorus, I realized that it had taken me years to arrive at this place in my life. After I caught my husband in bed with a friend of ours, I'd fallen into a funk that had lasted for months.

My friends and family were supportive. But it was book club that allowed me to vent, to cry, to rage. Looking back, I would have felt foolish about some of the things I did or said with someone else, but not with them. Book club's our safe haven, our therapeutic session. We've all spent time on the couch.

Checking my e-mail, I noticed my younger sister, Jessica, had sent me a link to some news show about people living longer when they're in a committed relationship. "But of course they do," I said loudly to no one as I hit the delete button. She just can't let the subject go.

I decided to eat lunch first and not go shopping on an empty stomach. The last time I did that, I ended up with a freezer full of ice cream. I reached into my pantry and pulled out a can of tuna. Opening the can, I remembered how I used to cringe every time I visited the grocery store after my ex's betrayal. Because my high-school-aged sons ate so much, I had had to go two to three times a week.

My pulse would quicken even before I stepped foot in the door. Every aisle I turned down held its own surprise. Sometimes I'd encounter blank stares from women I knew casually from high school sports events. Sometimes women in conversation would huddle close and whisper when they saw me. But the worst was when people I barely knew came up to me and said how sorry they were. What was I supposed to say, cornered between the coffee and cereal aisles? I always kicked myself for not practicing a response in a mirror, one that would allow me to appear unaffected and care-free. Like it was the best thing that ever happened. I dubbed this my *Shop Rite Walk of Shame.* I started going out of town to buy groceries. I didn't want to talk about the demise of my marriage. But my withdrawing backfired, causing even more rumors and speculation, completely twisting the truth.

My stomach still quivers when I think about that time. Now I pranced down the aisles of my local store, daring them all to look or whisper. But they're not interested anymore. They've moved on to someone else.

*

Maxwell was gone for two weeks on business. He called and texted me every day. When he returned, he invited me over for dinner at his house. I packed an overnight bag with dessert, my most seductive nightie.

He lived a half hour away in the bucolic town of Ridge Lake. His house was a renovated 1910 Hapgood-style charmer with two large gable bays in a pleasing soft biscuit color, typical of the arts-and-crafts design of the time.

I knocked on the exquisite mahogany beveled-glass front door. When he opened the door, I smelled garlic and fresh bread. He wore a tight-fitting pair of straight leg jeans and a polo shirt. It was the first time I had seen him with his hair down, so to speak. I liked him dressed up, but this relaxed look was irresistible. When he asked if I wanted a glass of wine, I said yes, even though my thirst was elsewhere.

"So, this is a bachelor's pad? Nice," I said, following him through the living room, taking in the oriental rugs and the warm rich tones.

"Well, that's one way of looking at it." He stopped in the kitchen. "I just had it renovated."

It looked it, with its brushed stainless-steel appliances set into cherry cabinets and finished with a sandstone countertop.

But it was the view beyond that held my interest. "That's beautiful," I said, looking out the sliding glass doors to the lake below.

"I looked for almost a year before I found this place. I fell in love immediately."

"I can see why."

Maxwell brought me a glass of wine. "This is a favorite burgundy of mine."

I took the glass. "I smell garlic and bread, I think. What's for dinner, chef?"

"I'm grilling up some salmon. I have a cheese tray with meat, fruit, and nuts on the deck. Shall we?" He reached for my hand and led me outside.

The backyard sloped down to the water with stairs leading from the deck to the dock. Two landings were built into the stairs, just a step to the lawn. One set of stairs ended by a hot tub and another led farther down the lawn to a set of Adirondack chairs. Rosebushes and hedges lined the property.

A table was set up on the dock with lanterns and candles all around. "Are we eating on the dock?"

"Yes, as soon as it gets dark." Maxwell handed me a piece of cheese on warm bread. "Charlie, could you hand me one of the plates by your arm?"

"Charlie? I don't think anyone has ever called me that before."

"Is that okay?" He cracked a huge grin, looking half teasing and half serious.

Jeez, what's all this? Romance…nicknames…next thing you know, he'll be flying me off to Paris. Unsettled, I gulped down my wine.

He went inside to get the bottle.

By the time I had finished my second glass, I got back into the swing of the date and helped him finish making the salad and grilling the salmon. We fixed our plates and brought them down to the dock where the last remnants of sun reflected off the lake. Maxwell had another bottle of wine breathing on the table, which was set with glasses, silverware, and a low bowl filled with roses from the bushes. He put his plate down, lit the lanterns and the candles covering the dock, and sat down, proud as a peacock.

I was speechless. Why had he done all this? *Say something, say anything, idiot.* "This is really beautiful." It came out as a whisper. I looked out over the water, suddenly feeling tired.

I started to eat and gradually pulled myself out of my funk. Maxwell didn't seem to notice that I had checked out for a few moments.

It was a warm night and the stars began to flicker to life as we finished dinner.

"Mary called and invited us to a small dinner party tomorrow night. Two of my other fraternity brothers and their wives are in town. I know its last minute, but I hope you can come."

Without thinking, I nodded yes.

Maxwell brought our dishes up to the house and came back with a gift bag. "I got you a little something." He handed me the gift.

"Why?" I gingerly opened the bag and pulled out a book. "Wh...?" Surprised, the words wedged in my throat. I looked inside the front cover. "I never thought I'd see one of these," I said as my hand glided over the copyright page. "A first edition..." I couldn't finish the sentence and looked out over the lake. "How did you find this?"

Maxwell grinned and sat up straight in his chair. "A friend of mine owns an antique book store in Boston. I called and asked him to track one down."

"You didn't have to do this." *Why did he? Oh, come back, Mr. Bond.* I shivered, hoping he was like this with all his other dates, too. I didn't want to be anybody's special person. I just couldn't.

He came over to my chair and held out his hands. I rose. He kissed me deeply. Instead of thrusting my hips into his, I felt my whole body drawn in. My stomach fluttered. Warmth overwhelmed me. I broke off the kiss and leaned on his chest trying to catch my breath.

Maxwell guided our lovemaking that night with plenty of fore-play and tenderness. I floated in and out, detached one minute, engaged the next, like diving into a warm turquoise ocean, then fearing a shark and scrambling away.

I woke early the next day. I thought he was still asleep, but when I rose, he stretched his arms over for a hug.

"Shhh. Go back to sleep. I have an early appointment. I'll see you later." It was an excuse. My heart raced. I needed to get out. I didn't want to meet his friends tonight, but I'd already agreed.

*

"Hi, guys, so glad you could come." Mary beamed at us at the front door. I'm sure Mary couldn't wait to tell me: "I told you he was perfect."

We were the last to arrive. There were two other couples. As Maxwell had mentioned, the men were also fraternity brothers. They formed a tight group, leaving me with Mary and the other wives.

"Charlotte, this is Cindy and Donna." As Mary introduced everyone, she gave me some background. The couples had all been friends for more than twenty years. I wandered around the kitchen, picking at the appetizers, listening to the three women talk as only long-term friends can, finishing one another's sentences.

My ex and I had shared a group of close friends, all couples. We went on vacations together, to dinners, plays. Our children played with one another growing up. I loved feeling so connected to that group, but it ended with the divorce. My ex kept our couples friends, almost as if he won them in the settlement. Why do they always seem to stay with the man?

Maybe it was my penance for obtaining the house. Divorce had chopped up all the pieces of my life, leaving only slivers by which to navigate. The wives initially reached out to me but slowly disappeared. I missed our friends in the beginning, but eventually I moved on and made my own. At least the book club stayed loyal to me.

I've avoided these cozy couple kind of dates since my divorce. I don't see why I should make an effort when the relationships seem to fritter away anyway.

Mary gave me a cosmo and I drank it down in three gulps. I kept walking around the kitchen, almost pacing, and hoped the drink would calm me. I wasn't sure why I felt this way: pegged into a hole where I no longer fit.

The second cosmo lasted only four gulps, but I did stop pacing and sat down.

The ladies started asking me questions about myself and Maxwell. I felt dizzy. *Damn, those drinks were strong.*

"We are so glad Maxwell has met someone he really likes," Mary said, putting her hand on my shoulder.

"He's great. Thanks for introducing us." I looked up at Mary. The ladies were talking too quickly or maybe the cosmos were catching up with me. I struggled to keep up.

"Don't forget to bring some sneakers with you next week. We walk a few miles in the morning on the beach," one of the wives said.

Wait a minute. "What beach? What are you talking about?"

Mary gave the ladies the cut sign under her chin. "We are all going to Kiawah Island for a week. Donna must have assumed Maxwell had asked you to come." Mary glared at Donna for a second. By the time she turned toward me, she'd resumed her usual sunny face mask.

God, I don't want to go on a couples' week. That's it. I'm done. "No, Maxwell hasn't asked me to go, but we aren't exclusive. We both date other people."

Mary's eyebrow rose. "That's not what Maxwell told us. I think he's really into you."

I gave her the *nuh* wave with my hand. "Why would anyone want to settle down again?" I wobbled as I stood, bracing myself on the back of the chair.

The women just stared at me. I wanted to go home and have sex. These women still live in their snug little worlds. I walked over to the counter and poured myself a Diet Coke.

The men joined us and we moved to the backyard. Another warm blue-sky day was giving way to a moonlit night. I enjoyed the conversations much more after the men joined us.

Maxwell went to help with the grilling and I noticed at one point that Mary was in deep conversation with him. *God, I hope he doesn't ask me on that trip.*

I smiled frequently at the dining table as the group discussed politics and the latest late-night commentary. Even though we sat outside, I felt cramped, claustrophobic. I took deep breaths while they shared funny YouTube videos on their phones. I leaned back into my chair trying to disappear.

Maxwell was quiet on the trip back to my house. He told me he was tired and left as soon as he dropped me off.

*

"Where the hell is he? I told you men are dogs and only good for one thing," I said pushing a tree branch out of my way.

"Jesus, the way you talk about men," Bri said. "Maybe he's on a business trip."

"For three weeks? Not likely!"

"I thought you wanted a Bond type, here and then gone."

"I did. It was that damn gift. It messed with my head," I said, winded. I had been talking nonstop during our entire walk.

"Why don't you call him or send him a text?" Bri suggested.

I gulped down a few deep breaths. "I tried that. I can't figure it out. One minute I think this is going way too fast, and the next he's gone." My head ached.

"Maybe he sensed you don't want a commitment. Maybe he does."

"Hmmm... You think?" I stopped, resting against a tree. "I did tell the women at Mary's dinner party that we weren't exclusive. I didn't want to get invited to a god-awful couples' week. You don't think that got back to him and he took it the wrong way, do you?"

Bri smiled in exasperation. "What's the right way to take that?"

*

I wasn't going to let Maxwell upset me anymore. I needed to get back on the circuit. I called Staci and Hanna for a last-minute rendezvous at Bradley's.

"Hanna, I can't believe you managed to come tonight," I said.

"My husband's away, of course, so I asked my babysitter last minute." Hanna sipped her drink. "I feel kinda bad that I blew out of the house as soon as Ally got there." She grimaced. "Maybe not that bad."

"Who are you texting?" I asked Staci.

"I'm not texting. I'm trying to fill in all the information on this online dating site." She held up the app for me to see.

"Eww....The *marriage-minded dating* site," I said, imitating the man on the commercials. "Why not have some fun first? Try Tinder and enjoy a few hookups before you look for something so serious."

"No, thanks. I've had enough of the love-them-leave-them types." Staci's voice caught.

Hanna looked around the bar. "Charlotte! Guess who's here?"

"Who?" I spun my head around.

"That young man we met here in the beginning of summer." Hanna pointed over my shoulder.

"What the hell was his name?" I asked.

Hanna chuckled. "I don't remember."

As I laughed I realized I needed the ladies room. On the way back, I looked through the open French doors into the dining area. At a candlelit table in the corner Maxwell sat with a woman with shoulder-length red hair. I could almost see the sparkle in his eyes. My knees went weak.

My eyes watered. I took a few deep breaths before rejoining my friends.

The young tadpole from across the bar came over. I tried to smile but felt like I needed a crane to pull up the corners of my mouth. I guzzled my cosmo and pretended to listen.

I told them I had to go back to the ladies' room again, that the drinks must be getting to me. I walked toward the restroom but made a left and walked around the outside of the dining area, so that Maxwell's back would face me. I had to see his date. *Who was she? How did he meet someone already? Maybe he had been dating her all along?* She had on a well-tailored black suit with a lavender silk blouse. The color was gorgeous with her hair. I thought she looked pretty, with small features, but all I could dare was a quick glance in candlelight. *I'm a damn fool.*

I rejoined my friends and ordered another cosmo. I wasn't

driving. I'm the one who didn't want to get involved. *Why is this bothering me?* The young man, Chris, noticed some of his friends were leaving and went to say goodbye to them.

"Girls, Maxwell's here with some young bimbo having dinner." I gulped the last of my drink down. "Can you believe that? He isn't who I thought he was."

"Oh, isn't that the pot calling the kettle black?" Staci said. "All you ever say is how you don't want to get involved. So isn't he perfect for you?"

"Funny, very funny." I motioned for the bartender. "I'll have another."

"Three cosmos in an hour? I'm not carrying your ass out of here." Staci groaned. She flagged down the bartender and asked for a large glass of water. "I don't want you getting sick in my new car. Drink this first and slow down."

She was probably right. My hands shook and my heart felt like it was beating out of my chest. I was growing angrier and angrier.

"Why are you so upset?" Hanna asked. "Oh...I get it. You like him. You actually like a man."

Oh...my head spun as I sipped water through a straw. I wanted that cosmo, but Staci would kill me if I didn't finish the water first. I thought back to the night at Maxwell's house. I should have left before we'd fallen into bed. Then that couples' dinner. *What the hell is the matter with me? I'm going to confront him.*

I stood up, determined.

"Don't tell me you have to go to the ladies' room again."

"Yes. What of it?" I stormed away.

I walked right into the dining room. My walk felt like the opening of a TV crime show where the actors saunter over to you in slow motion.

"Hello, Maxwell. Funny running into you here. Don't you believe in returning calls?" I turned away from the surprise in his lovely eyes. They must have cast a spell on me. But no more. I see him. I know the type. "And who is this? Your latest conquest?"

The woman pushed back in her chair facing me. Her jaw clenched and her eyes narrowed.

Maxwell jumped up and apologized to his date. He thrust his arm into mine, marching me out of the dining area.

"What the hell are you doing?" he asked.

"What am I doing? What are you doing?" I pulled my arm away and almost fell, saved only by the wall behind me. I wanted to ask if he had given her a gift, too. Out of the corner of my eye I saw Chris approaching.

"Is everything all right?" Chris asked.

Maxwell looked at me. "You're dating children now?"

"Hey, watch who you're calling a child!" Chris tried to move between us, but I blocked him with my arm.

"I guess I don't know you at all!" Maxwell turned to walk away.

I grabbed his arm. "Wait."

I turned to Chris. "I would like to speak to my friend privately. Please." Chris turned on his heels in a huff and headed back to the bar.

I stepped closer. "I'm not dating him." I could see Maxwell's date over his shoulder. "Though he certainly did ask." I spat out.

He said nothing. I looked into his eyes, remorseful. I was acting like an idiot. "I'm sorry. You have a right to date whoever you want." I turned, but this time he grabbed my arm.

"She's the human resource manager of a client of mine," he hissed at me. "It's not a date."

What had seemed like such a good idea had turned into a catastrophe. "I'm really sorry." I turned quickly and walked away before he could see me cry. I collected Staci and Hanna and got out of there fast.

*

My head hurt in the morning and I couldn't tell if the pounding was the cosmos or my humiliation. I ate a small piece of bagel so I could take some aspirin. Sitting down, I closed my eyes to give the aspirin time to work. But all I did was replay the scene from the night before, over and over.

"Enough," I shouted and stood. I made some coffee and put on my sweats and sneakers. Acid rose from my stomach when the coffee hit, but I drank it anyway.

I went out for a brisk-paced walk, mile after mile until my hips throbbed and my knees creaked.

The acid still danced in my stomach so I chewed a few antacid tablets. I got into my car. A half hour later, I parked down the street from Bri's home and waited for Eric to leave for work. 8:00…8:05…8:10…my finger tapped out each second on the steering wheel. Finally, I saw Eric's BMW pull onto the street and leave.

I pounded on Bri's door. I barely gave her time to open it before barging in. "I think I blew it last night."

Bri stood aside and let me in. She looked bleary eyed, yawning. "What? Blew what?" she asked as she closed the door.

I told her the story while she made us coffee.

Bri and I have been friends since our teens. She'd helped me cope with the death of my father, and then my mother within a year.

In our early twenties, we had shared an apartment. We did what all our peers did—dated, danced, and drank. At least until I met my ex, who proposed after a whirlwind six-month romance.

"I'm sorry," Bri said.

"So that's it. Right?"

"Well, what do you really want? You said you wanted a man like Bond, but that's not what I'm hearing now."

"I don't know. I don't know." I felt exhausted and slumped further into the chair. "I didn't just fall off that damn seesaw of yours, I feel like someone threw me off."

Bri had helped me pick up the pieces after my divorce. I kept asking over and over. "Why? Why me? Didn't I go through enough as a kid?"

I remembered what she'd said that day. She sat down next to me and held my hand. "I kind of look at life like a seesaw. Sometimes you can balance in the middle, but usually it moves one way or the other." Bri had given me a warm hug. "You've managed to balance in the middle for a long time. Just stay on the seat. The fall is temporary. You'll soar again."

I needed my friend right now to tell me everything was going to be all right. "Bri, I didn't land well. It happened so fast. Like the person jumped off the seesaw and sent me crashing down." I choked back tears.

Bri said nothing for a minute or two. Then: "Pick up the phone and call him. You have nothing to lose."

*

I hoped beyond all hope that Maxwell would call me back. A week went by and no call, no text.

After the scene I caused, it was no wonder he stopped calling. I thought about the look in his eyes when he gave me the book, and how different his hugs were from anyone else's. Never stiff and superficial, but filled with vulnerability and need. He breathed me into him.

I had wiped my kitchen counter five times working up the courage to text Maxwell again. This had to end one way or another. *I miss you. Can we talk?* I clicked send.

*

I arrived at the bar early. I thought it was better to be there first. But the minutes ticked by like hours.

My hands shook as I rummaged through my purse for my lip gloss. "Damn it!" I said as I threw my crap all over the table. Nothing. I probed in the bag's pockets with my fingers. Nothing.

Panic set in. I squeezed my lips together, realizing gloss was still on them. I calmed a bit. I must have left it in the car.

When Maxwell entered the restaurant, my breath caught and all my rehearsed words flew away. He approached me. I stood up and my wallet fell to the floor. I must have left it on my lap.

He bent over and handed it to me.

I froze. *Should I kiss him? On the cheek?* Indecision made me sit down.

Tongue-tied, I motioned for the waiter. I ordered a white wine spritzer, but what I really wanted was a few shots of tequila. I knew I had to behave tonight. Maxwell ordered a glass of red wine.

Neither of us spoke. The few minutes stretched uncomfortably before the waiter returned with our drinks.

"Cheers," I said and moved to click his glass.

He clicked glasses but didn't say anything.

I took a sip and set my glass on the table. "I'm sorry for the way I behaved at the restaurant."

Maxwell just stared into his drink.

A shiver of dread ran through me. I took another nervous sip of wine. "Ah…I overreacted completely." I bowed my head. Without thinking I added, "But I was angry at you. I haven't heard from you in weeks and then I saw you with another woman."

He seemed like he was deep in thought. Tension stretched even tighter between us.

My foot began to tap up and down under the table, faster and faster.

Maxwell finally looked up at me. "Charlie, I'm sorry I left you hanging after Mary's party. I was away for some of it, but I needed time. I've been where you are now. Dating, drinking, and enjoying life like a twenty-year-old. But I'm through with that."

I watched him place his glass on the table, speechless.

"I'm ready for a relationship, but I'm not sure we're at the same place." He looked directly at me. The creases in his brow softened.

"Well, yes, no…" I placed my hand on his forearm. "I mean that I haven't dated any man exclusively since I was married. But…"

He grinned, but it faded quickly. "I've been there." Maxwell brushed a hand through his hair. "I went out of my way to feel whole again after my divorce. I dated a lot of women, worked crazy hours, and drank more than I should have. All that did was give me a quick self-esteem boost that never lasted."

Sort of what I'd been doing for years. I sat back in my chair.

"One day the craziness ended. I felt ready to start a new life." He leaned across the table.

I held my breath, afraid of what was coming.

"I immediately connected with you." He reached over and cupped my hand. "But I'm not sure you felt the same."

Words left unsaid screamed inside my head. My confusion about wanting a relationship was tempered by the pain and rejection I'd experienced.

Thankfully, the barmaid came over and asked if I wanted another drink. I immediately asked for a wine spritzer. Maxwell shook his head.

My mind spiraled trying to find the right words. "Maxwell, I agree that we definitely connected from the first moment we met." I clung to my drink. "Why would you think otherwise?"

"You acted really strange at Mary's dinner. Aloof. Then you told my friends that we weren't exclusive in a way that suggested you were just waiting for something better." He leaned back in his chair.

I felt a pang. That must have hurt him. "That's not what I meant at all." I unwrapped my hands from my glass. "Being at that dinner was really hard for me. When I got divorced I lost all my couple friends." Tears filled my eyes and I looked away.

Regaining my composure, I explained that I had avoided all couples' events since my divorce.

"You should have told me you were uncomfortable. We didn't have to go."

I grinned weakly.

"Charlie, all I want is to give my full attention to one woman and see where it goes. I was hoping it would be with you."

And, there it was. The one thing I'd avoided like the plague—monogamy. My foot was jumping so hard under the table he must have felt the vibrations. The moments ticked past as I tried to figure out what to say.

"Well, I guess I have my answer." Maxwell pulled fifty-dollar bill out of his wallet out and placed it on the table.

"Wait." I reached out to him as he stood.

He stopped and looked at me.

"Give me some time. Please."

Maxwell bent down and kissed me tenderly on the lips. Then he left.

*

We. He wants to be a we. I lay in the dark in my bathrobe on my bed, curled like a frightened child. All I needed was a small, dirty blanket to complete the picture. The nagging voice in my head kept reminding me that I failed at this once before. I looked at the clock: 3:30 a.m. Too early to get up. I rolled over. I pulled my phone from the nightstand and listened to his voicemail message again and again. His voice soothed me to sleep.

*

I kept up my vigil for a week. I called family. I walked miles with friends. I went out every night. Anything not to be home and alone with myself. He haunted my thoughts, my mind, my heart. I saw his face in the crowd wherever I went.

After a week, I called him. He told me to come over. I went.

He opened the door the moment I reached up to ring the bell. Barefooted, in shorts and a T-shirt, his hair windblown. I wondered if he had been out on his boat.

I looked at him and tried to smile. I hadn't prepared what to say.

Hell, I couldn't keep my thoughts together enough to say anything. But I was there. I figured that was worth something. *Jeez, look at him. Who wouldn't want him?*

Awkwardness permeated our small talk as we sat on his deck overlooking the lake.

"Ah. I thought about what you said last week and I'm ready, too." I twisted my hands together.

"You don't sound so sure." He reached over and plucked one of my hands from my lap.

"I am. I think…It's just that…I don't know. I don't know."

Maxwell squeezed my hand. "This is scary for me, too. But I want to give it a chance. If we continue to date other people it will get complicated."

Date other people? Was he dating? I turned away and looked out over the lake. "Grant smashed my life to pieces like a hammer on a glass table. Sometimes I still find shards of glass in unexpected places."

A boat drove past and the sound of the motor caught our attention. I could hear voices but not make out the words.

"Sometimes you have to take a leap of faith and go for it." His voice was warm and sensual.

I wanted to leap all right, right into his pants. No, I wanted more than that.

"Okay…I'll leap."

He stood and pulled me into his arms and we hugged for a long time. Maxwell retreated into the kitchen and brought out a bottle of wine and two glasses. We sat on his deck and talked for hours. It was the first time I'd talked that much to anyone, much less a man. I was hoarse by the end of the evening.

We made love somewhere in the wee hours of the morning. Slowly, a little tired at first, but then something happened. This raw sensuousness came over me, way beyond anything I had felt before, jolting yet soothing, as if every cell in my body were charged, merging into a million sensations over and over again.

"Wow! That's all I can say." Light-headed, heart pounding and every nerve tingling, I closed my eyes and took a few deep breaths.

"Amen." He sat up on the bed and pulled me into his arms. "That's what happens when two people really click."

I tried to laugh. "Oh yeah."

"Really, I read it somewhere. There's a name for it. I can't remember it. I'm lucky I can remember anything right now."

We both laughed.

"It had to do with feeling really secure with someone where you both have a physical and emotional union and it creates this ultra-aroused sex. Or something like that."

"What?!"

"Seriously. Look it up."

"I can think of a few more things I'd rather look up." I kissed his cheek and got out of bed grabbing his bathrobe from the back of the chair. I slid open his bedroom sliders and went out to the deck overlooking the lake.

I leaned on the railing.

"That's a hell of a sunrise," Maxwell came up behind me and wrapped his arms around my waist.

"You bet it is." I let out a blissful sigh, and wrapped myself tighter into his arms. "It's the best I've ever seen."

TESS

THE AWAKENING

"LIZ! HI, SWEETHEART. It's great to hear your voice." I said pulling back on Mac's leash and leaning on the boardwalk's railing.

My daughter and her boyfriend had just returned from a two-week holiday in Europe. Except for a few e-mails, we hadn't communicated much. Hearing her voice, I realized how much I'd missed talking with her.

"Did I catch you at a bad time, Mom?"

"No, not at all. I'm walking Mac, watching an amazing sunset and some die-hard surfers cresting the swell. I can't believe I've been down here three weeks already. Thanks for sending the pictures of Rome and Paris. I felt like I was living vicariously through you. Looks like you had a great time."

"It was wonderful. I'll tell you more about it later. Rob and I still need to unpack. I wanted to check on you first."

"Check on me...you make me sound about a thousand years old." I couldn't help laughing slightly. "I've been decompressing big time. Puttering around, reading, napping, and taking care of the new man in my life."

"Man? What man?"

"See, your old mom isn't so old after all is she? He's right here with me. He's very good looking, too: blond, fit, likes long walks on the beach. He also walks on four legs and guzzles kibble like there is no tomorrow."

"Mom! You're talking about that dog you're taking care of."

"Yup. Mac. He's loyal, loving, and the best part is, he doesn't talk back. He does sometimes want to go outside in the middle of the night, but that comes with the territory."

"I see you haven't lost your sense of humor. I'm glad to hear you're doing okay. Jackson is worried about you, too."

"Jackson? Worried? About me?" My low-key son seldom worried about anything.

"All right. It's me who is worried about you being down there all alone. But he does care."

That's more like it, I thought and looked down at my fingernails. The nails were growing. I guess I hadn't been picking at them much lately. "No need to be worried. I'm keeping busy and I've met some nice people."

"Good. Okay, I love you."

"Bye. I love you, too, sweetheart." I hung up and looked at the dog, who had waited patiently. "Well, Mac, my friend. I guess roles really do change as we age. The child is now worried about the parent. Let's head home."

Mac stretched and yawned.

*

The next morning, I took care of Mac and headed to my new guilty pleasure—the outdoor shower. My morning ritual was both peaceful and invigorating. Me, the birds in the trees, the blue sky above, and the occasional praying mantis hanging from a wall.

Still, I hadn't completely abandoned my big-city ways. I liked my shower with plenty of hot water, especially when the morning air was a bit crisp.

Shower complete, I turned the water off. The left faucet handle twisted a bit farther than usual. Then it fell into my hand.

Huh. I didn't think I was that strong.

I tried to screw the handle back on. No dice. The whatchamacallit would not connect to the thingamajig.

"Oh, no. I'm not giving up my hot showers," I said aloud. My praying mantis friend stared at me, silent. "I guess I'm going to have to call Brian."

I shuddered at the thought of seeing him again. Not that I didn't want to; I was just embarrassed at what a fool I'd made of myself last time we'd met. But I didn't have a choice. I threw on my robe and headed inside. Grabbing the emergency list, I punched Brian's number into the phone hanging on the wall.

Please go to voicemail, please go to voicemail, please...

"Well, hello, sunshine!"

Definitely NOT voicemail.

"Um...Brian, this is Tess."

"I know. The caller ID came in as David's number. Unless Mac has grown opposable thumbs and learned how to dial, I figured it had to be you. Or do you have someone staying there with you now?" The playfulness of his voice took me aback.

"No, just me and Mac and the occasional praying mantis staring at me in the shower."

"Lucky praying mantis."

"Umm, yeah, well, speaking of showers. I just need some help... nothing major...just a little fix..." The jabbering teenager was back.

"Hold on, slow down. What's up?"

"I was in the shower this morning and the hot water faucet knob broke off in my hand."

"Interesting. And what were you doing that you had to grasp the hot water faucet knob so tightly that it broke?"

"Nothing. I swear. I just...it just broke off...I got the water shut off...nothing is spewing out. But I can't get it back on again. I'm sorry to bother you."

"It's definitely no bother. In fact, I'm finishing up a job this afternoon and not starting another until tomorrow morning. I could easily come over tonight."

"That would be, um...great. What time? Would you like dinner?"

Please say you're busy, please say you're busy.

"Dinner would be wonderful. How about I come over about seven-thirty? Would you rather go somewhere?"

"No, dinner here is fine." I mentally kicked myself. "Seven-thirty sounds great. I'll...well...see you then, I guess. Anything special you like?"

"Nope, I'm really easy. Speaking of easy, it should be an easy fix on the shower. I'll bring my tools and some extra parts just in case."

"I really appreciate it. I know how busy you are this time of year. Hey, why aren't you working right now?"

"I AM working. I do, however, pause to take phone calls from special VIP customers."

"Right, see you later."

All right, Einstein. Now what do I do? I looked at Mac. He yawned and curled up on his kitchen rug.

*

It was a warm evening. I changed into a bright yellow sundress with spaghetti straps. I hoped it was nice enough. He probably wouldn't be staying long, anyway.

"This is *not* a date," I said to Mac. He blinked a couple of times and yawned. "True, he is a very attractive man. Plus, he *is* single. Stop fussing, Tess! He's only here to fix the faucet. You're being silly."

At 7:30 on the dot, there was a rap on the screen door. Mac gave a welcoming "woof" from inside.

Butterflies did somersaults in my stomach.

This is ridiculous for a woman of my age, I thought, heading toward the door.

He looked every bit as breathtakingly handsome as he did at the bookstore. He was wearing the same style white polo shirt and khaki shorts, complementing his deep tan and muscular body. I reminded myself to breathe.

"Hi, you're very prompt. Please come in." A whiff of freshly laundered clothes mixed with a hint of musky cologne followed him. His hair had that just-rolled-out-of-bed messy look. He held a grocery bag.

"I wanted to bring something, so I brought a killer apple pie."

Suddenly he seemed shy and nervous. The awkward moment was interrupted by another "woof" and a silky blond head gently nudged his side.

"Hey, Mac. Looks like you haven't missed many meals since I last saw you." He scratched behind Mac's ears.

"Um...I'll take the pie into the kitchen so you can give Mac some much needed attention before he wags his tail off."

He was still holding the grocery bag.

"Were you able to find all of the parts?" I asked, motioning to the bag.

"Yes, I think I have what I need. It's all in the truck. Didn't want to drag my tools inside."

"Then what's in the bag?"

Reaching in, he pulled out two paperback books and an empty cardboard coffee cup stamped with the Browse and Brew logo.

"I don't understand."

"You left the shop so quickly the other day that you forgot your latte and your books. I couldn't bring the latte—it would be a little cold by now and I'd probably spill it all over the inside of the truck—so I brought you this."

He handed me the paper cup. Inside was a folded piece of paper.

Still confused, I opened it and read the handwritten note: *This certificate (actually just a piece of paper) entitles Tess to one latte courtesy of Brian. No expiration date.*

I stared at him, confused.

Clearing his throat, he shuffled his feet. "I was sorry my teasing chased you away, leaving your coffee and books. I hope this makes up for it."

I studied the books. They were the two I had been holding when he startled me in the bookstore.

"That is so sweet. You really didn't have to—"

"Tell you what, I'll go fix the faucet before dinner. Mac, want to join me outside?" At the word "outside," Mac sprang to his feet.

Breathe in, breathe out... I had opened a bottle of wine earlier. Hoping I picked a good bottle. The two dusty wineglasses I pulled from the cabinet were functional, but mismatched. Clearly, David wasn't much of an entertainer...or a wine drinker.

Feeling a little more in control, I went outside to see how Operation Shower Faucet was progressing. As I turned the corner of the house, Brian emerged from the enclosure carrying his tool belt and the old handle.

"Good as new. Nice place you have in there. I'll have to remember it," he said with a playful wink.

Did he just wink? Did the man just wink at me? I couldn't help but smile back. It was nice to have a handy man around the house. Stephen could barely screw in a light bulb.

"How much do I owe you?" *I should keep things professional, shouldn't I?*

"Nothing. Remember, David said any repairs would be on his tab. Let me put my tools in the truck."

When Brian came back in I told him I had opened a bottle of wine. Mac, perhaps sensing our guest was going to be there for a while, curled up on his kitchen rug and softly snored.

"No wine, thanks. I'll have water or if you have club soda would be great."

I carried our drinks to the screened porch. "I found some lime for the club soda."

"Great," he said.

We settled in to a rather awkward silence and then both tried to speak at the same time.

"Ladies first."

"I was just wondering what brought you to Clear Lake? Have you been a carpenter all of your life?"

"No, I have definitely not been a carpenter all my life. I've been here about five years Before that, I lived in Maryland, but spent most of my time in the Middle East. I did a few tours in the Army."

My eyes opened wide. "Really, you were a soldier? What did you do over there? That must have been scary."

"Yes, it had its moments." Brian looked at his feet. "I'll tell you about it someday. But right now, I want to hear all about you."

My life would seem boring in comparison, so I ignored the change in subject. "How did you end up here and not in Maryland?"

"My wife—"

"Wait. You're married?"

"Yes, I mean no. I'm divorced. Being married to a soldier isn't an easy life and she wanted out. We went our separate ways."

"I'm sorry." I wanted to reach out and cup his hand but the moment passed.

"David told me you lost your husband about a year ago," he said.

"I did. We were married a little more than thirty years." My throat tightened. I took a large sip of my wine. "We have grown twins, a boy and a girl; one in New York City and the other in California. They're amazing—I'm so proud of them. They're both on their own now."

"What do they do for a living?" He seemed genuinely interested.

"Jackson is a video producer/filmmaker and my daughter, Liz, is an attorney on Wall Street." I smiled at a memory. "Last Thanksgiving, I finally met Jackson's partner, Christopher, when they came home for the holiday. Liz brought her boyfriend, Rob. It was the first time we were all together since the funeral. I'm lucky to have such great kids."

Pausing, I studied the wine in my glass. "It's all so strange. I thought that retirement would mean having time to travel the world with the love of my life. Having new experiences. Learning new things. I couldn't have imagined being in this position."

"I'm sorry," Brian said softly and sipped his club soda.

I took a few breaths. "That's enough about me. Tell me more about you."

"Not much else to tell. Wandered around a bit after I left the service and finally settled here. My father was handy around the house and, somehow, I've always been, too. "So I guess I came by it naturally."

"Cheers…to happy wanderers then," I said, lifting my glass to meet his.

We sipped our drinks in silence, listening to the sounds of the evening. We emptied both of our glasses. I had not eaten much all day and the effects of that first glass of wine hit me faster than I expected.

"Why don't I get us some refills and then I'll get dinner?" I'm a lightweight when it comes to wine. Standing up, I tried to hide how unsteady I was on my feet.

Back in the kitchen, I felt like dancing. I was feeling more alive than I had in a long time.

Mac followed me onto the porch.

"Here you go. Freshly refilled," I said, handing the glass to Brian just as a rabbit sprinted across the lawn. Spotting prey, Mac jumped up, hit my legs and threw my already wobbly self completely off balance. The contents of my wineglass sloshed out and landed directly on the front of his white polo shirt.

"Oh, my God! I'm so sorry. Bad Mac! Let me get something to clean that up. That's going to stain." Words spilled from my mouth. "Let me go get one of David's old T-shirts or something that you can wear. I'm so, so sorry." Hastily setting down both glasses, I turned and almost sprinted into the bedroom. Digging around in David's dresser, I found a tie-dyed Grateful Dead shirt. It would have to do.

"I'll be right there!" I started to turn toward the door.

"You don't have to shout, I'm standing right here."

The voice was soft and sensual. Brian was standing just inside the bedroom door, naked from the waist up. "I put my shirt in the sink to soak. I hope that's okay."

His six-pack abs commanded my attention.

"Oh, yes, that's fine. Here's a T-shirt you can wear," I said, the heat rising from my neck all the way to my temples.

He took the shirt from my hand and tossed it to his right. It landed on the bed. Before I could say another word, he took three steps toward me, cradled my face in his hands and kissed me. Stunned, I kissed him back.

Gently holding my face in his hands, his eyes locked with mine.

"You are the most beautiful woman I've ever seen. I've thought that from the day I walked in the door. You might not have noticed, but you took my breath away." His voice was a whisper.

He smiled and his lips met mine once again, this time with more urgency and desire. My body responded in a way I hadn't felt in a long time. I pushed my hips into his, enjoying the tingling and warmth rising within me. I gasped a little through the kisses as I felt his excitement growing and pressing into me.

Suddenly he stopped. I was afraid he was going to say this was a mistake. Instead, he slid his fingers under the spaghetti straps of my sundress and gently pulled them off my shoulders. My dress fell to the floor. He stepped back and let his eyes roam over my body. I fought my self-conscious impulse to shield myself with my hands.

"You have the most beautiful breasts."

He gently guided me to the bed. I lay back and he lowered himself onto me. His kisses grew hotter and more intense as he worked his way down from my lips to my neck. He didn't stop until he reached my breasts. One after the other, he tenderly caressed their curves with his tongue, moving slowly from one breast to the other and back again. I couldn't suppress a groan of pleasure.

"If you think that felt good, wait until you see what else is in store." His voice was like velvet.

This is happening too soon. The thought raced through my mind. But body overruled my thoughts.

My breathing grew more and more rapid. While his tongue traveled the contours of my upper body, his hands were working their way lower. With one swift movement, he removed my panties. I didn't have much time to feel embarrassed by my nakedness.

His fingers found their target, and I gasped when he began slowly stroking and rubbing. I was surprised at how easily his fingers slipped in and out, but even more surprised at how aroused I was. I felt more than heard an unfamiliar moan coming from the very depths of my being.

"Oh my God…oh my God…oh my God!"

Like a roller coaster, the feeling grew. Climbing to the top, teetering for a split second, then exploding in a fury of motion. I felt like I was on the best carnival ride of my life.

"I told you that you had no idea what I had in store for you."

Brian unzipped his khaki shorts, and within seconds he was back on top of me, kissing, licking, sucking my lips.

"I want you so badly," I said aloud, surprising myself.

I heard him respond with a soft groan and within seconds he was inside me. It felt like he was plunging into my depths and I still couldn't get enough of him. The more he gave, the more I wanted. Afterward, we both lay in the king-sized bed panting, our hearts pounding outside our chests. Neither of us could muster the strength to speak.

Finally, Brian rolled onto his back.

"You know, this is entirely your fault. If you hadn't spilled that wine on me…"

He playfully kissed me again. This time all I could do was giggle. "I'll gladly take the blame."

*

I was poised at the escalator again. Trying to decide which way to go in the airport terminal. This time, there was someone beside me. Brian. He gently guided me by the arm. But which way? Neither of us knew.

*

A loud bang on the bedroom door roused me from the dream. Brian lay beside me. Both of us jolted wide awake, wondering what was going on. Another crash came from the bedroom door. It followed by a deep "woof."

"Mac!" We had left him on the porch. Brian must have closed the bedroom door before our…my mind started to drift back to earlier in the evening…

"Woof! Woof!"

"Poor guy, he probably needs to go outside."

We scrambled to find our clothes in the dark. My head was spinning from the wine. Brian quickly moved to the door and flung it open.

Mac stood on the other side. Confusion crossed his face. He obviously had expected me to open the door. Looking at Brian, it was as if to say *Are you friend or foe?*

"Mac, *treat!*" Brian said brightly.

The golden's mind was immediately made up…definitely friend.

I finished dressing and then walked from the bedroom into the living room just as Brian was letting an eager Mac out the front door.

"Oh, my goodness, we must have fallen asleep. Oh dear, poor Mac."

"Well, his loss was definitely our gain, don't you think?" Brian said with a mischievous grin.

The rumble of an empty stomach broke the mood. Not sure whose it was, we both laughed.

"I'm such a terrible hostess. Do you want something to eat?"

"I don't feel very hungry right now. I feel—well, rather satiated. Besides, I really should be going. Some of us have to work in the morning."

Brian gave me a kiss on the lips and turned to go.

"Wait…your shirt…don't you want it?" I asked.

"That's okay, I'll pick it up the next time I'm here. I can assure you there *will* be a next time."

His voice was husky and he leaned down to give me another, more passionate kiss. And he was out the door.

It was only 11 p.m. I felt alive and giddy as I locked the front door and headed back to the bedroom.

*

I couldn't believe how long I had slept. It was after 10 a.m.

Stretching, I thought of the events of the night before. Then it hit me. The pang of guilt about being with someone who wasn't Stephen. Was it too soon?

My phone buzzed from the other room. Too late, I answered right as the call hung up.

Looking at the display, I saw four missed calls. I must have slept like the dead. All of the calls were from Ava, my good friend and the Realtor who was listing our house. I hit redial.

"Ava, it's Tess. I'm so sorry…"

"Tess, I've been calling you for hours. I was afraid that a riptide might have gotten you. I was about to call the local police to go on a search and rescue mission." A smile came through her words.

Ava and I had both joined the book club about the same time and while careers and family absorbed most of our time, we had always enjoyed each other's company. Her voice sounded truly concerned.

"I'm sorry. What's up?"

"Someone's interested in your house."

"That's great."

"So, I have some good news and some bad news and then some more good news and some more bad news."

"Is this a puzzle?"

"The good news is they made an offer on the house."

"Great. That is good news. What about the rest?"

"The bad news is they want to move in four weeks. The other good news is it's an all-cash deal, full asking price. The other bad news is, they want to buy most of the furniture."

"Well, all I hear is good news."

"You mean you're okay with moving out that quickly?" Everything Ava did was with much precision and planning. To her, it must have sounded like a snap decision.

"Ava, I essentially moved out a long time ago, at least emotionally. And I was getting rid of stuff long before I began my house-sitting adventure. What is left can easily be put in a storage unit until I figure out what to do with it. I don't see it as a problem. Can we close that soon, though?"

"I think it will be okay. If we can't, they are willing to rent until things officially close. The husband is being relocated back to the United States from Singapore. They want to buy most of the furniture so they don't have to pay to ship theirs from Singapore. The wife came over early to find a place and fell in love with yours. She's staying with family, but eager to have a place of her own."

"Get the paperwork pulled together and I'll be there next week. I will see if Liz can come over and help me for a day or two. Just tell me when and we'll get it done."

"But where would you live?"

"I don't really know."

Rather than feeling distressed, it was as if a huge weight was lifted off my shoulders.

"Okay then, I'll work it out. Meanwhile, how are you doing? I mean, really doing?" Ava's voice was filled with genuine concern.

"I'm fine. It's beautiful here and I've made some really good friends, including one with four legs. I've never been so relaxed in my life. I do have to start thinking about the future soon, but I'm procrastinating."

"If you need anything, call."

"Thanks. We'll talk more next week. There is one thing. I will have to bring Mac with me."

"Mac?"

"Yes, the four-legged love of my life."

"Oh, sure, bring him along. It's still your house."

*

About 3 p.m., my phone rang again. This time it was Brian.

"How are you doing today?" His voice had that same husky quality as when he left the night before.

"I feel great! So that you don't think I have any regrets and have skipped town, I need to head up north next week. My Realtor has a buyer for my house and I have to complete the paperwork and clean things out. I'm taking Mac with me."

"You *are* coming back, aren't you?"

"Of course, I have to take care of David's place. Plus, I have to be here for you to retrieve your shirt from last night," I teased.

I could almost hear the relief across the phone.

The next couple of days were a whirlwind of activity. I had forgotten how much goes into selling a house.

I pulled together documents, sent e-mails to my attorney, to Ava, to David, and, of course, to my children. Liz agreed to come to New Jersey the evening after I arrived.

"I am looking forward to meeting Mac, even if I'm not much of a dog person," she said.

"Don't worry, he will win you over at first sight."

Brian was busy as the summer season was now in full swing. He called nightly to see how things were going. It was wonderful falling to sleep with his voice echoing in my head.

*

"Come on, Mac, let's go for a ride."

Mac eyed me warily. Car rides usually meant one thing: a trip to the vet. He was easily bribed, though, with a handful of treats.

It seemed like no time before we were pulling into my old drive-way. Everything seemed so much bigger than before. I was growing accustomed to cottage life. It looked, sounded, and smelled the same, but it no longer felt like home.

Entering the house, Mac took his time sniffing around the unfamiliar setting. After surveying his surroundings, Mac looked at me as if to ask, *What now?*

"Good question, my golden friend. Good question."

Where to start? Ava had said the buyers would consider anything I wanted to leave behind. Movers would be there in two days to pack up whatever was going into the storage unit. I had to sort out what would go into storage, what to leave behind, and what was going straight into the trash.

True to her promise, Ava had left a supply of packing boxes, tape, and wrapping paper.

"No time like the present, huh, Mac?"

I wasn't aware how much time had passed until I heard a familiar whimper. Mac. I had forgotten about him. He had curled up on an old rug and napped the afternoon away. I let him out to explore the huge backyard while I got his dinner ready.

I was suddenly hungry myself, and very tired. I had thought to bring Mac's food and water bowl, but nothing for myself.

"How about a brief tour of the neighborhood, Mac?" We hopped into the car and drove to the nearest drive-thru.

Later that night, I crawled into a bed I had slept in for thirty years, minus a few weeks. It was comforting, but empty. It was no longer the place for me.

*

I awoke to my phone buzzing. A little groggy, not sure where I was.

"Mom, don't forget I'm coming over tonight." It was the voice of my all-business-and-no-play daughter. "I'll be there at six-thirty and then we can go get dinner and catch up. See you tonight."

"Okay," was all I managed to say before she hung up.

Hours flew by as I separated things into *sell*, *donate*, and *storage* piles.

After walking Mac and taking a quick shower, I felt refreshed and ready to meet my daughter.

"Mom, oh my God, you look wonderful! I don't think I've ever seen you with a tan before!" Liz kissed my cheek. "Home still smells the same. Hey, is this your new 'boyfriend?'"

She bent down and scratched Mac behind the ears. Mac closed his eyes and lolled his tongue, clearly in love.

"Honey, I've only been gone a few weeks, of course it smells and looks the same."

I spent the next thirty minutes walking Liz through the house, making sure she agreed with all of my decisions.

"Mom, I'm fine with all of this. I just want you to be happy. That's what Jackson wants, too."

We picked a Chinese restaurant for dinner. "Tell me everything. What have you been doing, who have you been doing it with, and don't say you've just been hanging out with the dog. You are glowing too much for that to be the case." Liz unfolded her napkin.

"The town is small, but quaint. Mac and I walk a lot, which

explains the tan. I'm four blocks from the beach and downtown is only three blocks away."

"What about the house, how big is it?"

I laughed before I could respond.

"It's a dollhouse. I could fit the entire place inside the family room and kitchen of our soon-to-be-old house. There's a combination living room/eating area that blends into the kitchen, a lovely screened porch, a very large bedroom with king-size bed and a delightful outdoor shower."

"Wait, back up a minute, back up. What was that about a king-size bed?"

"David combined two bedrooms into one and filled it with a huge bed. It's comfy."

"Hmm…all alone in that big bed?"

"Well, there was one night last week…" I trailed off and started thinking about that wonderful night, but I quickly came to my senses. "Last week we had a brief, but loud thunderstorm in the middle of the night. I had a hundred pounds of golden retriever next to me after the first crash of thunder."

"Oh, Mom…I thought you were going to say you'd found someone special,"

I didn't know what to say. Should I mention Brian or not? I was relieved when she didn't give me the chance. I didn't know enough about him to talk to her about him anyway. I would have to fix that.

"You've always been there for me, for Jackson, for Dad, for everyone," Liz said now. "Never for yourself. It's time you thought about yourself for a change. You really have no idea how beautiful and wonderful and caring you are. You deserve to be happy and to be loved."

I could feel my eyes filling with tears "Thank you, sweetheart. These things take time.".

She dropped me off at the house, promising to visit me and

Mac at the shore before the end of the summer. Her words echoed in my head.

You deserve to be happy and to be loved.

*

The next day was filled with more e-mails, phone calls, and conversations with attorneys and real estate agents.

As I crawled into bed that night, I felt homesick. But how could that be? I was in my home.

I miss the cottage and I miss Brian!

Grabbing the phone, I hit the speed dial for his number. He answered almost immediately.

"Hi there, stranger."

"I didn't wake you up, did I?"

"Not at all. I was just lying in bed hoping that my phone would ring and a beautiful, sexy woman would be on the other end."

"Well, sorry to disappoint. I was just missing you and wanted to hear your voice."

"No disappointment at all. There is a very sexy woman on the other side of this conversation."

I blushed and then told him all that was happening and how Mac was adjusting. He filled me in on his busy schedule.

"If all goes well, I should be home tomorrow night late."

"Great. Call me when you get within about fifteen minutes of the house and I'll meet you there."

"But it will be late."

"It's never too late."

I recognized the husky voice and could feel myself melting into the bed.

*

Bright and early the next morning, I gave the house one last look-through, taking my time going through each room, checking drawers, and under beds. All that was left was the final paperwork.

The buyers had bought most of the furniture, as well as the appliances, lawn mower, and other home maintenance equipment.

"The buyer's Realtor told me that the wife felt like the stars had aligned when she saw your house. She also told me that the couple is expecting their first child," Ava had said on the phone the day before.

It all reminded me of myself decades before, moving into a big home where I would raise a family. My life had changed.

I was not moving out, I was moving on.

*

Mac and I hit the road later than I planned.

It was close to midnight when I called Brian with my fifteen-minute heads-up.

He was standing on the front steps as I pulled into the driveway. I couldn't get out of the car fast enough. Mac and I clamored over each other to see who would get to Brian first. He was leaning nonchalantly against the front door, arms crossed in front of him.

"What took you so long?"

This time we didn't even attempt the pretense of dinner or chitchat. As soon as we were in the house and I got Mac fed and settled, we were in the bedroom.

Afterward, we lay basking in the glow of lovemaking. He pulled me close to him, intertwined his hand in mine. "I missed you so much."

"I missed you, too."

Over the remainder of the summer, we made love more than I ever thought I'd experience at my age. We had picnic lunches, long afternoon boat rides, and late-night walks on the beach. These simple pleasures with Brian helped lift the weight of my mourning.

Weeks passed in this dreamy bliss until it was time for me to make some decisions. I was going to have to find another place to live. David would be home soon. I liked this new life and seemed to be falling in love again. I wanted nothing more than to stay here with Brian and enjoy my new easygoing life. Maybe I'd look for a small place to buy or rent right here.

*

On one of our long afternoons together, Brian and I were eating lunch in a neighboring town. A large man with a weight-lifter's body squeezed into a too-tight T-shirt and shorts approached.

"Brian, man. Is that you?"

Brian stood and faced him. "Hock? Hock? No way!"

They slammed into each other, arms encircling in a man hug.

"How have you been?" Hock asked.

"Great. Just great!" Brian replied. "Man, look at you all beefed up. What're you up to?"

"I train business suits to look like warriors. They pay a lot of money to get the look." Hock flexed and did a bodybuilder's pose "So, I have to keep myself up."

Brian chuckled. "Hock, this is Tess."

I rose and shook his hand.

"This man," Hock began and went over and slapped Brian's back. "He's a hero, you know that? He saved my ass...ah, life in Afghanistan."

"I'm just glad your ass didn't look like it does now or I'd never have been able to move you."

Brian and Hock roared with laughter.

I looked at Brian and I felt a huge rush of pride. *A hero, I'm dating a hero.*

*

I couldn't even bear the thought of being away from Brian long enough to attend the annual Build-a-Home fund-raiser that Bri and Madeline were chairing back in Chester. I lied through my teeth when I left my excuse on Bri's voicemail.

231

"I'm so sorry, Bri, but I can't make it back. I'll put a check in the mail though."

*

"I have to leave early this morning. I have sort of a breakfast meeting. I'll feed Mac and take him outside first," Brian said, leaning over to kiss me.

"Mmm...okay." I rolled over, welcoming the chance to be lazy.

An hour later, I forced myself out of bed.

I decided to grab a cup of coffee and a pastry from the Browse and Brew. It was one of those beautiful end-of-summer days with a few fluffy clouds dotting the sky. I couldn't help but smile as Mac and I walked the now-familiar route.

I was still smiling when I opened the door to the coffee shop. One step in, my smile froze. There on the Brew side was Brian. He sat with a woman whose back was to me. She had shiny long blond hair and I could tell she was young. They were deep in conversation. Brian's eyes looked directly into hers. He didn't notice me when I'd walked in. I didn't know what to do. I felt like I had been punched in the gut.

I have to get out before he sees me. But before I turned away to leave, Brian's eyes met mine. I quickly turned around and ran for the door.

"Tess, Tess..."

I could hear him calling. I grabbed Mac by the leash and stumbled home. My eyes stinging with disappointment that Brian had not followed me, I collapsed on the couch. The stress and strain of the past couple of years all came crashing down. I slid from the cushions onto the floor, sobbing in a heap. Mac stood patiently by my side.

Thank God I have you, Mac! I hugged him tight. He didn't seem to mind.

When the tears ebbed, the hiccups began. Mac's head lay on my lap. I scratched him behind his ears.

I ignored the knock on the screen door.

"Tess... Can I come in?"

"Sure," I said, hiccupping. I wiped tears away with the back of my hand.

"I'm so sorry. I should have told you earlier."

"No, it's okay. She's beautiful, Brian." Another round of tears formed behind my eyes.

"She is. She's my daughter." His voice was almost a whisper.

"What?"

"We need to talk." He held his arms out to me and gently pulled me up off the floor.

I just stared at him, too stunned to think.

"How about I make us some coffee? It's a beautiful day, we can talk on the porch. Okay?"

I collapsed onto the porch chair.

Brian came back with two cups of coffee and sat in the chair across from me.

"Tess..."

"You didn't tell me you had a daughter." I blurted out.

"It didn't come up." He couldn't even look me in the eye. "But I should have told you."

"I told you all about my children. Why wouldn't you tell me about your daughter? What else don't I know?"

"If I told you about my daughter it would lead to something I wasn't ready to talk about. What I told you was the truth, but I didn't tell you the whole story." Brian put his coffee mug on the side table and leaned over the chair resting his elbows on his legs. His hands cupped the outside of both of my legs.

"I *was* married when I was in the Army. I left out that I was in Special Forces. Without going into detail, I was someone who was gone too often, not able to tell anyone, not even my wife, where I was or what I was doing. I rarely saw Emily when she was a baby." He stared at the ground.

When Brian looked up his eyes were moist. "We fought a lot when I was home on leave. I started drinking a few beers at night, then a few more." He coughed and sat back. "My drinking picked up in the Middle East." He stopped talking and looked off as if remembering something,

"That's why you never drank wine or anything else when we went out to dinner?" I realized. I hadn't put it together until now.

"After a while, my wife decided that it wasn't the life she wanted for herself or for our daughter. She was right. To her credit, she waited for me to come home to tell me and didn't send me a Dear John letter while I was deployed.

"I left for Iraq and started drinking all the time. During a training maneuver, I fell, hit my head, and blacked out." He paused for a few seconds, staring into his coffee cup. "If that had happened during a real maneuver, I could have endangered myself and my squad."

Brian stayed quiet for a few minutes. I didn't know what to say.

"I had such a strong desire to serve my country, but it took its toll. My commander arranged for me to be honorably discharged and I returned home. My wife had moved from Maryland to Pennsylvania with our daughter." His voice was filled with regret.

"I wandered around a bit, drank way too much, and somehow found my way here. David helped me pull myself back together."

I took another deep breath.

"Today was the first time I've seen my daughter since she was five years old. While you were gone last week, I did a lot of thinking. Meeting you made me see that it was time to let others back into my life. I had to right an old wrong, to atone. I called her mother and asked if she could tell Emily I really wanted to get to know her. Emily agreed to come to meet me this morning. She lives in Philadelphia. She's been close by me all this time."

Brian stopped. He stared at his hands for a minute and then looked into my eyes.

"I hope you can forgive me, Tess. I didn't mean to keep any part of my past a secret. I didn't mean to hurt you. I'm ashamed." His eyes clouded with tears. "I know this is probably a lot to take in, so I think I had better leave and give you some time."

He stood and wavered for a minute, as if he wanted to lean down and kiss me, but didn't. He turned to leave.

"Brian. Stay." I called out after him.

He hesitated at the door. The beginning of a smile tipped the corners of his mouth and eased his frown lines. I rose and walked over, throwing my arms around him. He had a daughter. She would be about Liz's age. I wondered if she had his blue eyes, his dazzling smile. His charm.

Mac sat at my feet looking up at the two of us wrapped together. I could feel his wet nose on my thigh. Maybe he was giving his approval.

Brian and I sat on the couch and talked for hours—touching and loving. We tumbled into bed in a frenzied state of passion. Afterward, I stroked Brian's back until he fell asleep. As my eyes began to close, I turned on my side. The alarm's slight glow illuminated a picture on the nightstand of my family in California. We had all been so young. I looked at Stephen. God, I loved him and I always would. It was so hard, but I knew he would want me to move on. I grabbed the picture and held it as I slept.

*

Once again, I was face-to-face with the airport escalator. Brian was by my side. I looked at his clear blue eyes, back at the escalator and back at him. I felt, rather than heard him ask, "Well, where do we go from here?"

A few yards behind Brian stood another man. Stephen. He smiled, nodded his head, and disappeared.

I took Brian's hand in mine. I finally knew where I was going. Together, we walked toward the gate marked "Italy."

TEMPTING FATE

S UMMER DRIFTED ON, languid and relaxed, a great break from the hectic school year. In Japan, the Everall deal hit some snags, so Mark and his colleague, Bruce, took advantage of the delay to travel to Singapore and then California to cope with other emerging deals. By the time they returned to Japan, almost two weeks had passed. Communication between Mark and me consisted of rushed calls in the middle of the night, and texts squeezed between meetings, business dinners, and airline flights. He tried hard to keep in touch, but the demands of his job and the time difference made it tough.

Although Mark had never been gone for this long at one stretch, I adjusted to his absence and even took a certain pride in how I efficiently managed the household. Over our son Brandon's "man of the house" objections, I hired a landscaper to mow the lawn. Mark would miss his therapeutic weekly chore, but I was afraid if the grass grew any taller the neighbors would start a petition about the condition of our property.

The morning I signed the contract with the landscaper, I walked the property with him to point out a problem bald area. Mark could never figure out why grass didn't grow there. As we passed it, the landscaper kept staring at the eyesore in the corner. Funny, many days I simply blocked out the massive unfinished wreck of tree house wood that sat on the lawn waiting for Mark to build it. Other times I kept the curtains closed so I wouldn't have to face it.

I was so focused on the landscaper's reaction that I didn't see the bucket of nails stashed under a tarp. I knocked into it hard, spilling the nails onto the grass and gouging my shin with the edge of the bucket. *Damn it, Mark!* For a second I considered heaving the bucket over the fence and crying.

The landscaper eyed me nervously, handed me a clean bandana to stop the bleeding, and said a quick goodbye over his shoulder as he almost ran to his truck. That's one way to chase a man away—look like you're about to break into tears.

*

Chester emptied in July as my neighbors fled to vacation homes up and down the East Coast. At the gym, even the training group thinned out. Thomas and his family left for a good portion of the summer, and the supermodel moms split their vacation time between Nantucket and Bay Head homes, leaving Jim to train with me one-on-one several mornings a week. We fell into the habit of stopping at the Grounds Crew to grab an iced coffee or tea as we cooled down.

The time spent alone with Jim—his humor, the intent way he looked at me, the electric current when we happened to brush against each other—preyed on my mind. The story about his ex-wife made him more attractive to me. To keep me from fixating on him, I doubled up on long walks with the dogs, watercolor classes, lengthy solo runs, and household chores. But even so, I fantasized about Jim stretching me out after a hard run, his hands inching up my shorts, fingers grazing my panties, culminating in torrid sex on the gym mats. I'd tuck the kids into bed early, revisiting my daydreams with a glass of wine. One week, overwhelmed by the intensity of my imaginings, I decided to stay away from the gym.

Three days later, Jim called. "Hey, are you okay? I was worried when you didn't show up. You never miss a session. Did you injure yourself?"

"No, no, not at all," I stammered. "I'm fine. I…I just had a crazy few days and couldn't make it. It's nice of you to check on me."

"Glad to hear it. We…missed you," he stuttered, then stopped. The pause felt long to me. "Now that Thomas's back in town," he finally said, "we came up with an idea for this week. Friday is supposed to be absolutely perfect weather."

Where is he going with this?

"We're planning on driving down to the beach and doing a trial shore run. We'll go over the course of your September race. I'm going to bring Gracie and make a day of it. Thomas and his boys are coming, too. It'll be good practice for all of you, and testing your stamina in the summer heat will prepare you for the races you and Thomas will run in the cooler fall weather."

I hesitated, not wanting to seem overeager. But I was elated.

"I think that we should be able to go on Friday," I said. *Why didn't I just tell him that Brandon and Katie wouldn't be able to join me?* They already had plans for the day as well as sleepovers at friends' houses on Friday night. I'd planned to work around the house, and log some miles running. But Jim's proposal was much more fun—if not particularly safe.

·I purchased a new one-piece suit, teal with little cutouts at the sides. I loved the color, and it was practical for swimming, with a touch of sexiness at the midriff. After all the running and training, my body was toned. I could've comfortably worn a two-piece, but after two decades of sporting a maillot, donning a bikini for a man other than my husband was a line I couldn't bring myself to cross.

Friday dawned crisp and bright, a glorious day. Each family was to drive to the shore separately and meet up at Surf Bright Beach.

I wore my running gear, threw my swimsuit, sunscreen, and towel in a tote along with my watercolor set and paper, and filled the big cooler with some water bottles, a batch of homemade Snicker doodles for the kids, an antipasto snack platter and a six-pack of beer for the grown-ups. *All bases covered*, I thought. I tossed a beach chair into the back of the Expedition, then hopped into the car and got a jump on what would definitely prove to be heavy traffic.

At the Surf Bright Beach parking lot, I texted Thomas and Jim. I hoped that we would get in our thirteen-mile run first and enjoy the beach for the rest of day. Jim pulled up with his daughter, Gracie. Immediately afterward, a minivan with two other girls and their moms slid into the spot next to him. I froze in my car seat, watching the group. Jim hugged Gracie goodbye as she hurried off with the two women and their daughters. The little girls, slathered in sunscreen, sprinted onto the beach, flip-flops shooting sand up the backs of their calves so their legs were coated like shake and bake chicken pieces. The mothers followed behind, laden with beach paraphernalia.

I watched as Jim glanced at his phone, smiled, and began glancing around. I clambered out of the SUV before he spied me ogling him.

"Hey," I yelled across the row of parking spaces.

"Hey, yourself." His eyes beamed and his wide smile looked brilliant against his tan. "My sister, my niece, and their friends just headed onto the beach, if Brandon and Katie would like to join them while we run. Thomas just texted me that he won't be able to come today. His kids are sick and his wife is away, so he's playing nurse. I think he's jealous that we'll be logging extra miles today. You know how competitive he is."

"Uh, um... my kids ditched me. They got better offers and decided to pass on a day with Mom at the beach." I cringed, afraid Jim might think I'd orchestrated this kid-less arrangement.

His smile lit up his whole face, contrasting with his next words.

"Too bad. Gracie was looking forward to seeing Katie. But it's a great day for a run and I'll make sure you get home in plenty of time for the kids' dinner."

I pursed my lips, trying to decide if I should tell him about the kids' evening plans. I opted to keep quiet.

We double-checked the map of my half-marathon's route, and set out jogging at a reasonable speed.

I stopped twice to retie the perfect bow in my shoelaces, eager to steal a few moments of rest.

At about the eight-mile mark, he pointed. "Here's the sign where you'll begin entering the steep incline." And later: "See how the path narrows here before the brush? You'll need to jockey for position when you approach that point."

After the run, we cooled down at a picnic bench. "Want to hit the beach now?" he asked.

"Sure." I squirmed a bit, unsure what Jim's sister would think of me: some woman with a wedding band spending a day at the beach with her divorced brother.

"You know," he said slowly. "Your kids aren't here…and my sister loves having Gracie around…and Gracie is crazy about my niece's friends. I'm sure she's having a ball. Why not take advantage and be grown-ups for a change? Let's sit by ourselves on the beach."

"Sounds good to me."

We rinsed off in the open outdoor showers, then disappeared into the restrooms to change into our suits and slather ourselves in sunscreen. Jim bought two daily beach badges and we plopped blankets down and set up our beach chairs.

The crystal clear blue sky was spectacular. Fluffy white cumulus clouds moved slowly high in the sky. I was relieved that we'd avoided the usual New Jersey summer humidity. American flags fluttered in the soft breeze. Surprisingly for a Friday, there was ample room. Usually, beachgoers were packed in like sardines.

I looked around. On the newly repaired wooden boardwalk, a

healthy crop of runners and walkers of all ages strolled, and at the concession stands, customers lined up for hot dogs, hamburgers, and milkshakes. Kids used boogie boards in the pristine blue-green sea, fishing boats dotted the horizon, and kayaks plied the water closer to shore. Above, propeller planes trailed advertisement banners, the hum of their motors pleasant. The boom of the crashing waves, the squeals of happy children, the caws of seagulls, and the rhythmic thumping of beach paddle ball volleys—all part of the din of the Jersey Shore, music to this Midwestern gal's ears.

"Want to go for a dip?" Jim asked, already up and heading toward the water. He waded into the surf, diving through a breaking wave. I took my time adjusting to the water temperature, cool in contrast to the warm air. When I finally dunked my hair, I swam out to Jim, who was floating near the boogie-boarders and body surfers just beyond the breakers, waiting for that dream wave to deliver them to shore. I looked out to sea, where entwined couples were oblivious to the world around them. I was glad Jim didn't seem to notice. He swam over to me. We chatted, bobbing in the waves. I can't recall ever feeling so carefree at the beach. No children to keep an eye on, no multiple trips toting cargo gear from the car. Unadulterated bliss.

As we exited the water, I noted women of all ages staring at him admiringly. I found it endearing that he seemed oblivious of his good looks. Surreptitiously, I checked Jim out. Funny. All that time training and I had never before seen him with his shirt off. His chest was as impressive as I'd pictured in my daydreams. His swim trunks were slightly baggy but deliciously snug around his muscular rear.

Drying off, draping my damp towel over the back of my beach chair, I noticed him glancing at my chest, the cutouts at the side of my bathing suit, and my rear end. I blushed, feeling a twinge below. *How can he do that without even touching me?*

We ate the antipasto and drank some water, then each had a beer.

"You really will be able to clock a great time at the race," he said, "if you keep training as intently as you have been. You'll be amazed how well you do in September."

He opened another Bud, took a lengthy swig, then added, "You look fantastic. And you owe it to your hard work."

I took a few moments to savor the compliment. "Thank you," I gushed. "I owe it all to your training. I feel so strong, so good."

I hadn't drunk so much daytime alcohol in a while. Several families were beginning to pack up, probably wanting to beat the traffic north.

"Do you get down here much in the summer?" I asked.

"We used to come a lot as a family. Since Marci left, we've only come to the beach a couple times, usually with my sister and her family."

There, he had broached the subject.

"If you don't mind me asking, what happened with Marci? If it's none of my business, please say so." It felt somehow liberating to talk while staring out at the beautiful blue sea, similar to how a car ride can loosen passengers' lips and inhibitions. There is something to be said for avoiding eye contact.

He swigged some beer and sighed before he answered. "She tried to tell me that she was unhappy for a long time. I thought it was just a phase. Then she hooked up with the contractor building the addition at our house. I wanted to work through what I assumed was a one-time 'indiscretion;' I said that I could forgive her and move forward. But she said that she was falling in love with the guy, that he gave her emotionally what I didn't anymore." Another sigh. "Now she's living with him in Florida and only sees Gracie about every other month." He polished off the rest of the beer in one gulp. "What about you? I don't see your husband around much."

He turned and looked directly at me. I was tongue-tied. I had spent hours thinking about my deteriorating relationship with my husband. But I still didn't know how to describe it to someone else, especially Jim. I'd lain in bed most nights this week creating sexual fantasies about him, yet somehow I still felt disloyal bad-mouthing Mark.

"It's hard to explain. He's gone so much lately, traveling for work, and we've drifted apart. Sometimes I feel like I don't know him. It's…it's exhausting. Lonely." The beers were getting to me, but talking did seem to help.

We both sat staring at the ocean as the early evening sun sank lower in the sky and our words sank in. He finally broke the silence. "Pretty sunset."

I rose a bit wobbly from my chair. "Yes, I'd like to paint it."

My alcohol haze lifted as I unpacked my watercolor set and painted broad strokes, trying to capture the shifting pastels of the summer sunset. I didn't realize that Jim was standing behind my chair watching me work. He gently brushed my hair off my neck. "You truly are a woman of many talents. That's unbelievable."

I thrilled at his words and his touch, silently continuing to paint. *What am I doing?*

His phone buzzed and he checked the text message. "My sister wants to take Gracie for ice cream, a round of mini golf and then for a cousin sleepover. You probably need to be getting home soon, huh?" His head was bent over his phone as he texted.

I hesitated a beat before answering. "Actually, I'm covered myself until after dinner." I still didn't feel ready to advertise that I was on my own that night.

He flashed an impish grin. "In that case, why don't we continue being grown-ups and meander over to the tiki hut for a quick bite and listen to some music before we head home?"

"Sounds great to me. Let me just finish this up."

The tiki hut was a Caribbean seaside bar relocated to the middle of the Jersey coast. A live band played island music, daiquiris and margaritas flowed, and the tables were populated by couples from barely legal twentysomethings to gray- and blue-haired couples. The sky was stained in breathtaking color and everyone seemed to be in a great mood after such a spectacular summer day. We each had a strawberry daiquiri and shared some clams oreganata. Jim wiped some breadcrumbs from my cheek and pushed my hair behind one ear as the breeze picked up. The alcohol warmed me from inside and I closed my eyes at his touch. I had to resist kissing his hand as it traveled across my face. His eyes looked even bluer against his sun-kissed face. As he squeezed my knee while making a point, instantaneous warmth snaked between my legs. Just then, my phone buzzed. *The kids*, I thought with a start.

Lots of action going on here! The text was from Bri. I glanced frantically around the bar. *Was she here? Had she seen us? No, I'm tipsy. She's back in Chester.* But what could she be talking about? She had offered to let our dogs out today while I was gone. I fumbled with the phone, texting her back. *What?*

"Problem?" Jim asked.

"No, but I probably should be getting back home soon. This has been such a perfect day. I can't tell you what a nice time I've had—I always have—with you," I blurted. Then, to my shock, I began crying softly. He brushed my cheek to wipe my tears away.

He started to say something but stopped, his hand now resting gently on my chin.

"Let's have some coffee and sober up and I'll follow you up the parkway to make sure you get home safely." His voice was soft.

Bri never texted back. I guess it wasn't anything important.

We sat for a while longer and switched to coffee before our drive home. Twilight began its descent. Tapping my foot in time with the music, my flip-flop fell off. Jim pounced off his stool, knelt down and put it back on my foot, Prince Charming style, lingering on my arch, rubbing my instep. As the wind picked up and I caught a chill, he rubbed my arms to warm me. We probably look like just another married couple enjoying a romantic night by the beach while a babysitter watched the kids.

I was thrilled by this undivided attention. I reached out to touch his wrist, playing with his watch, circling my fingers around his pulse. His eyes widened, then closed, seeming to savor my touch.

"Actually…" *Could I say it?* "Actually," I cleared my throat and launched into my best—but still awkward—coquettish voice. "I don't have to be home tonight." A quiet nervous laugh as I awaited a response.

Surprise and relief crossed his face before he smiled and grabbed my hand. "If you're okay to drive, let's head north."

We walked to my car. I leaned against the door and looked at him. He turned to me, gingerly touching my shoulder, then, taking my silence as a cue, leaned into me and kissed me on the lips, softly at first, then more insistently. I opened my mouth wide for his tongue, and pressing myself against his body, felt him grow hard against me. I wrapped my arms around his neck and pushed against him. His breath quickened, and I began kissing him, ravenously, almost desperately. Sober as I was, I couldn't blame the passion on alcohol. It was pure Jim. I couldn't stop myself.

"Oh, babe," he moaned softly.

I froze. *Mark.*

What the hell am I doing? Can I really throw my marriage away like this? I began crying and he pulled away slightly.

"I…I can't do this," I stuttered between sobs. "I want to but I can't. I shouldn't be here. I'm so sorry. I think we would be great together, but I just can't do this," I babbled. "I'm sorry." I peeled myself from his body.

He backed away from my longing body but his hand remained tenderly on my shoulder. He looked wistful but not angry.

"It's all right. Don't cry. It's okay. I dream about being with you all the time, but I guess it isn't right for you now." He nuzzled his face into my neck and we rested there for a minute. "If things change…" his voice trailed off.

Without a word, I climbed into my car, heaved a sigh, wiped my face, and carefully drove off, locking eyes with Jim as I passed him.

I navigated safely home, forcing myself to concentrate on the road rather than replaying his luscious kisses. I wanted to make sense of the day. Heartbroken, guilty, and lonely, I looked forward to collapsing into bed, hoping that sleep would somehow magically ease my guilt.

Pulling into the driveway, I was startled at the light spilling from my backyard. The kitchen lights were on as well. About to call the police, I realized that Bri was probably inside letting the dogs out again. I walked around back and into a blaze of spotlights. In the mammoth corner oak tree was a massive tree house, complete with rope ladder, tire swing below, and slide curving down from an opening in one of the tree-house walls. The roof was only half finished, and pieces of lumber still littered the grass, but it was a nearly completed tree house, almost fifteen feet high. The sound of hammering reached me as I approached. Some music was playing as well.

"Hello?" I called out uncertainly.

Mark peeked his head over the wall. He was sweaty and covered in sawdust, his smile beaming down on me.

"Oh my God, why are you home early?" As soon as the words left my mouth I realized how guilty they sounded.

"Come on up, babe! I wanted to surprise you. I want to talk to you."

"Is this thing sturdy?" I wobbled on the rope ladder. The rickety ladder swayed and my flip-flops slipped on the rungs.

Suddenly, the lights went out and the music stopped. I stopped my ascent. "Mark. What's happening?"

"Don't worry. I have a light up here."

Light streamed above and I continued up the ladder.

Once I reached the top, the transformation was unbelievable. Two of the walls were painted pink, and the other two blue, the kids' favorite colors. A large macramé rope hammock hung from one corner, and a small bookcase occupied one wall. A floor below enclosed a reading nook with big pillows depicting Bill the Buddy and Princess Penny, beloved cartoon characters from the kids' early childhood. Built-in benches lined one wall. Through an opening in the tree-house wall, a chute slide spiraled to the ground. I had forgotten what a skilled handyman Mark had been during the early years of our marriage.

"Check it out," he said as he hoisted the rope ladder up through the opening and closed a hatch door in the floor, essentially sealing us off from the ground. Seeing how thrilled he was, I didn't have the heart to point out that we might not want the kids to be able to lock themselves away from us so easily.

"What's this?" I pointed to a rectangular section on the wall.

"I thought it would be nice if you painted some kind of picture here for the kids. I bought you a bunch of paints. Are they the right kind? We can exchange them if they aren't."

I looked at the small cans of paint, then back at Mark.

He stood up straight, looking around, and smiled. He continued talking about what he was going to do to this nook and that wall. And my heart fell, recalling what I had been doing a mere hour ago.

"I couldn't wait to get home to see you," he said. "This was one long, wild trip. The deal finally went through. But I have something weird to tell you, babe. Come here, sit down on this bench."

A paper coffee takeout cup and two empty beer cans were strewn on the wooden planks of the floor. "Here's a bottle of wine for us. I don't want you to hear this from anyone else, so I jumped on a plane right away." He poured us each some wine into a mason jar, which I hoped hadn't held nails earlier in the day.

"What is it?" Apprehension crept into my voice. Maybe I wasn't the only one with a secret.

"Don't worry. Nothing bad actually happened, but I have to tell you something." He was pacing along the walls of the tree house, ducking when he had to, gesturing with his hands, the headlamp beam swiveling around like a boat out on night patrol. I gently switched his headlamp off, removed it, and placed it on the floor.

"The deal was touch and go at the end. The whole thing threatened to fall apart at the last minute. When it finally did close, we all were exhausted, relieved, and in the mood to celebrate. Everyone from both companies went out for a huge dinner at the restaurant in our hotel. The liquor and sake were out of control. The waiters refilled glasses as soon as they were half empty. The Japanese especially were boozing it up. For Christ's sake, I've got forty pounds on the biggest one of them, and they were still drinking me under the table. Finally, I'd had enough, excused myself, and stumbled up to my hotel room."

He stopped pacing and faced me directly.

"Hanna, a naked woman was waiting for me on the bed. I swear I didn't touch her. It just shocked me out of my drunken stupor. Apparently, these 'gifts' aren't unheard of. When I asked her to leave, she looked embarrassed. Mortified really. It turns out she is married and this is how she makes a living. I'd heard rumors about this kind of thing, but I was still unprepared." He took a deep breath, looked at my stricken face, squeezed my hand, and continued.

"She got dressed and we talked a little bit. I didn't want her to be offended. I told her I was married to my best friend and lover and that I could never betray her. I couldn't wrap my head around the fact that she does this for a living. Talk about culture shock. As soon as she left, I packed up, took a cab to the airport, and booked the first flight out."

Pausing for breath, Mark looked me in the eyes.

"Seeing her sitting there looking so lost and sad made me miss you even more. I love you." Mark put his arm around me. "I probably don't tell you that enough. You've been such a team player taking on the house and kids by yourself. And to show my appreciation for all you do, I thought I'd get as much of the tree house done as I could today."

"How in the world did you get so much done in such a short time?" I asked.

"The base was already done. The rest is fairly easy," Mark moved closer to me. "I saw Bri when I arrived from the airport and she told me that you were at the beach for the day with your gym group and that the kids were spending the night out. So, I decided to get this done and surprise you guys." He kissed my neck. "What do you think? Not too bad for someone working on a few hours' sleep, huh?"

I looked into his eyes, and swept the sawdust from his tousled curls. "I love it. It's absolutely incredible."

He had on his old work jeans, a tool belt, and his Timberland boots. My husband pulled off the sexy construction worker look quite well. I grabbed his hand and kissed it. He led me to the hammock and we lay there, cuddling together. He began to nuzzle and kiss my neck, trailing his hand down the front of my cover-up.

"Mmm. You smell like the beach."

I froze for a guilty second.

Mark touched the back of my neck and swirled my hair. As he kissed me softly on the back of my neck, I melted into his arms.

I reached down, unfastened and removed his tool belt, letting my hand linger over the front of his jeans. He drew me close to him, and we turned to face each other, listing slightly in the hammock. Our hands roamed over each other's clothed bodies, as if exploring new territory. Mark's rippled chest and firm biceps surprised me. Had it been that long since I had touched him? I hoped he noticed my toned legs and core as well.

It took a while for us to find our balance, but our hands kept working as the perch swayed. Mark lifted my cover-up over my head, and kissed each shoulder before sliding down my bathing suit straps and peeling the suit off me. The cool air and breeze felt delicious on my bare chest and thighs as he rubbed his face between my breasts and over my belly, awakening my nipples and every nerve in my body. I unzipped his jeans and he kicked off his boots. He wiggled out of his pants and underwear, almost flipping us both out of the hammock in the process. The moonlight poured into our roofless loft, illuminating us both as we stared at one other hungrily, as if for the first time.

"I promise I won't neglect us anymore, babe. I love you and I'll give you the attention you deserve," he whispered as he glided his hands tenderly up my thighs and between my legs.

· I quivered with anticipation. "We can't let that happen again," I said breathlessly. "It almost ruined us."

His long legs straddled me and I let out a whimper as we entwined. I was on a rocking boat, rising to meet him, clasping his shoulders, letting my hands roam his muscular back and chiseled bottom. I was desperate to accept all of him and arched my back in pleasure. We couldn't get enough of each other, like a pair of over-sexed teenagers in love.

We rocked furiously in the hammock, the rope pressing against my bare skin. Mark carefully reached down to get the Bill the Buddy pillow, and gently propped it under my back and hips. *Not exactly an approved use of trademarked Buddy merchandise*, I mused, smiling. It had been ages since we had connected so closely, in tune with each other's bodies, seemingly reading each other's minds. Furiously, we rode the waves of passion until we both collapsed in ecstasy, sweaty and chilled.

Wrapped in each other's arms, we kissed and lay there catching our breath. Content, we stared up at the moon and stars.

Several minutes later, we heard rustling in the bushes. "Hey, are you guys up there?" Bri called. "Do you need me to take the dogs out again?"

"No, it's okay, Bri. Thanks. We'll let them out in a few minutes," I called down.

"Enjoying that little love nest? Do you have to put a sign up? You know: 'When the hammock's a rockin', don't come a knockin.'"

She chuckled at her joke, and after a few seconds Mark and I laughed as well.

"I'm glad that you're both home. Stop by for a drink tomorrow night if you're around. Eric and I will be home enjoying some cocktails outside on the patio. I promise we won't talk about the Build-a-Home gala!"

We let the dogs roam the fenced yard and thoroughly confused them when we disappeared into our tree loft with provisions of water, more wine, and some cheese. My husband and I rested in each other's arms and talked for hours—about our personal hopes and dreams, our marriage, the children, our fears, Mark's job, and my renewed love of art and running. We condensed two years' worth of meaningful dialogue into one night of intense sharing. I almost broached the subject of Jim, but didn't. I felt that our relationship was strong enough to weather that storm, but I didn't want anything to derail it. We vowed that night to reconnect at least one night a week, regardless of the demands on our time.

By the end of the night we had fully mastered the logistics of "hammock time."

For the rest of the night, we lounged, my head on Mark's chest, both of us overflowing with happiness and satisfaction. Arms and legs intertwined, our bodies snug against each other. The jigsaw puzzle pieces were fitting together perfectly once again.

BRIANNA

THE PATH TAKEN

THE DAYS TICKED by. My vacation glow had all but diminished. I wasn't in the mood to attend Eric's annual firm picnic, but I knew it was important to him.

It was as bad as I thought it would be. I was still brooding about it the next morning when Charlotte called.

"Hey, Bri. How are you? How's the charity event coming?" Charlotte asked.

"Fine." I sighed.

"That was a big sigh. What's wrong?"

"Nothing," I slowly answered.

"Yeah right—come on. What's up?"

"Do you think I need Botox or something?"

"What? What are you talking about?"

"Eric's secretary and paralegal came up to me at the end of the law firm's picnic and said that they knew why Eric married me—I'm so funny!"

Charlotte uttered, "You are funny."

"Yeah, do I look so bad that the only reason Eric's with me is that I'm funny?"

"You're beautiful. Anyway, what do they know, they're twentysomethings," Charlotte soothed. "They were probably trying to connect with you and didn't realize how they came off."

"I guess. I've got to go. I'll call you later."

I hadn't told any of my friends that my mammography had come back with a spot. My appointment for a biopsy was in an hour. I'd barely mentioned it to Eric an hour before my appointment and only did because he'd be mad if I hadn't. I'd rather handle things myself.

Madeline had told me a million times if I vented more it would relieve my stress. Like she's one to talk. I don't want to burden anyone, ever.

*

Eric came in and surprised me while I was filling out the medical forms for the biopsy. "What are you doing here?" My mouth hung agape. "I thought you were in court today."

"Bri, come on, this is where I need to be. I sent an associate in my place, it was only a calendar call." Eric sat next to me, took hold of my hand, and kissed me on my cheek. "Why didn't you mention the biopsy when you made the appointment? It would have been easier to rearrange my schedule earlier rather than last minute. How were you going to get home, anyway?"

"Logan dropped me off and is coming to pick me up. It's no big deal."

My husband shook his head. "Let's hope so." He squeezed my hand tighter. "I can't believe Logan just dropped you off and left."

"I told him it was just a checkup. I didn't want him to know."

"Well, I'll call Logan and tell him that I'll bring you home."

I looked at him and smiled wanly, relieved I no longer had to pretend I wasn't scared.

"We'll deal with this no matter what happens. Don't worry," he assured me.

*

A week later, the doctor called and told me that the spot was a benign growth. My muscles relaxed and I took a deep breath for the first time in a week.

Eric took me out to dinner to celebrate. Dinner was romantic despite spending much of the time talking about his cases and the charity event. The kids were out when we got home, so we fixed drinks and sat next to each other on the deck, holding hands under the stars.

The idea of having the house to ourselves in a few weeks and our relationship shifting back to just the two of us was looking better and better to me. I'd always loved being a mother, but now perhaps I could indulge in being a wife again.

*

My friends insisted on celebrating my fiftieth birthday. Charlotte told me she was cooking a meal I would remember for another fifty years.

We headed out to Charlotte's deck with our martinis. I hadn't spoken to Ava for a while. She seemed to be avoiding my phone calls lately.

"So, Bri, how does it feel to be fifty?" Ava asked after she sat down next to me with her drink.

"Awful!" I slumped in my chair. "Fifty. I can't believe it. I still feel like I'm forty—hell, twenty-nine."

"You look great." Ava's bangs, as if on cue, fell into her eyes.

"Hey, turning fifty is better than the alternative," Staci laughed, spilling her martini on her lap. With an annoyed gasp, she blotted the material with her cocktail napkin.

I nodded. "I'm so glad you came tonight, Staci. Have you heard from your friend in Vermont?"

"No. I'd call you in a heartbeat if I heard from John." Staci sighed. "It's been weeks. But I did get an article I wrote about a band that played at the festival in the *Burlington Free Press*. Maybe he'll see it and think of me. At least it's nice to know there are still some good men out there."

"That's the spirit." Charlotte smeared on some lip gloss.

Staci lifted her cosmo and took a long sip. "Do you want to see what he looks like?"

"You had a picture of him and never showed me?" I threw my hand up. "Give me, give me."

"Actually, I didn't take any pictures of John." Staci blushed. "I went on the Devil's Bowl Speedway website and copied the picture posted of him the night he won that race."

We all grabbed for the phone at once, but, of course, Madeline got to it first.

"Darling, he doesn't look anything like a farmer." Madeline passed the phone to Ava. "He's very handsome, but you can do better."

Ava rolled her eyes. "I don't know about that. He's hot!"

They handed me the phone last. "Wow, nice!"

We went inside and sat at Charlotte's beautifully set dining table. I sat at the end of the table and my friend brought out this sumptuous dinner of salmon in a glazed sauce with fresh vegetables and a champagne risotto. The aroma fired up my hunger.

"What an amazing meal, Charlotte," I said. "Really amazing. You didn't have to do all this."

Charlotte smiled widely. "Of course, I did. You're my best friend!"

We ate with gusto. I loved the wine she served with dinner. It was light, but gave the dinner a perfect finish.

Madeline talked about the charity event through most of dinner. As she droned on about the centerpieces, Ava cleared her throat loudly.

"Super. Can't wait," Ava announced. "By the way, who is this Natasha Hanson person?"

Without missing a beat Madeline replied, "Oh, she's darling, just lovely. She moved into my neighborhood in June. I'm going to ask her to book club."

"I don't know if that's a good idea. I see her all the time with Eric and with Charlotte's ex at Fairfield Racquets," Ava said.

"She better be careful with my ex." Charlotte grunted.

"What? What do you mean with Eric? My Eric?" I sat ramrod straight in my chair. Eric never mentioned that he'd seen or talked to Natasha since Madeline's party in June.

"Take it easy, they were just talking. But I wouldn't trust her for a second with my husband." Ava reached for more wine.

"You know, when I met her at Madeline's party, there was something about her, something that didn't sit well with me." My hands shook, growing annoyed at Eric, at Natasha, and maybe even a little at Madeline. After all, she had brought this person into our circle of friends.

"Oh, come off it, you're overreacting. All you saw was them talking." Madeline's face reddened. "Why are you starting trouble, Ava?" Madeline leaned in closer, almost threateningly.

"I know what I saw. I see this kind of thing all the time. You need to wake up, Madeline. Bri is right; she's a fox and getting ready to pounce on someone's husband. The question is whose."

"Maybe I should introduce her to George. She sounds like his type," Staci slid in.

"That's complete and utter nonsense." Madeline's cheeks flared a darker red. "Talking isn't cheating."

"Keep telling yourself that." Ava leaned back in her chair. "I don't like the way she stands so close to the men she's speaking with. The way her body seems to almost curl around them, like a snake. She's trouble."

"Not everyone is a scoundrel," Madeline spit out.

Madeline was clearly referring to Ava's husband. I thought the comment was below the belt.

Charlotte intervened before I did, gingerly moving the topic of conversation back to the charity event.

It took a good ten minutes of Charlotte's talking nonstop to relax Ava's flared nostrils and the pulsating vein in Madeline's neck.

We dropped all discussion of Natasha. Maybe we should have thrashed it out then and there. The atmosphere grew strained and it ruined my birthday dinner. I barely made it through to the cake.

The drive home seemed to take forever. I was livid. Just what the hell was going on with my husband? I didn't need to hear about another woman at my birthday dinner. I went from angry to sad to scared then back to angry every other minute.

The kids' cars weren't in the driveway when I got home. "Eric!" I roared, slamming the front door.

"I'm in the family room," he yelled out.

I threw my purse on the table and marched in. "Explain to me, please, why I have to hear from my girlfriends—at my birthday dinner—that my husband is spending time with Natasha Hanson?" I hollered, hands on my hips. I nearly choked.

"What are you talking about?" Eric jumped up and walked toward me.

"Ava told me that you spend a lot of time with Natasha at the tennis club. She said every time she's there you're always with her. And she's like curled around you like a snake. What exactly are you doing with her?"

"That's ridiculous. Natasha and I are just friends. We play in the same league and talk after the matches. Since when is that a crime?" His own temper flared. "Are your friends spying on me?"

"Don't be ridiculous!" I screeched, finding it hard to contain my fury. I turned away and stormed into the kitchen. I tried to calm myself. Eric should have left me alone just then. But he was right behind me.

I pivoted to face him. "How would you like it if your friends told you I was always in the company of a handsome man, talking to him, standing close? Someone I never mentioned to you. What would you think?" I found it hard to breathe. "I hear *ad nauseum* about all your cases, the people you see every day and yet you neglect to tell me about Natasha. I find that very interesting. What exactly do you two talk so much about anyway?"

"Nothing, just small talk. Why are you asking me about another woman? I thought you were friends. Just listen to yourself." Eric threw his arms up. "I've never seen you so angry. Screaming like this. All we did was talk. You can't be angry—not seriously."

"If the roles were reversed, you'd be annoyed—too." My body shook. My thoughts grew jumbled as I tried to regain control of my emotions. *I need to calm down. Inhale. Am I overreacting? I don't seriously think Eric is cheating. Do I?*

"I can't believe there's gossip about this." He approached me and touched my arm. "All I ever did was talk to her."

"There's always a touch of truth in gossip before it gets twisted out of control. Maybe Natasha is inspiring some of it. Stay away from her," I demanded.

"All right, but I still feel persecuted when I haven't committed a crime." Eric moved in front of me and smiled that irresistible infectious grin of his. He wrapped his arms around me. "You know I love you. Why would I jeopardize that?"

I exhaled and returned the hug. My shoulders relaxed, but my stomach was still tight.

"By the way, you are sooo sexy when you're mad. That mad vibe is hot. Where has it been all these years?"

I put my head on Eric's shoulder. Busy or not, I hadn't noticed any change in Eric's schedule. He always keeps the exact same agenda. I silently vowed to watch more closely. *But trust me, Eric, Natasha will never be my friend.*

He hugged and kissed me gently, and I felt truth in his words. He was a terrible liar anyway, especially for a lawyer. Eric could be a controlling pest, but he was an honest man, one I had grown to trust, and trust was hard for me. Our life together had its difficulties, but only small bumps compared to some of our friends whose relationships had already ended in divorce. How does anyone ever know if their marriage will last?

Now, here in Eric's arms, my worries subsided and I closed my eyes. I had a feeling this little kerfuffle wasn't over, but in his embrace my angst was weightless and floated away.

*

Any solace I had imagined about both children leaving for collage collapsed the day we dropped Logan off. Julianna had left a few days before in her own car, not needing us to bring her back and forth from college anymore.

Eric tried to talk to me after we left Logan's campus, but nothing penetrated my sadness. My baby was gone and my sense of worth along with him. It had all happened so fast, their entire childhoods. I so missed my mommy hugs and kisses and the sweet baby faces of my children with their flyaway hair.

Eric reached over and held my hand as we drove home. Both of us were quiet. "Say something, Bri. I know you must be struggling."

"No, I'm just tired. It's a lot of work getting the kids ready for college and dealing with the charity event." I tried to steel myself. *Stay calm. Breathe.*

The house was deadly quiet when we arrived home. Logan's essence was stripped from the house: no loud talking on the phone, no singing or slamming doors, no bouncing balls in the driveway, nothing.

"I'm tired, Eric. I'm going to take a nap," I said.

"It's six p.m. If you nap now, you'll be up all night." Eric stood at the foot of the bed with a look of surprise on his face.

Tomorrow I would pull myself together and act like an adult, but not now. When Eric realized I couldn't be deterred, he decided to organize a game of tennis.

Sleep came immediately and I dreamt I was playing tennis with

Eric like we used to when we first met. He kept trying to instruct me, but I wasn't listening, just fooling around. He took the game seriously, while for me it was just a form of exercise.

Eric raced back for one of my awful lobs and brought that ball down just inside the baseline.

Then we finished playing and walked onto a path with leaves scattered about. Eric went up ahead. I froze, not wanting to be on this path. Eric kept walking. Natasha suddenly appeared and walked toward Eric in her slow deliberate, hip-swaying walk. Panicking, I finally broke free of the path and awoke, totally unsettled, breathing heavily.

Parts of the nightmare seemed familiar but I didn't know why.

I looked around and Eric was asleep next to me. He wasn't with Natasha. I got up and drank a glass of water. *What was that about?* The path looked like the one in the painting downstairs. I must be losing my mind. Staying in the bathroom, I breathed deeply for a few minutes before going back to bed, snuggling against Eric.

I thought of him, of us. Eric's intensity was sexy to me. I found his sharp intellect quite sensual also. He never seemed to get lost, always knew which direction he was traveling in. He could figure out complicated calculations in his head in seconds. Eric could be overwhelming at times, but he also had a fun-loving, adventurous side. Too much of either would be more than I could handle.

His passion could be just as intense. At fifty-four, he had a young man's libido, no Viagra needed, and no complaints from me.

The moments I treasured, however, were more intimate. Like the happiness in his smile when he walked in the door after work, or the way he spooned with me every night before going to sleep, or the way he brushed wayward strands of hair from my face.

Warm against him I fell into a dreamless sleep.

*

Only one week remained before our charity event. Madeline had taken the day off from work and we met the volunteers at the venue with Charlotte to review the silent auction items.

Right after that, we had an appointment with the company printing the program. Madeline had planned that we'd stop for lunch first.

We went to one of our book club's favorite restaurants, La Torre in Morristown. When no one felt like hosting book club, we'd meet there for dinner while we discussed the book.

Morristown's revitalization in the last ten years made it a popular spot for chic restaurants and entertainment. I was glad my ever-efficient friend, Madeline, had made a reservation because the place was packed.

We had just ordered when Madeline pointed to a table filled with men by the main window. "Eric's here, Bri."

His law firm was just off the square near the courthouse and the attorneys often took clients to lunch there.

I turned in my chair but the first person I saw was not Eric—it was Natasha. She approached Eric's table and put her hand on my husband's shoulder, bending down and whispering something in his ear. Eric immediately rose and appeared to be introducing her to the men at the table. Natasha hooked her arm into Eric's during the introductions. Eric gently broke away from her arm hook.

I got up from my table and walked over to Eric, never taking my eyes off him, boring into him, looking for—I'm not sure what.

"Hi, honey," I said as sweetly as possible. *Never let them see you sweat.*

Eric turned around, mouth dropping at the sight of me. He stepped back and put his arm around me and pulled me closer to the table. Once again there was another round of introductions, mostly unnecessary since I already knew all of his colleagues. Natasha stepped back, but didn't leave.

"It's such a nice surprise finding you here," I said.

"Same here, sweetie."

I turned around. "You, too, Natasha. What a surprise meeting you here. Are you with anyone?"

"No, I just stopped in to get a salad to go," Natasha answered.

What? That didn't make sense. As far as I knew, she didn't work in Morristown, but I guessed she knew Eric did. Had Natasha come here to see my husband, or at least had hoped to see him? No one goes to this expensive restaurant for a salad to go. I hadn't known Eric would be here, so how did she? Was she stalking him? Or was this a prearranged meeting? My mind was whirling, but the idea seemed preposterous.

"Natasha, why don't you join Madeline, Charlotte, and me for lunch?" I motioned to our table.

"Oh, no, I have to get going, I have an appointment in a few minutes. Thanks anyway. I'll see you soon. Nice to meet all of you," Natasha said, turning toward my table waving at Madeline. Then she sauntered out of the restaurant. I noticed she didn't wait for her salad. Had that been just an excuse?

I gave Eric a peck on the cheek and rejoined the ladies. "Don't you think it's a little odd to see Natasha here?" I said, picking up my napkin. "Madeline, did you tell her about this restaurant?"

"Maybe. Why? What difference does it make?" Madeline replied. "Honestly, Bri, you should get to know Natasha, you'd really like her. Stop listening to Ava's nonsense."

"Do you think Ava's right, Charlotte?" I asked.

"I don't know, but Natasha's name has come up a few times. She's trouble according to Ava." Charlotte raised her voice to be heard over the increasingly loud neighboring table. "Ava told me that Natasha was all over Eric again last weekend at the tennis club. But...I don't know. Ava can be dramatic sometimes." Charlotte looked away, opening her menu.

Eric never mentioned that he'd seen Natasha last weekend. It must have been after we dropped Logan off, when I crashed. My stomach tightened and I twisted my wedding ring around my finger under the table. I'd explicitly asked him to stay away from her.

Charlotte eyed me over the menu. "Is everything okay?"

"Of course." I smiled. I started tying my napkin into a tight knot under the table, rubbing hard against my skin.

"Charlotte, darling, how is Maxwell?" Madeline asked, her tones almost sickly sweet.

Charlotte said, "Great," while continuing to stare at me. Parched, I picked up my glass of water.

"Bri, why is your hand red? Did you bang it?" Charlotte asked.

"I don't think so. I think they're just dry." I dropped my hand back into my lap.

Eric came over to say goodbye and told me he'd be home after tennis.

"Okay, I'll see you then." I smiled up at him. Neither of us mentioned Natasha in front of my friends, but my mind kept drifting back to Natasha putting her hand on Eric's shoulder in such a familiar way. She seemed very comfortable around him. Would Natasha show up at the tennis club tonight?

We left the restaurant a few minutes later. We proofread, corrected, and approved the program and handouts at the printers.

Charlotte dropped me off at home. It was only 4:00 p.m. and I wandered through the house, anxious to talk to Eric. Or maybe just anxious, period.

Feeling lonely, I wandered into Julianna's room and looked at pictures arranged haphazardly around her desk. Remembering the moments frozen in time. I walked into Logan's room and picked up his trophy from swim team. He won it when he was only seven. Of course, all the kids were awarded trophies for participating whether they won a race or not. Logan was always in high gear, and nothing seemed to intimidate him, except maybe math. He made me laugh. His love of life was contagious. I could use some of that now.

Back in my own room, I continued down memory lane and

picked up a picture of Eric and me at his friend's wedding. We were in our twenties. I stared at the woman staring up at me. Smiling broadly, she was beautiful, smart, unafraid, energized, and ready for anything. I remembered how she'd always felt indestructible, special.

Where had that *chutzpah* gone?

Instead I was weighted down in the muck of a midlife crisis with out-of-sync hormones, hot flashes, loss of sleep, and restlessness. Adding this empty-nest component to the sludge, the mixture had the consistency of quicksand.

I sat down.

My cell rang, snapping me out of my funk. "Hello."

"Bri, darling, it's me." Madeline announced.

"Hi. What's up?"

"Wanted to see if you had the figures for the decorations from Ava?"

"No. I'll call and get back to you today."

"Everything okay? You sound distant."

"I'm a little tired. Let me call Ava now and I'll get back to you." I didn't want to talk to anyone, but especially not to Madeline right now. I wasn't sure if my reaction was because of how perfectly she conducted her own life, or if it was because I felt she was pushing Natasha on us all. I texted Ava for the information then forwarded her response to Madeline. There, done.

Movement. That's what I needed. I threw on some sweats and sneakers, picked up my phone and earbuds and off I went.

The music and movement worked their magic. My mind cleared and a little optimism peeked through like a ray of sunshine on an overcast day.

Back home, the message light blinked on our house line. Usually I ignored it, but this time I stopped and listened.

"Eric, just wanted to make sure you were coming to the invitational tonight." Natasha's silky voice resonated through my kitchen.

I almost threw the phone against the wall. "What balls she has to call here!" On the plus side, Eric must not have given her his cell number.

It was 6 p.m. so I grabbed a bottle of chilled wine and headed into the family room. Draining the first glass in two gulps, I poured a second.

I rested my head on the back of the couch and looked at the damn painting above the fireplace.

Could life be repeating itself?

I felt moisture on my cheeks and wiped away tears. The last memory of my father came into focus, the day he took me to live with my grandparents. We had been at a park walking on a tree-lined path just like in the painting. He told me he was bringing me to my grandparents to stay for a while. That they could take care of a child better than he could. I was only six and I never saw him again.

My mother had died in a car accident two weeks before. My father survived the crash. That's all I ever knew about any of it. My grandparents wouldn't speak of it or of my father. I always wondered what had happened and why he left me.

I loved my grandparents very much, but he was my dad. That accident robbed me of both my parents. Without any information or anyone to talk to, I blamed myself. I felt all alone.

I had pushed the hurt into a cavern down deep in my soul and left it there.

Uncertainty and doubt nagged at my sense of waning security. I felt like my six-year-old self, afraid and alone. I stood, wiping the tears away with my hand, and walked over to the bay window. Outside Hanna struggled with her dogs. The Saint Bernard pulled in one direction and the Lab in the other. "Isn't that just the way," I said to no one. I hoped Eric and I weren't pulling in different directions. I shook my head to dispel my gloom, but the intensity of the emotions just hurt my head.

I decided to take a shower. Standing with my eyes closed, I

breathed deeply. I had a lot to be grateful for. I just needed time to adjust.

I visualized every negative feeling being washed down the drain. Down, down, down went Natasha, followed by my father. Temporary or not, my mind felt lighter.

*

The garage door slammed shut.

"Can you believe one of Logan's professors insists each student buy something called an 'iClicker?'" Eric stormed into the dining room, still dressed in his tennis whites, complaining about how much Logan's books and other supplies cost. He had just received an e-mail from the college with the bookstore invoice.

"A what?" I looked up from the papers I'd strewn across the table.

"An iClicker. It costs forty dollars, which the college considers a nominal fee, by the way."

"What does it do?" I asked, more to placate him than because I really cared.

"Not sure exactly. They say it's for attendance and that it records a student's response to a teacher's questions. What's wrong with raising your hand? Why do we have to spend another forty dollars?" Eric pushed the bill back into his briefcase and clicked it shut. "College costs are completely out of control." Eric paced up and down along the dining room table. "Every other institution and business has to bring in costs, but not colleges. I asked the bursar's office: 'What is the thousand-dollar student fee for?' They told me something about labs, and I told them that our son didn't have a lab. They said it didn't matter, every student has to pay it. Can you imagine if I told my client they owe me a thousand dollars just because?" He stormed into the kitchen to fix a drink.

I really didn't care. "I'm exhausted, I'm going to bed."

"It's only nine something. Are you feeling okay?" Eric came back into the dining room.

"Working all day on this fund-raiser has tuckered me out." I stood and left the room. I didn't tell him about Natasha's call or what I had heard. The hell with it. Either I just didn't want to know or the muck had clogged up my senses. I simply wasn't up for it tonight.

*

It was 5:30 a.m. on the Saturday of our charity event. Wide awake, thinking of all the things that still had to be done, I quietly rose and went into the bathroom. Eric was sleeping soundly. When I came out, Eric turned over and asked, "How about a little morning sex?"

I laughed. "Ooh, I'm so stimulated, great foreplay." I went to the dresser to get a top.

"Jump back into bed and I'll show you a little foreplay." He held out his arms to me from under the sheets.

Normally, when already dressed and focused on my day, I would have requested a raincheck. But dear Natasha, ever present in my mind, made me reconsider. My arms reached out to his. Natasha wasn't the only reason for our increased lovemaking over the last few weeks. It was also our newfound freedom. Now we could do whatever and whenever in our home. I enjoyed this aspect of empty nesting.

Eric got up twenty minutes later and made us breakfast while I showered and dressed again. Madeline had already texted me and said she'd be at my house by 7 a.m.

"Why don't you go back to bed?" I said to Eric, rubbing the back of his neck, wanting to slip back under the covers with him and feel his warm embrace.

"That's okay, I'm going to try to get a tennis game today and maybe go into the office for a few hours this afternoon. If you need help, call me."

Our moment was over. "Thanks, but don't wait on me for

anything today. I'll be lucky to get home to get changed for the party. By the way, it's a casual event, so think business casual."

The doorbell rang, Madeline was right on time.

"Did you hear that a big rainstorm is coming in tonight?" Madeline pulled the bags she was carrying through the door and plopped them on the floor.

"Oh, no. Last I heard it would be here tomorrow." I had checked the weather yesterday.

"Don't worry. It's supposed to start after midnight." Madeline picked up one of the bags and brought it into our dining room. "We'll be out of there before the storm hits."

I grabbed Madeline's other bag and brought it into the room. I turned on the Weather Channel while I made Madeline a cup of coffee. Armed with our fuel, we tackled all the last-minute phone calls and preparations. I spoke with all the volunteer managers, letting them know that cleanup had to be done quickly tonight because of the storm. Around 11:30 a.m., Madeline and I left for the arboretum to begin setting up.

On the drive over, Madeline said, "I thought I'd bring Natasha to help."

"What? No, don't. Absolutely not! Is she coming tonight?" I demanded.

"Yes, she's coming. She's my friend, why wouldn't she come? Don't tell me you still think she's trying to steal your husband? Really, Bri, that's just ridiculous." Madeline's finger began tapping the steering wheel. "I've had a great time with her this summer."

"That's great, so happy for you." My cheeks burned. "I can't do anything about her coming tonight, but she's not helping set up."

"Are you kidding? Are you losing your mind?" Madeline continued tapping her finger.

I knew she was upset, but so was I. "Hey, when have I ever said I don't want someone around? Huh? I'm always the one including people in things. But clearly, I have issues with *this* woman." I slapped my hand on my lap. "As your longtime friend, your loyalty should be with *me*. Not her!"

"This isn't a loyalty issue. Natasha is a lovely person and a lot of fun and would never go after a married man. You're being petty and jealous for no reason." Madeline sounded angry.

"Fine!" I shouted and looked at the window, silent for the rest of the ride.

We pulled into the venue parking lot to calls of "Madeline" and "Bri" from all corners. *Time to let things go and get this thing done.*

Hours passed in minutes. Sweaty, tired, and a little light-headed by the time I took a break at 3:00, I needed some water and food. We ordered pizzas for the volunteers. Looking over the volunteers, I didn't see Natasha. Thank God.

By 4:00, Madeline and I were joking around, the morning's squabble forgotten. She dropped me off at home so I could shower and change.

I went over all the details of the evening in my mind as I was getting ready. Something always comes up and I wanted to have a game plan when it did. Brushing my hair, I rummaged through the closet, throwing clothes everywhere looking for my black silk cardigan just in case it got cool tonight. It was the only thing that matched my new Elie Tahari maxi dress. I went for sexy. Deep plunged with ruching from the waist to the hip in effervescent shades of violet, red, and yellow. Each color blended perfectly into the next like an oasis sunset. This dress should catch Eric's eye—at least until he saw the price tag.

Arriving at five o'clock exactly, I noticed some missed calls on my phone. The parking lot was filling up for the six o'clock start.

"Bri, everything looks great!" Ava called out. We hugged and kissed.

"Thanks, Ava, sorry I missed your call before, I was too busy to call back."

"I only called to see if you needed any help."

I noticed a sparkly clip in the side of Ava's hair and moved closer to see it. "That's a beautiful barrette and it matches your dress so well."

"Thanks. At least tonight I'll be able to see." Ava laughed.

"Let's go down to the pond and make sure the bar is up and running." I pulled Ava along. We joined Staci and Hanna at the bar.

"Let's have a drink before everyone gets here," Ava suggested.

"Bri, you look radiant." Staci looked me up and down. "That's quite a sexy number you have on."

"Thanks. I'm feeling pretty good," I said.

"Girls—guess what I did?" Staci twirled. "I have a date from an online dating site." She pulled out her phone to show his profile.

We all laughed, pulling at the phone to snatch a peek of him.

"I'm glad you're moving on." I touched Staci's arm.

Madeline and Charlotte found us. Armed with our drinks, we clinked our glasses. It felt so good to have most of the book club back together again.

As patrons made their way to the bar, we headed up to the barn for the dinner dance. The band began to play. I stopped by the silent auction and started the bidding on a few items. I looked up and saw Eric staring at me from a few feet away.

"Honey, you look amazing!" He had that look in his eyes that I know so well, and a shiver slinked up my spine. I walked over and answered him with a kiss. We headed to our table.

On the dance floor, I noticed Natasha shimmying. She was quite a number in fuchsia, as if anyone could miss her no matter what she wore. I swore to myself that nothing was going to deflate my good feeling tonight. I simply positioned Eric so he couldn't see Natasha on the dance floor in all her Lycra glory.

Tess was the only one who didn't make it. I couldn't wait till our next book club. I didn't know all the men my friends were with and couldn't wait to catch up with their stories. As I looked out over their smiling faces around the table, I realized my worries about our group going separate ways were nonsense.

"Bri, did Tess tell you she met a man?" Ava announced.

"No, when, where? I haven't spoken with her recently." I answered realizing that I owed Tess a call.

"Not sure of the details," Ava said. "Is she coming to book club next week?"

"Yes," I said. "I guess we'll find out then."

Natasha had been scurrying around all evening—anything to be noticed. Madeline spent a great deal of time sitting with her at a different table. They danced together and I noticed Madeline introducing her to friends and neighbors. Except for dinner, which Madeline ate with us, she spent the rest of the evening with Natasha. Maybe I *should* be more inclusive, I thought. After all, Natasha hadn't ventured near Eric all night.

After the winners of the silent auction were announced, people started to leave little by little. As the barn emptied, Madeline and I decided to put away some of the now-vacant tables and chairs. I asked Eric if he could bring a few of the tables to the small storage building right behind the barn.

I nabbed Staci, Madeline, Hanna, and Charlotte, and asked each to carry a few folding chairs. I looked for Ava but didn't see her. We marched in a line through the big doors of the barn to the storage building. We were joking around, excited about the event. Entering the storage building first, I turned right to line the chairs up along the far wall. My peripheral vision picked up movement and a blur of fuchsia as I placed one armful of chairs down. I started to turn back to release the remaining chairs when my head snapped around.

What? I mouthed the word. Air rushed out. Dizzy, I dropped the chairs. The clatter echoed through the space. I felt eyes swivel toward me.

Run, I willed my legs. But I just stood there openmouthed, watching Natasha's arms wrap tight around my husband. Her mouth on his.

"Aah!" I heard Charlotte gasp next to me.

Ava flew toward Natasha.

"No, no," I cried out. I heard nothing else. I saw nothing else. Time stood still. I turned and left the barn. I stopped before I reached my car. I had to finish the event. I had to. I walked to the bar area that we were using as our cleanup command center. My shoulders were heavy, my head fuzzy, and my heart broken.

"Bri, Bri are you okay?" Staci grabbed my arm.

I looked around. My friends were running down the path to the bar. "No, how could I be?" I wanted to lock myself in my car and drive far away. *I knew she was after my husband.*

I glared at Madeline. "How could you bring that viper into our circle of friends? This is all your fault." I turned away, head lowered, choking back tears.

Madeline looked at the ground then turned and went back up the walkway.

Unbalanced, I felt like I was free-falling, plummeting down the first drop of a roller coaster. I collapsed on a bench and looked at the grass, breathing deeply, trying to recover. This wasn't the time or the place to fall apart.

My husband approached. I stood facing him and raised my arm to signal him to stop. "Eric, leave!"

"What? What are you so upset about?" Eric said, still wiping lipstick off his mouth. "Please give us some privacy," he said to my friends.

My friends stepped back a few feet.

"Not here, Eric. Not now." I turned.

Eric grabbed my arm. "It isn't what you think."

"Are you kidding me? I saw you and Natasha!" I hissed, poking my finger into his chest and yanking my arm away.

"*She* kissed *me*."

I moved close to him and said in a low, deep voice. "Get the hell out of here now." My stomach plunged over another huge drop, twisting, falling.

Eric stared at me with narrowed eyes. He looked as if he wanted to say something more, but instead turned and left. I sat down, looking out over the pond. Slowly, my friends came over to me.

Ava bounded into view. "I told that bitch to leave, and followed her to the parking lot," she said, continuing breathlessly. "When we were gathering up chairs, I saw Natasha race after Eric into the storage room. I followed her." She moved closer to me. "If it's any consolation, Natasha kissed Eric when he had both arms filled with tables. I think he was as shocked as we all were."

I didn't say anything.

"Bri, did you hear me?" Ava asked.

Turning toward her, I found my voice. "Huh. Thanks." I put my hand on Ava's arm. "I warned him about her." My eyes felt moist.

"Bri, Eric loves you. It was her, she did this." Staci sat and put her arm around me. "We've all seen the way he looks at you."

"I don't want to talk about it. Let's finish up," I mumbled.

Nobody said anything for a minute. "Go home!" Charlotte wrapped her arm around me. "Now."

"I need to finish up."

"There's nothing but a little clean up and we have plenty of volunteers to help with that. Come on, I'll follow you home." Charlotte insisted. She grabbed my tote under the table in the volunteer tent and fished out my car keys. "If you don't want to go home you can stay with me," she whispered.

I shook my head no. "I want to be alone." I took my tote and keys and without another word turned and left. I pulled out of the drive just as the catering truck left. The skies opened up and drenching rain pounded the pavement.

The rain was so heavy that motorists dropped their speed to ten miles an hour. My rain-sensing wipers worked overtime to keep up.

The rhythm soothed me for a few minutes like a hypnotist's watch. My hands released their death grip on the wheel. But then my mind wandered back to the barn and Eric and Natasha. Was Ava right about Natasha making the move? Could Eric have feelings for her?

A tear slowly dropped down my cheek followed by another. I pulled into a closed gas station. I reached into the glove box to get a tissue. Before I could blow my nose, an avalanche of tears fell. My chest constricted, my breath grew short. My mind circled back to the kiss, over and over. The way she touched Eric at the restaurant. The way she looked at him. More tears. It was my father all over again. Layers of repressed emotion peeled away like the skin of an onion. I sobbed until all that was left were spasms.

It took another half hour before I pulled out of the gas station and drove the five miles home. The rain was still teeming; it seemed like it would never stop. In the garage, I found it hard to summon up the energy or the desire to leave the car. I exhaled and breathed deep, slow breaths. Flipping the driver's mirror down, I looked at my puffy face, mascara trailing on my cheeks. I didn't want Eric to know how upset I was.

I quietly entered through the kitchen and kicked off my heels. I ran cold water and splashed some on my face to banish the red flush.

"Brriii, Bri! I'm down in the basement. I need your help, quick," Eric screamed up the basement stairs into the kitchen.

Instinctively, no matter how raw my emotions still were, I responded to his to call for help. I ran down the steps two at a time. "What!" My stomach was simmering hot, aching like the time we ate Cajun shrimp creole in New Orleans.

"Back here, come quick," Eric hollered. The door to the laundry area was open, Eric crouched over one of the sump pumps in bare feet and sweatpants, desperately trying to mop up the water spewing out of it with towels and a mop.

"What the hell is going on?" I shrieked, not knowing how much more I could handle tonight.

"The motor isn't pumping and there's too much rain coming down. The French drain and the other pump are overwhelmed. It's going to ruin everything," Eric screamed, frantically mopping up the water spraying out of the pump and onto the floor. "Bri, come over and start mopping, while I try to figure something out."

I yanked the mop from his hand. "Shit," I spat out. Slamming the mop on the floor I pushed water back into the working drain, over and over again. But the water just kept coming.

Looking out through the door of the laundry area, I could see the full-length mural my mother-in-law had painted. It really would be awful if the water seeped into the finished part of our walk-out basement. We used the basement like a pool house with a bar, pool table, and a small second laundry area for towels and bathing suits. The kids gathered there with their friends all the time.

I redoubled my efforts. Ten minutes later I noticed my dress was wet to mid-calf, clinging to my legs. "Shit!" The dress was ruined before we even received the bill. *Good, let the asshole pay for a one-time wear—penalty points.* "Jesus, Eric what the hell are you doing? Call a plumber for God's sake." I mopped furiously, but couldn't catch up. The water reached halfway to the door of the laundry area, and was inching closer and closer to the brand-new carpeting. I heard Eric banging at the runoff sink by the washing machine.

"What are you doing?" I yelled.

Christ, I hate it when he just ignores me. The water was almost at the door separating the laundry room from the finished basement. My back and arms ached.

"We need another motor," he uttered, then gave me his famous I'm-thinking-don't-bother-me look.

What an ass! I've just had the shock of my life and all he cares about is a motor. Part of me wanted to rant and rave at him. Hit him with the mop. Another part wanted to run into his arms. *Don't leave, stay with me.*

"Move," Eric commanded. Cradling something in his hands,

he pushed past me, reached down into the sump pump, and started to connect hoses to the motor. The makeshift pump immediately began operating and sucking the water down the drain.

I stood there watching the water draw down. Exhausted from mopping, exhausted from the event, exhausted from worry. "You ready to talk?"

"I didn't do anything. There's nothing to talk about."

"What? That's bullshit and you know it."

"Let's get this mess cleaned up first."

"You can't talk and clean up at the same time?" I gave Eric a scathing look and threw the mop on the floor. "Go to hell." I stormed up two flights of stairs, slammed the door to our bedroom, and locked it.

Shivering, I peeled off my soaking wet dress and flung it onto the bathroom floor. I showered and threw on some workout clothes.

I opened our bedroom door and heard Eric downstairs in the kitchen.

"Do you have any idea what it feels like to see your husband with a woman wrapped around him? Kissing? In front of all your friends?" I shouted, entering the kitchen.

He was washing his hands in the sink. "You are overreacting! She kissed me when I had my arms full of tables. I couldn't just drop the tables—they've ended up on my toes. I was going to tell her to leave me alone as soon as I put the tables down. But all of you walked into the room before I had a chance." He began to dry his hands.

"That's it? That's your explanation?" I wanted to rip the dish towel out of his hands and slap him with it. "You're not taking this seriously! Maybe you should find another place to live!"

"Now you're really going overboard." He placed a hand on his hip and the other on the counter.

We locked eyes.

I had his attention now. "I repeatedly asked you to stay away from Natasha. You just ignored me. And look what happened."

"Bri, don't you trust me?" He came close and put his hand on mine. "You know I love you. Come on, it was nothing."

I lowered my head. "I'm so disappointed in you. And to just stand there and dismiss my feelings…" I shook my head, turned, and walked out of the room.

"Bri." Eric reached for me but I pulled away. "Don't be mad."

"I'm more than mad. Put yourself in my place." Not knowing where to go or what to do, I plopped down in my favorite chair in the family room.

"All right, I'm sorry." He flung his arms in the air. "But just so you know, I did tell Natasha to cool it at the tennis club last time I was there. She came on too strong and I told her I was happily married and wasn't interested." Eric collapsed onto the couch. "I didn't want to tell you because you were so upset about dropping Logan at college that day. You wouldn't even talk to me about it. The last thing you needed to hear was about me talking to Natasha."

"Don't even think of blaming me for any of this!" I stood up, my arms folded against my chest, my anger bubbling like lava.

"I'm not trying to. I probably should have put a stop to it when we first talked about it." Eric stood and moved closer to me.

I held out my arm, keeping him back. "Probably should have? Are you dense? Can't you admit when you're wrong? We're supposed to be a team and listen to each other!" I shouted. "I don't always agree with you, but if you feel strongly about something, I go along with it. The give and take has to have a balance for both of us. It can't be just what you want."

Eric raised both hands, surrendering. "You're right." He looked down at the floor. "I screwed up. I'm sorry."

I turned away from him and stared at the painting above the fireplace. "And, another thing, I hate this painting."

"Why do you hate the painting so much? I can bring it into my office, if you prefer," Eric quietly said.

The arrogant attitude gone, a softness filled his voice and made me turn toward him. Eric walked back to the couch and sat.

I unclenched my arms. "This whole thing with Natasha…Does it mean something?"

"No, nothing." Eric looked up at me. "Absolutely nothing."

"Flirting might not be cheating, but it still hurts."

Eric looked away. "I really am sorry."

"It just adds to a growing list of shit I feel I'm wading through," I blurted out, walking away. I could hardly keep my own head up. I felt as wrung out as the rags I'd been mopping the floor with.

Eric stood up and moved toward me. I turned away, but he grabbed my arm and held me close. "What's wrong? Is it the kids being away? Come on, Bri, what's the matter?"

I pushed away from him and paced around the room. "Everything is changing." I dropped my head. "I feel unhinged, lost."

"The kiss meant nothing. Honestly. It was a mistake." Eric slowly approached. "And the kids' leaving is an adjustment for me, too."

"It's so much more than that." I sighed, holding back my thoughts.

"I was wrong with this thing with Natasha, but I rarely know what you're thinking. You need to talk to me more."

"Well, I certainly let you know how unhappy I was after my birthday dinner. You didn't listen."

Eric paused. "You did. Well, maybe this Natasha situation has done us some good in getting you to open up." Eric reached both arms out to me.

I jumped back. "What? No, way. Don't you dare! You want me to share my feelings? Well, here goes. First, I'm mad as hell with you because you spoke with Natasha last weekend after you promised me you'd stay away. Then, you never told me about it, and covered it up."

Eric tried to respond, but I held up my hand.

"I think you knew Natasha wanted more than just talking. That's how affairs begin. It happens that fast—the infatuation trap." I stood confident in my argument.

Eric spoke up. "You're right, I did let it go on too long. I thought I could control it. It was just a little flirting, nothing more." Eric shook his head, regret and guilt evident in his face. "It really wasn't what you think. I'm sorry. I never met to hurt you."

"She had to sense that you *were* interested. Is your ego so small you need another woman's adoration?" I breathed hard, my hard-fought calm melting away.

"Bri, stop it," Eric bellowed. "I would never do that to you, to us, to our family." He looked directly at me.

I turned away and walked to the fireplace.

He relaxed his stance and held out his arm. "I'm truly sorry. Forgive me."

I unclenched my hands and sat on the couch. A silence settled between us.

Eric sat down next to me and dropped his head onto the couch back. I stared at the painting above the fireplace, my anger dissolving as my breathing slowed. So many thoughts raced through my head.

I said nothing. Exhaustion overwhelmed me.

Eric inched closer to me. He placed his hands on both sides of my face and looked directly into my tearstained eyes. "I love you and only you, Bri. I'm truly sorry. I swear this won't happen again. I promise."

I believed him. "I love you, too, but I won't tolerate this a second time."

As Eric kissed me, the tense lines on his forehead relaxed. He put his arms around me and I let my head rest on his chest.

We sat for a long time without saying anything. Perhaps we were both thinking what life would be like without the other, realizing how close we had come to the edge.

Relief flooded me. He wasn't my lustful love from my twenties, nothing so mundane. He was my confidante, my partner, my best friend, my companion, and my desire. The person I wanted to be with always.

Breaking the embrace, I said, "You know, you are very handy to have around. You saved the basement."

"Let me show you how handy I really am," he whispered into my ear. His voice warm and deep. A tingle began in my neck and moved down my spine.

I looked at Eric's intense sapphire eyes. He cradled me in his arms, then kissed my lips, gently at first. He touched my neck and nibbled my ear. His kisses turned more urgent as he caressed my breasts. I could taste the smoky flavor of the cabernet on his tongue as it mingled with mine.

My earlier anguish vanished as I lost myself to the intimate place where only Eric and I existed. I looked up at him, his face liquescent, his eyes exploring my every inch. He lay me on the couch, sliding his hand down my stomach. I shuddered at his touch. His kisses on my body awakened a need and desire so strong, I struggled to control myself.

Eric pushed the table away and threw some of the pillows and throws from the couch on the floor. We lay down and wrapped ourselves around each other. The light from the lamp glimmered on his handsome face.

I kissed him, then tugged at his earlobe. He moaned. Our passion built again, intensifying, and I welcomed him into my body. We moved with the seasoned harmony of a long-together couple who know every point of pleasure and every sign of delight.

Eric stopped and said, "Shhhh, Bri. Shhh." He brushed my hair out of my face. "Bri."

I grudgingly ceased my rhythm, opening my eyes and looking into his.

"I love you," he said, gently stroking the side of my face.

Emotion overwhelmed me. Our lips met again in a long devouring kiss, and our bodies began their familiar tempo as we melted together.

A million sensations merged into one shimmering, intense moment of brilliance, and even our skin seemed to glow with the aftereffects of our lovemaking.

Trying to catch my breath, I murmured, "Wow." I lay a hand across Eric's chest. "Let's fight more often."

"Agreed," Eric said, his heart against my palm pumping hard.

Beyond drained, I rolled onto my back, staring at the painting above our fireplace.

"You know, I think that painting reminds me of the last time I saw my father," I said almost to myself. "I seem to remember my father and me walking on a path in a park the day he dropped me off at my grandparents, never to be seen again."

"So that's why you don't like it. It reminds you of your dad."

"When I was young I blamed myself, but since the kids, I can't understand him at all. How could he do that—abandon me like that?" Putting my father and my children in the same sentence provoked an intense burning in the pit of my stomach. "I could never have left Julianna or Logan, not for any reason."

"You've never mentioned your father," he said. "Do you want us to try to find him?"

"No! I've worked hard to try to forget him. But... I guess with everything going on, those feelings have resurfaced." Suddenly I understood. "The last few months I've been feeling like that six-year-old girl again, discarded, lost." My eyes welled with tears.

Eric placed his hand on the side of my head and slowly pulled me into him. He kissed me on the forehead and held me.

"Your father was a weak man and an idiot."

A single tear escaped, traveling down my cheek. Eric wiped it away and held me tighter.

Quietness enveloped us.

"Believe me when I say that I've never wanted anyone but you," he murmured.

I snuggled under his ear. "I love you, too."

We hugged, fighting exhaustion.

"Let's go to bed. I'm tired." Eric stood and offered me his hand.

"Go ahead, I'll be right behind you." I put the cushions and throws back on the couch and brought the wineglasses to the kitchen.

I stood in front of the painting. It didn't seem so sinister anymore. I didn't see loss, or death, or endings. Instead I saw the magnificence of a brilliant autumn day with its promise of release. I felt a warmth rise up inside me. It was time to let go of the past and sow the seeds of a new season.

Brianna

BOOK CLUB

I ARRIVED LATE TO book club deliberately. I didn't want to repeat my story every time another member arrived. I knew they were concerned by the number of calls and texts I'd received. God, it had only been a week. It felt like months.

Drawing a few deep breaths at Charlotte's door, I paused, then opened it. The murmuring stopped as everyone looked in my direction. "Hi," I whispered and walked into the kitchen.

I heard hey's and hi's. Then someone asked, "Are you okay?"

"Yes, fine." I waved my hand dismissively. "Eric and I put that whole thing behind us." My eyes darted around the room and I walked over to the island and poured myself a glass of wine.

No one said anything. I took a sip. "So, did everyone like the book?"

Charlotte waved her lip gloss tube like a maestro halting a symphony. "Oh, no you don't. What *happened?*"

A slow inhale. "We're fine, really. We've talked a lot and even spent a few days by ourselves in Cape May." I sat down next to Staci on a stool, staring at the countertop, I didn't want to explain further, but these were my closest friends and they deserved to know.

"Eric didn't kiss Natasha, she kissed him. I watched the whole thing go down," Ava interrupted.

I forced my head back up, determined, but still uneasy about sharing my feelings. "I know that, Ava." I noticed how chic her hair looked. I barely remembered her old bangs.

I looked around the room. "You've all been so supportive, and I know I tend to be closed lipped about how I'm feeling…"

"Really?" one of the girls said, and a giggle circulated around the room.

"Hey, I did tell all of you that I thought Natasha was after Eric." I hesitated, not wanting to talk anymore. "We all have problems." I twisted my hands together. "I don't want to bore you with mine."

Charlotte cleared her throat. "Listen, we don't want you to feel uncomfortable. But we're concerned."

"I know. I'm good now. Better than I've been in a long time." My eyes welled up. "And I love you all for caring so much."

"We're always here for you," Staci said, wrapping her arms around me. "And we're glad things worked out with Eric."

Madeline stepped up from the back of the kitchen and stood across the island from me. "I want to apologize, Bri. I honestly didn't think Natasha was like that." She looked down at the counter, her finger tracing the granite's veins. "We had a lot of fun over the summer, and I never got that vibe from her. I'm really sorry." She reached across the island and patted my arm.

I wanted to steer the conversation to anything else but I had to tell her how I felt. "It hurt me when you just disregarded what I was saying. We've been friends a long time and I thought that would carry more weight than a new acquaintance."

Then I gave Madeline a big hug. I knew eventually we'd get past this. We had too many years of friendship invested to let it all go.

"Holy shit! Did Madeline just apologize?" Ava pulled her phone out of her pocket. "Say that again, Madeline. I want to put it online."

"And we're off," Hanna said, laughing.

I let out a long whoosh and laughed with my friends. Everything felt normal again: jabs intermixed with laughter. As always, the books could wait.

"Hanna, the tree house looks great. Mark worked so hard and so quickly," I said, glad to be talking about something other than me.

"My husband decided to cut down on the time he travels and spend more time with us." Hanna's freckled-face smile was contagious. "Mark and I have taken our relationship to another level."

"Oh, Jesus. And what pray tell does that mean? A different level?" our uptight Madeline asked.

Just as Hanna was about to answer, Madeline put her hands over both ears. "Never mind. I don't think I want to know."

Hanna grabbed one of Madeline's hands away from her ear and whispered something into it.

"Oh, double yuck." Madeline's face turned red and she squirmed away.

"Sex, it has to be about sex. I know," Charlotte threw out. "Hanna's made a red room out of that tree house. That's it. It's an adult tree house. Ha!" Her lip gloss, a lighter shade, accented her summer tan.

Hanna doubled over with laugher and the rest of us joined in.

"Let's have October's book club in Hanna's red room," Charlotte said.

"Enough!" Hanna bellowed. "It's for my kids. There's nothing red about it. Although…" She paused, then plunged ahead, "we did have great sex in there before we finished it."

"Tell us more!" Charlotte clapped, stomping her feet.

That was it. Everyone's saucy sexcapades was now the evening's main topic of conversation.

"How about you, Bri? Did you guys have makeup sex?" Hanna asked to rousing cheers.

I threw up my arms, laughing. "Yes, we did." My face grew

warm. "Actually, it was the best sex I think we've ever had. And we're still having it. I guess we need to fight more often."

Whistles and high fives erupted. Tess and Ava were trading stories by the sink. From the looks on their faces, the stories must have been good.

Just as I was going to ask them what they were talking about, Charlotte interjected, "Ladies, that's not makeup sex, that's wall-socket sex."

"What? Where do you come up with these things?" Madeline broke in, her hands folded across her chest.

"In a book, where else? This *is* a book club." Charlotte seemed amused by her own quip. "Wall-socket sex? It's the best sex of all." She held up a finger. "A therapist wrote a book about it. He was helping an empty-nest couple who felt estranged after their children had grown up. He told the couple to tell each other the truth about everything in their lives. Slowly, through the honesty, something amazing happened to them. They started to have incredible sex."

"Yeah, fine, that's enough," Madeline said and sat down at the counter.

"I don't know if that's true. If I told Eric every time I bought a pair of shoes I don't think we'd be having wall-socket sex. He'd be cutting up my credit cards." I laughed.

"Well, it can be challenging at first, but I'm telling you it's a real thing. I know. When you really confide in each other it creates this safe place and that allows you to be totally free sexually. The sex is this incomparable, out-of-this world kind of intoxicating electricity between you. Hence the name. Get the book; it will explain it better than I can." Charlotte turned to us before continuing, "And guess what? The therapist believes that young people aren't grown-up enough to have this type of sex. Ha! Sex does get better with age!"

Madeline sat speechless, shaking her head.

"Hey, let's read that book next month," Hanna shouted. "You know, I think Mark and I had that kind of sex!"

"Only you, Charlotte, would come up with that." Tess laughed, looking like a new person after relaxing for a full summer at the shore. She was sporting the best tan of us all, and her nails had grown and were polished. No more soreness around the cuticles. "I guess this is a good time to tell you all. After tonight, I'll be living at the shore all year long. For this year, at least."

The room quieted immediately. Tess, who had barely uttered a word last spring, was positively beaming with happiness.

"I'm going to stay at my friend David's house. His sabbatical was extended and he asked me to stay on to take care of Mac."

"Come on, Tess, you don't get that kind of glow just from walking a dog. Spill it." Charlotte leaned forward, practically drilling a hole through Tess with her eyes.

"You're right—there is someone other than Mac. His name is Brian and he's divorced and has a newly rediscovered daughter Liz's age. Long story short, the sex has a certain, what did you call it? Wall-socket feel?"

Everyone smiled as the heat rose in Tess's cheeks.

"Anyway, I'll come up for as many book club meetings as I can."

"Tell us more about Brian," I said.

Staci interrupted, looking down at her phone. "Well, sex with John was amazing. But, I don't think I'm gonna have it with anybody I've met so far online." She held up her phone on a man's profile.

Tess and Charlotte said in unison: "Let's see the guys!"

Staci handed over her phone.

"I didn't think I'd ever date again after Stephen died, so I understand your race-car driver's reluctance," Tess said to Staci as she reached for her phone. "We all get over grief in our own time. You'll meet someone, don't worry. Look at me."

Staci smiled and shrugged.

"Yeah. Me, too. Look at everything I went through. It took a while, but I found him." Charlotte was still radiant after her summer with Maxwell.

Ava joined the group looking at Staci's phone. She seemed as jubilant as the rest of us.

"I enjoyed talking with Neil at the event," I said. "You two fit together nicely."

"Thanks. I always thought so. I can't believe we've been given a second chance." She beamed.

Ava turned to Madeline. "You're not your normal opinionated self. Is everything all right?"

"Yes, everything's fine. Still trying to figure out what that electric term really means." Madeline smiled. "You'd think they could come up with a better name than wall-socket sex."

Charlotte butted in. "Of course, you'd find something wrong with it. But you'd sure know it if you had it." She jabbed Madeline's side slightly.

"And that reminds me. Let's go to the Dain Shoppe one Saturday and buy some sexy lingerie and other stuff," Charlotte said.

Madeline started to protest. Charlotte gave her another jab to the ribs. "Don't be such a prude. Try it, you might like it," she taunted.

All the girls agreed to go. Even me.

"Oh, before I forget. Promise me girls, if I die, one of you has to clean out my lingerie drawer so my sons don't see what's in there," Charlotte announced.

Madeline covered her ears again. "Need to know!"

I shook my head. I could just see us at the store. God help the place.

Four hours passed, and we still hadn't talked about the book. For once I didn't care. We shared our summers, our lives, our loves, and our fears. We teased each other, and comforted each other, like we'd been doing for the past ten years.

As the group began to pack up to leave, Hanna came over to me. "Bri, you told me you recently had a biopsy. My older sister just texted me and asked me if I could drive her to the surgical center. She has to have a biopsy." Hanna kept looking at the text on her phone.

"The doctors tend to err on the side of caution. So, try not to worry too much," I said draping my arm around her shoulders. "I'd be happy to go with both of you."

"Thanks, I really appreciate that." Hanna inhaled deeply and put her phone in her purse.

"Come on let's help clean up," I said.

Charlotte protested but we all picked up our glasses and plates. At the sink I heard vibrating and looked around. Staci had left her phone on the counter after the girls finished with her online dating site.

"Staci, your phone is ringing."

"Thanks. Who could possibly be calling me at this hour?" Her laugh abruptly stopped when she saw the caller ID. "Bri, Bri…" Staci stared.

"What, Staci, what's wrong?" She didn't reply. I grabbed her phone and looked at the caller ID.

She'd missed the call. John Marshall had called and left a message.

"Oh, my," I said, smiling.

"Is that the sexy race-car driver from the beginning of summer?" Charlotte asked.

"It sure is," I answered.

The other ladies gathered around, wanting to know more. Staci took her phone back and ran her finger over the screen, touching John's name.

She shifted her gaze at me, a look of intense astonishment on her paling face. "I'm too nervous to call him. Look, my hands are shaking."

I touched her arm. "Go home. Have a glass of wine, then call him back. You'll know what to say."

I watched Staci bound out the door and a rush of euphoria

seemed to wash over me. I watched her race into her car through the window, smiling widely.

Did my friends feel it also? This transcendent feeling of freedom, being at a crossroad of life? We've met society's expectations. You know the ones: marriage, kids, education, careers. Now we are gloriously free to be and do whatever the hell we want without some pesky voice asking: "Don't you think it's time to…?"

No need to conform anymore. We're ready to say no. We don't want to do that. We've finally accepted that we're fine just the way we are.

Acknowledgements

I want to thank my fellow writers and book club members for coming on this amazing journey with me. I'm forever indebted to my dear friends Patty, Fran, Denise and Jeanne. You all hold a special place in my heart. This wouldn't have happened without you.

I want to convey my thanks to Ellyn A. Draikiwicz, Esq. of Bourne, Noll & Kenyon for her invaluable advice and service.

I'd like to thank our editor, Lara Robbins, for her editorial skills and direction.

I also want to give a special thank you to The Writer's Circle and my incredible writing workshop mates: Veronika Roo, Mary Rahill and Devon Villacampa who have been with me through numerous drafts and rewrites and have given me the support I needed to grow and continue. They're such accomplished writers whose names you will soon know.

A very special thank you to Michelle Cameron of The Writer's Circle for her dedicated work on *Novel Women*. She took our entangled mess and weaved it into a coherent story. I, and my fellow writers, owe her a debt of sincere gratitude for her incredible guidance, editing, and her unwavering support.

Lastly, but most importantly, to my family who saw me through this book. And to my husband for believing in me even when I didn't.

Come and see what we're up to at Between Friends Book Club by clicking on our website at http://betweenfriendsbookclub.com. We post a review of the books we read and would love to know your thoughts.

Also, come and visit us at http://novel-women.com and join in the discussion. We'll keep you updated on our book tour and our upcoming books.

FIC BETWEEN

**Between Friends Book
Club
Novel women**

06/26/19

CPSIA information can be obtained
at www.ICGtesting.com
Printed in the USA
LVHW090037100619
620628LV00003BA/492/P